Vaetra Unleashed

Book Three of the Vaetra Chronicles

Daniel R. Marvello

 Published by Magic Fur Press
An imprint of Logical Expressions, Inc.
P.O. Box 383, Ponderay, ID 83852-0383, USA

VAETRA UNLEASHED

ISBN: 978-1-61038-027-0 (paperback)
978-1-61038-028-7 (EPUB)

Vaetra Unleashed is dedicated to "Mama Marvello," as my mother has started calling herself. She was one of the first supporters of my fiction writing and one of my first Vaetra Chronicles fans. Thanks for your love and support, Mom.

Books by Daniel R. Marvello

<u>The Vaetra Chronicles</u>

Vaetra Unveiled

Vaetra Untrained

Vaetra Unleashed

THUNDERHEAD COLLEGE
RIVERVIEW
THE ARCHIVES
DUSK
NORTHSHORE
DUNVER
DELTA
PLAINS END
CASSANDRIA

CHAPTER 1

THE RUNEGATE

"Are you ready?"

It was a simple question, but the twisting knot in my stomach kept me from giving a simple answer. "As ready as I'll ever be."

Professor Marlene Delano stood just behind me on my left. She lightly patted my shoulder in encouragement. "Don't anticipate failure; anticipate success. Both are self-fulfilling prophecies."

Benjamin Morrison was behind me to my right. When I glanced over my shoulder at him, the young sorcerer smiled and nodded once.

We stood at the bottom of a rocky ravine about a quarter mile from the Archives castle. My target was a boulder about fifty yards away. Down here in the ravine, my efforts would be unlikely to hurt anyone, and the noise I made would only disturb a few random deer and ravens.

Not that a little sorcery practice would alarm anyone at the Archives. Sorcerers filled the half-underground mountaintop complex that had become my home. In addition to being a training facility, it lived up to its name as a repository of knowledge and artifacts related to sorcery.

The walls of the ravine concentrated the gathering heat of the day, so I welcomed the light breeze that stirred my loose shirt. The gloriously sunny day was a good omen for my first attempt at casting lightning.

"You can do it, Jaylan." The supportive words came from directly behind me. Daisy Morrison, Benjamin's twin sister, had joined my little field trip. The three of us studied together in Professor Delano's incantations class.

"Okay, here I go."

With a tingle of excitement running through my chest, I mentally opened a channel from my internal well of vaetra to the casting orb in my palm. I stretched my arm out toward the boulder and began the incantation I'd spent the past week memorizing.

White and pinkish striations within the orb's crystal shimmered in the sunlight. Those features had been the inspiration for the name its creator had given to it: Froth. Every time I used it, I felt honored by the gift from my good friend Wizard Ebnik Vlastorus.

After the first few phrases, the plum-sized orb accepted the flow of vaetra I offered it. I was careful to maintain tight control over the flow since my goal today was to demonstrate basic manifestation, not destructive power.

Things went fine until I got about half-way through the incantation.

My vision blurred and tension began to build in my chest right below my sternum. My concentration slipped as I steadied myself against a disappointingly familiar wave of dizziness.

For reasons no one could explain, my spell work had been hampered by these strange symptoms since I first learned I could cast. No amount of rest or practice seemed to make any difference, and the healers had been unable to do anything for me.

My heart began to race, and I took deeper breaths between each phrase of the incantation. I tried not to rush the vocalizations because cadence was as important as pronunciation. I was determined to complete this spell.

I made it about three-quarters of the way through the incantation before everything unraveled. My flow of vaetra to the orb slowed and the growing manifestation noise from the spell stuttered.

Ben shifted from one foot to the other and muttered, "Uh, oh."

I tried desperately to maintain my channel, but it snapped free of the orb before I could complete the spell. The last couple of words I hissed before my muscles went limp were definitely not part of the incantation.

The malady that interfered with my casting had never been this severe. In the past, it varied from lethargy to dizziness, but I'd never actually passed out before.

Except I hadn't truly lost consciousness. I felt hands grab my arms from both sides as Ben and Professor Delano eased me down to lie on the rocky ground. A small stone dug into my back, but I was helpless to do anything about it. My eyes were closed, but I could still dimly see what was going on around me in shadowed, strobing images.

The channel I'd opened to my internal well was still active somehow, even though I'd lost the connection with Froth. As if it were sneaking away from my incompetence, the orb slowly rolled out of my slackening grip. The sensation of dizziness increased and it seemed as though I was floating away from the others through a dark, dense fog.

I'm not sure exactly how long I floated, but eventually the fog cleared to reveal a tall, arched gate made of gray stone blocks. I couldn't tell if I had moved to the arch or it had come to me. Either way, my feet seemed to rest on solid ground again.

Runes decorated the stones at the top of the arch. The runes were familiar because I'd been seeing them for weeks. Every time I tried to cast a spell, one or more of those runes had intruded upon my concentration.

The opening created by the arch was utterly, frighteningly, black. I couldn't tell if the portal was open or closed. No light or image reflected from it. I automatically reached out, but hesitated before touching what seemed to be the surface. Would my hand go through? Would I be sucked into the portal? I drew back my hand, afraid to find out.

I studied the runes on the arch. I recognized the first rune from my Artifacts and Implements class studies. Implements were driven by a sequence of runes, and this rune was usually one of the first ones in the sequence. I had not advanced far enough in my lessons to try my hand at smithing, the art of creating implements, so I had no idea what function it performed.

Was the gateway a giant implement of some kind?

As if to confirm my supposition, I noticed a hand print recessed into one of the stones at chest height on the left gate pillar. I went closer and positioned my left hand just above the depression in the stone. It seemed to be a perfect fit.

I glanced over at the right pillar and saw it had a similar depression that looked to be a match for my right hand. Why two hand imprints? I couldn't possibly reach across the wide opening and place my hands in both depressions at the same time.

I was distracted from the puzzle by a disturbance in the fog behind me. I turned around and stumbled as the vertigo returned. The fog thinned, and I saw a hazy image of Daisy reaching toward me. Her voice called my name, but it came to me in echoes as if from a great distance. I called back to her, but she didn't seem to hear me. My voice sounded muffled and yet close, as if I were speaking with my fingers in my ears. Her image faded back into the fog after a moment, so I went back to studying the archway.

I wasn't sure what to do. I was in some kind of lucid dream and the gateway was obviously important somehow. But was this a good dream or a nightmare? I shrugged and decided there was only one way to find out. I placed my left hand into the depression.

Nothing happened.

Well, that made sense. Implements needed a power source and something to activate them—usually a trigger word. I tried to open a channel to the gate, but I couldn't sense my internal well. My alarm at that discovery faded when I noticed the gate vibrating faintly beneath my palm. I suspected the power it needed was there, somehow.

Next came the trigger word. Smiths usually kept the trigger word simple. I spoke the word "open" and was rewarded with a swishing noise that sounded like a single sweep of a broom on a gritty floor.

The blackness of the opening parted like a curtain to reveal a stairway going down into a rough-hewn tunnel.

I pulled my hand back from the imprint slowly. The gateway remained open. I moved to the center of the opening and peered down into the tunnel. Dim lights floated slowly up the stairs toward me. I took a couple of steps back as they came closer. They hovered just inside the opening, apparently disinclined to join me in the fog.

At first I thought the lights came from someone ascending the stairs, but as they got closer, I saw that they floated independently, shuffling around one another. As I watched them, a few lights winked out and others came into being, some brighter and some dimmer. Each time they moved or appeared, they made a tiny noise, like a mosquito buzzing near my ear.

I stared at the lights for a while, uncertain of what to do next. If they were alive, I didn't think it would be polite to just walk through them and investigate the tunnel. I wasn't too excited about going down into the dark tunnel in any case. I'd have to hope the lights would stay with me so I could see where I was going.

While I had been considering the lights, they had apparently been considering me. With a chorus of squeaks, they made their move. They swarmed out of the gateway and surrounded me. When I failed to do anything but freeze in alarm, they pushed me toward the opening. At least, that's what it felt like. The lights didn't touch me, but increasing pressure on my back forced me to take a step toward the opening.

My alarm turned to panic. This dream was taking a turn for the worse and I'd had enough of it. With a flash of insight, I knew what I needed to do.

I leaned, shifting my trajectory so the pressure from the lights pushed me toward the right side of the archway. I reached out my right hand and placed it in the depression on the pillar. It was another perfect fit.

The pressure at my back disappeared as soon as my hand touched the pillar, and the lights streaked into the gateway just before I said the word "close." The curtain of black slid shut again with the same swishing sound, sealing the pesky lights within their dark domain.

I turned away from the gate and started walking. I didn't know where I was going or even if I'd just find myself standing in front of the gate again. All I knew was that I wanted to get back to the others and leave this strange place behind.

I only took a few steps before the vertigo returned and I floated through the fog again. When the fog cleared, I was back on the ground in the ravine. Benjamin and Professor Delano were trying to lift me to my feet with my arms draped over their shoulders. They held me steady as I coughed and shook my head to clear it of the residual dizziness.

I took my arms off their shoulders and patted their backs. "It's okay. I think I can walk."

They slowly let me stand on my own as I took a few deep breaths and rubbed at the sore spot the rock had left on my back.

Professor Delano kept a light touch on my arm and watched my eyes with a worried frown. "Are you sure? You had us worried. We were about to carry you back to the healers."

"Something strange did happen, but I don't think the healers can help. Thanks for catching me."

We all stared at each other for a moment, and then Benjamin asked, "Do you want to try again?"

"No thanks," I answered without hesitation, and we all chuckled.

I could tell that my brief sojourn had not only left me physically tired, but it had also taken a toll on my internal well of vaetra. I'd have to rest before I tried to cast again.

"What happened?" Daisy asked as she handed Froth to me.

I tucked the orb into the specially designed pocket I'd added to my belt. "Let's head back and I'll tell you on the way."

Dream or no dream, the experience had me worried that I'd never be able to use an incantation to cast a spell. What would I do if the same thing happened on my next attempt and I faced the gateway once more? Were the lights trying to help me, or were they setting me up for trouble? Part of me wanted to give Froth back to Ebnik and be satisfied with using implements. If that was good enough for Sulana, it was good enough for me.

Deep down, I knew I would try casting again. Maybe facing down the gateway was some kind of mental test I had to pass. But that line of thought was no comfort. If it had been a test, it was anyone's guess as to whether I had passed or failed.

CHAPTER 2

DESPERATE MEASURES

On our way back to the Archives, Professor Delano suggested I take the rest of the day off and rest. My head was starting to pound, so I gratefully accepted her offer. The twins volunteered to let Lissy, my alchemy instructor, know why I was absent.

I considered going back to my room to lie down for a while, but the frustrating event had left me too tense for sleep. Instead, I went in search of the one person who would truly understand the disappointment of my spell casting failure. I wouldn't be able to relax and process the bizarre experience until I shared it with Sulana and got her perspective.

As I reached the door to the sparring room, I heard the characteristic clang of parrying practice swords. The cadence of the routine was slower than normal, so I was pretty sure I knew who would be on the other side of the door. Weaponsmaster Talon Destry had slowed his pace for Sulana.

Sulana Delano was the Sword Sorceress of the Archives. It was her duty to enforce the Sorcery Accords and ensure that sorcerers did not try to influence mundane affairs. She was both a skilled sorceress and an accomplished swordswoman, or at least she had been, until a tragic incident that happened a little over a month previously. While I was helping Sulana escape from a rogue band of sorcerers who had captured her, their leader Dumont Fortenz fired a lightning bolt at us that nearly killed her. She survived, but the lightning had damaged her strength and agility. It had also affected her ability to channel vaetra.

If we didn't find a way to heal the lightning damage soon, Sulana would have to resign her Sword Sorceress commission.

I dutifully followed the weaponsmaster's protocol for entering a room while a sparring session was in progress. After opening the door slowly, I slipped into the room and settled quietly on a bench that was positioned along the wall.

My butt had just touched the bench seat when the slap of steel on skin was followed by a cry. Sulana yelled, "Son of a bitch!" and threw her sword to the mat. She brought her hand to her cheek, tested for blood, and then moaned as she slowly rubbed at the place where Talon's blade had caught her.

I was on my feet instantly, but Talon reached her first.

"I'm so sorry, Sulana. Are you okay? Let me see that." Talon gently moved her hand away and guided her chin to the side so he could take a look. "You'll be okay. It's not bleeding and it doesn't look like your cheekbone was broken. You'll have a colorful bruise though."

The mark on Sulana's cheek was already bright red and her eye was watering on that side of her face. She took a couple of unsteady steps back and eased herself down on a nearby bench. Talon and I held out our hands, ready to catch her if she stumbled. She waved our help away impatiently. "I'm fine. Really, I'm fine."

Talon and I sat down next to her.

"Sorry if I distracted you," I said. "I didn't mean to disrupt your session."

Sulana shook her head and growled, "It wasn't your fault. I missed the parry."

"Maybe we need to take it a little slower," Talon offered.

She glared at him. "If we go any slower, I'll be going backward. This isn't working. I'm not getting any better. In fact, I think I'm getting worse." She continued to glare at him, as if daring him to deny it.

Talon shrugged one shoulder and sighed. "I think you may be right. Even last week, you wouldn't have missed that parry."

Sulana dropped her chin to her chest and a couple of tears rolled down both sides of her cheeks. She took a deep breath and blew it out. "What am I going to do?" she mumbled.

I sat next to her in silence, unable to answer her question. My heart was heavy with the guilt of how I had contributed to her condition. It was during my rescue attempt that she was caught in the crossfire of spells that nearly killed her. Through a miracle of luck, timing, and intuition, I'd been able to save her, but it was starting to look like she'd never fully recover.

Talon cleared his throat. "I have an idea, but you may not like it. I'd also appreciate it if you never mention to your mother that I suggested it."

Sulana sniffed and her lips twisted into a wry smirk. "What? Have we actually missed a routine from the basic training manual? I sure can't handle anything advanced right now."

Talon laid a hand on Sulana's forearm. "I'm serious. Before I came to the Archives, I patrolled with the Imperial Guard. My squad covered an area that included a spirit refuge over on the eastern side of the province. The monastery at that refuge already had a reputation for being the best healing center in the empire. I've heard that it is now the main training center for all druid healers. Maybe you should go there and see if they can help."

Sulana chuckled and shook her head. "Right. You say that like the druids would let me step one foot onto the refuge, much less agree to help a heretic sorcerer."

From what little I knew of sorcerer and druid relations, I was inclined to agree with Sulana. Druids believed vaetra was a gift from the spirits and that sorcerers used that gift frivolously, or even blasphemously, with no regard to the well being of the spirits or the environment.

But would the druids turn away someone who was hurt and needed their help because of that enmity?

Sulana went on. "I see why you don't want my mother to hear about that idea. She thinks druid healers are incompetent compared to ours."

Talon squinted at her. "What do you think?"

Sulana sat in silence for a moment. Then she spoke slowly. "I believe the spirits have more to offer than we give them credit for. I've encountered a few of the spirits that inhabit the area around the Archives, and they don't seem to have any particular antipathy for sorcerers. But the druids are another matter entirely." She turned her head toward Talon and added pointedly, "It doesn't matter if druid healers are competent if they won't help me."

Talon's suggestion got me thinking while they talked. I started to like the idea of getting away from the Archives for a while. Even if the druids wouldn't help us, maybe a road trip together was just what Sulana and I needed to clear our heads. Sulana had considered going on an excursion by herself after she discovered how badly the lightning strike had affected her, but she talked herself out of it, much to my relief at the time.

Talon had just opened his mouth to say something more when I interrupted. "Let's do it. You've wanted to get away for a while now. Here's our chance."

Sulana turned an incredulous look my way. "Are you serious? You'd be willing to abandon your studies to go on a trip that might be a waste of time?"

I snorted. "Abandoning my studies might be just what I need right now." She looked at me questioningly. "I'll tell you about it later."

I took her hand in mine and looked into her eyes. "Think about it. Just the two of us on the road together. No Council politics. No lectures. No weapons training." I ducked my head toward Talon apologetically and he smiled back with an encouraging nod. "We could use a break."

Sulana tilted her head and seemed to seriously consider my suggestion. Her lips curled into a slow smile that turned into a wince from the pain in her cheek.

I gave her a sympathetic look and squeezed her hand. "Even if the druids turn us away, we can come back refreshed for another try. What do we have to lose?"

Sulana stared at me for a moment and then answered, "Only time, I guess. What about Dumont Fortenz and Thunderhead College?"

I shrugged and tried to dismiss the concern. "What about them? We haven't heard anything for a few weeks now. They are probably still licking their wounds from the last time they tried to mess with the Sword Sorceress."

Sulana flipped her hand under mine and pinched me. "Very funny. I can tell you without a doubt that Dumont Fortenz is not going to give up just because he lost his hostages and a couple of men."

I took a deep breath and sighed. She was right, of course. By casting the lightning strike that nearly took Sulana's life, Headmaster Dumont Fortenz had effectively declared war on the Archives, a war he was much better prepared to undertake. My unexpected counter-attack had wounded the headmaster and his compatriots, but as Sulana intimated, time was probably on their side.

"Well, I think we just concluded that we are getting nowhere by trying to force your recovery here. I can report that my problems with casting are getting worse too." Sulana raised an eyebrow but didn't interrupt. She knew I'd give her the full story later. "It's time to try something different."

Talon stood up and nodded. "Good. I'll draw you a map. And try to figure out what we'll tell your mother."

Sulana and I stood as well.

She shook her head at Talon and said, "Let me talk to her. Our healers have been unable to do anything for me, so she won't be in much of a position to argue."

Talon leaned over and picked up the practice sword Sulana had dropped. As he carried it away, he said, "Good luck with that."

CHAPTER 3

HEIR DESIGNATE

Headmaster Dumont Fortenz paced slowly back and forth in his second floor office at Thunderhead College. He was pleased to note that his leg didn't give him a single twinge of pain as he walked. The healer's vaetric splint was doing an admirable job of protecting the fracture from the pressure of his weight while it held the mending bone together.

He heard steps coming down the hallway outside his office and paused to watch the open doorway. Sorcerer Paeter Thoron strode into the room and stopped just inside the opening. He had a half-smile on his face and a mischievous glint in his eyes.

Dumont smiled at the man. "You look positively smug, Paeter. I take it your lovely wife was successful in her mission?" As Dumont walked behind his desk to sit down, he waved toward the chair on the other side, inviting Paeter to join him.

Paeter sat in the offered chair and folded his hands in his lap. "Yes, Master. Governor Brachus announced this morning that he has chosen Astin as the heir designate."

Dumont nodded. "Then congratulations are in order. I'm sure your son will make a fine Governor one day soon. How did the good people of Dusk react to the announcement?"

Paeter chuckled. "They were confused at first, but overall, I'd say the reaction was positive. Astin is a popular young man among his peers and the adults appreciate his work ethic and enthusiasm."

Dumont leaned back in his chair and folded his hands behind his head. "Excellent. What about Malcolm Brachus?"

Paeter's expression grew sour and he shrugged. "The governor's son was shocked, naturally, but he didn't make a fuss. I can't tell if he is secretly relieved that Astin has replaced him or if he is plotting something. We'll keep a close eye on him for a while."

"Give Uriel my thanks for carrying out my orders so splendidly." Dumont leaned forward and raised an eyebrow at Paeter. "Since you are here to deliver this news personally, I assume you have something for me?"

Paeter grinned and reached under his robe to slide a thick cloth sack from under his belt. The contents of the bag clinked as he dropped it on the desktop with a triumphant flourish. "Indeed I do, Master. Here are the amulets you requested."

Dumont took the bag and loosened the strings that held it closed. Peering inside, he saw four sparkling amulets. He couldn't help but smile broadly when he looked back up at Paeter. "Thank you, Paeter. You just made my day."

"What next, Master?"

Dumont pushed the bag of amulets aside and gave Paeter a grim nod. By delivering the amulets, Paeter had kept his part of the bargain that would put his son in the governor's seat, but Dumont trusted no one with the full scope of his plans. "What's next is going to be tricky and delicate, but it's nothing you need to be concerned about. I just wish we'd gotten further along before attracting the attention of the Archives."

Paeter frowned and sighed. "If only Lohan had found some other way of dealing with the Sword Sorceress and her team. He knew we were trying to move secretly. Capturing them was a stupid mistake."

Dumont waved a hand apologetically. "I'm afraid that's partly my fault. Before you and I left for Dusk last month, I told Lohan to detain anyone who showed too much interest in our activities here. When I came back to discover he had the Sword Sorceress in our dungeon, I was amused enough to try and take advantage of it. That was my mistake. I underestimated the Archives, and my attempt at distracting the Council did nothing but focus their attention on us."

Paeter raised an eyebrow. "Do you dare move forward then?"

Dumont took in a deep breath through his nose and let it out slowly while he thought about his answer. He'd been debating the same question with himself for nearly a month. He placed his hand on the bag of amulets. They were the final key to his plans. Everything was in place and conditions around the empire were the best they'd ever been. He could wait to act, but who knew what might change in the meantime? Yes, the Archives was watching, but he still had the advantage there as well.

Finally, he looked intently at Paeter and said, "I don't think I *dare* wait. The Archives hasn't been interested in us long enough to have placed spies yet. Meanwhile, our own spies tell me the Council has other problems to deal with. Their Sword Sorceress was badly hurt during her escape, and Jaylan Forester, their current candidate for her replacement, is having serious problems with his casting."

Paeter snorted. "I've had my share of trouble from Forester. He seemed plenty dangerous when you tried to stop his rescue attempt."

Dumont absently rubbed his thigh where the bone had been broken when Forester's moving wall of force had blasted the wilderness around him. "Tell me about it," he growled. "I'll deal with Forester eventually. In the meantime, we still have momentum and the advantage of surprise on our side." He picked up and hefted the bag of amulets. "Nothing is holding us back now."

CHAPTER 4
CONVALESCENCE

Sulana stood patiently in front of Senior Councilor Gregor Rissik's desk while he collected and tidied the parchment papers that were spread across the top. He stacked the papers in a single pile and thumped a stone paperweight on them. Keeping a wary eye on the tall stack as it slowly tilted and adjusted to the stone's weight, he folded his hands on his desk and gave Sulana a brief smile. "Sorry for the mess. I've been reviewing sanctuary reports most of the day."

Sulana returned his smile. "I understand, Councilor. You sent for me?"

"Yes. The Council has authorized me to tell you that your request for a leave of absence has been granted, effective immediately. If your leave extends beyond three months, they'd like you to check back and request an extension."

Relief washed through Sulana. The leave was generous. Hopefully, she wouldn't need anywhere near that much time.

"Thank you, Councilor. What is your opinion on how the discussion went and what the Council currently thinks about my condition?"

Councilor Rissik's mouth twisted into a frown and he seemed to consider his next words carefully. "I'll give you the truth, Sword Sorceress, because I think you'd want nothing less."

Sulana nodded as dread made her stomach drop. She *did* want the truth, but his face and tone told her she wouldn't like it.

"The Council is very concerned about the recent conflict with Thunderhead College."

Sulana rolled her eyes. "It's about time."

Councilor Rissik bowed his head slightly in acceptance of her criticism. "Yes, well, that concern has prompted the Council to make an unprecedented resolution with regard to the Sword Sorcerer program."

Sulana braced herself. *This is the part I'm not going to like.*

"The Council has resolved to find as many training candidates as possible and strongly encourage them to enter Sword Sorcerer training immediately. As part of that initiative, Jaylan Forester's application has finally been accepted."

Sulana went silent as she reacted to the news with a range of emotions. Several potential responses battled for prominence in her mind. She was disappointed that the Council seemed to have lost faith in her, although it was satisfying to learn that the Council was finally taking the threat of Thunderhead College seriously. She was excited that Jaylan had been accepted into the training program but worried about what that might mean for their upcoming journey.

Sulana decided to address the most pressing concern first. "Jaylan and I hoped to take some time off together. Do you think that will still be possible?"

The councilor nodded. "Yes, Jaylan has been granted leave to accompany you." He raised an eyebrow and gave her an impish grin. "In fact, I believe you'll have more company than either of you intended for your private trip to visit the druids."

Sulana frowned. At Lissy's suggestion, she had been careful to tell only a few trustworthy people about her trip to visit the Grand Cedars Spirit Refuge with Jaylan. She had intentionally omitted that information from her leave request. As far as anyone was supposed to know, they were headed to the capital city of Cassandria to speak with the imperial healers there.

Sulana was aware that Lissy and Councilor Rissik had a close relationship, but she was still surprised to learn that Lissy had shared their true destination with him. Lissy had warned Sulana that she believed a spy was leaking information from the Archives to Thunderhead College, and even members of the Council were suspect.

"Yes, Lissy told me," the councilor confirmed quietly. "Your secret is safe with me, Sulana. And I wish you luck."

Sulana trusted Lissy's judgment enough to accept her apparent faith in the councilor. "Thank you, Councilor. You said something about extra company on our trip?"

"I'm sure you and Jaylan were looking forward to some time alone, but the Council doesn't want both our Sword Sorceress and our only current candidate for the training program to travel unprotected. Your entire team is going with you."

The news wasn't entirely unexpected, but Sulana would not have *asked* for the escort. Jaylan would probably be more annoyed that they wouldn't be traveling alone than she was. The thought of visiting the druids made her nervous, so it was comforting to know she'd have the support of her team. The most surprising thing was that the Council was willing to spend the funds.

Sulana gave the councilor a wry smile. "That was generous of them. Please give the Council my thanks for their consideration."

Councilor Rissik laughed and said, "You're welcome."

He stood up and his expression became serious. "I sincerely hope you find the help you need. Thunderhead College has been quiet for a while now, but I don't think the peace is going to last. We need you, Sword Sorceress Delano. We need you here and we need you whole."

Sulana bowed slightly to him. "That's the plan, Councilor. I appreciate your confidence, and I'll try not to let you down."

As Sulana left Councilor Rissik's office, she thought back on his comment about how the peace would not last. She agreed with his concerns. Thunderhead College had an agenda that no one at the Archives fully understood. Everyone believed it was only a matter of time before they would try something new. When that happened, she and Jaylan needed to be ready.

CHAPTER 5
LOST CONFIDENCE

Patches danced around more than usual when I tried to saddle him for our trip. I think he caught on to my excitement at the idea of leaving the Archives for a while. His step was quick as we headed down Alpine Lakes Trail toward the valley. I grinned at Sulana. "I think Patches is a fan of this idea."

Sulana's horse Stardust tossed her head and Sulana had to hold the mare back from breaking into a trot. "His enthusiasm seems to be infectious," she said with an answering smile.

It was high summer, so even though we were leaving early in the morning, the sun was already shining brightly through the trees and burning off the morning mist that rose from the waters of Castle Tarn. With sixteen-hours of daylight each day, our trip to the spirit refuge would go quickly.

As was his preference, Talon rode ahead of us on his black charger. His horse usually out-paced ours, but this morning we were keeping up just fine. Daven rode behind us and Barek followed in the rear guard position. It was just like old times, except that on this trip, I was a full member of the party.

Before we left, Sulana went over our roles and responsibilities. In the event of trouble, I was supposed to back her up with the small arsenal of implements I had stashed on my person. Daven would protect Sulana and then me from physical threats while we used vaetra. Talon and Barek would take the fight to the enemy.

We weren't expecting trouble, partly because few people knew where we were actually going, but Sulana wisely refused to take any chance at being caught unprepared on this outing. We'd start moving even more cautiously when we entered unfamiliar territory.

The trip down the mountain from the Archives to the valley floor went by too quickly. The open vistas that spread before us when we came to the rare breaks in the trees along the trail were breathtaking and filled me with a deep contentment. The mountaintops covered with tall green pines, dramatic outcroppings of moss-covered granite boulders, and a deep blue sky dotted with puffy clouds had always meant home to me.

We slowed down when we reached the valley floor and approached the intersection with Trench Highway, the main thoroughfare that connected Riverview with Northshore.

At that point, we had to make a decision. The spirit refuge was only about 35 miles to the southeast. However, the Trollhaven Mountains blocked our passage for many miles to the north and south. We'd have to go north to Riverview and cross at Gorge Pass, or go south to Northshore and travel through Heron Pass. Either way, our trip would be more like 90 miles.

We stopped at a clearing near the trailhead, just before a small bridge that crossed the fast-running creek bordering Trench Highway. Dismounting, we led the horses to the creek and let them drink.

Sulana and I stood next to each other while Patches and Stardust slurped at the stream and nibbled at the tender grass along the banks. "What do you think? Do we continue toward Northshore like you were planning?" I asked her.

Sulana observed the sky to the north and then to the south before nodding her head. "The weather still looks just as good in either direction. I see no reason to risk going north."

Going north through Riverview would bring us uncomfortably close to Thunderhead College. Under the circumstances, we wanted to avoid a confrontation with them. I nodded at her comment and let out an exasperated sigh. I was certain that, at some point, we would be forced into another conflict. But that wasn't what bothered me. I was concerned about being ready when the time finally arrived.

Sulana reached over to pat my arm and said, "Don't worry. Try to have faith that we'll figure out what's wrong with us and fix it."

I narrowed an eye at her and gave her a twisted grin. "I won't worry if you won't worry. You could use a little of your own advice."

She shrugged and smiled. "I know. I'm trying. It's really hard sometimes."

I reached over and gave her a one-armed hug. "We're doing what we can. We'll have to take this one step at a time and move on to the next idea if the druids can't or won't help you."

She leaned into my hug and returned it. "I just hope we don't run out of time."

"You and me both."

We fell silent at the sound of rhythmic tromping coming from the highway to the north. Soon a jingle overlaid the thud of boots, and Barek lifted his head to listen. Handing his reins to Talon, he jogged over the bridge toward the road just as a group of six Wintermen loped by the trail intersection.

The Wintermen slowed to a halt and turned to face Barek. He greeted them in his native language and exchanged words with the oldest man, who seemed to be the leader of the group. The other warriors watched us warily, except for the single young female warrior. Her attention never left Barek, and she assessed him with a hint of recognition.

The warriors from the northern tribes were dressed in gray leather armor with thin chain mail riveted to the chest and back. Each carried a claymore strapped to his or her back and a long dagger at the waist. Two of the men rested their hands on the hilts of their daggers.

All in all, the group looked thoroughly dangerous.

The tone of the conversation between Barek and the leader seemed cordial, but I wasn't surprised when Talon and Daven shifted their positions so they were between Sulana and the Wintermen. Sulana and I had automatically put some extra space between us in case we needed room to maneuver.

Barek concluded his conversation and saluted the Winterman leader by crossing his arms across his chest and bending forward in a shallow bow. The other man returned the gesture.

The warrior woman had shifted her gaze to Sulana at some time during the exchange. Her narrow, considering expression transformed into a smile, and she saluted Sulana in the Winterman way. Sulana dipped her head in acknowledgment.

The warriors formed up into two columns of three, and when the leader barked a command, they continued their loping jog toward the south.

Barek returned to us at a walk, his impassive face giving away nothing about what he'd learned. Talon handed him the reins to his big, gray war-horse Boulder, and he accepted them absently, his look distant.

Sulana waved her hand back and forth in Barek's direction, trying to get his attention. "Well, are you going to tell us what they said?"

Barek focused on Sulana and cleared his throat. "My countrymen are following a caravan from Thunderhead College."

"Why?" I asked. It wasn't unusual for Wintermen to travel within the empire for trade, but an armed group with a mission of trailing our citizens warranted explanation.

Barek looked at Sulana and I could swear he blushed. "The tribal elders have lost confidence in the Archives. They are sending small teams to monitor sorcerer activity within the empire."

Sulana's expression darkened. "That sounds like an invasion. Is the emperor aware of this *monitoring* activity?"

Barek shrugged. "They claim that he is."

Sulana shook her head and glared at Barek. "How are they even aware of what's going on? We haven't exactly advertised our conflict with Thunderhead College or my … difficulties."

Barek's blush deepened, and I noticed out of the corner of my eye that Talon was looking at the ground and shuffling his feet.

Sulana put her hands on her hips and stepped close to Barek. The move was meant to be authoritative, perhaps even intimidating, but the effect was spoiled by the disparity in their heights. Barek had to practically rest his chin on his chest to maintain eye contact. When Sulana moved forward, Stardust had to follow the pull of her reins.

"I think I get it. It's you. You've been spying for your people this whole time. *You* are the one who told the elders what has been going on at the Archives."

Barek took a breath and his eyes hardened. "Yes," was all he said.

Sulana also noticed Talon's guilty behavior and turned to him. "You knew about this? How long have you known? And why didn't you tell me?"

Talon spoke quickly, his tone defensive. "I've known for quite some time, but you weren't told because you didn't *need* to know. Until now, it hasn't mattered."

Sulana shouted, "Hasn't mattered? The tribes may be allies of the empire, but they've never been fond of sorcerers. I can't imagine what the Council would think about this." She turned around and ran into Stardust's nose, startling the horse into taking a step backward. She pushed the equine's head to the side and threw the reins at me. I caught them and pulled Stardust out of Sulana's way.

She started pacing, as she often did when she was distressed. When she glared over at Talon, he tilted his head to the side and shrugged, looking down at the ground again.

She stopped in front of him with a look of suspicion on her face. "Wait. The Council already knows, don't they?"

Talon looked back up at her. "Yes and no." He glanced over at Barek, who gave him a subtle nod. "Councilor Rissik knows."

Sulana resumed her pacing, but her steps were slower. "And now I know." She glanced at Talon with a thoughtful expression. "But only because I need to know." She stopped again, looking back and forth between Talon and Barek. "What changed?"

Barek's answer was direct and painful to hear. "The Archives no longer has a Sword Sorceress, and the Council has been infiltrated by an Integrationist spy." He glanced at me, but continued to address Sulana, "You defeated Thunderhead College at your last battle, but you probably would not prevail against them again. Meanwhile, you have made little progress in learning their ultimate goal. The time for subtlety is past. My people are here to ensure that the Accords are preserved."

My mouth went dry from the shock of Barek's words. His callous review of our current situation was as cruel as it was accurate.

Sulana face paled, and her reply came out as a croak. "Just go." When he didn't move, she waved the back of her hand toward the highway. "Go join your *people* and leave us be."

Barek still didn't move. When he spoke, it was in the softest tone I'd ever heard him use. "My duty to my people does not change my duty to the Archives. I must report what I see, but I wish to help however I can."

Sulana folded her arms across her chest. "How can I ever trust you again?"

Barek shrugged. "My oath to the Archives and to you still stands. Nothing has changed."

"Sure, nothing has changed," she said in a mocking tone.

"He's right," I interjected. Sulana looked over at me with raised eyebrows. "Barek's duties to his people have not prevented him from being a loyal part of your team up to now. Besides, this is good news. We need more time, and having Wintermen underfoot is going to be a huge distraction for Thunderhead College."

Sulana considered my comment for a moment and then stared at Barak for a moment more. She finally shook her head and held her hand out to me for Stardust's reins. As she mounted, she addressed Barek again. "Okay. I'll go along with this. I just hope you don't ever have to choose between your loyalty to the Archives and your loyalty to the tribes."

Barek's face clouded and he frowned. As he stepped up into his saddle, I heard him mumble, "That would be unfortunate."

CHAPTER 6

DEEP RIVER CAMP

Our journey south along Trench Highway was uneventful and the tension slowly eased among the members of the team. To his credit, Daven distracted everyone with simple conversation about the weather and food. After a while, we were all able to enjoy the day again and share some laughter.

That evening, we camped at a site routinely visited by highway travelers. We had to stop a little early in the day to take advantage of it, and we were rewarded with a spot right on the small adjoining lake. Daven and Talon did some fishing while Sulana and I set up camp. Barek tended to the horses. The weather was so nice that we decided to forgo the tent and everyone rolled out their blankets near the fire.

We struck camp and set out just after dawn the next morning.

Several miles before we reached Northshore, the forest ended abruptly and gave way to fields. Rather than go through town, we turned onto the dusty track that the farmers used to carry their goods to market. The farm road took us east through ripening fields of golden grain and then south through plots of cabbage and squash. A few of the field hands noticed us and some waved, but they kept to their business. The farm road eventually met up with Shoreline Road, which meandered along the edge of Teardrop Lake from Northshore to Delta.

I was secretly disappointed that our agrarian detour circumvented Northshore entirely. The desire to see the familiar faces and shops of my old home grew stronger as we approached, even though I knew it was not in our plans. I couldn't help but sigh when I turned Patches onto Shoreline Road with Northshore at my back.

Unfortunately, there was no way around Delta. The small but sprawling lakeside town filled the river valley between the rocky cliffs that rose to either side of the pass. We were forced to go straight through town, hoping that our deviation from the route to Cassandria would not be observed by anyone who might recognize us.

Luckily, the residents of Delta were far too busy with their own lives to pay much attention to a party of riders who were just passing through. I watched carefully, but didn't notice any lingering looks from the people we passed.

The only person I did recognize was Penny, the proprietor of the Eagle's Rest boarding house. I'd stayed at the Eagle's Rest a few months ago, long before I learned I could work vaetra. That seemed like a lifetime ago. But Penny didn't look up from sweeping her porch, her blond curls bobbing around her face as she worked. Although I was tempted to wave and wish her well, I resisted the urge and rode past unnoticed.

After a long day of riding, it would have been nice to stop for the night in Delta and enjoy Penny's cooking and soft beds. But even friendly questions might reveal details that would lead to irresistible gossip and mark our passage through town.

Instead, we continued a few miles into the mountain pass beyond Delta. We finally got to slide out of our saddles when we reached a nearly deserted camp site perched above the rushing waters of Deep River. The only other camper, a hearty fur trapper with a wild mop of hair and suspicious eyes, watched us settle in and ignored my greeting.

Setting up camp and making dinner was a quiet and perfunctory affair performed in the ruddy light of the long summer sunset. The mist floating over from the nearby river rapids inspired us to set up the tent this time. The four-person tent could not hold all of us comfortably, but since one person was always on watch, it wasn't a problem.

The next morning's dawn made fiery streamers of the high thin clouds that had slid across the sky overnight, presaging a change in the weather. Having taken the final watch shift, I was treated to a brief light show. While the clouds brightened from deep red and orange to pale pastels, and then finally to white, the fur trader gathered his belongings. I waved as he left the site and headed toward Delta, but he ignored me again.

I heard rustling from the tent and turned to see Sulana emerge, adjusting her blanket around her shoulders against the morning cool.

"Not quite the intimate excursion we had planned, is it?" she said quietly as she sat next to me.

I put my arm around her and pulled her close. "No, but the wariness of that trapper reminded me why it isn't wise to travel these mountains alone. With just the two of us, one would always be on watch. That would have taken all the fun out of the trip."

Sulana patted my chest. "They do call them the Trollhaven Mountains for a reason, I suppose."

I shrugged. "From what I understand, trolls are no more common here than in any other northern range, but these mountains have fewer settlements and fewer guard patrols to keep the females from creating lairs near the roads and camps."

"I could do without meeting another female troll," Sulana said with a shudder as she huddled closer. Sulana and the rest of her team had battled an enormous troll just a few months back, and it had been a difficult fight. A carefully timed strike by Sulana had ended the encounter and won her a bit of acclaim.

I smiled and kissed the top of her head. "I'm not worried. I have Sulana Delano, Sword Sorceress and Trollbane by my side."

Sulana poked me in the ribs. "You've been spending too much time with Ebnik."

Wizard Ebnik Vlastorus was a mutual friend of ours. He was the first person to jokingly dub Sulana a Trollbane upon hearing about her triumph. The title had stuck, especially among Sulana's friends.

"I miss him," I said with a sigh. "Particularly now that I'm having all these problems with casting."

Sulana looked up at me. "He said you should call for him if you need him. When we get back, let's see if he'd be willing to return to the Archives for a while and look into the problems you're having."

Ebnik's home was in Plains End. He had been at the Archives for a while helping Sulana investigate the thefts of a couple of vaetric artifacts, but he'd gone home before the trouble began with Thunderhead College. Ebnik was retired from his position as a Senior Councilor of the Archives, but he was still a powerful sorcerer with useful connections.

I nodded slowly, considering her suggestion. "I hate to bother him, but I'm not sure what else to do."

"It's settled then. Contact Ebnik when we get back. I'm sure he'll have some ideas. Or he'll know someone who does."

The canvas tent flap slapped open behind us and Daven came over.

"Hey, you two. Get a room," he said as he kneeled and extended his hands over the fire.

"Too much work," Sulana replied. "We'd have to throw all the lazy men out first."

"Hah. Not lazy. Just trying to get some rest. It's hard to sleep with that bear of a Winterman snoring right next to you. Good thing it's not winter or we'd have to worry about getting buried in an avalanche."

We chuckled at Daven's joke, then Sulana grew serious.

"Tell me the truth. Do you think the druids will help me?"

Daven glanced at her, seeming surprised at the change in subject. "How would I know?" His voice grew bitter. "But from what I've seen, they have no tolerance for sorcery."

Sulana nodded slowly. "That's what worries me. But you spent a lot of time with the druids before you came to the Archives, so I was thinking you'd know more about their commitment to healing people in need. Would it outweigh the fact that I'm a sorceress?"

Daven looked into the dwindling fire, his eyes unfocused. Finally, he shrugged. "When I was little, the druids always seemed helpful and concerned for the welfare of all life. My parents never let us miss a temple gathering. But then my brother was expelled because he was able to use vaetra. As far as I was concerned, the druids as well as my family betrayed him. My father didn't even try to stop me when I denounced their prejudice and followed Terrence to the Archives."

I knew Daven had gone to the Archives with his sorcerer brother when he was in his early teens, but this was the first time I'd heard any details about how that happened. His brother had apparently been faced with the same decision I had. He could either go to the Archives and learn sorcery, or he could ignore his abilities and try to continue life among the mundane, hoping his friends and family didn't hold his sorcery potential against him. But I had since learned that the druids offered a third option: the sorcerer could submit to a Binding ritual.

Being Bound meant permanently giving up the ability to use vaetra. The druids could manipulate biology to harm as well as to heal. The Binding ceremony made it impossible for a sorcerer to channel vaetra. However, it left the subject's sensitivity intact. The former sorcerer was forever aware of sorcery, but no longer able to use it. Binding was the only way a person with the ability to use vaetra would be allowed back into the temples and truly be able to rejoin the mundane.

"Your brother didn't want to be Bound?" I asked tentatively.

Daven gave me a challenging glare. "Would you?"

I grimaced and shook my head. "No, but I didn't grow up in a devout family with the temple a prominent part of my life."

Daven went back to staring at the fire. "My parents were so offended by his ability to use vaetra that they didn't even *ask* him if he would agree to be Bound. Their attitude convinced him that the sacrifice wouldn't make any difference."

Sulana looked down into the dying embers of the camp fire. "So, there really isn't much hope."

Daven shook his head. "I honestly don't know what they'll say."

We all stood as Barek and Talon appeared. Barek immediately went to work breaking down the tent. Talon looked at the three of us standing around the fire and made a shooing motion with his hands.

"We're wasting daylight," he said, as if he had been the one waiting.

We put out the fire, gathered our things, and packed up the horses. As I sat astride Patches waiting for everyone else to mount, I looked down the road that would lead us toward

Grand Cedars Refuge. The wide path was carved into the side of a steep, rocky cliff. Wildflowers and grasses grew in small clumps across the sporadically traveled roadbed, quivering in the morning breeze that often followed sunrise. From here, we would be leaving civilization behind and entering the deep wilderness.

CHAPTER 7

ABANDONED VILLAGE

For most of the first day, we followed the winding path of the river. The road took us across wide open meadows of green-gold grasses and up along cliffs where we enjoyed commanding views of the tree-lined river below. The river narrowed to raging rapids and widened into peaceful sloughs where we stopped to rest ourselves and the horses.

About mid-afternoon, we came to a junction of road and river. Cedar River flowed out of a deep fold in the mountains to the north and merged with Deep River. To continue east, we'd have to cross the narrow bridge that spanned the tributary. But our destination was to the north on the road that followed Cedar River back into the shadows of the thickly forested canyon.

As we entered the canyon, something large and furry ran across the pathway about fifty yards ahead of us. Talon's horse shied to the side and danced a little, but the rest of the horses just froze and stared up the trail with their ears perked.

"Troll," Talon said. "Just a small one though. Probably a male. I doubt he'll bother us, but keep your eyes open anyway."

Daven looked around and commented, "There's not much point in readying my bow. Too many trees. It would be on us before I got a shot off."

Talon watched the trail and nodded absently. "I wouldn't worry about it. We're too large a group. He has other things on his mind."

On average, female trolls were much bigger than the males. They set up permanent lairs and viciously defended the territory around them. They welcomed the nomadic male trolls only during the fall mating season, chasing them away or even killing them the rest of the year. At the height of summer, male trolls were busy locating female territories and fighting off the other males while carefully avoiding a direct encounter with the females.

Avoiding an encounter with a female troll sounded like a sensible plan to me.

The horses weren't happy about continuing forward, but they eventually obliged after some encouragement. Patches took in big snorts of air as we continued down the road. He shuddered when we passed the spot where the troll had crossed the trail.

All of us stayed on high alert while we traveled north through the canyon. A couple of tense hours later, the road curved near an abandoned village. In truth, calling it a village was a stretch. Three small, rotting log cabins sat back against a tumble of moss-covered boulders. A crumbling rock palisade surrounded the cabins and a small patch of meadow. Its wooden gateway had long since collapsed. I could barely see the remains of the gate through the grass and white daisies that had grown up around it.

Sulana surveyed the area inside the palisade. "It looks like we aren't the first travelers to stop here. We won't make it to the refuge today anyway, so this is probably a decent place to camp."

She exchanged a glance with Barek and Talon, and they both nodded. "It will do," Talon agreed.

We rode through the gateway and over to the cabins. The cabins had no doors and light streamed in through holes in the roofs, but the walls seemed sound enough, and the dirt floors had been cleared. Three large fire rings set in front of the cabins showed signs of recent use. We unburdened the horses and staked them out where they could browse on the tall grass in the enclosure.

As evening fell, we set fires in all three of the pits. Like most forest creatures, trolls had a healthy fear of fire. We also decided that making enough light to shoot at anything entering the palisade was more important than trying to maintain our night vision. That night, we kept two people on guard rather than one.

Barek and I had the second shift. Even with the light of the fires, bright stars twinkled down at us between the gathering clouds in the moonless midnight sky. With the exception of an occasional mosquito and the vigilant watch for a troll attack, it was a lovely night.

I came back to my seat after adding a log to one of the fires. Barek sat cross-legged on the ground and alternated his attention between the open gateway and a broken-down section of wall that had a narrow, V-shaped gap. Sulana's crossbow rested next to his leg.

I sat back down on the thick section of log I was using as a stool, careful not to step on Daven's bow. I had one arrow nocked and another sitting outside of the quiver, but if something charged us, I was pretty sure I'd only have time for one shot.

I looked down at Barek and asked him something that had been bothering me since our encounter with his countrymen two days ago.

"Should we be worried?" I asked quietly.

He looked up at me and narrowed his eyes. "About ..."

"About the fact that the emperor has invited the Wintermen to help him keep an eye on the empire's sorcerers."

Barek grimaced and slowly nodded. "I have been expecting that question. And the answer is yes."

"You said they've lost faith in the Archives. Does that mean we're being watched as well?"

He chuckled slowly and gave me a wry grin. "You mean by someone other than me?"

I rolled my eyes. "Point taken. But yes, by someone other than you."

He frowned and looked through the flames of the fire. "You can count on it."

I mused to myself, "I don't understand why the emperor would use Wintermen when he has the Imperial Guard."

Barek cleared his throat and took a deep breath. "The treaty between the empire and my people says that the emperor must enforce the Sorcery Accords, using our help if necessary. The guard has close ties to the regions that host them. If the emperor has doubts about the loyalty of a governor, he cannot have confidence in the guard for that province either."

My back straightened in reaction to the accusation. I'd once been an Imperial Guard captain myself, and I resented the implication that the guard would disobey the emperor. "The chain of command for the Imperial Guard cascades down from the emperor himself. His word is law."

Barek raised a hand in a gesture of peace. "I understand. But there are many ways to interpret and execute orders."

He was right, of course. I'd seen it firsthand. Subordinates could get creative with orders they didn't understand or support. One of my responsibilities as captain was to minimize that kind of creativity by always issuing clear and direct orders. It was easier said than done.

I nodded my head in understanding. "There are many layers of *interpretation* between the emperor and the guardsmen who carry out the orders. That's a lot of opportunities for miscommunication."

Barek sighed. "Exactly. Winterman patrols give the emperor a mobile set of eyes that are not biased by local politics."

"But Winterman patrols are not directly under the emperor's control. They may support the goal of enforcing the accords, but their agenda is directed by the tribes."

Barek nodded and looked up at me with a serious expression. "That is why I said we should worry. I will do what I can, but the failure of the Archives to enforce the accords may be seen as going along with the violations."

"Guilt by association," I mumbled.

Barek shrugged. "It may not come to that. If the druids can help Sulana and you can overcome your difficulties, the Council will appear stronger and more capable of performing its duty. It will then be up to the Council to prove its commitment to the Accords by taking appropriate action."

Barek made it sound like the future of the Archives, and maybe the fate of all the empire's sorcerers, rested on Sulana's shoulders and mine. Just a few months ago, I was a bored innkeeper looking for adventure. I should have been careful what I wished for. "What about the expanded training program the Council is starting? Doesn't that help?"

"It does. But it comes too late. The recruits will be months behind the Lightning Corps."

That was a new term. "Lightning Corps?"

He looked at me and raised an eyebrow. "That is the name the Thunderhead College forces have given themselves, according to Turel, the commander of the patrol I spoke with."

The warrior sorcerers of Thunderhead College had a name. An identity. I knew that would improve their solidarity and morale. It would draw more sorcerers to their banner from around the empire. Sorcerers who were tired of being looked down upon would long to join with others who rejoiced in their abilities. It wouldn't occur to them that creating an organized, and armed, society of sorcerers would draw an even sharper line between the sorcerers and the mundane than already existed. They would achieve the opposite of their supposed Integrationist dream. No wonder the emperor was concerned.

"Why haven't you told Sulana any of this?" I asked.

Barak stared resolutely at the fire, not willing to look me in the eye. "She wasn't ready to hear."

I took a few deep breaths, letting a flash of anger subside. Barak had a point. Sulana had been mostly ignoring him since the encounter with the Winterman patrol. His tentative attempts at conversation with her had been met with curt responses.

I stood up and paced back and forth a few times. We needed to do something. I added more logs to the fires while I thought through what Barek had just told me.

The distant howl of a wolf reminded me that the world was filled with predators and prey. I was starting to feel like prey, and it rankled.

I sat back down with a frustrated sigh. *One thing at a time.* We were already doing what we could for Sulana. I would have to put my problems on hold for the moment, but as soon as we got back to the Archives, I was going to send for Ebnik.

As if reading my mind, Barek looked up at me and said, "Let's just see what happens tomorrow."

Tomorrow we would arrive at Grand Cedars Refuge, and we'd find out whether or not the druids would be willing to help Sulana.

CHAPTER 8
GRAND CEDARS REFUGE

Daybreak arrived as a slow brightening of the low, gray overcast that had moved in during the late hours of the night. Because of the change in the weather, everyone went through the morning routine of breaking our fast and preparing to leave in a monosyllabic shuffle. Even the horses seemed subdued. Only the mosquitoes were energized by the warm moist air that the clouds had trapped around us.

Once we got going and the yawning subsided, I rode close to Sulana and told her about my fireside conversation with Barek. She was as alarmed as I had been and berated Barek for not telling her sooner. But then she conceded that she had not been the most receptive listener lately. Talon and Daven overheard our conversation and drew Barek back into it with additional questions. By the time we had exhausted the subject, Sulana and Barek had achieved an uneasy truce. I think she was starting to see that Barek could be a source of valuable information for us as well as for his Wintermen brethren.

We saw the first border markers for the Grand Cedars Refuge after a couple of hours on the road. Every ten to twenty yards along both sides of the road, a tree had its lower branches trimmed away and a hand-sized square cut out of the bark at waist height. I'd learned at an early age that those marks meant "no trespassing." Strangely, the branches and shrubs along the border had woven themselves into an abnormally thick tangle. I had little doubt that the druids had created this living fence to discourage road travelers who failed to heed the markers.

The road eventually led to an entryway built from two tall, thick posts with a cross-member connecting their tops. The horizontal piece was carved with the name of the refuge. As we passed through the entrance to the refuge, the clouds released a light drizzle that made us all put up our hoods.

"I hope this isn't a sign," Sulana said, with a glance at the clouds.

"It's not," I replied with forced confidence. "This storm has been coming our way since before yesterday. We're just lucky it didn't arrive last night. I don't think those cabins would have given us much protection. Actually, I think this weather is a good sign."

"How so?"

"This is an unusual storm for summer. They normally come in with wind and lightning and then dump buckets of rain. This drizzly overcast may be gloomy, but it sure beats a downpour."

Sulana shuddered and flashed me a quick smile. "I'll go along with that."

With a low whinny, Patches came to a halt, and I looked ahead to see why. Talon had stopped with his hand raised. About a dozen yards ahead of him, three riders blocked the road. All of them were dressed in green and carried swords. Like us, they had their hoods up, so it was difficult to see their faces.

Rangers. They found us sooner than I expected.

The center man rode forward a few paces. A serious pair of eyes observed us from under the shadow of his hood. "Welcome to the Grand Cedars Refuge," he said. "May I know the reason for your visit?"

The greeting was friendly enough, but our answer to his question would probably determine whether or not we'd be allowed to proceed.

I expected Talon to answer for us, but before the ranger finished speaking, Daven eased his horse to the front of our group and responded with an urgent tone.

"My mistress is ill and her healer has not been able to cure her. Grand Cedars has the best healers in the empire, and she seeks their help."

The rest of us sat still and wisely said nothing while the lead ranger looked each of us over in turn. His gaze lingered on Sulana, undoubtedly noticing that she didn't look particularly sick. "What is the nature of her illness?"

"She was struck by lightning and suffers from lingering weakness."

The ranger sat back in his saddle and considered us again. He motioned toward the trees by the side of the road behind us, and as I turned to look, three monks slid silently out of the forest in knee-length, tan robes. They arranged themselves in a semi-circle behind us. Two of the monks had quarterstaves in hand, and one held a sling at the ready. We were surrounded.

The ranger narrowed his eyes at Daven and said, "Keep your horses at a walk and follow me." He turned his mount around and rode away from us. His fellow rangers fell in alongside our group, casting occasional glances our way. The monks followed on foot.

Our procession moved down the road without further comment for a couple of miles through some of the largest cedar trees I'd ever seen. They truly were grand. Some were so thick around the base that I doubted four people linking hands could reach all the way around. The forest was awash with wildlife. A snowshoe hare zig-zagged down the track ahead of us, its white feet flickering before it disappeared into a shrub. A squirrel bounced across the road with tail held high and spiraled up a tree trunk, coming to rest on a branch where it sat and scolded us as we rode past.

I couldn't help but feel like a prisoner, in spite of the fact that our "escort" had allowed us to keep our weapons. For the moment, they appeared to accept us at face value, but the lead ranger obviously had his doubts.

His caution was understandable. As the martial branch of the druid Hierarchy, rangers and monks were responsible for protecting the priests, temples, and refuges. The monks behind us were probably stationed permanently at the monastery here on the refuge. The rangers, as their title implied, patrolled the forest and moved around the empire; they were the mobile eyes and ears of the druids. Rangers would see armed strangers within their domain as a potential threat.

Daven speaking up like he did had surprised me into silence. He'd apparently had the same effect on the others. The shock was giving way to concern over how the druids would react when they learned the truth about Sulana. Daven hadn't lied, exactly, but he'd knowingly left out information that he knew would be important to the druids.

There was nothing to do but see how things would turn out when we met the high priest of the Grand Cedars Monastery. And it looked like we'd get that chance soon. The tall log walls of the preserve materialized out of the misty rain. The rangers led us through an open gateway into a wide square. A two-story monastery building squatted near the gray shoreline of Cedar Lake. A covered walkway curved from the front of the monastery to the nearby dock.

Word of our coming had apparently preceded us.

I had never seen a high priest or priestess in person before, but the woman who stood waiting under the protection of the walkway had a presence that left no doubt as to her identity. The symbol of the druid priesthood on the breast of her violet cloak was familiar, but different from others I'd seen. Her badge of office had the usual three concentric circles outlined in black. The center was filled with silver as it seemed to be with all priests, but the middle circle was filled with bright red. All the priests I'd seen before had symbols with a blue, green, or empty middle circle.

Standing next to the high priestess was a tall older ranger whose raptor stare never left us as we approached. On her other side was a young woman who wore the purple cloak of a druid.

The ranger leading our party held up his hand in a "hold here" gesture. As we came to a halt, I caught the end of a conversation between the high priestess and the young woman.

"I am grateful for your faith in my abilities, Your Grace," said the young woman with a shallow bow.

The high priestess smiled and placed a hand on the young woman's shoulder. "You do not have to be a priestess to be a good healer, Karla. I would be a fool not to see that the spirits have other plans for you. Of course you may keep your cottage and continue your work here." She removed her hand and turned her attention our way. "Now, let us see what the storm has brought."

The lead ranger saluted the high priestess and the ranger standing next to her by placing his right fist over his left shoulder and bowing his head. The young woman apparently did not rate such a greeting. Once she had turned to fully face us, I was able to see that the druid emblem on her cloak had a blue middle circle.

The ranger addressed the high priestess. "Greetings, Your Grace. I bring a young noblewoman who seeks the help of our healers."

The high priestess narrowed her eyes at Sulana. "Odd attire for a noblewoman. I am Medwina Chalker, High Priestess of this refuge. How may I address you, my dear?"

Sulana blushed and lowered her head. "My apologies, Your Grace. I am not a noblewoman. My compatriot may have chosen his words poorly when he introduced us." Sulana glanced over at Daven with a frown. He shrugged in response as if to say it wasn't his fault that the ranger had read into his words.

High Priestess Chalker raised her eyebrows but said nothing as she waited patiently for an explanation. The lead ranger's face went rigid upon Sulana's confession and he started to draw his sword. He stopped when the ranger who stood with the priestess motioned him to stand down.

We should probably just tell them the truth. I hoped Sulana would reach the same conclusion, but I didn't dare say anything that would interrupt the delicate moment.

Sulana took a deep breath and returned the priestess's direct gaze. "I was struck by lightning several weeks ago, and the healers I've seen so far have been unable to help me regain my strength and coordination. Your healing college is renowned for its skill, and I hoped to be accepted as a patient here. I can pay for my treatment, of course."

Before the priestess could respond, the young druid woman took a few quick steps forward and put her hand on Sulana's leg. She smiled encouragingly up at Sulana and spoke with enthusiasm. "Of course we can help you. Lightning strike victims are rare, but the spirits must have guided you here because I actually have experience treating it. No two patients seem to suffer exactly the same symptoms, but I'm sure we can find a way to help you get better."

The high priestess cleared her throat loudly and extended her arm toward the druid girl, signaling her to return to the sheltered walkway. "Karla, come away from there. We have more to learn about our visitors before we start offering our services."

Karla looked around at the rest of us, her eyes lingering on our weapons and armor. She lifted her hand from Sulana's leg as if stung and then backed away as directed.

Once Karla had returned to the priestess's side, the older woman addressed Sulana again. "Thank you for explaining the purpose of your visit. However, I'm still not sure how I should address you."

Here it comes, I thought. *She wants to know exactly who we are.*

Sulana took in another deep breath and let it out as a sigh. She answered clearly and plainly. "My name is Sulana Delano, Your Grace, and I am Sword Sorceress of the Archives."

Karla gasped. I could hear the monks behind us mumbling and fidgeting. The rangers shifted their horses closer to the priestess.

The senior ranger standing next to the high priestess folded his arms and nodded his head with a rueful smile, as if he had expected Sulana's declaration.

The high priestess gave no indication that she was shocked either, but when she spoke again, her voice was tight with disapproval. "Well, Sorceress Delano, I'm afraid that it's impossible for us to accept you as a patient. Frankly, I'm surprised you would ask. Surely, our healers would not able to help you when the great healers of the Archives have failed."

Sulana's face turned grim. "Druid healers have an advantage that ours do not: the guidance of the spirits. I had hoped you would see past my occupation and have the compassion to treat me as a fellow human being."

Karla turned pleading eyes to the high priestess. "We can help her, Your Grace, I'm sure of it."

The priestess growled, "Silence, Karla. Do not say another word." The younger woman cringed. The priestess then tilted her head back and gave Sulana an appraising look. "A sorceress of the faith? How unexpected. And impossible. Sorcery is an abuse of vaetra. Your *occupation* does not respect the spirits or follow their guidance. Your kind consumes without giving back. It would be blasphemy to let you remain on the sacred ground of the refuge."

Sulana looked around at the rest of us. I shook my head and had nothing to offer. Daven glared at the high priestess and returned Sulana's glance with an apologetic grimace. Barek and Talon both gave Sulana a sympathetic shrug.

Sulana turned back to the high priestess. "I'm sorry you feel that way, Your Grace. I respect the spirits, no matter what you may think about sorcery, but I understand that you must obey the policies of the Druid Hierarchy. I apologize for wasting your time."

The high priestess nodded curtly at Sulana. "Goodbye, Sorceress Delano. I wish you luck in finding the help you need, but you shall not find it here." She then addressed the senior ranger standing next to her. "Marshal Shields, please have your men escort the Sword Sorceress and her companions off the refuge."

The marshal nodded toward the lead ranger escorting our party, confirming High Priestess Chalker's order.

Karla bit her lip and gave Sulana a pained, sympathetic look. She appeared to be genuinely sorry that she couldn't help. As our group turned our horses to leave, I half smiled at her in gratitude.

Before I turned my back on the druids, I caught a glimpse of the marshal's face. His eyes were on Sulana and his look was contemplative. I wasn't sure how to read the expression, but it made me uneasy. When I turned around again to get a better look at him, his gaze had shifted to me, and his eyes had narrowed in assessment. I was suddenly glad that he was not part of the escort that formed up around us to herd us off the refuge.

The monks and rangers stayed behind us and were silent the whole way back to the entryway. By unspoken agreement, no one in our party said a word either. I don't think any of us wanted to give them the satisfaction of commiserating in their presence.

Along the way, the rain transitioned from the gentle drizzle it had been most of the morning to gusty bouts of driving rain. We huddled in our wet cloaks as we passed back under the Grand Cedars Refuge sign. When I looked back over my shoulder, our escort had vanished.

CHAPTER 9

DRUID HEALER

Daven turned in his saddle and watched the road behind us for a moment, making sure our escort was truly gone. He turned back around with a sigh. "Well, that failed."

Sulana cleared her throat. "Thank you, Mr. Obvious. Do you have any constructive thoughts?"

"Hey, I warned you. The druids have even less tolerance for sorcery than I anticipated. But I am sorry, Sulana. I was hoping they'd accept you."

The rain had stopped again, so Sulana removed her soggy, clinging hood. "Thanks for trying to ease the introduction. The look on the ranger's face when he learned I wasn't a *noblewoman* was priceless." She and Daven shared a chuckle, but Barek and Talon and I remained silent. My sense of humor had fled me.

Interrupting their exchange, I said, "So what now? Back to the Archives? Back to a treatment plan that wasn't working?"

Sulana gave me an exasperated sidelong glance. "Settle down. We all knew this was a long shot. We'll just have to try something else."

"Sorry. I guess I had my hopes up. That druid healer … Karla? She seemed pretty sure she could have helped you."

"Maybe she could have, and maybe not. I guess we'll never know." Sulana gave me a sheepish look and added, "Part of me is glad it didn't work out."

I was genuinely surprised. "Why?"

"We all know how druids feel about sorcerers. I wasn't looking forward to spending a lot of time among them. Talk about a hostile environment."

We had ridden out of sight of the refuge entrance, and I felt our last hope of getting help for Sulana slip away. Like she said, we'd try to figure out something else, but no one had any other ideas that I'd heard. I couldn't stop myself from complaining about the druid rejection.

"What's the big deal, anyway? Sorcerers use vaetra, and druids use vaetra. Why is our way *dirty* and theirs *sacred?* Okay, I get that they work with the *blessings of the spirits,* whatever that means, but the end result is pretty much the same isn't it?"

Sulana's expression was incredulous. "Don't ever let a druid hear you say that. Druids are the spiritual leaders of the mundane. You're trying to make them out to be just another kind of sorcerer. Tarring them with the same brush as us would undermine their power."

"Well, *aren't* they just another kind of sorcerer?"

"Not really. Their methods are supposedly quite different from ours. We use incantations to shape vaetra into a physical manifestation. They pray to the spirits for a physical manifestation and offer vaetra as a sacrifice."

"But the end result is often the same," I insisted.

Sulana was getting the look that told me I was asking too many questions again. "Yes and no. There is some cross-over, but druids can easily do some things we find nearly impossible, and the reverse is true as well."

I rode in silence for a while, considering the insights Sulana had shared. *The most basic theory of working with vaetra says that every manifestation must come from an incantation of some kind. Did the druids get their incantations from the spirits?* I glanced over at her with my lips pursed, and she gave me a narrow look. She probably knew I was holding back more questions. I decided to give her a break and think about it some more myself.

I didn't get far in my ruminations.

We were exiting the refuge border when Talon pointed toward the living fence that angled away from us along the right side of the road. "There's someone ahead."

If the druids wanted us to leave, there would be no good reason to have someone cut us off. This encounter was something else. Possibly an ambush.

Daven uncovered his bow and had it strung in seconds. His ability to perform that maneuver from the saddle was nothing less than amazing. A couple seconds later, he had an arrow nocked and ready.

"Don't shoot," cried a female voice from the trees. The druid girl Karla stepped through the border fence as if it had melted around her to let her pass. She had her hands up in surrender and her eyes were wide with alarm. Her breath came in gasps, and I realized she had run through the forest to catch up with us. Daven lowered his bow, releasing the tension on the string, and she slowly dropped her hands.

Karla looked a lot less tidy than the last time we'd seen her. Her plum-colored woolen dress had a couple of small tears, and it was splattered with mud. Her damp hair was in disarray and a few red scratches marked her face and hands. She seemed to realize how wild she looked. As she walked slowly toward us, she made a half-hearted attempt to draw a few tendrils of hair behind her ears.

"I'm so glad I caught up to you," she panted with a hand on her chest.

Daven positioned himself in front of Sulana and demanded, "What do you want?"

Karla stopped a few yards from Daven and blinked in surprise at the anger in his voice.

"I … I want to talk to the Sword Sorceress."

Sulana urged Stardust alongside Daven, and she grabbed his arm when he started to interpose himself again. "It's fine, Daven. She's not here to attack us."

Karla smiled tentatively, as if uncertain of whether or not Sulana was joking. "Attack you? Me?" She shook her head in confusion. "I'm a healer. I wouldn't know how to attack you. Even if I wanted to, which I don't."

Sulana waited patiently for Karla's nervous chatter to stop. "That's good to know. Perhaps you can tell us what you *did* have in mind?"

Karla spread her hands. "I want to help you, of course. Why else would I run all the way out here in the rain?" She looked back at the refuge border, seeming to realize for the first time that she stood alone against sorcerers and armed warriors. She looked up at Sulana with a worried frown. "I swear by the spirits that I'm telling the truth."

Sulana smiled down at the druid. "I believe you. You have nothing to fear from us." She gave Daven a significant look. He rolled his eyes and started to put away his bow.

She turned back to Karla. "We weren't formally introduced. As you know, I'm Sword Sorceress Sulana Delano, but you can call me Sulana. I'm not feeling very Sword Sorceress-y lately."

Karla took her cue and straightened her back. "I'm Karla Scoles, Druid Adept of the Grand Cedars College of Medicine." Then she dropped the formal tone and her voice became bitter. "Please call me Karla, though. Hearing people call me 'Adept Scoles' always makes me cringe and now the term is too much like a mean joke." Karla's eyes took on a far-away look.

Sulana prompted, "Nice to meet you, Karla," and waited for the druid to continue.

Karla gave Sulana a blank look for a few moments before realizing Sulana was waiting for her to speak. "Oh. Sorry. I'm here because I would like to try to heal your lightning injury."

Sulana's eyebrows went up in surprise. "Right now? You can do that?"

Karla gave Sulana a sideways look through a furrowed brow. "No, not *right now*. It could take weeks, maybe months, to uncover the true nature of the injury and apply the proper therapy."

Sulana's shoulders slumped. "Months? I don't have that kind of time."

Karla shrugged with an apologetic look. Apparently there was no way to treat Sulana quickly, even with the help of the spirits.

To me, the important thing was that Karla was offering hope where we'd had none before. We would achieve nothing if we went back to the Archives right then.

"What choice do you have?" I asked. Barek, Talon, and Daven nodded in agreement as soon as the words left my mouth.

Sulana took in our acceptance of Karla's proposal and opened her mouth a couple of times to speak, but no words came out. She turned back to Karla and asked, "What will you need me to do?"

Karla looked nervously down the road in both directions. "The first thing we need to do is get off this road. Someone could come by at any time. If word gets back to the high priestess that I was seen talking to you, I could get in big trouble." Karla waved toward the place where she had exited the forest and started backing up in that direction. "Follow me to my cottage, and I'll do an examination. I might be able to give you a better idea of how long your treatment will take."

Sulana nodded and nudged her horse to follow Karla, but Talon stopped her with a gesture. "We'll meet you at the forest edge," he said to the druid. "Everyone else follow my lead."

Talon walked his horse back toward the refuge for several paces and then turned around and headed away again. The rest of us followed him like children on a pony ride, understanding his goal of obscuring the hoof prints we'd left behind when we stopped to talk with Karla. When he reached a spot where the roadbed turned to hard stone, he led us off the road and onto the meadow that bordered it. He angled toward Karla, who stood at the forest's edge with a puzzled look on her face.

When we arrived at Karla's position, I saw that she hadn't used druid magic to get through the refuge border after all. The entrance to the forest trail was cleverly concealed by an overlapping section of the living fence. I didn't even realize a gap was there until she stepped into it, waving for us to follow.

Talon dismounted before following Karla into the forest, and the rest of us did the same. It was obvious that the trail was too overgrown for mounted travel at this point. Wet branches were swept forward by our passage, springing back to spray the next member of the party with droplets of water. I was following Daven and got slapped in the face by a whipping branch more than once before I put more space between us. From the occasional curses around me, I wasn't the only one.

The forest is rebuking us for invading the sanctity of the refuge.

As we went deeper into the forest, the shrubs and smaller trees were choked out by the interconnecting canopy of the giant cedars that dominated the refuge. The ground was dark with moist humus and littered with dead cedar fronds of orange, rust, and brown. Ferns clustered in the few places where sunlight filtered through the canopy. In one stretch, the trail followed the length of a fallen cedar, its rotting horizontal trunk thicker than I was tall.

With the increased spacing between the trees came the distinct impression that we were being watched. I saw and heard nothing unusual, but the feeling persisted.

It was hard to keep track of which direction we were traveling, since I couldn't see far enough to orient on any landmarks. My best guess was that we were heading deeper into a cleft in the mountains away from the monastery.

After about twenty minutes, the trail widened into a clearing. In the center of the clearing squatted a mossy, stone cottage with a sharply peaked, shingle roof. A substantial mound of firewood was piled near the house. A well-used ax leaned against an upright log and a few chunks of split wood littered the ground nearby. The giant cedars seemed to keep a respectful distance from the cottage grounds, their branches arching protectively over most of the clearing.

Karla motioned toward a small hitching post next to the cottage and said she'd be right back before running inside. The posts wobbled as we tied our reins to the rail. Barek stepped back and frowned doubtfully at the arrangement. Daven chuckled and said, "Don't worry, the horses will hold it up."

Karla came back out of the cabin with a leather satchel over her shoulder. She disappeared around the opposite corner of the cabin with a wave for us to follow.

When we came around the corner, Sulana halted and stared pensively.

Karla was using a hand broom to brush twigs and fronds from the surface of a stone altar. The three concentric circles of the druid faith were chiseled into the front of it. Karla looked over her shoulder, raised her eyebrows, and called, "Well, come on, I can't examine you over there."

Sulana moved forward with hesitant steps. "What exactly is involved with this *examination?*"

Karla rolled her eyes. "Don't worry. It won't hurt. All you have to do is lie still on the altar and let me call the spirits. The rest is up to them."

Sulana didn't seem convinced. She was probably wondering what "the rest" would entail, as was I. Sulana glanced at me and I shrugged. She took a deep breath and sat on the altar. Karla instructed her to remove her boots and socks and helped her lie down. I moved to the side of the altar and Daven took a position on the opposite side. We both looked at Karla and then each other before nodding simultaneously. Neither of us would let Sulana come to harm. Barek and Talon stood at the foot of the altar opposite Karla.

Karla noted our protectiveness and smiled reassuringly. "Just don't touch her while I work," she warned. She extracted a bottle from her satchel and popped the stopper. Bowing her head, she said a prayer to the spirits as she poured the water into a shallow bowl recessed into the end of the altar near Sulana's head. "Spirits of water and earth, air and wood. Sprites, nymphs, faeries, and dryads, heed my call. Bless us with your help in healing this woman. Come to me now and give me the understanding and strength to carry out your will. May the spirits guide me."

Karla set the bottle on the ground. She placed one palm across Sulana's forehead and the other hand in the pool of water she had poured. She bowed her head again and closed her eyes.

We stood quietly for what seemed like several minutes. It gave me time to notice how quiet the forest was. I heard an occasional bird chirp in the branches high above us, but otherwise, the ancient forest was as silent as an empty temple.

Sulana started fidgeting, and Karla pressed her hand harder against Sulana's forehead in admonition. Sulana sighed and then remained still.

After a few more moments, I heard a soft hum from all around me. I'd come to recognize this particular quality of sound as vaetric manifestation noise, so I knew that none of the others could hear it. At first, I felt satisfaction that my suspicions about druids being a kind of sorcerer were right after all. Then I realized that Karla wasn't doing anything to trigger the manifestation. She wasn't chanting or praying, or whatever the druids wanted to call it. She was simply standing there with her eyes closed, waiting.

As the hum grew louder, it broke apart into tendrils of sound that teased at my comprehension. It was like overhearing several people whispering in a foreign language. I closed my eyes and concentrated, but I couldn't make out any intelligible details. The whispers flowed toward Karla and concentrated at her position.

I opened my eyes to see that Karla was smiling blissfully with her eyes still closed. Sulana had closed her eyes as well and her breathing had slowed. After all of her fidgeting and frequent glances at Daven and me for support, I nearly reached out and touched her to make sure she was all right. I stopped myself when I remembered Karla's warning not to touch Sulana while she worked.

Karla's face became a mask of concentration. She opened her eyes but kept them focused on Sulana, as if she were in some kind of trance. She moved slowly around the altar, using her wet fingers to draw lines and arcs on Sulana's face, in the palms of her hands, and on the bottoms of her feet. The whispering followed Karla as she moved around the altar. Daven and I stepped back when Karla came toward us, giving her space to work. Sulana twitched a couple of times, but otherwise remained still.

After Karla completed her circuit, she placed both palms on either side of Sulana's head and closed her eyes. Sulana gasped and tensed, but then relaxed again. Daven and I both came to full alert and edged closer to Karla, but Sulana did not seem to be in pain.

I was starting to wonder how much longer this was going to take when the whispers intensified in volume and Sulana let out a low whimper. I automatically reached out and grasped her hand to reassure her I was there. Daven glanced at Karla, and then gave me a questioning look. I figured he was wondering if he should interrupt Karla. I shook my head. *Not yet.*

Karla opened her eyes and glared when she saw that I was holding Sulana's hand. The whispering rose in volume until it was like the roar of a waterfall inside my head. I dropped Sulana's hand and took a step back from the altar.

A cascade of images flashed through my mind as the whispers intensified. I closed my eyes and raised my hands to my ears in a futile attempt to block out the visuals and the sound. The whispers became insistent and the chaos that raged through my mind made me shout in frustration. Desperate to make it stop, I did the reverse of what I'd seen Karla do. I plunged a hand into the pool of water and begged the spirits to leave me. The whispers departed in a rush that left me unsteady on my feet. When they were gone, I nearly collapsed with relief and put my hands on the altar to steady myself.

"Are you okay?" Sulana was sitting up on one elbow, regarding at me with concern.

"I think so."

Karla had her arms crossed as she considered me with a look that alternated between hostility and curiosity. "How did you do that? Have you had druid training?"

"No. What just happened?"

"I *told* you not to touch her. You interrupted the session."

Sulana groaned and lay back down. "Does that mean we have to do this all over again?"

Karla went to Sulana's side and helped her sit up. "No, I was almost done and I got what we needed."

Karla handed Sulana her socks and boots and went on. "Usually, I ease us both out of the examination trance while the spirits slowly depart." She tilted her head at me and added, "But Mister Overprotective here touched you and drew the spirits to him instead. I've never seen anything like it."

I felt bad about forgetting Karla's warning; however, her sarcastic comment confused me. "Sorry I interrupted the examination. But you must have expected the spirits to do what they did or you wouldn't have warned us not to touch her."

Karla stared intently at me before answering. "You really don't understand, do you? I warned you not to touch her because that can make the spirits depart immediately and disrupt the session. I've never even heard of someone drawing the spirits *into* them like you did. Only druids are supposed to be able to do that, and only when they call the spirits with prayer. It felt to me like the spirits went to you spontaneously."

The druid healer went around the altar and looked me over as she came to stand in front of me. "Maybe you should consider joining the order. Even if you don't have inclinations for the priesthood, you could become a monk or a ranger."

Sulana chortled in anticipation of my response.

I shook my head slowly. "I'm having enough trouble with sorcery, thank you very much, and I'm starting to think your spirits have something to do with it."

Karla took a step back. "You're a sorcerer too?" She looked around at the rest of the team. "All of you are sorcerers?"

The others shook their heads, and I answered her. "No, just Sulana and me."

Karla rubbed her forehead and stared over at the pool of water on the altar. "I don't understand what this means. Sorcery is an abomination. The spirits should have been repelled." She seemed to realize how offensive her words might seem to us, and she had the grace to duck her head in apology. "Sorry, the rhetoric of druid doctrine becomes automatic after a while. I don't really have anything against sorcerers personally, although I do believe the use of vaetra should be guided by the spirits."

Sulana slipped off the altar and stood next to me. "We'll save the debate about the proper use of vaetra for another time. Right now, I want to know what your examination revealed."

With relief evident in her voice, Karla jumped at the change in subject. "It was good news mostly. I'm sure I can help you with the lightning damage. With several weeks of therapy, we should be able to bring your strength and coordination back to normal."

Several weeks. I looked at Sulana and saw the disappointment in her eyes. Several weeks was a long time, but what choice did we have?

"What about my channeling? Can you fix whatever is blocking me?"

Karla's face got a pinched look of discomfort at the return to the subject of sorcery. "I don't know anything about that. The spirits didn't address it. Honestly, I think we should be thankful that they were willing to help at all."

"Maybe the spirits aren't as repelled by sorcery as you've been taught," I interjected.

Sulana put a hand on my arm to stop me from saying more and addressed Karla. "You said several weeks. Are we talking three or thirty?"

Karla shrugged. "It depends on how hard you are willing to work and how well your body responds to the treatment. But I can't imagine it will take fewer than six weeks or more than six months."

Sulana's hand dropped limply from my arm. "Six months?" she muttered in dismay.

Karla spoke quickly, trying to reassure Sulana. "That's the worst case. You seem very motivated, and that will be a great help."

I was processing the implications of Karla's news when Daven said, "How are you going to treat Sulana when the high priestess has banished her from the refuge? Aren't you taking a terrible risk by helping her?"

Karla blinked at Daven a few times, and I got the impression that she hadn't fully considered the issue herself. She finally answered him with a resolute tone.

"I'm a healer first and a druid second. I thought I wanted to be a priestess once, but now I know that's not possible. The worst thing that can happen is for me to be expelled from the faith and thrown off the refuge. The healer in me is willing to trade that risk for the opportunity to treat a patient who has asked for help and who I know I can heal."

"Is it safe for us to hide here?" I asked.

Karla looked around at our group and grew pensive.

"Stop," Sulana said, waving her arms. "*We* aren't hiding here. *I* am. The rest of you need to get back to the Archives, especially you, Jaylan. You can't stay here with me and do nothing for months while I undergo treatment. You need to get back to your training." She paused and added pointedly, "*And* you need to call Ebnik to help you."

The idea of leaving Sulana alone here at the refuge was too painful to consider. I would not be able to help her or protect her. Her supportive words as well as her hugs, smiles, and kisses were what sustained me when life at the Archives became overwhelming.

But I couldn't stand in the way of this opportunity. I didn't entirely trust Karla, but the woman seemed certain she could help. I knew how much it would mean to Sulana if the druid could deliver on that promise.

Seeing the reticence in my eyes, Sulana drew close and rested her hand on my arm. In a lowered voice, she said, "I'm not thrilled about the idea of hiding here alone for months. I'll miss you terribly, but we both have things we must do. For now, we can't do them together."

I was inclined to agree with Sulana, but the image her words had conjured of her hiding here alone was more than I could stand. I was about to argue for another solution when Daven spoke from right behind Sulana.

"You aren't staying here alone. Your safety is my primary responsibility. If I go back to the Archives without you, I might as well resign right now."

Sulana turned to argue with him, but Talon cut her off. "Daven is right, Sulana." He glanced over at me and continued. "And if you think about it, Daven staying here is a good compromise."

Sulana raised an eyebrow at me questioningly.

I did feel better about the idea of *someone* staying with Sulana, but I wasn't excited about the fact that it would be Daven. Although I trusted Sulana and her commitment to me, it was she who had once told me that "geography is destiny" where relationships are concerned.

I ground my teeth and addressed Karla. "Is this workable? Can you keep these two safe while they stay with you?"

Karla shrugged. "I believe so. I can count on one hand the number of times I've had visitors out here in the past year. I'm off the main border trails, so I rarely see rangers. If we get a surprise visit, we can pass Sulana off as a mundane healer trainee. As long as I make my regular appearances at the college, no one will have a reason to come check on me."

I tilted my head at Daven. "What about him?"

She looked at Daven and considered. After a moment, she said, "He can be her brother, working off the fee for her training." She grinned at Daven and added, "I *could* use some help with the firewood."

Daven glanced over at the ax and the stack of wood waiting to be split. He then bowed toward Karla with a wry smile on his face.

Sulana nodded and said, "Good, it's settled then."

I cleared my throat loudly, but before I could say anything, Sulana turned pleading eyes my way. "Please don't make this harder than it has to be. We really don't have any other choice."

I tried to come up with a compelling reason for why she should return with me, or why I should stay with her. All of the thoughts that occurred to me sounded like lame excuses. We both needed help—help that she couldn't get at the Archives and that I couldn't get here.

"I don't like it, but I don't have a better idea. What really bothers me is that we won't be able to communicate while you're here. I'll have no idea how you are progressing or if you are in danger."

Karla interrupted. "You can move messages through your sanctuary network and I have access to the temple network. The networks intersect in Northshore and Riverview. I'm sure we'll be able to exchange notes."

I raised my hands in surrender and sighed. "That would be appreciated."

I reached out and took Sulana's hand in mine. She looked up at me, and I could see the fear that lurked behind her determination. "Are you sure you want to do this?" I asked her.

Tears began to pool in her eyes, and she quickly hugged me, burying her face in my neck. "Not if there were any other way," she mumbled into my chest.

I gently lifted her chin and kissed away the salty tears that had spilled onto her cheeks. When our lips met, I kissed her deeply, like it was the last we'd ever share.

When the kiss ended, we both let go of each other and stepped back with sad smiles on our faces. "Wow," she said. "That should hold me a while."

As the warmth of her embrace faded, cold tension slithered into its place. I looked over at Daven, who had half turned away and was frowning at the ground. He returned my stare as I addressed him. "Thanks for volunteering to stay. Please watch her back."

He nodded, and without a trace of sarcasm or mockery, he soberly promised, "You can count on it."

With the decision made and nothing more to be done about it, we all said our goodbyes.

As Barek, Talon, and I led our mounts away from the healer's cottage, I trailed behind and glanced back at least a dozen times to see Sulana slowly waving. Just before we walked out of sight, I waved back to her, my own eyes beginning to brim with unshed tears.

Trudging along the narrow trail that returned to the road, I slowly pushed away the sadness and regret at leaving Sulana behind. If we were going to make this sacrifice, it was damn well going to count for something. I was relying on her to make the best use of our time apart to make herself whole again. I made a promise to her and to myself right then that I would do the same.

When Sulana and I rejoined, we'd be ready to take on whatever challenges Thunderhead College could throw at us.

All we had to do was hope they would hold off on their plans until then.

CHAPTER 10

DEFENDER MARSHAL

Easing back behind the cedar tree trunk that hid him, Defender Marshal Nigel Shields took several deep breaths to calm his pounding heart. With so little ground cover around the clearing, it had been difficult to find a spot close to the healer's cottage where he could remain unseen. It would have been an impossible task, if it weren't for the fact that the trees were large enough to hide a horse.

His mind reeled trying to understand the meaning of what he had just witnessed. The spirits had not only accepted the young Sword Sorceress as a patient, but they had blessed her sorcerer companion as well. The foolish man obviously didn't comprehend or appreciate what the spirits had done, but that didn't make it any less remarkable. Or worrisome.

Nigel had followed Karla when she left the monastery preserve, suspicious of her sullen acceptance of the high priestess's decision regarding the Sword Sorceress. Initially, the young woman was far too upset and preoccupied to notice his presence behind her, but the moment when she decided to approach the strangers on her own had been obvious. He had to follow more carefully after she started moving furtively and checking the trail behind her.

When Karla reached the old roadway trail and started running, he knew it was only a matter of time before she returned to her cottage, with or without the strangers. Rather than follow her and risk being seen, he searched the area around the cottage for a good vantage point and settled back to wait.

Nigel's suspicions proved to be well-founded, but he was still surprised when Karla strode into the clearing with the Archives delegation in tow. He considered confronting them right then, but it would just be him against their five. In truth, he was curious to see what would happen.

The druid Hierarchy strictly forbade the presence of sorcerers at druid ceremonies. However, Karla was only an adept, so she could not perform true blessings. If he ever had to defend this spontaneous decision to allow Karla's examination, he knew he would be equivocating to claim that Karla was merely communicating with the spirits, not manipulating vaetra. Part of his job as Defender Marshal of the Northern Region was to ensure that sorcerers, and more importantly, the mundane, never had reason to equate druid blessings with sorcery.

He couldn't decide if he had made a terrible mistake, or if he was somehow meant to observe the miraculous events that had transpired.

The spirits were clearly interested in helping the Sword Sorceress. The proof of that was in the unusual number and variety of spirits that had answered Karla's call as well as the success of the examination. It was equally clear that the man accompanying the Sword Sorceress had a strong affinity for the spirits, or they for him, even though he seemed oblivious to the potential implications.

Nigel had little doubt that this incident should be reported to the druid Hierarchy immediately. He should go directly to the top, to the Archpriest himself, and confess his failure to prevent the adept's examination. He might be censured for his poor judgment, perhaps even lose his position.

He instantly rejected the idea. It wasn't that he was afraid of destroying his professional career. It was the tingle of excitement in his chest. It was the faith that had brought him into the druid fold so long ago. He was meant to witness this remarkable event. Fully believing in the druid valediction, "May the spirits guide you," he was certain that the spirits had guided him to this moment.

But it wouldn't hurt to be sure. Nigel would pray for further guidance later.

He peered around the tree again to see that the group from the Archives was splitting up. It looked like the Sword Sorceress and one of the male agents were staying behind. The other three, including the young man who had received the spirits, were leaving.

Good. If he allowed the Sword Sorceress to remain on the refuge, he would have to help keep her presence a secret. That would be much easier with two intruders instead of five.

After the three Archives agents had departed, Karla helped the other two bring their belongings into the cottage. While they worked, Nigel slowly picked his way back toward the monastery, sneaking silently from tree to tree until he was far enough away to move without being detected.

CHAPTER 11

BOUGHT OUT

Something was different about the Snow Creek Inn. It seemed newer somehow. Meldon must have put a lot of effort into the painting and carpentry tasks I'd left behind. I admitted to myself with admiration that his work was better than mine would have been.

As I tied Patches to the railing alongside Barek and Talon's horses, a townsman walked by and did a double-take. His curious stare turned to a surprised blink of recognition and then a quick look away. He moved away from us at an increased pace.

His behavior was more disappointing than surprising. Northshore wasn't a large town. Word would have gotten around quickly that one of their own, a former city guard captain and short-term innkeeper, would have "turned magician." Since our entry through the east gate, three other people had a similar reaction upon seeing me.

I resolved to shake off my funk and keep my wits about me. No one had been outright unfriendly, but I had detractors here that predated the discovery of my sorcery abilities. I doubted anyone would try to take me on with Barek and Talon at my side, but I wasn't sure of that, and it would be best if we could move on without raising much attention.

Our trip from the druid refuge had gone by in a blur because I was preoccupied the entire way. I would go to say something to Sulana only to realize she wasn't there. My thoughts spiraled into horrible scenarios involving our enemies at Thunderhead College. On more than one occasion, Barek or Talon had asked me if I was okay. I'd realize that I was glowering with anger or wide-eyed and twitchy with the distress of my imaginings.

Talon had made only token resistance when I requested that we swing through Northshore on the return trip. His objections evaporated when I promised a good hot meal at the Snow Creek Inn and Barek gave him an encouraging nod. Although we were trying to avoid attracting attention on our journey, I argued that Sulana knew I had some final business to wrap up at the inn. And she did. It was also true that she would be happy to miss out on this particular visit.

Barek and Talon preceded me into the Inn. Meldon's voice called, "Sit anywhere you like," as they entered. Talon led the way over to a table that happened to be my favorite. I wasn't sure if he remembered the day we met or if he just appreciated the location the same way I did. From that table, at least two of us would be able to watch the door and have no one at our back. Talon waited for me to pick a chair first and I uncharacteristically chose the one that put my back to the room. I trusted them to keep an eye on things, and I was hoping to surprise Meldon.

I looked around the dining room over my shoulder. Not much had changed. It was still the cozy space it had always been. It had the same big fireplace and tables, and there was still a long bar at the back. The only thing that was different was me.

Meldon glanced up from the tankard he was drying at the bar, but he went back to his task without a hint of recognition. We had arrived at mid-afternoon, between the lunch and dinner crowds. The only other patron was an old man sitting at the bar staring into his flagon.

I turned back around to find that Talon was staring at me. He quietly said, "Does it feel strange to be back?"

I nodded. "It's like returning home to find someone else living in your house." In this case, it was literally true.

I could tell by the synchronized movement of my companions' eyes that someone was coming up to the table from behind me. I snickered to myself and resisted turning around, knowing that things were about to get interesting.

"Get you something to drink?" Meldon asked.

"Ale," Talon and Barek answered in unison.

"Do you still have the spruce tip ale?" I asked, finally turning in my chair and making eye contact with Meldon.

Meldon's face broke into a big grin. "Jaylan!" He held out his hand and we shook. "I had no idea you were coming."

I held out my hand toward my table mates. "We are just passing through, but I had to prove to my friends here that the Snow Creek Inn serves the best meal around. You remember Barek and Talon?"

"Sure, I remember them now. I seem to recall you had a couple of other friends with you when we last parted."

I knew that he was really asking about Sulana. My leaving with Sulana had cleared the way for him to court Dela—a successful courtship as it turned out. "You mean Sulana and Daven? They had other things to do and couldn't come with us on this journey."

He seemed relieved, but was polite enough to say he was sorry to hear that.

I guess neither of us was sure what to say next. After a moment of awkward silence, Meldon stepped back and said, "Let me get you those drinks. The spruce tip has been going fast, but I'm sure I can find some for you. In the meantime, think about what you'd like to eat."

Barek eyed me and asked, "Still think this was a good idea?"

I shook my head and shrugged. "Had to be done sometime. They deserve a chance to move on with their lives without worrying about my interference. Meldon wants to negotiate for my share of the business, and I owe them my blessing on their nuptials."

I pulled a tightly wrapped bundle from my jacket and set it on the table.

From behind me, a feminine voice said, "I'll take those over." I glanced over my shoulder to see that Dela had entered the dining room and was picking up the tray of tankards that Meldon has just filled. He opened his mouth to object, but she was already on the move. Once again, I watched my companions track her progress as she approached.

"Here you go, gentlemen," Dela said as she set a mug in front of Talon and Barek. She finally looked at my face when she leaned over to set the last mug in front of me.

"Jaylan!"

The exclamation was accompanied by an arm spasm that spilled a foamy glop of brew into my lap. True to her years of experience, she guided the mug the rest of the way to the table without dropping it.

Her face went crimson and she pulled a towel from her shoulder. She reached down to wipe the foam off my leg and froze when my hand intercepted hers.

"It's okay. I got it," I said, taking the towel from her.

She spoke rapidly, still in automatic server mode. "I'm so sorry. That one's on the house."

Meldon stood beside her and put his arm around her. She smiled at him and calmed instantly. Funny, when I used to do that, it always seemed to have the opposite effect.

As I dabbed at the ale soaking my pants leg, I said, "Don't worry about it. After a few days of travel, I can stand a little sprucing up."

Everyone groaned.

Dela gave me a serious look. "Why are you here?"

"I got your note. You said you wanted to negotiate for my share of the inn." I picked the bundle up from the table and handed it to Dela. "I also wanted to congratulate you on your wedding."

She took the package from me hesitantly. "What is it?"

"Open it and see."

Dela untied the strings that held the canvas wrapper closed and gasped when the wrapper fell open to reveal the gift. "It's lovely. But you didn't have to give us anything." She turned the wood carving of a sitting arbolynx around in her hand, showing it to Meldon.

"I know the carver. I knew you'd like it from the moment I saw it, so I bought it for you and Meldon as a wedding present. I hope you both have many happy years together."

Dela smiled at me and said, "Thank you. For the gift and the blessing."

Meldon nodded my way in appreciation, and said, "I'll be right back." He jogged out of the room.

To fill the uncomfortable silence that settled in his absence, I took a swallow of my ale. It was just like I remembered. It had a sharp, piney aroma that complemented a light, delicately balanced body.

Meldon came back to the table carrying a leather sack and set it down next to my mug.

"We've put a lot of thought into this, and we think that should be more than fair compensation for your share of the inn. We can still negotiate if you want, but I'm sure you'll see we aren't trying to cheat you."

I opened the heavy purse and tilted it to roll the coins around inside. It was all gold. And a fair amount of gold too. I squinted up at Meldon and Dela, who both had anxious looks on their faces. "This is rather generous. Are you sure it isn't too generous?"

When I had left, the inn was doing better than ever, but the repairs we had planned were still sucking most of the profit out of it. The amount of gold in the purse surely represented my original investment plus at least two years' worth of profit, not counting renovation costs. I would never have asked for so much from them.

Dela beamed with pride as she answered me. "The inn is doing well now. Father would be so proud. We converted your apartment into a suite for our most prosperous visitors, and it's almost always booked. That was Meldon's idea, and it was probably the smartest thing we've ever done." Meldon blushed and kicked at the dust on the floor.

I pulled the purse ties closed with a quick tug. "In that case, I accept."

My abruptness put them both on alert and they looked at me with trepidation. Dela tentatively reached out a hand and touched my shoulder. "You aren't mad, are you?"

The news of their success and obvious happiness together did grate on me, but not for any reason that made sense. When I left Northshore to begin my training at the Archives, I had hoped that Meldon would act on his interest in Dela and do a better job helping her with the inn than I had done. Those hopes had been realized more quickly and completely than I would have predicted.

Thanks to Meldon, I had a nice chunk of savings and Dela seemed happy and relaxed. I guess it was the speed with which I was replaced at the inn and as the target of Dela's affections that stung a little.

I did my best to give Dela and Meldon a sincere smile. "Mad? Of course not. I'm a little stunned is all." I turned toward Talon and Barek, who were quietly watching the scene play out between sips of ale. I raised my own mug into the air. "Here's to the Snow Creek Inn. May it be a blessing to its owners and their descendants forever more." My table mates clacked their mugs against mine and we all drank.

Meldon got a thoughtful look on his face and Dela giggled when she saw his expression. "Thank you, Jaylan. Let me get you gentlemen something to eat while Meldon considers the ramifications of *descendants.*"

Meldon blushed again, and we all laughed at his expense. Barek's stomach rumbled and Dela took that as her cue to rush off to the kitchen and get us something special.

Throughout the meal, Meldon sat with us and gave us the news of Northshore. Dela bustled around the dining room preparing for the evening meal and making sure our tankards stayed full. Dela's mother came out from the kitchen and visited for a few moments as well. For a while, I was distracted by the feeling of being a guest in the place I used to call home. My last tie to my mundane life had just been reduced to a sack of coins.

By the time we left the inn to continue our travels, I was ready to leave the past behind and focus on the future. The gold that once represented my investment in the Snow Creek Inn would become a new investment in something for Sulana and me. It wasn't an ending, it was a transformation.

CHAPTER 12

THE WIZARD RETURNS

The main gate of the Archives was a welcome sight. Patches flared his nostrils and picked up his pace, anticipating fresh fodder and a cozy stall. I eagerly looked forward to the culinary skills of the Archives kitchens myself. With the exception of our one delicious meal at the Snow Creek Inn, we'd had to endure too many days of our own trail cooking.

At the stables, I dismounted and started to unbuckle my gear from Patches's saddle. A bath would be one of my first tasks. Everything I owned smelled like horse, road dirt, campfire smoke, and my own sweat.

"Excuse me, Sorcerer Forester?" a voice called from the stable doors. I turned to see two castle guardians eclipsing the incoming light.

"Yes?"

One of the men stepped forward. "Please come with me, sir. I've been instructed to escort you and Sorceress Delano to Councilor Rissik's office as soon as you arrive."

"Can it wait a few minutes? I need to rub down my horse and take my bags back to my room."

"Sorry, sir. Those are my orders. The groom can take care of your horse, and Guardian Frakes here can deliver your bags to your room." He looked around the stable. "I don't see Sorceress Delano. Is she here?"

"No, sorry. She was delayed by other responsibilities."

A confused look passed over the guardian's face. He probably wondered what other responsibilities might have delayed Sulana, but knew it wasn't his business to ask.

Talon came over from the stall where he had started unloading his own horse. "What's this about, Guardian?"

Upon recognizing Talon, the guardian immediately came to attention again. "I really don't know, Weaponsmaster Destry. We were instructed to watch for Sorcerer Forester's return and bring him to Councilor Rissik without delay."

At the bidding of the second guard, a groom ran over and took the reins from my hand. Patches stepped back from the young man and shook his head up and down. I petted his neck to calm him and asked the guardian, "Am I in some kind of trouble?"

He looked surprised at the question. "I don't think so, sir. We weren't asked to disarm or restrain you, just to provide an escort."

I looked at Talon, but he just shrugged.

Stepping back from Patches, I looked down at my dirty clothes and spread my hands helplessly. "Lead on," I said with a sigh.

I followed the guardian into the stone halls of the Archives. We took the main stairwell up to the Council level landing where we encountered a stern-faced guard. He stopped my escort and asked the purpose of our visit before allowing us to pass through to the restricted hallway beyond.

When we reached Councilor Rissik's office, the guardian knocked softly on the closed door. A muffled voice from within the room called, "Enter."

The guardian opened the door and announced, "Sorcerer Forester is here, Councilor."

Senior Councilor Gregor Rissik rose from his seat. "Thank you, Guardian. Please find Lissy Aragon and ask her to join us here. You can return to your normal duties after that." He waved me into the room. "Jaylan, please come in and close the door behind you."

The room's second occupant had also risen from his seat, and I was surprised to see that it was none other than Wizard Ebnik Vlastorus, former Council member and one of my first sorcerer friends.

"Ebnik! It's so good to see you. What brings you to the Archives?"

Ebnik's grin matched my own as we exchanged an enthusiastic hand shake. "You do, for one thing," he replied. "I hear you could use some help refining your casting technique."

I sighed. "That's one way to put it. I'm not sure how you'll be able to help, but I'm grateful for your assistance."

He let go of my hand and patted my shoulder. "Don't worry about it. We'll figure something out. In the meantime, tell us about your trip. I gather Sulana is still in the care of the druids?"

I wasn't surprised that Councilor Rissik had told Ebnik the true destination of our journey. I'd have done so myself.

"Yes. And she'll be there for a while it seems."

I told Ebnik and Councilor Rissik about our journey to visit the druids and about how the young healer had volunteered to help Sulana. I tried to play down my doubts about Sulana's safety and my distress at leaving her behind, but I could tell that neither man was fooled.

"That was a dangerous choice," Councilor Rissik observed at the end of my tale. "But I suppose it was really the *only* choice."

I shrugged. "That's definitely the way Sulana saw it."

Ebnik said, "She'll be fine, Jaylan. I have friends in the Northshore sanctuary, and I'll tell them to watch for messages from this healer. We'll make sure we can stay in touch with Sulana."

"Thanks. I appreciate that. So, what are the other things that brought you to the Archives? You said my casting problem was just one thing."

Ebnik's face grew serious, as did the councilor's. "Some disturbing news recently arrived at the sanctuary in Plains End. It seems that Governor Brachus of Sunset Province has named Astin Thoron as his heir designate."

It took a moment for the news to sink in. The Brachus family had been given the governorship of Sunset Province when the previous governing line, the Thoron family, had no eligible heir at the time of Governor Darius Thoron's unexpected death. Paeter Thoron, ineligible for rule because he was a sorcerer, never accepted his father's replacement. As a result, the Thoron family, who remained a powerful influence in the capital city of Dusk, waged a quiet feud with Governor Brachus.

It made no sense that Governor Brachus would choose Paeter Thoron's son Astin as his heir designate. If I remembered correctly, he had an eligible son of his own.

"I thought Governor Brachus had a son."

Ebnik nodded. "He does. A young man named Malcolm."

Suspicion tinted my voice. "Did something happen to him?" But before Ebnik could answer I shook my head and said, "Doesn't matter. I can't imagine a scenario under which Governor Brachus would willingly choose a Thoron as his heir designate."

Ebnik and Councilor Rissik nodded their heads simultaneously, seeming pleased that I understood the implications of the news I'd just received. Ebnik leaned toward me. "Are you sure you can't imagine *any* circumstance under which Governor Brachus would behave completely out of character?"

Ebnik was hinting at something. When I realized what it was, I gasped. "Paeter's amulets. They've put one on the governor."

"That's our belief as well," said Councilor Rissik. "If we're right, we've got big trouble coming."

I wasn't convinced of the amulet theory. Such a plan was not only audacious, it was exceptionally risky. "But they wouldn't dare put an amulet on Governor Brachus. Using sorcery on a member of a ruling family carries a penalty of death. It would be like the Grassgate Dispute all over again. The Archives and the emperor would step in and the sorcerers responsible would be executed."

Both men were silent for a moment. Then the councilor spoke softly. "The comparison you just made is interesting. Do you by chance remember the names of the families involved in the Grassgate Dispute?"

I searched my memory for the information. I had read about the Grassgate Dispute during my studies here at the Archives, but the detail of the family names was lost in the flood of other information I'd had to learn. I shook my head.

Ebnik answered for me. "The emperor issued a Ruling Proscription against both families, but he executed the patriarch of the family he judged most culpable. That family's name was Fortenz."

"As in Headmaster Dumont Fortenz?" I asked incredulously.

Ebnik nodded. "The very same. It was Dumont's father who was executed."

I was speechless. After a moment of shock, my mind started to put some connections together. Most important was the connection between Paeter Thoron and Dumont

Fortenz. The emperor had taken away Thoron rule over Sunset Province and had prevented the Fortenz family from ever entering the ruling class. But there was more than one way to rule. If you couldn't hold the reins yourself, the next best thing would be to control the person who did.

I took a deep breath and let it out. "That's a serious allegation. You'll have to prove it before the emperor will take action."

The councilor folded his arms and inclined his head in my direction. "Yes, we will."

His subtle use of *we* to my *you* was not lost on me. "Hey, I'm up for it. What does the Council have to say about the mission?"

Ebnik and Councilor Rissik exchanged a glance. "That's where it gets tricky," Councilor Rissik answered.

I was about to ask what he meant when a soft knock came from the door behind me. I opened the door and let Lissy slip into the room before closing it again.

Lissy gave me a quick hug and whispered, "Welcome home."

With four people in Councilor Rissik's office, we were pushing the occupancy limits of the room. Ebnik gestured to Lissy that she should take the chair he had occupied in front of the councilor's desk. As she sat, the councilor did as well. Ebnik and I stood shoulder-to-shoulder in the remaining space.

"How is Sulana doing?" Lissy asked me. She leaned forward in her seat, eager for my reply.

"I'm not sure, honestly. The druid healer seems to think she can help, but it could take weeks or months."

Lissy's face fell. "That's not good. I don't know if we have that much time."

"So I gather. I think the councilor and Ebnik were just getting to that."

Councilor Rissik nodded and held up a hand. "In this room and in this company, please call me Gregor. Both of you." He smiled briefly and then continued. "As we were just about to explain, we need to verify and prove that Governor Brachus is under the influence of one of Paeter Thoron's mind control amulets." He stopped and looked at Lissy, who nodded to show she was aware of the conclusions we had discussed before she arrived. "My viewpoints are currently out of favor with the Council, so we can't expect much support there. However, if we *can* prove that Governor Brachus is under the influence of sorcery, we can swing Councilor Underwood's vote back our way."

My jaw clenched as I thought about what Gregor was leaving out. I'd had my share of difficulties with the two Integrationist Council members, Velna Asher and Rikard Shepherd. Their influence had always been mitigated by Gregor's vote and the fact that the other Senior Councilor, Boris Underwood, didn't entirely trust them. But after Underwood learned that Gregor regularly met with the emperor and gave him updates on Archives activities, his support had become less reliable. Sometimes it seemed like he sided with Asher and Shepherd out of spite rather than genuine agreement.

Sulana had been somewhat disturbed when she learned of Gregor's clandestine meetings with the emperor as well. Maybe it was because I had worked for the emperor as an imperial guardsman before I came to the Archives, but to me Gregor's role made sense. The Archives was granted its powers by imperial charter and sorcerers were citizens of the empire. The emperor had every right to know how well we were policing the activities of the sorcerer community.

"I think I know how we can get the proof we need without alerting our enemies," Lissy said. "Next month is the Harvest Festival in Dusk. It's the biggest celebration of the year, and the city will be mobbed. Traditionally, the governor *always* makes an appearance, even if he is so ill that he has to be carried. In the chaos, we should be able to get close enough to verify that he's wearing an amulet."

I shook my head doubtfully. "Thunderhead College knows the stakes. They'll have people everywhere watching for us. We'd never get past the main gates."

"We won't go in through the main gates. We can travel by journey room directly to the Dusk sanctuary."

"They'll be watching the sanctuary even more than the front gate," I argued.

Lissy nodded. "Probably. So we give them something they expect to see. The twins are from Dusk, and they are going home to visit their parents during the festival. You and I will tag along with them. No one in Dusk has ever seen us, although it might be wise to leave the sanctuary under a Veil."

"Paeter Thoron has seen me," I said with a wry face.

"I didn't say there weren't risks. It won't be easy to get close to the governor, and the amulet may be hidden under his clothes. But you have an advantage; all you have to do is get close enough to *hear* the amulet."

I saw many points of failure in Lissy's plan, but we still had a few weeks to refine it. I looked at Gregor and Ebnik, and both nodded their heads, agreeing with Lissy's proposal.

"Do the twins know about this? Your plan may put them and their family in danger."

Lissy pursed her lips and looked at the floor briefly before answering. "Not yet." Then she added with a sardonic lift of her eyebrow, "But I can't imagine they'll be resistant to the idea."

I snorted. "Not those two. We'll have trouble convincing them to stay out of it."

Councilor Rissik rose to his feet. "For now, we'll go with Lissy's plan. I'm sure I don't have to warn you to keep this conversation a secret. We know that Thunderhead College has spies in the Archives and probably an informant on the Council. They will expect us to check on Governor Brachus, but we must not let them find out who we are sending or when we'll make the move."

We all agreed with Gregor and shook hands before parting. When Ebnik opened the door, a refreshing draft flowed into the room, which had become stuffy from too many bodies and intense discussion.

As we left the office, Ebnik suggested that I meet him in the library to discuss my casting problem in an hour or so. That would give me time to clean up from the trip and change my clothes. Lissy went back to her class preparations in the Alchemy lab. But first she made me promise to meet her in the dining hall later so she could hear about Sulana's visit with the druids.

About three weeks. That was how long I had to prepare for the trip to Dusk. It would be nice if I could cast reliably without passing out in a heap by then.

CHAPTER 13

NOTHING TO LOSE

Ebnik did his best to help me, but after a week of testing, practice, and meditation, my situation was no better. In fact, it was worse. All I had to do was open a channel and *think* about casting, and I could trigger the deep trance that drew my awareness into the strange gray fog.

One afternoon, Lissy asked if she could sit in on one of my sessions. I readily agreed, hoping that her unique blend of intuition and perspective could pick up on something that no one else had. She met us in a sorcery casting lab that Professor Delano let us use for our research into my problem.

I gave Lissy a full history of the problem and demonstrated it by trying to cast a simple light spell that I used to be able to perform without difficulty. As soon as I started the incantation and began channeling vaetra, my surroundings dimmed and I once again entered the dream of gray fog.

After my experience with the gateway and the beings that tried to pull me inside, I was careful not to move while I was in the fog. Eventually, the fog would dissipate and I'd regain consciousness, surrounded by the concerned and confused faces of the friends who had been observing me.

This time was no exception. When I woke up, Ebnik was propping me up with what had become a practiced hand. Lissy stared at me thoughtfully.

"Tell me exactly what you are doing before you pass out," she demanded.

I'd answered that question so many times by then that it was beginning to annoy me, but I knew she was just trying to help. "I'm doing what I was taught to do. I open a channel and begin the incantation. I used to be able to fight off the trance and finish the incantation, but I can't seem to do that anymore. Now, I start to lose consciousness almost as soon as I begin channeling."

Lissy ignored my surly tone and jumped to her next question. "Do you think this is related to your low resistance? Are you draining off all of your internal well somehow?"

That was a good question. Ebnik and I had only recently considered it ourselves. "Not as far as I can tell. The channel stays up and I lose some vaetra while in the trance, but it doesn't drain me completely."

Ebnik nodded approvingly at Lissy's questions, but remained silent.

"What about using an external well?"

Most sorcerers cast spells using the natural store of vaetra that came from within their own bodies. However, vaetra also tended to pool in minerals such as stone and gems. Sorcerers could augment and even replenish their internal well of vaetra by drawing from an external source, if they could find one.

Unfortunately, replenishing your internal well required an incantation. I had done it successfully in the past, but lately, I didn't have much interest in replenishment. By the time I had exhausted my internal well in futile attempts at casting, I was too dispirited to continue trying.

I shook my head. "I don't think I can replenish any more. I'd never finish the incantation."

"That's not what I mean. Have you tried drawing from an external well as your sole source of vaetra?"

Ebnik's bushy eyebrows drew together and his face got a thoughtful look.

Lissy was suggesting a somewhat advanced technique that I'd tried only once before outside of the classroom, and that was under desperate circumstances. It was possible for a sorcerer to cast a spell using vaetra drawn directly from an external source. The problem was that it was much harder to establish and control a channel from an external source than it was from your internal well.

The last time I managed it, Sulana had been dying in my arms. I needed vaetra to cast the spell that I hoped would save her, but I'd already exhausted my internal well, so I had to borrow vaetra from a reluctant Daisy Morrison. I was so focused at the time that I didn't even stop to think about the difficulty of what I was attempting. I just did it.

"I haven't tried using an external source in a while. If I can't even manage simple spells, it doesn't make much sense to try something advanced."

Lissy tilted her head one way and then the other. "Maybe it doesn't make sense at first glance, but you have an unusual situation. Why not try an unusual approach to solving it?"

Ebnik blushed and folded his hands. "She's right, of course. An old friend once told me, 'If you don't like where you are going, change direction.' It doesn't seem to matter what incantation you cast, what you use for a focus device, or how much vaetra you have at your disposal."

I interrupted, seeing where he was going. "So, we might as well experiment with the link and the well."

Lissy smiled and said, "Exactly." She reached out and took hold of my right hand with hers. "Try again, but this time, draw from me instead of yourself."

I was reluctant to do as she asked. Sorcerers are taught that it is unethical to draw vaetra from any living creature without consent. Paeter Thoron had been expelled from the Archives partly for his disregard of that rule. I reassured myself that it was okay in this situation because Lissy was offering it freely.

I steeled myself for another casting attempt and realized that I was reaching the limits of my patience. It had been so long since I had last succeeded at casting that I was beginning to think it would never happen again. Pushing aside my doubts, I took a deep breath and opened a channel to Lissy through our joined hands.

I expected to have difficulty establishing the connection with her, but the link snapped into place instantly, and her power flowed into the channel, ready for work. Lissy's eyebrows lifted in surprise at the same time mine did, then she dipped her head, urging me to continue.

I raised Froth with my left hand, and spoke the light incantation while channeling vaetra directly from Lissy into the crystal orb. The power flowed easily and the orb lit up the moment I finished the incantation.

I was so startled that I let go of Lissy's hand, dropping the channel and causing the orb to go dark.

Ebnik looked back and forth between Lissy and me. "What happened? Are you all right?"

Lissy looked at her hand in confusion. "I think so. The linkup came easily, and we all saw the manifestation."

I finally recovered enough to answer for myself. "It worked perfectly. I dropped the channel out of surprise." I rubbed my forehead thinking through the ramifications of what had just happened.

"Try again," Ebnik suggested.

Lissy offered her hand, and we went through the process again. This time, I kept the spell going until after the three of us had shared a triumphant grin.

When I let go of her hand, Lissy said, "You've certainly mastered linking to external sources. I can't even do it that easily." Lissy had years more experience than I did and was considered an accomplished sorceress, so coming from her, it was quite a compliment.

My grin faded as I realized what this new discovery meant. "Thanks. But what am I going to do when I don't have you standing next to me?"

The three of us exchanged glances.

Ebnik scratched his head. "You might be able to carry a few conjuring stones, but that wouldn't give you much to work with. To duplicate your internal well, you'd just about have to carry your weight in gems."

Lissy added thoughtfully, "If you happened to be near a basin, you'd have almost unlimited power."

I sighed. "So my choices are to travel with a wagon load of conjuring stones or find a basin and convince my enemies to come to me. Not very practical."

"Let me think about it," Ebnik said. "This is a unique challenge, so it may take us a while to devise a good way to deal with it."

Lissy folded her arms and shook her head at Ebnik. "This was a good discovery, but I'm not ready to give up on Jaylan being able to cast with his internal well." She turned to me. "Tell me more about the time you found the gateway in the fog."

I once again related my experience with the arched gate, answering her questions when she interrupted me for additional details. When I finished, she closed her eyes in concentration for a moment.

When she opened her eyes again, she asked, "So, other than the fact that the beings tried to push you into the gateway, you didn't get any sense of danger or malevolence?"

"No, not really. What made it scary was that I couldn't see what was inside. What are you thinking?"

"Something you won't like."

I believed her. "You think I should go back there."

"What do you have to lose? It's just a dream, right?"

I turned to Ebnik for support. He was frowning, but he didn't object to Lissy's suggestion.

"It isn't really a dream, exactly," I answered. "I'm aware and in control of my movement."

"Have you ever found anything other than the gateway?"

"I tried to explore the fog a few times, but I always ended up standing in front of the gateway."

"So, it's almost like the purpose of this trance is to give you access to that gate."

I couldn't argue with her logic, although I wanted to. "Okay, suppose you're right. What would be the purpose?" I waved my arms in frustration, "And why doesn't anyone else have this problem?"

Lissy ignored my irritation. She just smiled sweetly at me and said, "There's only one way to answer those questions."

CHAPTER 14
THE RUNEDREAM

Ebnik, Lissy, and I left the sorcery lab and moved to my sleeping chamber so I could lie down comfortably for my journey into the gateway. My little room seemed even smaller with three people in it.

I looked up at them with trepidation, and Lissy's gaze grew tender. She sat next to me on the bed and took my hand in both of hers. "Don't worry, we'll give you a nice burial if you don't come back."

"Oh, thanks. You're hilarious."

She looked up at Ebnik. "How long should we wait before we give up? Do you think he'll just stop breathing?"

I snatched my hand back and pushed her off the bed. "Go away. You're not making this any easier."

She reached down and patted my arm. "Sorry, just trying to lighten the mood. If you are going to do this, you should try to be positive and take control of the situation."

I closed my eyes and sighed. "I'll try."

Ebnik, standing at the other side of the bed, also patted my arm. "We'll be right here keeping an eye on you."

Lissy added, "Unless we get hungry or something."

Ebnik laughed, and I couldn't help but join him.

I reached over to my nightstand and palmed Froth. My hand tingled around the heavy orb as I thought about going back to the mysterious gate. What awaited me on the other side of the opening? What were the beings I'd seen? Why did they want me to go inside? Like Lissy had said, there was only one way to find out.

"Good luck," Lissy said. Ebnik just smiled and squeezed my arm.

I opened a channel and started the familiar incantation for light. The gray fog descended upon my awareness and surrounded me immediately.

I waited for a moment to see if the fog induced any of the negative feelings Lissy had asked about. If it did, I might have a good excuse not to enter the gate. But it was just fog with no sense of malice or impending doom.

Be positive and take control of the situation, Lissy had told me.

Fine. Let's get this over with.

As soon as I decided to start searching for the gate, it appeared in front of me. Maybe Lissy was right that the entire purpose of this trance was to transport me to the gateway.

I placed my hand into the depression on the left column, as I had done the first time I visited the gate. I spoke the trigger word and the gate opened. The dark tunnel yawned before me, but I didn't see the little lights this time.

I held my breath as if I were about to go under water and took one tentative step into the darkness. Then another. After a few more steps, I turned around. The gateway was still open, but what it showed on the other side was not the fog I expected. The opening was like a rain-streaked window that let me see back into my chamber. Lissy and Ebnik were leaning over me and talking to each other, although I could not hear what they were saying.

Curious about this phenomenon, I went back toward the gateway to see if the vision persisted on the other side. But I couldn't return to the gateway; it receded away from me as I walked toward it. Was the gateway a one-way portal? I swallowed hard. Apparently, I was stuck here until I discovered another way out.

I turned around to follow the tunnel, but stopped before I had taken a single step. In the distance, a glow approached. As I watched, the glow resolved into a luminous being with a vaguely human female shape. Like flies drawn to a picnic, a cloud of tiny lights floated around the apparition. When she moved, the lights followed her like a trail of smoke from a torch.

Is this being in charge of this place?

"Hello? Can you understand me?"

Her answer came to me the way I'd "heard" the spirit fish when I was with Sulana at the pier on Castle Tarn. The being's voice was not so much sound as an impression of meaning that came directly into my mind.

"Yes, I understand you," she answered.

"I am called Jaylan. Can you tell me who you are and where I am?"

"Your people know me as Tritia, although it has been a long time since the last runemaster visited the Runedream."

Tritia. Why was that name familiar?

A disturbing thought crossed my mind. "Are you a spirit?"

"I am many spirits."

That answer didn't make much sense to me, but I was more concerned about where I was and why I was here.

"You called this place the *Runedream?* What does that mean? Where is the Runedream?"

"The Runedream is everywhere and nowhere. It is wherever you want it to be."

Well, that explained ... absolutely nothing.

"Why am I here?" I asked her.

"Because you came. You answered the call of the Runedream."

I raised my arms helplessly. "Am I trapped here? I tried to leave, but I can't reach the gate."

"You can't reach the gate because you are not ready to leave."

I looked over my shoulder at the translucent door. The spirit was right. I didn't want to leave yet. This experience was too unique to ignore.

"What should I do now?"

"Whatever you wish. You are the runemaster."

"What is a runemaster?"

"A runemaster is someone who can answer the call of the Runedream, as you did."

I was starting to see a circular pattern in her answers. Getting useful information out of Tritia was probably going to be a challenge.

"Will you stay with me?" I asked.

"If that is what you wish."

While we were speaking, the top half of the spirit's form had sharpened from a fuzzy female outline to a detailed image of a woman in a blouse or dress. Her lower half still faded out before it reached the floor. I couldn't tell if she was making herself more distinct or if it was something I was doing.

"You're changing," I commented.

She shrugged apologetically. "It has been a long time since I last needed to present a shape for a human."

Since I couldn't go back through the gateway, my only choice was to go forward. I went around the spirit and proceeded down the passage. She floated behind me, her glow conveniently providing enough light to see. Maybe I could find some place more interesting. Perhaps I'd find a door—just like the one that suddenly blocked the end of the passage in front of me.

"Very good," the spirit said from behind me. I didn't bother asking her what she meant.

I tried the handle to the door, but it was locked. I pulled harder to no avail.

"What is beyond the door?" I asked the spirit.

"I won't know until you do," she said.

Great. A spirit guide who didn't know her way around her own domain.

Did the layout of the Runedream correspond to the real world in some way? I thought about where my chamber was in relation to the rest of the Archives, and estimated that the door might lead out into the utility level. I gave the door handle another pull and it opened to reveal a narrow corridor that led to a larger hallway. I walked down the corridor and stood at the intersection. It looked like the main hall of a lower Archives level. At least I wasn't totally lost.

That was when I noticed the illuminators. They were on, as I would expect them to be, but they didn't have the same high-pitched whine I normally associated with them. I walked over and stood under one of the devices, staring up at it. The noise it made was a series of sounds, more like a song than the monotone I was used to hearing. In fact, I recognized part of it. It wasn't a song; it was an incantation. I had used that incantation myself to conjure light on many occasions.

If I had Froth with me … wait, I did have Froth with me. Its telltale weight tugged at my pocket. I took out the casting orb and held it in my hand. I tried to open a channel to it, but nothing happened. I couldn't even sense my inner well, much less open a channel to it. I could not perform sorcery.

"Something's wrong," I said.

The spirit's quick response sounded genuinely concerned. "What is it?"

"I can't channel vaetra."

She paused for a second and then chuckled. "You *are* channeling vaetra, silly human."

"No, I can't," I insisted. "I just tried and failed."

"What were you trying to do?"

I held up Froth and waved it toward her. "Make the orb light up."

One of the floating lights broke away from the spirit, and disappeared into Froth. Light burst forth from the orb so brightly I nearly dropped it. The light waned to a comfortable level, and I stared at Froth trying to make sense of what just happened. Was the spirit helping me cast? Had she somehow cast the spell herself? Stranger still, Froth was emitting the sounds of the light incantation I'd been about to use.

Canceling the spell, I put Froth back in my pocket. I went back into the corridor and walked to one of the other doors. I stopped with my hand on the handle. The door *should* open into a room on this level. But what if it didn't? What if it opened up into my chamber instead? I closed my eyes, opened the door, and stepped into the room. Then I opened my eyes. There was my bed, my dresser, and my little table in the corner. It was my chamber. But it was empty. Where were Ebnik and Lissy?

Floating next to me, Tritia clapped her hands together. "Wonderful! That was fun. Where shall we go next?"

Where, indeed? It seemed I could go wherever I wanted. But where I might go wasn't as interesting a question as what I might do there. I could cast without speaking an incantation; without even thinking one.

"But is it real?" I mused out loud.

"Oh, yes," the spirit answered.

"I thought you said this was a dream."

"No, I said you are in the Runedream. It is as real as I am," she said with her arms spread wide.

I smirked as I looked at her, an insubstantial figure shimmering and floating above the floor. "Not to be rude, but I'm not entirely convinced that you *are* real."

She smiled and folded her arms. "I could say the same of you. The Runedream was here before you came, as was I. Your presence here is a temporary illusion. The Runedream and I will endure long after you are gone."

That's what I get for arguing philosophy with a spirit.

I decided to take the "reality" of the Runedream on faith, which was an uncomfortable concession for me to make. Faith and spirits. I sincerely hoped I wasn't having some kind of religious experience.

A new question started to nag at me. *What's the point of the Runedream?* I didn't bother asking it out loud. The spirit had already proven herself to be spectacularly unhelpful with any question that didn't involve a yes or no answer. In fact, she was being *so* vague that I thought I might be undergoing some kind of test. Maybe she was more of an examiner than a guide.

The Runedream was like a regular dream in a lot of ways. My mind conjured what appeared before me. The main difference was that I was lucid. I had conscious control, more or less. When I had wanted Froth to light up, it did. And it sang the light incantation.

I thought I'd try something different. I reached for Froth out of habit, then let it fall back into my pocket. Instead, I raised my hand and tried to conjure a shield just by willing it to exist. As with the light spell, one of the tiny lights flew over from Tritia's cloud and the shimmering shield appeared, singing the rune phrases of the incantation I would have used to create it.

I looked at the spirit to see if she had anything to say about what I was doing, but she just watched me with an annoyingly smug smile.

Okay, raising the shield was interesting, but still not terribly useful. I already knew how to cast a shield. What about something I *didn't* know how to do? On a couple of occasions during our recent road trip, Sulana had started the camp fire using a spell. It was one of the many useful spells I hadn't gotten around to learning yet. Such a spell was rarely needed inside the Archives, where illuminators were common and lamps often had spark crystals. Sulana could have taught it to me, but we had other things on our minds at the time.

A lamp sat on the side table next to my bed, just as it did in my real room. I pointed at the lamp and said, "Fire." One of the tiny lights following Tritia zoomed over to the lamp, and as I had visualized, the wick started burning. I went closer and crouched down next to the flickering lamp. Just as with the illuminators, the flame emitted a short, repeating series of sounds. I mimicked the sounds as best I could using variations on the vocalizations I'd learned for other spells. Once I could reproduce the flame's song reasonably well, I stood and extinguished it with a thought.

I turned to the spirit with a triumphant smile, but she was gone. Had I passed the test? Did she leave because I no longer needed her guidance? Or had she been the product of my imagination all along?

I shook my head and turned around to face the door of my chamber. When I opened the door, I saw exactly what I wanted to see: a passage that opened into the chamber containing the arched doorway. Through the translucent door, I could see Ebnik and Lissy talking. Lissy was starting to look concerned when she glanced down at my sleeping form. How long had I been unconscious?

This time, I was truly ready to leave, and the gateway did not recede when I approached it. I stepped back out into the gray fog and turned around to face the entrance. Unsure of the protocol here, I decided it would be a good idea to close the gate behind me. Placing my right hand into the depression on the right column of the gateway, I said, "Close."

The door closed without incident, and I finally allowed myself to believe that I had successfully entered and escaped the Runedream. I turned around and faced the fog, confident that I could return here safely. According to Tritia, the dream was mine to control. With that thought in mind, I willed myself back to my chamber where Lissy and Ebnik waited.

Back on my bed, I opened my eyes and turned my head. The movement caught Lissy's attention, and she placed a hand on my shoulder.

"Are you okay? How do you feel?" she asked.

I sat up on my elbows and answered, "I feel fine. That was without a doubt the strangest experience I've ever had."

"What did you learn?" Ebnik asked.

"I'll explain later. First, I have to try something." Lissy stood up to get out of my way and I swung my legs over the side of the bed. I asked Ebnik to give us some extra light, and he obliged by casting a light spell on a narrow rock shelf that stuck out of the wall over my bed. That was a useful trick I'd have to ask about sometime. I only knew how to create light directly around the casting orb.

Facing my nightstand, I blew out the lamp that had previously been our sole source of light in the room. Normally I would reignite the wick by touching the lamp base and triggering the spark crystal. This time, I was going to try the simple incantation I had just learned in the Runedream.

Froth was still in my hand, so I opened a channel and began the incantation. But I had forgotten a small detail. As soon as I started the incantation, the fog began to settle over my awareness once more. I exhaled in frustration and held my hand out to Lissy.

"Would you please loan me some vaetra again?"

With a curious half-smile, Lissy nodded and took my hand.

This time, I channeled the vaetra from Lissy to Froth and spoke the incantation. The lamp's wick popped and guttered for a moment before settling into a steady flame. I squeezed Lissy's hand before letting it go.

"I did it!" I exclaimed, grinning up at her.

Ebnik had moved around the bed to stand behind Lissy. "What happened during the trance, Jaylan? Do you feel okay?"

Lissy gave me a concerned look. She spoke slowly and carefully, as if she were speaking to a child. "I saw you light the lamp, Jaylan. Honestly? Your technique could use a little work. But what's the significance? We already proved you can cast when you have help."

"True. But there's something you don't know. I've never cast fire before." I held my hand out toward the lamp. "That was my first time."

"You mean you've never tried the incantation before now?" Ebnik asked.

"No, I mean I never *knew* the incantation before now."

Lissy shook her head in wonder. "How is that possible? You literally dreamed up the incantation for fire?"

I shook my head, wondering how I was going to explain my bizarre encounter with Tritia to them. "Not exactly. It was shown to me. By a spirit, I think."

Lissy and Ebnik both gave me blank stares. This was going to take a while.

I stood up and urged them toward the door. "Let's go to the dining hall and get something to eat. I'll try to explain what happened, although I'm confused about a lot of it myself."

As we left the room, I tried to assemble what had happened into some kind of order that would make sense to Lissy and Ebnik. Maybe then it would start making sense to me too.

One thing was certain: I was going back to the Runedream. I had a strong feeling that it was the key to defeating Thunderhead College.

Chapter 15

Secret Knowledge

Sulana watched Daven's movements carefully, waiting for the shift of balance that would presage his strike. She maintained her position facing him as they circled each other. When the thrust came, she was pleased with her reaction time and the satisfying clang her sword made as she deflected Daven's blade away from her torso.

The space they used as a sparring ground was about a quarter mile from Karla's cottage. It was set back deep in the woods, away from the main trails, in the direction of the refuge border. An overgrown game path connected the small clearing to the trail Karla had used when she first brought them to her cottage. Sulana had explored the difficult path beyond the clearing and learned that it meandered close to the border. If she could find another break in the border fence, it might make a good emergency escape route.

Daven saluted her with his sword and stepped back. "It's only been a couple of weeks, but your blade work is definitely getting faster and more accurate. I think Karla's treatments are working."

Sulana sheathed her sword and sat on a mossy log at the edge of the clearing. "I think you're right. I'm not tiring as easily either."

Daven sat next to her. "Well, don't push it. Karla said exhausting yourself will slow down the healing."

She raised her palms, indicating their current sitting position. "Hey, I'm resting, aren't I?"

Daven nodded and gave her a half-smile. "You seem more relaxed than you've been in months."

Sulana stared off into the forest. "I think I needed a break. A break from the politics of the Archives, a break from responsibility, and even a break from Jaylan." She looked sharply over at Daven. "But please don't tell *him* I said that."

Daven shrugged and kicked at the ground with the toe of his boot. "You've both had a lot to deal with. It's probably hard to build a relationship under those circumstances."

The comment was surprisingly insightful and understanding coming from Daven. Daven was usually brusque on the subject of Jaylan. Sulana wondered what might have prompted the change. Then she realized that her own preoccupation and self-involvement might have blinded her to what was going on with the people around her.

"Are you interested in Karla?"

Daven's eyebrows went up. "Me? What gives you that idea?"

Sulana searched her recent memory for clues. They were subtle, but they were there. The way Daven did whatever Karla asked without complaint. The way Karla watched Daven while he worked. She became more certain of her suspicions and gave him a sly look.

"You are interested. And so is she."

"I don't know what you're talking about," Daven said defensively, but it didn't ring true. Then he kicked at the ground again and nonchalantly asked, "Why, did she say something to you?"

Sulana laughed like she hadn't in months. Daven and Karla. That would be an interesting match.

"No, she didn't say anything. But maybe *you* should."

Daven stared down at his boots. "There's no point. I have responsibilities and duties and so does she. I can't stay here, and I'm sure she wouldn't want to leave."

"You don't know that. From what she's told us, she lost a lifelong dream to become a priestess and is focusing on her healing skills now. She can heal from anywhere."

Daven scoffed. "Even the Archives? You know how she feels about sorcery. Do you really think she'd willingly go to work at the castle of iniquity?"

Sulana paused, reticent to give voice to her thoughts. But Daven was a friend and deserved to hear what she was thinking. "Not long ago, you were pondering another life. A life away from the Archives."

Daven glanced at her. "Oh, I wasn't serious, just annoyed. I'll stay with the team until you don't want me any more."

Sulana scoffed and gave his shoulder a rough push. "Hey, don't put this on me. No one is forcing you to do anything. Decide what you want to do with your life and then go for it. No one else can know what you need to be happy."

Sulana regretted the words the moment they left her mouth. Daven often reacted poorly to criticism, particularly from her, and she braced herself for the expected outburst.

Daven just stared at her for a moment, saying nothing. Finally, he took a deep breath and nodded.

"You're right. I used to think I knew what would make me happy and I did go for it." He turned his head and looked at her seriously. "It didn't work out."

An uncomfortable silence settled between them. Sulana had ignored Daven's interest in her for a long time, hoping the crush would fade if she didn't encourage it. It wasn't until Jaylan came along that Daven finally faced reality and accepted that she would never be his. Not that he had accepted it gracefully.

But what she was seeing this time was something different. He not only seemed to accept the situation, he was turning his interests elsewhere. She almost envied Karla his attentions, but knew that feeling was just her own reluctance to accept change.

Sulana gave Daven a knowing smile. "If I'm reading Karla correctly, you'll have better luck this time."

Daven stood and held out his hand to help Sulana up. "We'll see."

She accepted his assistance and got to her feet, pleased by how little her muscles complained about being asked to move again after the long exercise and brief rest.

"Don't get your hopes up," said a strong voice from behind Daven.

Sulana and Daven both instantly drew their blades and whirled into a crouch. They eased apart to give each other room to fight.

A tall man with dark hair and a short beard, both going to gray, stepped smoothly out of the forest into their clearing. He moved so silently that Sulana briefly doubted her eyes and ears.

Once the initial surprise had passed, Sulana noticed the man's attire. He was a ranger. His green uniform was unmistakable, as was the gold, five-pointed star sewn into his leather breastplate. A silver circle connected the points of the stars. Sulana had seen few rangers in her life, but the configuration seemed unusual and significant.

Daven's sword wavered and he said in a puzzled voice, "You're the marshal who was with the high priestess."

Daven was right; this was the same ranger who had been standing next to the high priestess when they were ordered off the refuge.

They were in big trouble.

The ranger nodded with a grim smile and hefted his longsword in his left hand. "I think I'd like to see what the Sword Sorceress is made of."

Daven interposed himself between the stranger and Sulana. "She's done sparring for the day. She needs to rest now."

The ranger looked at Daven with raised eyebrows. "I wasn't asking for permission."

Before he completed his sentence, he was on the move. Daven barely had time to defend himself from the ranger's rush. Sulana tried to slip around Daven so she could engage the enemy as well, but she was nearly bowled over when Daven retreated from the ranger's onslaught. Daven tripped on her, but she managed to catch him and push him back to his feet.

With a growl, Daven charged the ranger and made a good showing of himself with several powerful blows. But it was no use. The ranger's sword blocked each strike effortlessly. Seconds later, the ranger executed a flat-bladed strike to the head and a well-placed kick, and Daven rolled unconscious to the edge of the clearing.

The ranger faced Sulana with a grim expression. "Guard yourself for true, Sword Sorceress." And then he attacked.

When she was at her best, she could defeat Daven in most of their sparring sessions. But she wasn't at her best. After what she had just witnessed, she had little doubt as to the outcome of her battle with the ranger. But it was not in her to give up. She gritted her teeth and brought every ounce of her energy and training to bear.

After they traded several blows, the ranger said, "Not bad for an invalid. It would have been interesting to fight you when you were at your peak."

Sulana narrowed her eyes at him and spoke between strikes and parries. "Just give me some time. I'll get back to my peak and we can try again."

The ranger, who was barely winded, chuckled and shifted the sword to his right hand. "Perhaps," he said.

The change in the angle and direction of his attacks briefly disoriented Sulana. With dismay, she realized that the ranger was an even better swordsman with his right hand than he was with his left. She started losing ground as she tried to adjust, but she never got the chance.

With a quick flick of the ranger's sword, Sulana's weapon twisted from her grip and clanged to the ground a few feet away. Feeling the sharp point of his blade at her throat, she stood completely still and looked directly into his eyes.

They stared at each other for several seconds.

The ranger put a small amount of additional pressure on his blade, and a sharp pain told Sulana that his steel had bitten into the soft tissue at the base of her throat. A few drops of blood leaked around the blade and trickled to the top of her tunic.

"Your life is mine, Sorceress Delano."

Sulana eased back enough to swallow without suffering additional damage. "What are you going to do with it?"

The ranger withdrew his blade, but kept it ready. He glanced quickly at Daven, who was still out cold.

"For now, give it back to you."

Sulana shook her head in puzzlement. "Then what is this about?"

The ranger gave her a sidelong glance. "You'd rather I killed you?"

She ignored the question. "I'm just trying to understand what you want with me."

The ranger set his sword point on the ground and rested both hands atop the pommel. He pursed his lips and looked her up and down as if seeing her for the first time.

"You represent a unique difficulty, Sword Sorceress. On the one hand, I am sworn to keep you and your kind away from all druid ceremonies and out of all druid lands."

Sulana saw where this was going. She looked at the ground and nodded. "You want me to leave."

The ranger continued as if she hadn't spoken. "On the other hand, I have prayed for guidance, and the spirits clearly want you to remain with the healer." She looked up at the unexpected words, and the expression on his face revealed that he found the admission disturbing.

"Then what is the point of all this?" Sulana demanded, waving an arm at Daven's prone form.

"To get your undivided attention. I needed a private conversation to impress upon you the dangers of staying here."

Sulana raised a hand to the small wound on her neck and looked down at her bloody fingertips. "Tell me about it," she said with a droll tone.

He chose to treat her sarcastic comment seriously. "The danger is not just to you and your companion. My duty to the Hierarchy is clear. By allowing you to stay, I put myself and my career at considerable risk."

In spite of her annoyance with him, Sulana was intrigued. "Then why let us stay?"

The ranger shifted uncomfortably and looked up at the trees. He took a deep breath and let it out. "I am Defender Marshal of the Northern Range. My territory includes all of Lakewoods Province, so I know something about what has been happening at the Archives and Thunderhead College."

"You have spies?" Sulana asked, genuinely surprised. She had a hard time imagining a druid who would subject himself or herself to "filthy sorcery," even for the purpose of spying.

He shook his head. "Nothing so … useful. But rangers move around. We hear things. We see things. We also have many friends who hear and see what we do not."

"And your job is to assess and act upon the information you gather," Sulana guessed.

He inclined his head to her in a shallow bow. "You are perceptive."

The man still wasn't making much sense. He seemed to be dancing around the subject he had come here to talk with her about. It was starting to get on Sulana's nerves.

"So, what have you decided? Are you here to tell me that you are siding with the Archives? Against Thunderhead College? In spite of the Hierarchy's wishes?"

He held up a hand to stop the flow of questions. "Nothing so dramatic. Or official. I'm here to tell you that I will not report your presence, but you must be extremely careful that you are not discovered. By anyone."

Exasperated, Sulana waved her arms and slapped them to her sides. "What more can we do? We *have* been very careful." Then she considered her current situation and added hesitantly, "At least I thought we were."

"Your secrecy has been adequate up to now. I've known you were here since you arrived. But I think the healer overestimates the privacy of her remote location. Her behavior during her visits to the college has changed, and others have noticed it. Curiosity is something none of you can afford right now."

Sulana wasn't sure she believed his claim that he'd known about their presence since the first day. "What took you so long to come warn me?"

"My *plan* was to throw you off the refuge and be done with you. But something stopped me. I spent some time in prayer and asked the spirits for guidance. That led to some research, which took more time. I could not approach you until I fully understood what I needed to do."

When he stopped speaking, Sulana prompted him. "And what would that be?"

He looked at her for a moment through squinted eyes. He then straightened and sheathed his sword. "Let's just say that we share a common enemy. I believe it is in the best interests of the druids for you and the sorcerer who was with you earlier, Jaylan Forester as I recall, to prevail against Dumont Fortenz and his Lightning Corps."

His words revealed that he knew far more about Archives business and current events than she had guessed. Being able to move and communicate freely among the mundane definitely had advantages.

Sulana didn't trust the ranger, and she wanted to strangle him for his heavy-handed tactics, but she believed his words were sincere. "What should we be doing to better protect ourselves?"

"Karla has always been enthusiastic and helpful at the healing college. Lately, others have noticed that she has been distracted and eager to leave once her duties have been satisfied. Some are blaming it on her failure to attain the priesthood, but others are beginning to wonder if it isn't something more. The next time she returns, ask her if your sessions have changed anything about her schedule. She'll probably recognize the danger by herself. If not, suggest that she behave as if nothing has changed, even if that means shortening or delaying your healing sessions."

"You're her superior. Why don't you tell her?"

His response was quick and vehement. "No. She must never know we've met. You must promise me that you won't tell any druid that I allowed you to remain on sacred ground."

Before she could react, he stepped forward and grabbed her arm so hard it hurt. "Promise me," he demanded.

"Okay, fine." She pulled at his fingers with her free hand, and he slowly let go. "I promise."

He looked into her eyes to gauge her sincerity, then nodded once. "Believe me, it's for your sake as well as mine." He stepped back a couple of paces to widen the distance between them.

Sulana rubbed her arm, wondering why this man had to make everything so *physical*.

The ranger looked up into the canopy and went back to the edge of the forest. "I have to leave now. Be careful, and tell no one that we've met." He glanced down at Daven, who was starting to groan and rub at his sore head. "Convince your partner to do the same." With that, he was gone.

Sulana ran over to Daven and knelt at his side. Seeing a small cut on the side of his scalp where the skin had split, she got up and retrieved their supply pack. Back at his side, she helped him sit up and cleaned the wound with a wet cloth.

Daven looked up at her gratefully and then froze when he saw the cut on her neck. He stopped his hand in mid-reach toward her. "Your neck is bleeding. Are you all right?"

She put his hand over the makeshift bandage to hold it in place on his head and then wet another cloth to clean off her own wound. "I'm fine. It's just a scratch. Looks worse than it is."

"What happened? Did we do this to each other?"

Sulana stopped and looked at Daven with concern. "What's the last thing you remember?"

He gritted his teeth against the pain in his head for a second, and then his words came slowly. "We were sparring. No, wait. We were done sparring and we were talking." Sulana nodded encouragingly when he glanced at her for corroboration. "We talked about Karla." He gave her another glance. "And me." Daven straightened and his eyes widened. "We were attacked by a ranger." He looked around the clearing and tried to get up, but Sulana put a restraining hand on his shoulder. He collapsed back on his bottom with another groan.

"Relax. The ranger is gone."

Daven put his hand on his forehead as he recalled the brief fight. "He was so fast. And he was so much better than me."

Sulana chuckled and patted Daven's leg. "I know exactly what you mean. And that was with his *left* hand."

Daven gave Sulana a confused look. "What?"

"Never mind. I'll tell you more about it later. For now, you need to promise me something." When his eyes locked onto hers, she continued. "We can't talk about the ranger. We gave each other these wounds while sparring." He seemed about to object, but she overrode him. "It wouldn't be the first time that happened." He tilted his head, conceding the point. "It's essential for our safety and Karla's that we don't tell her. At least not right now."

"But why?" he asked.

Poor Daven. She was expecting him to make promises he didn't understand. But this was not the time to explain everything. "I swear I'll explain later, but we need to get back before it starts getting dark. Just promise me you won't say anything about the ranger."

"Okay," he said with a strained voice and an exaggerated nod. Then he twisted his body and vomited into the shrub next to him.

Sulana handed him a cloth to wipe his mouth. When he finished, she stood to help him get to his feet. He wobbled for a second or two until she handed him his sword, which he used as a makeshift cane to steady himself.

"Who was that guy, anyway?" Daven asked.

Sulana picked up her own sword and wiped off the dust. With a frown, she turned slowly back around to Daven. "You know, he never told me his name."

CHAPTER 16
INCOGNITO

Lissy and I followed Daisy and Benjamin Morrison into the crowds of people filling the streets of Dusk. I tried to resist gawking at the unfamiliar buildings and the astounding glimpses I got of the valley below the tiered city. It was like the city had been constructed in the clouds.

"Feel free to look around," Lissy said softly. "We aren't the only first-time visitors." She angled her head to indicate a wide-eyed and smiling young couple we were overtaking. The pair pointed and chattered, slowly making their way through the city streets.

Her arm was entwined with mine, and I gave it a squeeze to acknowledge her comment. We both wore loose, light clothing and wide-brimmed sun hats, playing the part of a landowner couple attending the Sunset Province Harvest Festival.

I didn't expect to be recognized, but I was careful to tilt the brim of my hat away from the occasional guardsmen and anyone who had an official look. I noticed that Lissy did the same.

It was hard to believe that about fifteen minutes ago, we had been standing in the journey room at the Archives many miles from here. Councilor Rissik had escorted the twins to the fascinating transport facility for their trip to the Dusk sanctuary. The guard dutifully wrote Ben's and Daisy's names into his log book, unaware that Lissy and I had slipped into the room with them under a Veil. I felt a little guilty about bypassing the enhanced security measures enacted by the Council, but Councilor Rissik assured us it was necessary. If knowledge of our intentions got into the wrong hands, we would be in great danger at the festival.

Councilor Rissik explained the operation of the translocation orbs to Daisy while Lissy and I remained hidden. We dropped the Veil just before Daisy activated the orb and transported the four of us to the journey room in the Dusk sanctuary. We had to abandon the idea of using a Veil once we reached the sanctuary and moved onto the city streets. All it would take would be for one person to bump into us, and the Veil would shatter. Then we'd have a lot of explaining to do. Instead, we had chosen to disguise ourselves.

The twins had grown up in Dusk, so they moved confidently through the city toward their home. Lissy had asked them to choose the least busy streets, but it seemed to me that every avenue was filled with people. The twins waved at other folks they knew and shouted greetings. Fortunately, no one insisted on stopping them to talk. Lissy and I had to stay close to keep from losing the twins in the crowd, but we didn't want to make it obvious that we were traveling together. If someone did decide to speak with them, it would be best to avoid introductions. Our background story was as thin as it was fictitious.

We reached the Morrison household at last, and Ben held the door open for us, inviting us in with a grin and a wave of his hand. We stepped into a great room with a wide fireplace and a set of stairs leading to the upper level. A large, rough-hewn dining table sat to our right, and a modest kitchen was nestled under the second story overhang.

A large gray dog woofed and levered itself to its feet with a growl as we entered. When Daisy shushed him, the animal wagged and limped over to her.

Daisy kneeled and gave the dog a scratch behind his ears before sending him back to his place on the rug in front of the fireplace. "Old Rojie doesn't see too well any more, but he's still a brave defender."

A stout, middle-aged woman appeared at the top of the stairs in a worn dress and apron. "Is that you, Daisy?" She paused to take in her children and the two strangers who accompanied them before coming swiftly down the stairs to embrace her daughter.

After receiving similar treatment from his mother, Ben introduced us. "These are the friends I mentioned in my letter. Jaylan is a fellow student, and Lissy is our potions instructor."

Mrs. Morrison looked us over carefully before bowing her head and giving us a knowing smile. We'd met her husband at the Dusk sanctuary, and he assured us she was expecting our arrival. She understood we had come on a mission of some delicacy. "Dressed to blend in, I see. Well, any friends of my children are welcome in this house." Her look turned serious. "Just try not to make too much trouble for us while you're here, if you please."

I returned her bow. "Thank you for your hospitality and understanding, Mrs. Morrison. I assure you that our most fervent wish is to complete our visit and leave without attracting any attention whatsoever." At my side, Lissy nodded her head vigorously in agreement.

The woman considered us both for a moment and then smiled. "That's good enough for me. Now, let me feed you something. If it's been more than an hour since Benjamin last ate something, I'm sure his stomach is growling."

Ben rolled his eyes, but he didn't resist when his mother grabbed his arm and dragged him toward the kitchen. We all enjoyed a nice mid-day snack of fresh, warm bread and cheese.

After the meal, Daisy and Ben left the house to visit with friends and explore the festival. Lissy and I stayed behind to wait until later in the afternoon when the governor was scheduled to appear. We needed to minimize the amount of time we might be recognized, so we let the twins determine the best way to approach the podium where the governor would give his speech.

Lissy and I exchanged pleasant conversation with Mrs. Morrison for quite a while, and then she went back upstairs to finish her chores, leaving us at the table alone. I took out a pendant with a long neck chain and laid it on the table. Lissy picked up the chain and dangled the pendant. The center stone was a piece of convex, green glass, and it sparkled in the sunlight streaming in through the kitchen window. This was the last of the mind-control amulets Paeter Thoron had created and tested on the villagers of Buckwoods. Fortunately, it had not been among the others of its kind when my former friend Lohan broke into the Archives armory and stole them.

"I really wish you would reconsider using this thing," Lissy said with a sidelong glance at me. "We've learned a lot about it, but we haven't been able to test it with other amulets."

We'd been over the pros and cons of using the amulet, and I understood her concerns. With it, I might be able to verify that the governor was wearing a similar device. The risk was that it would alert others to my presence. They wouldn't know *who* I was, but they would know *where* I was. I had little to fear from other amulet bearers; they'd most likely ignore me. But Paeter would probably be around and he'd be wearing a "master" amulet. From the moment I activated my amulet, he'd know that something was wrong.

Still, I wasn't willing to give up on the idea of using such a potentially valuable tool. If the plan worked, it would be all the proof we needed. "How about we make a deal? I won't use the amulet unless you agree it's necessary."

Lissy looked suspicious of my offer, but nodded her head and set the amulet down. "That's fair. Just don't make the decision without me if we get separated at the festival."

She had a good point. The festival would be crowded, particularly when everyone gathered to hear the governor speak.

I put the amulet around my neck and slipped it under my shirt. Until I activated the implement, it was just a pretty bauble. "We need to do our best *not* to get separated. I knew we'd be surrounded by people, so I brought implements that are limited in power and range. If we get into trouble, you'll have to handle the spell work."

Lissy frowned and stared down at the table. "I hope it doesn't come to that."

"You and me both." I looked over at the front door of the house. "I wonder what's keeping the twins?"

Lissy checked the strip of sunlight streaming in through the window. "The governor's speech won't be for a while yet. They probably ran into some friends and lost track of time."

As if our words had summoned them, the front door opened and the twins walked in. They were followed into the room by a young man and a girl of about their age. Ben wore a sheepish expression, but Daisy's determined look was what caught my eye. Sensing something was up, I rose to my feet.

Daisy introduced the newcomers. "Jaylan and Lissy, these are good friends of mine. This is Malcolm, and this is Hayli. They have some important information that I think you both should hear for yourself."

This was good. None of us knew much about what was happening in Dusk, so any additional information from locals would be welcome.

But Ben broke into the conversation as soon as his sister finished speaking. "I tried to tell Daisy this was a bad idea." He looked over at Hayli apologetically, but the girl ignored him.

Lissy got up and stood next to me. "What's the problem?"

Ben waved his hand at his sister. "Daisy's introduction was incomplete. This is Malcolm *Brachus* and Hayli *Thoron*."

The Thoron name stopped my heart for a moment. I narrowed my eyes at Daisy, but she stood resolute.

Daisy crossed her arms and subdued her brother with a quick glare. "Yes, this is governor Brachus's son and Paeter Thoron's daughter. But I know them both, and we can trust them. They have their own reasons for helping, but for now, let's just say their goals are in line with ours."

My initial thought was to take Lissy by the arm, leave the house, and get back to the Archives as quickly as possible. If the Thorons knew what we had planned, the mission was too dangerous to continue. I exchanged a glance with Lissy and her wide eyes told me that she was thinking along similar lines.

Daisy was about to say more, but Hayli touched her arm and interrupted. "I know you have no reason to trust me, and maybe lots of reasons not to trust me, but I'm not here to get in the way of your plans, whatever they are. I would like to know one thing, though. Are you here to hurt my father or brother?" Her direct gaze held my eyes while she waited for my answer.

I was still trying to come to terms with the fact that Paeter Thoron's daughter was standing here talking to me, so it took me a moment to answer.

"No, we aren't here to hurt anyone. But to be honest, your father may be in serious trouble if he has done something to violate the Sorcery Accords."

Hayli dropped her eyes to the floor and nodded her head. "I understand. I don't want to get him in trouble, but I think we need to stop whatever is happening before it goes too far."

Now we're getting somewhere.

"What do you think is happening?"

Hayli took a deep breath and let it out before answering. "My father has been acting weird lately."

Malcolm snorted. "*Your* father is acting weird? What about mine?"

Hayli looked at Malcolm with sympathy and nodded once. "They both are," she amended.

"What can you tell me?" I asked her. I was excited by the opportunity to get some real inside information for a change, but I didn't want to push Hayli too hard.

Hayli paused and looked at her friends for support before continuing. "My father used to spend a lot of time with me. He gave me sorcery lessons and encouraged me to stay at home rather than go away for training. Then he went on a long trip, and since he's been back, he's been secretive and gloomy. I used to help him with his projects, but everything he works on now is some big secret. When I ask about continuing our sorcery lessons, he says I have to go to Thunderhead College, even though he knows I want to go to the Archives and study with my friends."

Her complaints revealed more than the self-centered concerns of a teenage girl. Paeter was still working on secret projects. Maybe more amulets. Or maybe something else.

"I'm sorry to hear that, Hayli. But why are you telling us this?"

The young woman glanced at her friend. "I told Daisy that I wanted to go to the Archives to study with her. She said you might be able to help me get there."

"What would your father think about that?"

Hayli looked down at her feet. "He'd be mad." Then she folded her arms and narrowed her eyes at me. "But I don't care. He's the one pushing me away, and I'm old enough to decide for myself where I'm going to go."

In spite of Hayli's claims of independence, I was certain her father would see us helping her as an abduction. Part of me wanted to help her just to spite him, but I wasn't sure if the trouble I'd cause would be worth it. On the other hand, maybe it was time to stop laying low and whack a hornet's nest or two.

Lissy raised an eyebrow when I glanced at her to gauge her reaction to what we'd just heard. I wanted to discuss the possibilities with her, but not there and then.

"Let us think about it and get back to you. In the meantime, I suggest you seriously think about how your parents will react. I know you want to train alongside your friends, but going to the Archives against their wishes will have serious consequences."

Hayli shook her head. "I'm not stupid. Believe me, I've thought about all that. It's *all* I've been thinking about. Please let me know soon what you decide. I'm tired of waiting and being ignored. I have to *do* something."

I nodded my understanding and turned my eyes to Malcolm.

"You said your father was acting strangely as well. Would you care to elaborate?"

Malcolm rocked back on his heels and gave me a look of helplessness. "Where do I start? For years my father and Sorcerer Thoron have been enemies. They still aren't exactly buddies, but father tolerates him like never before. And now he has appointed Astin Thoron as the heir designate. It doesn't make sense. He was so proud at having single-handedly raised the Brachus name into the Ruling Families. He would never willingly turn that honor back over to the Thoron line." He looked at Hayli apologetically, but she gave him a nod and a half-smile to show she wasn't offended.

What stood out to me about his analysis of the situation was that I didn't detect any disappointment or anger at his father for appointing Astin Thoron over himself.

"Yet he did appoint Astin Thoron. How does that make you feel?"

Malcolm took a deep breath and ran his hand through his sandy hair. "Surprised, mostly. And maybe a little relieved. To be honest, I wasn't looking forward to being the next governor. But I know my duty, and I would have done my best."

Lissy chimed in with a question of her own. "You said your father wouldn't *willingly* give up Ruling Family status. Do you think he was forced?"

"I can't prove it, but there's no other explanation. He's been grooming me as heir designate since he became governor, even though he knows it's not what I want. I'd rather spend my time in the forest hunting, but he won't hear of that." He shook his head and smiled at some memory. "He used to say I could chase rabbits on my own time after the work is done."

"And now?" I prompted.

"Now he doesn't seem to care what I do. 'Do what makes you happy, son.' He's like a different man."

I glanced back and forth between Hayli and Malcolm. Their information corroborated our theories on what was going on, but the evidence was all circumstantial and could have many explanations. We needed something definitive.

All the same, I had to be careful not to ask leading questions if I wanted genuine observations from them.

"Have you noticed anything else different about your fathers lately?"

"Like what?" Hayli asked.

"Changes in routine, like places they visit, what they eat, what they wear, anything."

They both looked at each other and thought about my question for a few moments. Malcolm spoke first.

"We haven't been spending much time together. At first, I was glad his attention was on other things. I didn't think anything was wrong until Astin's appointment. Since then, I've only had a couple of conversations with him, and each time, he brushed off my concerns and made it sound like he was doing it all for me. That just isn't like him."

I looked at Hayli to see if she had anything to add.

She shrugged. "I already told you Father is being secretive. I opened the door to his basement lab once when he left it unlocked. Before he yelled at me to get out, I saw he was working on an implement, but that's nothing unusual."

Her remark caught my attention, but I kept my face neutral. "Did you see what it was?"

Hayli shrugged again. "No. He was blocking most of my view and I was too busy being shocked that he would yell at me like that. Like I said, he used to let me help him."

I gave Lissy an exasperated look. This wasn't getting us anywhere. Malcolm and Hayli were both at the age where they had other things to do than hang around with their parents. At nineteen, Malcolm would be apprenticed to a trade or working the fields by this point if he weren't the governor's son. Hayli was a couple of years younger, but she seemed ready to leave home and get started with her own life too.

Still, the conversation wasn't a complete waste of time. I was more certain than ever that we had made the right decision to come here. Everything the teens said supported the theory that the governor was being influenced by one of Paeter's amulets. I had nothing left to lose by asking a direct question.

I looked at Malcolm until our eyes met and I could tell I had his full attention. "Have you noticed your father wearing any new jewelry lately?"

Malcolm's brows twisted in confusion at the unexpected question, and then he pursed his lips in thought.

"Not that I've noticed. He still wears his wedding ring to honor Mother's memory. He usually wears his signet ring too." He looked at me curiously. "Are you looking for anything specific?"

I glanced at Lissy, and she gave me a subtle nod.

"Actually, yes. Have you noticed him wearing a new neck chain? Maybe one with a pendant?"

Malcolm shook his head slowly. "Not that I recall. But he's always cold, so he bundles up. He could be wearing a dozen neck chains and I'd never know."

So much for the direct approach.

While Lissy and I talked to the four teens, Mrs. Morrison had slipped down from the upper level and quietly cleaned up the table behind us. At this point, she came forward and stood next to Lissy.

"It's getting late," she said. "You should get going if you want to get a good position for the governor's speech."

Once I learned he was the governor's son, I had hoped that Malcolm would be able to give me the evidence I needed to bring back to the Archives. That didn't happen, so we needed to get on with the original plan.

I addressed Daisy and Ben. "Did you find a good vantage point?"

They both nodded, and Daisy said, "We can show you."

Daisy's mother wrung the dish towel she carried. "Please be careful."

To ease their mother's mind, I pointed at the twins and said, "I just want you two to point out the way. Stay back from us once we get into the crowd. If you see anything that looks like trouble, don't do anything. Just get away or hide."

Daisy nodded, but Ben looked offended. "We aren't helpless, and we're part of this team."

I softened my voice. "Absolutely. Your help has been invaluable. But we each have our tasks, and this last task is for Lissy and me. If something bad happens, I'm counting on you to get word back to the Archives."

Ben didn't seem convinced at first, but after Daisy put a hand on his arm and they exchanged a long look, he nodded once and responded in a serious tone. "Okay. You can count on us."

"What are you going to do?" Malcolm asked.

"We're going to hear the governor speak," I answered cryptically.

Malcolm gave us a suspicious look. "You're just going to listen? That will tell you what you want to know?"

Lissy and I exchanged a grim smile.

"I sure hope so."

CHAPTER 17
HARVEST FESTIVAL

I led Lissy through the milling crowd in the town square, her hand securely gripped in my own. The sun was low on the horizon, casting an orange glow over the many colorful vendor banners and the festive garments of the pedestrians who flowed around us. The people of Dusk bustled around one another with frequent smiles and dips of the head. Most of the men who drifted close to us did a double-take when they saw Lissy, but that was nothing unusual. Few men could resist the allure of Lissy's face and figure. Other than that, we passed without gathering undue attention.

As part of our orientation for the mission, Ben and Daisy had explained the layout of the city to us. The town square had roads merging into it at each of the four compass points. The east road went straight to the front gates of the governor's mansion. The west road descended the mountain toward the valley below. The north road splintered into the avenues of Cliffside, the affluent district of Dusk. The south road led into the Mountainside district where the sanctuary was located.

Looking over the heads of the people filling the square, I could see musicians playing on a stage near the intersection to the governor's mansion. The stage was our destination, since that was where the governor would appear.

Following the twins' recommendation, we slipped toward the stage through a gap between the loitering celebrants and the customers haggling with the vendors along the edges of the square. I stopped when I got close to a roped-off area in front of the stage that was reserved for special guests and those who were willing to pay an admission fee. A guard stood at the corner post that secured the ropes. If we went forward any further, we would be in plain view of the stage and too close to the guard for my comfort.

"Are you sure this is close enough?" Lissy whispered close to my ear.

"I think so, but we are near the limit of my range."

My sensitivity to the sound of vaetric manifestation was both a curse and a blessing. During my studies at the Archives, the endless din of nearby manifestations was often distracting and tedious. However, for the mission at hand, it would help us determine whether or not the governor was under the influence of sorcery. Sight sensitives like Lissy were far more common than sound sensitives, but she would not be able to see a manifestation glow through clothing.

We were counting on the fact that different manifestations produced different sounds. If things went as planned, the governor would give his speech and I would listen for a manifestation noise that was similar to what I'd heard in Buckwoods. Back at the Archives, we'd briefly activated the amulet I was wearing as a reminder. Normally, the sounds weren't unique enough to be a reliable identification method, but any manifestation I heard coming from the governor would be suspect. If the sound closely matched Paeter's mind-control amulet, it would be enough evidence to take to the Archives Council. If not, I'd have to risk activating the amulet I wore to be certain.

We waited for several minutes, shifting our position occasionally to keep other spectators between us and the guard. There was no reason to believe that the guard would recognize either of us, but if anyone else did, it would be best to be as far away from the guards as possible.

Finally, the musicians ended their bright dancing tune and began a marching fanfare. Behind the stage, the governor's procession approached slowly down the road toward the square. Four guards carried a large padded chair attached to a litter from which the governor smiled and waved. I'd heard he often had trouble with gout, which painfully afflicted his feet and knees. The guards marched up a ramp at the back of the stage and set the litter down between two rows of flanking musicians. The players ended the tune and scrambled off the stage while attendants placed chairs at either side of the governor.

Several of the spectators cheered as Governor Brachus rose slowly and painfully to his feet with the help of a cane. He grinned and waved again as he steadied himself.

The governor cleared his throat and took a deep breath before shouting, "Welcome to the Harvest Festival, citizens of Dusk. Are you enjoying yourselves?"

The crowd erupted into an enthusiastic cheer and many hands waved in the air.

"Glad to hear it! The harvest was excellent this year, which means good tidings for all of us in the year to come. I want to personally thank you for your hard work."

The governor continued his speech, but I stopped listening to what he was saying and concentrated on "listening" in another way. The crowd was respectfully quieter while the governor spoke, which was a big help. I closed my eyes and did my best to filter ordinary sounds from potential manifestations.

It was faint, but I was certain that I could hear something coming from the governor's direction. The sound didn't match my amulet exactly, but it was similar. I leaned forward and turned my head out of habit, but it didn't help. Then I heard a second, distinct sound that appeared near the governor. I opened my eyes to see what might be causing it and froze when I saw Paeter Thoron standing at the corner of the stage.

Lissy was watching my face and saw me react. She followed my gaze and asked, "Who is that?"

I growled in a voice just loud enough for her to hear. "Paeter Thoron, expert at mind-control spells and the talented smith responsible for this little piece of jewelry I'm wearing."

Thoron had line of sight to us through the crowd. We needed to back up to get more people between us and him. I looked behind us to see where we could go, but we were blocked by other spectators pushing forward for a clearer view of the stage. The hair on the back of my neck tingled, and when I turned around, my eyes locked with Paeter's.

He was staring at me with a puzzled expression. He didn't seem to recognize me, but he knew I looked familiar. Then his face cleared and his eyes narrowed. I blandly broke eye contact and looked away.

Nothing to see here. I only look like someone you think you know.

When I sneaked a glance his way a few seconds later, it was obvious he wasn't fooled. He was looking around the crowd for other familiar faces, but his gaze returned to me at regular intervals. He was making sure I was alone.

I kept my eyes on Paeter and spoke out of the side of my mouth to Lissy. "He recognized me. We have to get out of here."

"Did we get what we need?"

"The governor is definitely carrying an active implement, but the sound doesn't match this amulet."

A desperate edge tinged her voice. "That won't be enough for the Council. The implement could be for anything."

I looked directly at her. "There's only one way to be sure."

Her eyes widened. "It's too risky. Paeter is right there. He'll know exactly what you are doing."

I looked over at Paeter again. He was speaking to one of the governor's guards and pointing in our direction. "This is our only chance. Paeter already knows we are here, and we are running out of time."

Lissy's lips thinned and she glanced at Paeter. "Okay. But hurry."

I reached into the neck of my shirt and extracted the amulet. Across the square, Paeter's eyes widened in disbelief, and then he glanced up at the governor, understanding my intent. Considering me for a moment, he tilted his head to the side and folded his arms. I took that as a bad sign. It looked like he wasn't too worried about what would happen when I activated my amulet.

I gripped the pendant, opened a channel to it, and said, "Member." A familiar comforting sensation flooded my mind, and the amulet tried to find others who might be wearing amulets nearby. As I expected, it immediately linked with a hidden amulet Paeter was wearing. He smiled and nodded in my direction, acknowledging that he was aware of the link as well. He had apparently altered his master amulet, because the link was more tenuous than what I remembered from Buckwoods.

The vintage of amulet I wore took a while to adapt to its bearer. While the amulet tried to integrate its influence into my mind, it continued to seek other wearers. Over the next few seconds, it linked readily with three other members who wore the older amulets like mine. Their positions were like flickering flames against the backdrop of my awareness. One of them was the guard Paeter had sent to intercept us. Although I couldn't see him with my eyes, I knew he was moving behind the stage in our direction. The other two were farther away. One of them stood between us and the sanctuary.

Lissy gripped my elbow. "Well?"

Paeter grinned broadly at me. He knew he had us.

Then a new link slowly flickered into place in my mind. It was different from the others, but very similar to my link with Paeter. A jolt of adrenaline shot through me when I realized the link belonged to the governor. His amulet was different, but there was no question it was the same kind of spell. We had the proof we needed. To erase all doubt, the governor's voice stuttered to a stop in mid-sentence and his face got a confused look. He scanned the waiting crowd with a slow turn of his head until his eyes met mine. I smiled and nodded to him, but he just looked more confused, since he had no idea who I was. He shook his head and went back to his speech.

Paeter was no longer grinning. His face contorted in outrage, showing both anger and fear in equal measure. He started around the back of the stage in our direction, desperately pushing through the crowd leaving startled people in his wake.

"Time to go," I said.

I disabled the amulet and grabbed Lissy's hand, searching behind us for the fastest way through the crowd.

"Paeter's coming after us," Lissy warned.

"I know. Watch for the guard he sent too. That one and two others are under Paeter's control." I started pushing through the crowd. Most of the other spectators were happy to have the chance to move forward a bit more but a few grumbled about our rudeness as we jostled past them.

"I can't believe that after all this, we still don't have the proof we need," Lissy said bitterly from behind me.

"We got it," I contradicted her as we neared the edge of the crowd. I looked toward the street that would take us back to the sanctuary, but Paeter's guard had reached the intersection ahead of us and was talking to another guard. My guess was that the second guard was one of the other amulet bearers.

"Paeter is controlling the governor? You're sure?"

I evaluated our chances of slipping past the guards and decided they weren't good. We needed a distraction. I glanced around for a likely possibility. Spotting one of the vendor carts, my mouth twisted into a mischievous smile.

"I'm sure. It took a while, but the governor's newer amulet linked to mine through the master amulet somehow. It looked like even Paeter was surprised when that happened. Lissy, how good are you at casting fire?"

My change in subject confused her briefly, but she saw the guards I was watching and understood immediately. "What did you have in mind?"

I tilted my head toward the nearby vendor cart.

She giggled and said, "Oh, you're bad."

Thanks to the Runedream, I knew how to cast fire myself, but I'd have to borrow the vaetra from Lissy. It was faster and easier if she just did it herself. I changed my position so I was facing her, and she took out her small casting orb. It would look as though we were just having a conversation while she spoke the incantation. Hopefully, no one would look between us and see the orb.

Lissy cast the spell and then put her orb away. "Get ready."

A hissing noise erupted behind me followed by a whoosh as the first of several fireworks shot into the air. The festival had been good for the vendor, so his cart wasn't as full as I'm sure it had been earlier in the day. Still, two or three dozen rockets going off in chain reaction as one lit the next had everyone running for cover. We ran with the crowd.

By that point, sunset had progressed far enough to do the rocket explosions justice. After moving back far enough for safety, everyone turned to enjoy the show. We circled around through the spectators toward the intersection. Paeter's guard had joined the fleeing crowed and was at the front of the line of spectators. The second man was nowhere to be seen.

Lissy and I broke free of the crowd and ran through the intersection toward the Dusk sanctuary. I glanced over my shoulder to see that our haste had attracted the attention of the guard. He drew his sword and charged after us.

We got another hundred yards or so before the second guard stepped out of the shadows with his sword drawn.

"Nice distraction," he said.

My disguise made it impractical for me to carry a sword, but I did have a heavy dagger strapped to my hip. My arsenal also included a shield bracer on my arm and a wand of immobilization in a hidden sleeve pocket. I drew the dagger, activated the bracer, and waited for the guard to make his move.

At my back, Lissy faced the second guard who had caught up to us. I trusted her to take care of herself.

The street's pedestrians scattered away from the confrontation, but most stayed to watch, whispering excitedly amongst themselves.

"Is that a wand she's holding?"

"Spirits, I think she's a sorceress."

"I wonder what they did wrong."

"Do you think he's a sorcerer too?"

"Not going to do much good with that dagger."

The guard facing me grinned, seeming to share the opinion about my dagger versus his sword. But he stopped cold when Lissy triggered whatever implement she was holding. The other guard's body thumped to the ground and the man's sword clattered on the cobblestones.

She turned to stand by my side.

"Ready for one more?" I asked her.

"No problem," she answered.

The guard took a step back, his eyes widening in fear. "Don't use no sorcery on me," he begged. But before Lissy did anything, the man stared at the ground in front of him and screamed in fear before running away from us, waving his sword in the air.

"That wasn't me," Lissy said softly. She looked around at the spectators. Many had already disappeared. Most of the remaining people broke like a wave and ran as her gaze swept past them.

Out of the shadows stepped a robed and cowled female figure. Lissy and I squared off against the advancing sorceress to defend ourselves, but she made no aggressive moves as she approached.

"More guards are coming," said a vaguely familiar voice. "We need to get out of Dusk."

As she drew closer, Hayli Thoron's face resolved in the depths of the hood.

Lissy shook her head. "We can't take you with us."

"You *have* to take me with you. I helped you escape. I'll be in big trouble if I stay."

I frowned at her. "No one else knows you helped us, and we won't say anything. If you come with us, you'll be in even bigger trouble."

Hayli reached up and pushed her hood down. "I don't care. I'm not staying here one more day. I'll walk to the Archives if I have to."

Far down the street, people were shouting and directing the guards our way.

"There's no time for debate. We need to go," she said.

Shadows deepened and full darkness descended upon the streets of Dusk as we raced toward the sanctuary. The guards were far behind us, but they would be able to guess where we were headed.

I hesitated at an intersection, unsure of the correct direction, and Hayli took the lead. I appreciated her help, but I was still working on a way to convince her to stay behind. The farther she went with us, the harder that would be.

The torches at the gate of the sanctuary were a welcome sight. We were within fifty feet of the gateway when two men stepped forward and blocked our path. Both were dressed identically in dark clothing covered by a knee-length, long-sleeved jacket that they wore open in the front. The torchlight reflected off a silvery lightning bolt inscribed within a circle on the breast of their jackets. My guess was that these men were the Lightning Corps sorcerers from Thunderhead College that Barek had told us about.

The older of the two men stepped forward with a grin as we slowed to a halt in front of them. The hand he pointed at me held a short wand. "Not so fast. Don't you know it's rude to leave in the middle of the governor's speech?"

The man wore one of Paeter's amulets openly on his chest. He was a sorcerer, so like me, he would be able to activate it at will and use it to find other wearers. He touched a hand to his amulet. "Yes, I was in the square when you activated the Member spell. I knew something was wrong, so I took a chance and came straight here to head you off."

The younger man drew his sword and looked at his compatriot with admiration. "You were right. They came right to us."

When the men blocked our way, Hayli had let Lissy and me go around her. The man noticed her behind us and his grin faded. "Hold on. You look familiar. Aren't you Sorcerer Thoron's daughter?"

There was no point in having a conversation with these men. The guards would catch up eventually, and we needed to be gone by then. While the older man had been speaking, I opened a channel to my shield bracer.

When the man holding the wand noticed Hayli, I took advantage of his distraction to activate the bracer and draw my dagger. But he reacted quickly. He triggered the spell in his wand and its manifestation screeched against the hum of my shield.

I stepped forward without waiting to see if my shield would hold, and I punched his surprised face with my fist wrapped around the pommel of my dagger. He went down like a puppet cut from its strings.

The younger man gaped at his partner on the ground and then glared at me before dropping into a defensive crouch. Lissy started an incantation, but before anything else could happen, a figure stalked quietly out of the sanctuary gateway and whacked my opponent on the back of the head with some kind of cudgel.

Ben Morrison tossed the heavy stick to the ground and slapped his hands together with satisfaction. Daisy's face peered around the gateway and took in the scene before she urgently waved us forward.

I glanced over my shoulder at a shout from behind and saw torchlight bobbing at the far end of the street. Without another word, we all ran into the sanctuary and down to the journey room that would take us home to the Archives.

We didn't have time to argue about whether Hayli was going with us, and since she'd been recognized, I was sure I'd lose that argument anyway. Daisy activated the translocation sphere as soon as the five of us had crowded onto the platform.

When we appeared in the Archives journey room, everyone breathed a simultaneous sigh of relief, followed by a nervous chuckle at our narrow escape. Daisy plucked the translocation sphere from its pedestal to prevent anyone from duplicating our journey. She carefully carried the sphere over to the wall cabinet and stored it in the cell labeled *Dusk*.

The guard at the journey room door wouldn't let us out until he got authorization from the Council. Only Daisy and Ben had been checked through for departure, but they were coming back with three additional people. Daisy convinced the guard to call for Councilor Rissik, since he had been the one to escort them to the room originally.

While we waited, Ben grinned at me and said, "You sure caused a ruckus. Did you get what you needed?"

"Yes. There's no doubt that Paeter is using an enchantment to influence the governor."

Daisy noticed my tone of voice and the haunted look on my face. Lissy's expression mirrored mine. "What? Your mission succeeded. Why don't you look happy about it?"

Lissy answered for me. "Because we didn't really want it to be true." She glanced at Hayli who was frowning along with us. "This means Sorcerer Thoron is in direct violation of the Sorcery Accords." What she didn't say was that Paeter was probably facing a death sentence for that transgression.

I chimed in. "What's more, Paeter knows we know. That will make him determined and desperate. Dumont Fortenz is guilty by association, so both of them have nothing to lose at this point. They'll have to move fast to protect themselves, and I doubt we'll see a peaceful resolution to all of this."

Ben shrugged. "It sounds like you have enough evidence to convince the Council and the emperor. We'll arrest them and the emperor will sentence them."

"Yeah, I'm sure it will be just that easy," I said in a droll tone.

Ben was a little offended by my sarcasm. "Okay, I agree that they've been working to undermine the Archives, but they wouldn't dare oppose the emperor."

I shook a finger at him. "Don't be too sure about that. The thing that disturbs me most is how many people Thunderhead College has managed to recruit. Their Lightning Corps appears everywhere we go, and Paeter had control over three guards at the festival. I can't begin to guess how far they've spread their influence while we've been worrying about other things."

Even Lissy looked alarmed at the direction my thoughts had taken. "I've been meaning to tell you something. Before we left, Councilor Rissik mentioned that Headmaster Fortenz has been sighted in several provinces. He's apparently making arrangements to set up Thunderhead College campuses in each capital. We assumed he was trying to compete with us for potential students and that he wants his own sanctuary network. But what if he is after something more?"

Hayli had been silent while we spoke. She seemed cowed by the reality of her decision to join us, but her excitement to finally be here was betrayed by her fidgeting and darting glances at her friends and surroundings. Lissy's words penetrated her distraction and drew a bitter response.

"I don't trust that man. I'm sure he's the one behind all of this. My father would never have taken action against the governor on his own. He hated it when Governor Brachus took over, but he seemed to deal with it. Until he got involved with Thunderhead College. That's when he started disappearing for long periods of time without telling us why."

In my mind, I added fully debriefing Hayli to the many tasks that lay ahead. Hopefully, I had enough evidence to mobilize the Archives, but the truth was that we didn't have much to mobilize. Dumont Fortenz had been building his Lightning Corps while the Archives had been distracted by an incapacitated Sword Sorceress. The Archives had plenty of Isolationist supporters who could help fight against an Integrationist campaign, but we were way behind in terms of recruitment and organization. That had to change.

When Senior Councilor Rissik stepped in to escort us out of the journey room, I was last to exit. As I walked past him, he gave me a questioning look. "We need to talk," was all I said.

CHAPTER 18

PROGRESS REPORT

Headmaster Dumont Fortenz threw his cloak over the back of a chair and propped his feet up on the edge of his desk. He blew out an explosive sigh and stretched his neck back and forth before taking his feet back down and pulling off his boots. With a grumbled curse, he swiped at the dirt that had fallen off his boots onto his desk.

It was good to be back at Thunderhead College. He was mentally and physically exhausted after more than two weeks of intense negotiation and careful deception at nearly every province capital in the empire.

But it was all worth it. All but one of the province governors was the proud owner of a special gift from the headmaster. And Paeter's amulets were working even better than expected.

A servant scurried into the room with a decanter of wine and set a silver goblet in front of him. The middle-aged woman poured the wine and asked if he wanted anything to eat. Dumont asked her to get him whatever the kitchen had available, and she bowed her way out of the room.

He withdrew a small wand from his pocket and opened a side drawer in his desk. Wrapping the wand in a soft, velvet cloth, he placed it toward the back and locked the drawer.

The portal key that Lohan had stolen from the Archives for him had been invaluable. He would have spent weeks touring the empire on horseback, but the Portal Keep had given him near-instantaneous transportation between each capital city.

He had been prepared to encounter Archives forces each time he entered the keep, but his caution had proved unnecessary. The Archives' paranoia over losing their keys worked in his favor. That and the fact that the Archives relied more on their journey rooms for long-distance transportation.

Dumont had just slid his feet into his room slippers when heavy footsteps came down the hall. Guard Captain Peltor Mullan marched into the office and stopped a couple feet away from his desk.

"Welcome home, Headmaster," the captain greeted him with a bow.

"Thank you, Captain Mullan. Have you heard anything about Lohan's progress in Northshore?"

"No, sir."

That was disappointing news. Dumont needed subordinates he could rely on if he was going to expand his sphere of influence. Lohan had been tasked with getting an amulet on the governor in Northshore. The capital city of Lakewoods Province was fairly close, so Lohan wouldn't need to use the one portal key they'd managed to acquire.

Dumont frowned. "What could be taking him so long?"

"Incompetence?" Peltor suggested with a wry smile.

Dumont's mounting irritation found a target in Peltor. He pointed a warning finger at the captain. "Your attitude is only making matters worse. The two of you need to cease this endless bickering and find a way to work peacefully together. Don't make me choose between the two of you. You may not like the outcome."

Peltor clenched his jaw and stood at attention. "Yes, sir. I understand, sir. We'll work something out."

Dumont stared down his finger at the man for a moment more and then sat back in his chair. "See that you do. Now, how goes the recruitment and training?"

Chastisement over, Peltor's typical haughty expression returned. "Things are progressing well, sir. We are getting more recruits than I was led to expect, but so far we've been able to keep up. I've stationed about half our forces around the empire. They are raw, but they have basic skills, at least with weapons. I can't speak to their sorcery training." In spite of the fact that Peltor was working for the sorcerer sitting in front of him, his bias against sorcerers still came out as disdain in his voice.

"Sorcery training isn't your problem, Captain. Let Lohan decide when the sorcerers are ready."

Peltor gave a curt nod. "Yes, sir. Is that all, sir?"

Dumont thought for a moment about the delay in Northshore.

"No, that's not all. I have new orders for you. Leave the training to your lieutenants for now. Take a squad down to Northshore and see if you can help Lohan complete his mission. Don't take command, just offer your help. I want Lohan to finish this himself, but it's possible he needs additional support, or perhaps some kind of distraction. See what you can do *without* antagonizing him."

Peltor didn't look enthusiastic about the orders, but he stood at attention and nodded. "Yes, sir. I'll get my team together right away."

"And Captain, it's possible that Lohan is having a crisis of conscience. Remind him that what we are doing is the only way he will see his dreams of sorcerer integration come true."

Peltor raised an eyebrow. "Politics and philosophy are not my strengths, sir, but I'll be sure to remind him of his duty to you and to his cause."

Dumont chuckled at Peltor's understatement. "That will do fine, Captain. You're dismissed."

As Peltor was leaving, the servant returned with a trencher of some kind of stew and nearly half a loaf of bread. After many days of rich meals at the province capitals, the simple fare was welcome.

While he ate, Dumont thought about what was next.

The governors were finally under his control. Each governor appointed a Province Emissary to the Imperial Assembly, the governing body that handled the majority of the empire's affairs from the capital. He had already seen to it that the current emissaries would be replaced by others who were "recommended" by Dumont. Soon, he would be in a position to shape imperial policy. With all five province votes, even the emperor couldn't stop him.

His first policy change would be to pull the teeth of the Archives.

Chapter 19

Spiritual Healing

Sulana picked a few last flowers and checked the contents of the collection bag slung over her shoulder. She was proud of herself for finding everything Karla had asked for, from the tiny yellow flowers of the rosin rose to the bright purple petals of the giant coneflowers she had just added to the bag.

She stretched and closed her eyes for a moment while the setting sun warmed her back and shoulders. The nights were starting to get cool, but thankfully, the last sunny days of summer held back the inevitable dreary days of fall.

She left the open field and walked briskly back toward Karla's cottage, twirling once to revel in the smooth strength and balance that was returning to her movement. Thanks to Karla's ministrations, the stuttering disconnect between her intentions and her actions was nearly gone. Daven had new bruises to confirm that her skills with a sword were returning to normal, and the target they had set up for her crossbow practice showed a satisfying number of holes near its center.

The only dark cloud that periodically dampened her mood was her continued inability to channel. Karla had warned her that the treatments would only help her physically, but Sulana had secretly hoped that her channeling would return to normal as a side-effect. As happy as she was to have her combat skills restored, she had to swallow a lump in her throat every time she thought about never being able to properly channel vaetra again.

While walking the trail back to the healer's cottage, Sulana's mind wandered. Her thoughts turned to Jaylan, as they often did lately. The news in his most recent message had been both encouraging and alarming. In their missives to each other, they kept details to a minimum because they didn't entirely trust the networks that carried them. But she was able to glean that Jaylan was making progress on his casting problem. She also got the message that Thunderhead College had finally crossed the line of the Sorcery Accords and the Archives was taking steps to do something about it.

She longed to go back to the Archives and help the Council deal with the threat from Thunderhead College. It was her responsibility. But a broken Sword Sorceress was of little use to them. She believed that soon, she'd be able to return to duty, but would they want a Sword Sorceress who could no longer use vaetra? She stopped abruptly on the path and closed her eyes to hold back the pressure of tears that swelled behind her eyes.

No more crying. She'd done enough of that. She took a deep breath and started walking again, more slowly this time.

Most of all, she needed to feel Jaylan's arms around her again. She wanted to give him whatever support he needed with these new revelations about his casting. She commiserated with the frustration that came across in his messages. Anything that had Ebnik stumped must be truly challenging.

Lost in her thoughts of home, Sulana came around the wall of the cottage to find Karla and Daven embracing at the front door. She stopped. Neither seemed to notice her, their attention focused solely on each other. When their lips met in a tender kiss, Sulana eased back around the corner out of sight.

Well, that was no real surprise. The romance between Karla and Daven had been growing steadily over the past few weeks. Daven was still attentive to Sulana's therapy requirements, but he spent almost all of his free time near Karla. Karla shyly resisted his attentions at first, but that façade had lasted less than a week. Eventually, the two started disappearing together on various "errands" and would reappear with flushed and happy faces. Daven had finally found someone who returned his feelings.

Good for them. Sulana would be happy to give them a bit more private time together.

She went to the stream that ran behind the cottage and off into the forest. A narrow but well-traveled trail meandered alongside the stream to a rocky pool where they usually refilled the water bucket. In the fading light of the day, Sulana strolled to the pool and sat down on a large stone at the water's edge. This was one of her favorite spots for reflection when she wanted to be alone. At the head of the pool was a tiny waterfall. She closed her eyes and let its warbling trickle soothe her spirit.

While she sat there, the daytime birds quieted and the evening birds began their whooping call. The hummingbirds had left the area a little over a week ago, and most of the other birds would soon follow. When the last robins departed, the first snowfall would be close at hand.

Sulana set the collection bag down and kneeled at the pool's edge to get a drink. She cupped her hands under the clear water that was refreshingly cool all year long. Before she could raise her hands to her mouth, she felt more than heard a thump that seemed to press against her entire body at once. The compression effect in her lungs nearly made her cough. Disoriented, she stared at her hands under the water, unable to move them. Her vision magnified and receded as if she were looking through waves. She swallowed back saliva against a rising nausea and tried to pull her hands out of the water, but to no avail.

She peered out at the forest surrounding the pool, suddenly certain that she wasn't alone. Had the druids found out about her? The ranger, who eventually identified himself as Marshal Nigel Shields, had been back a few times to check on her. Had he changed his mind about letting her stay?

Before she could call out to Daven for backup, a familiar pressure pushed against her awareness, demanding her attention. It was similar to what she experienced when she communicated with spirit animals, but she saw no animals nearby. Taking a guess at what she needed to do, she opened a channel into the water through her hands and did her best to feed vaetra into it. The awful channeling resistance still held her back, but her effort was apparently sufficient. A cascade of images flooded into her mind.

At first, the images didn't make any sense. They just seemed to reflect what she could see with her own eyes. They showed her hands in the pool just as they were. Then she saw herself holding a rounded stone under the water. The rock began to glow, as if it were some kind of vaetric implement. Through the images came the impression that she was supposed to channel vaetra into the rock through one hand and draw it out through the other in some kind of channeling loop.

She'd never heard of such a technique, and she wasn't even sure it was possible. Even if it was, she had certainly never attempted it. But what did she have to lose? As soon as she resolved to give it a try, her arms unfroze and she was able to move her hands again. She dropped the channel at the same time and the images quickly faded away.

She picked up a rock from the bottom of the pool and cupped her hands around it as she'd seen in the image. But it looked wrong. This wasn't the rock she'd seen in the vision. Did it matter?

No sense taking chances. Get it right.

Her eyes searched the bottom of the pool for the stone she had seen in the vision. There it was, dark and rounded into an egg shape with white striations of crystal running through it. She picked up the stone and rolled it in her hands until the striations matched the pattern the vision had shown her.

Sulana opened a channel to the stone through her left hand and let vaetra flow into it. The stone accepted the flow just as if she were charging it up to use it as a conjuring stone. Next for the tricky part. How could she draw the vaetra back out of the stone through her right hand? She only had one channel. How could she connect two at the same time?

Smiling to herself, Sulana thought about how Jaylan would deal with this situation. It was one of those problems he would analyze to death until he seemingly stumbled upon a solution that would seem perfectly logical and obvious in retrospect. She didn't have the patience for that.

Letting her thoughts take a brief detour into thinking about Jaylan gave her a sudden insight. She didn't need to create a second channel. The whole point was to create a loop. She needed to feed the vaetra through the stone back into herself. Her right hand needed to link with her left through the stone, and she had to let her channel connect back to her own internal well. Was that even possible? Under normal circumstances, it would be a pointless exercise, so the Archives didn't teach it.

These definitely weren't normal circumstances.

The common druid saying sprung to mind: "May the spirits guide you." She had always taken it to be an expression of hope for spiritual guidance. But she realized it wasn't just that: it was a warning, almost a command. It might as well say, "*Let* the spirits guide you."

Sulana had never subscribed to the religious aspects of spirit worship, but nonetheless, she recognized this moment as her test of faith. The spirits were asking her to do something she had never done before. Something that maybe no one had done before.

Mentally shrugging, she decided to trust the spirits. In that moment of decision, the solution to her problem came to her so clearly that she felt stupid for not seeing it before. She pushed the channel through the striation in the stone and into her right hand. From there, she guided the channel back to her internal well where it snapped into place, replenishing her vaetra as she expended it. It was a weird sensation, and so personally intimate that it almost made her blush. She wondered what it would be like to join hands with Jaylan and cycle vaetra between each other this way. She licked her lips at the thought and promised herself they'd give it a try the next time they were together.

Just as she had foreseen, the stone actually glowed. She wasn't sure what that meant, but she smiled with the knowledge that she had managed to fulfill the vision.

Now what?

The vaetra trickled slowly against her channeling resistance while Sulana waited for something to happen. At first it seemed like the exercise was just as pointless as she expected. Then the flow of vaetra began to speed up. The change was subtle at first, but her resistance to the cycling flow slowly melted away. Her mouth dropped open in surprise as she realized that the rock was acting as some kind of filter cleaning out the impurities that clogged her channeling.

The promise of being able to use sorcery again made her nearly weep with relief. She fed vaetra through the loop as fast as she could, praying that the cleansing wouldn't stop until she was back to normal.

It didn't stop. After a couple of minutes, the flow of vaetra stabilized and all of the abnormal blockage was gone. Her resistance had returned to normal. After months of having her abilities strangled, she felt amazingly powerful and free.

Knowing that the task was done, Sulana dropped the channel and pulled her pale, numb hands out of the water. She held the stone to her breast and closed her eyes. She thanked the spirits for helping her while tears streamed down her face. With reverence, Sulana returned the stone to the place in the pool where she had found it. She didn't need it any more, so returning it seemed like the right thing to do.

The snap of a branch and the murmur of low voices told her someone was approaching down the trail.

"Are you there, Sulana?" Daven's voice called from the path.

Sulana lifted a wet hand toward them and waved it, not sure if they'd be able to make her out in the fading light. "I'm here." She wished she had thought to bring a lantern with her to the pond, but she hadn't expected to be here so late. A little light would be helpful.

To her astonishment, Sulana felt her channel open just long enough to let forth a small surge of vaetra. The surge went through her arm to her wet, waving hand, and a tiny glow appeared at the end of her index finger. The glow separated from her hand and drifted toward Daven and Karla like a soap bubble. It illuminated their shocked expressions just before it faded out.

Everyone was silent for a moment.

"That was druid light," Karla said with confusion in her voice. "How did you do that?"

Sulana stared at her hand, barely visible in the gathering darkness. She absently dried it on her skirt while she tried to comprehend what had just happened.

"Sulana, how did you do that?" Karla repeated, her voice growing insistent.

"I wish I knew," Sulana said, as much to herself as in answer to Karla.

Sulana groped around on the ground and found her collection bag. Blowing warm breath into her cold hands, she gingerly stepped toward Karla and Daven. "Let's get back to the cottage and talk there. I need to warm up my hands."

Karla led the way back to the cottage where a small fire had already been set against the evening chill. Sulana went straight to the fireplace and stretched her arms toward the heat. Her hands were beet red and tingling in a way that she knew would become excruciating within a couple of minutes.

Karla sat on a cushioned bench near Sulana and just stared, waiting for an explanation. Her expression was odd and unreadable.

At Daven's prompting, Sulana related her return from the gathering trip and her visit to the pool, skipping the part where she had seen the two of them kissing. When she described the joy of having her channeling abilities back, Daven congratulated her enthusiastically and gave her a hug. Karla said nothing and remained on the bench with that same unreadable expression.

"And then you two came along," Sulana said, nearing the end of her tale. "I had just put the stone back in the water when I heard you coming down the trail. I couldn't see very well, so I tried to get your attention by waving your way. At the same time, I wished for light, and just like that, the light bubble appeared."

Karla narrowed her eyes at Sulana. "Just like that?"

Sulana wasn't sure what was bothering the young healer, and the strange attitude was becoming annoying.

"Well, not exactly. I wanted light, and without really trying to do it, I opened a channel and cast it through the water on my hand."

Sulana's own words registered as she said them. She mumbled to herself, "I cast the light using the water as a focus." She grinned at Daven and shouted, "I *cast* the light!"

Karla looked down at her hands in her lap. "No, you didn't. I heard no incantation. It wasn't sorcery."

Karla was right. Sulana had known the incantation for light a long time ago, but she'd forgotten it along with most of the other incantations she'd learned. After she reconciled herself to the fact that she'd never be able to cast, there was no point in remembering incantations. So how had she cast the light? Karla seemed to have some idea.

Sulana kneeled in front of Karla and waited until the healer met her eyes. "Tell me what you're thinking," she demanded gently.

Karla shook her head and spoke hesitantly. "I don't understand how, but that was definitely druid light. I've seen it many times. The priest prays for light and the spirits respond with a blessing exactly like the one we just saw."

Sulana sat back on her heels and rubbed her forehead. "That doesn't make sense. I'm not a druid. I don't know anything about prayers or blessings."

Karla gave a sulky shrug. "I'm just telling you what I know."

Daven sat next to Karla on the bench and took her hand in his. "What is it? Why are you acting this way?"

Karla looked into Daven's concerned face and burst into tears before leaning forward into his shoulder. Daven gave

Sulana a look that said he had no idea what was bothering the girl. He patted her back helplessly, and her sobs began to slow. After a few deep sniffs, she turned away from Daven and wiped the tears from her face.

"I've been with the druids since I was little. I studied hard and prayed for the spirits to favor me. I did everything the priests asked of me, and I was so happy the first time the spirits helped me during a healing session. I was thrilled and proud when the priests said I had an affinity for the spirits. So I studied for the priesthood."

Karla looked up and returned Sulana's stare before going on. "But no matter how hard I tried, my prayers were never answered. The spirits never gave me a blessing. I wasn't chosen to be a priestess, just a healer."

Daven rubbed Karla's back and spoke softly. "You're an excellent healer. What you've done for Sulana has been remarkable."

Karla shifted under Daven's hand, ignoring his comments and refusing to be consoled. She looked at Sulana again, this time with a glare. "And now you come along. A broken sorceress with no faith. The spirits choose *you* to receive their blessings. It's just not fair!"

Karla leaped from the bench and ran out of the cottage, leaving an echo of her sobs behind the slamming of the door.

Sulana was too shocked to move. She looked over at Daven, who sat on the bench with his hand still reaching toward where Karla had been sitting.

"You'd better go to her," Sulana suggested. Daven nodded and walked out of the cottage in a daze.

Sulana got up from the floor and sat in a chair that was comfortably near the fire. She threw in a log to keep the flames going.

Karla seemed convinced that Sulana was some kind of priestess or that she could become one. How could that be? Druids and sorcerers produced manifestations in completely different ways. Or so she had always been told. What she experienced tonight was different from anything she'd seen before, yet it all felt so familiar. She had still channeled vaetra. She had still generated a manifestation using the water as a focus. According to sorcery theory, the only element missing was the incantation. Had the spirits somehow responded to her wish for light and given her the incantation she needed? Even if they had, she hadn't spoken the words. How had the manifestation appeared?

The sharp memory of her miraculous bubble of light pushed the confusing thoughts to the background. Who cared how it worked? The fact was that she could cast. She was finally a full sorceress ... of sorts.

Ebnik and Jaylan would probably spend hours theorizing about what had happened and what it implied. She preferred the more practical approach of focusing on what *was* rather than what *might be*. If only she were home at the Archives. She'd feel more comfortable experimenting with this new ability and seeing what she could do with it.

With that thought, she realized that she was nearly ready to leave the refuge. Karla had told her that morning that they were nearing the end of her treatments, and then the spirits had somehow helped her repair her ability to channel vaetra. Sulana would be able to return to the Archives soon. She looked forward to surprising Jaylan with her new casting ability.

That was, assuming she could duplicate it. Sulana pushed aside the doubts that began to stir and chose to believe that she had just started down a new path in her life. For reasons she didn't understand yet, the spirits had helped her. As much as she disliked the term, what had happened to her was undeniably some kind of *miracle*. She owed it to the spirits to take this new gift seriously and use it well. Leaving the Archives and joining the druids wasn't an option, but she would be sensitive to the will of the spirits.

Lost in thought while staring into the dancing flames in the fireplace, Sulana hardly noticed when Daven and Karla slipped back into the cottage. It wasn't until they were both seated on the bench across from her that she snapped out of her reverie and took in their stares.

Karla dipped her head and said, "I'm sorry, Sulana. None of this is your fault. I thought I had come to terms with never becoming a priestess, but what happened tonight brought it all back. I didn't mean to take it out on you."

Sulana smiled at the young healer. She knew all about the disappointment and pain that came from having your dream taken away. Now she knew the joy of having it restored. "Believe me, I understand. I don't know what all of this means yet, but I'm grateful for the opportunity to find out."

Karla nodded and looked down at her hands. "May the spirits guide you, Sulana."

CHAPTER 20

SCHOLAR'S REVELATION

The man who sat across from me was as pale as the full moon, his skin almost translucent from spending most of his life underground. He wore a simple woolen pull-over shift to keep back the chill of the spacious chamber he called home.

Ebnik sat next to me on a padded bench near the chamber entrance. He had just introduced me to this remarkable fellow. Arinot was an Archives scholar who was a sound sensitive like me. Except Arinot's sensitivity went far beyond mine. He could "hear" vaetric manifestation from miles away. According to Ebnik, his remarkable sensitivity was more a handicap than a gift. He lived here deep within the insulating stone confines of the Archives because the noise of nearby manifestation was too painful for him to bear.

I shivered, partly from thinking about his predicament, and partly from the chill of the room.

Arinot cleared his throat. "I apologize for the cold. The heat from the convectors doesn't carry over to my room very well."

"That must be unpleasant during the winter," I commented.

"Actually, it's almost too warm in the winter. The airflow through the convectors increases when it gets cold outside, and that somehow overcomes whatever interferes with the circulation."

"Maybe you should ask for better lodging."

Arinot gave Ebnik a knowing smile. They'd obviously had this conversation before. "This place suits me just fine. The temperature changes are the closest I get to experiencing the seasons down here."

It sounded pretty bleak to me, but Arinot was obviously at home. The surface of his desk was obscured by piles of parchment and open books. His bookshelves sagged under the weight of thick tomes that leaned haphazardly against each other.

A colorful, embroidered curtain separated the entry area and study from the rest of the chamber. When Arinot let us in, I caught glimpses of a well-cushioned cot and simple kitchen in the area beyond. Arinot seemed to have everything he needed in his underground apartment.

Ebnik cleared his throat and addressed the scholar. "You sent a note that you had found something interesting?"

Arinot nodded, but he looked at me as he spoke. "Ebnik asked me to see what I could find out about your remarkable casting experiences."

I barked out a laugh. "Remarkable? Well, that's one way to look at it."

Ebnik was intrigued. "What did you learn?"

"I wasn't making much progress until you passed along the terms *Runedream* and *runemaster*. I remembered seeing references to those words in some of our oldest records from the Wizard Wars. At the time, I dismissed them as mythic legend. Now that I've had a chance to review the material, I believe I understand what is happening with our young friend here."

I held my breath. *At last, I'm going to get some answers.*

Arinot reached over to his desk and picked up a sheet of parchment that was covered with scribbled notes.

"Prior to the Wizard Wars, sorcerers with Jaylan's ability to enter the Runedream were rare, but not as rare as they are now. In Wizard Rollek's time, three such runemasters served the sorcerers in power. They were carefully guarded because of their abilities, but in spite of that, all living runemasters perished during the wars."

It was comforting to know that the Runedream was real and that I *wasn't* the first to experience it.

"Why haven't more runemasters appeared since then?" I asked.

Arinot shrugged and waved the parchment toward his desk. "I have no idea. I can't find any reference to runemasters or the Runedream after the Wizard Wars. I sometimes want to weep at all the irreplaceable knowledge we lost in the violence of those wars. My guess is, once all of the runemasters were gone, no one was around to identify the gift in others and train them to use it."

"So, even if other people had this *gift*, they wouldn't recognize it for what it was. Just as I didn't."

"Exactly. From what I can tell, sorcerers with the ability to enter the Runedream occur only once or twice in a generation. In the decades following the wars, sorcerers were preoccupied with survival. When the ability to channel vaetra surfaced among the mundane, the gifted were more likely to hide their abilities or be executed for them than they were to seek out other sorcerers."

"Are you telling me that I'm the first runemaster in three hundred years? How is that possible?"

Ebnik had been listening with a thoughtful frown. At my question, he lifted a finger to interrupt. "Think about it Jaylan. If you hadn't met Sulana, you would never have learned you could channel. If you had decided to ignore your gift, you would never have come here for training. If you hadn't been willing to enter the Runedream, you'd have never learned anything more about it. I'd say we came quite close to missing *this* generation's runemaster."

Arinot nodded along with Ebnik's points. "Three hundred years is only about 15 generations. I'd say we are lucky to have uncovered a runemaster *so soon*."

"I don't believe it was luck," Ebnik said thoughtfully. He gave me a strange look, as if seeing me in a new light. "I think it was meant to be."

I squinted at him, hardly believing what I was hearing. "I hope you aren't thinking what I think you're thinking. No. Absolutely not. You'd better not say the word *destiny*, or I'll have to strangle you."

Ebnik smiled. "Then I won't say it. But that doesn't make it any less so."

Thankfully, Arinot wasn't buying it either. "Ebnik, just because an event is unlikely doesn't mean there's some kind of divine intervention when it occurs."

Ebnik shook his head. "Who said anything about divine intervention? I'm talking about fate. I believe we are in the middle of a significant historical event, and a lot of it seems to revolve around Jaylan. He's the one who uncovered and foiled Thoron's plans in Buckwoods. He's the one who rescued Sulana and her team from Thunderhead College. He single-handedly defeated the headmaster's entire pursuit force. He's the one who verified that Thoron is violating the Accords. And now he's our first runemaster in three hundred years."

My opinion of Ebnik's intelligence and objectivity was taking a hit. "You're kidding me, right? All those events were a matter of timing and circumstance. I just did what seemed right at the time. Any one of them could have turned out differently."

Ebnik sat back with a satisfied smile and folded his arms. "Thank you. You just proved my point."

Fate? No way. I was not "fated" to stop Thunderhead College. I was *determined* to stop Thunderhead College. It was a choice, not a destiny. But I could see there was no point arguing the subject with Ebnik.

"Whatever," I finally said, and I turned my attention back to Arinot, the other sane person in the room.

"What am I supposed to do with this *gift*? Do your records say anything about how it works or how I can use it to help us? I have no idea what being a runemaster means, and it seems that no one is left to teach me."

Arinot looked just as disturbed by Ebnik's pronouncement as I had been. He seemed happy to move on to another subject and brightened at my question. "Ah, I'm sorry to say that I found little information about the Runedream itself. However, I did find one intriguing reference to the Runedream as *the origin of sorcery*. I thought perhaps that might mean something to you."

The origin of sorcery? I had used the Runedream to learn the incantation for fire. But that was nothing new. Tritia must have known the incantation, and her spirit lights had demonstrated it for me. Was she the spirit of a dead sorceress? If I saw her again, I'd have to ask her about how she came to know sorcery. "I'm not sure what that means. If I figure it out, I'll let you know."

Arinot nodded and smiled. "Thank you. I will continue my research, and if I discover anything new, I'll pass it along to you as well."

Ebnik rose to his feet, signaling an end to our visit. "Thanks for your help, Arinot. I knew you would find something."

Arinot stood and shook hands with Ebnik. "I'm sorry I couldn't tell you more, but I'll keep looking."

I stood as well. "It was good to meet you. Thanks for all the research you did. I'm not sure what to make of it all, but I do feel better knowing that I'm not going crazy."

We said our final goodbyes, and Ebnik led me through the passageway back to the library. In the library, Ebnik sealed the door to Arinot's secret domain and turned to face me. His expression was thoughtful and serious.

"We may have a new problem."

I sighed in frustration. Why couldn't something just go right for a change? I motioned for him to continue.

"Too many people know about this to keep it a secret."

I frowned in confusion, unsure of where he was going. "Why would we keep it a secret? I need all the help I can get. I'll take suggestions from just about anyone at this point."

Ebnik tilted his head toward the door he had just sealed. "Arinot's research puts your situation in a new light. Before, you were a sorcerer with a casting problem. Now, you are a rare runemaster—the first in over three hundred years."

Unbidden, Arinot's words about the last living runemasters came to mind: *they were carefully guarded because of their abilities.* My chest tightened as I thought about what an overprotective Council might do to keep me "safe."

"You think the Council is going to keep me locked up here."

Ebnik nodded slowly. "Perhaps not literally locked up, but they may very well put an end to your career as a Sword Sorcerer."

I closed my eyes and fought back the desire to scream something obscene about the Council. Ebnik was right. They wouldn't want me out on missions putting myself in danger. But then a thought began to form. I opened my eyes and narrowed them on the face of my friend.

"I appreciate the warning, but the Council does not own me. Not yet, anyway. The only way they *do* own me is if I become a Sword Sorcerer. If they want to benefit from this *gift* of mine, they'll have to do it on my terms."

Ebnik gave me a sly smile. "I'm glad you feel that way. You'll have a hard hike up the mountain to make that case with the Council, but I'll support you any way I can."

Ebnik turned and walked toward the library exit, waving for me to follow. "In the meantime, I've been working on your casting problem, and I think I may have a solution."

CHAPTER 21

SORCERER'S STAFF

I followed Ebnik's long stride from the library up to the training level, breaking into a jog occasionally to keep up. "Where are you taking me?"

"You'll see."

"Is all this secrecy necessary?"

"Stay in your saddle, boy. This is something more easily shown than told." Ebnik grinned at me over his shoulder as he turned into an open doorway and entered the room beyond. I followed him in with my brow creased in puzzlement.

The Forge was one of the few rooms on the training level that was unfamiliar to me. This chamber was where the Archives' smiths assembled their creations. I would get a chance to try my hand at smithing once I completed my rune training.

A sorcerer sat at a workbench across the room hunched over his work. Several wooden wands lay side-by-side near his elbow. At another bench along the wall to my left, a sorcerer glanced up from polishing a crystal sphere. He went back to his work after deeming me unworthy of an interruption to his efforts.

Ebnik had gone to an unoccupied bench at a far corner of the room and came back toward me holding a staff. It came to about shoulder height on him, which was nearly head height for me.

"Is this what you wanted to show me?" I asked.

"Yes, partly. This is my vaenwork sounding staff."

My lessons at the Archives had taught me that the world was networked with underground flows of vaetra called the *vaenwork*. The flows, or *vaens*, merged at large wells, or *basins*. Long ago, sorcerers charted the vaenwork, identifying where the vaens flowed and where the basins were located. All but a couple of those charts were lost during the Wizard Wars. Ebnik once told me that he had made it his life's work to recreate those charts.

I looked the staff over from top to bottom. It was made of light-colored wood and had a metal spike capped onto the bottom. Near the top, several gem stones of different colors were embedded in a vertical line. A small, blue, crystal ball topped the staff.

"It reminds me of the resistance meter," I observed.

Ebnik nodded encouragingly. "Very good. It's based on some of the same principles."

"What does it do?"

"It measures how much vaetra is available at a given point along a vaen or at a basin. I designed it to help me recreate the vaenwork charts."

Ebnik went on to explain his creation. "Like the resistance meter, the gems illuminate in sequence. The more vaetra it finds, the more gems light up. Here, let me show you."

Ebnik pushed down on the staff, apparently to make sure the spike had good contact with the floor. He moved his hand over a metal band that ringed the staff at about elbow height. A few seconds later, the crystal ball at the top glowed brightly and about half of the gems along the side lit up.

"The crystal at the top drives the device. I made it glow so I'd know the thing was working in case none of the gems brightened." He pointed at the gems. "What it's detecting now is the Archives Basin. I calibrated the meter using the Archives as the midpoint."

The sorcerers who built the Archives had placed it on top of a major basin. The entire castle was made from stone, so vaetra from the basin seeped into the structure, effectively adding the Archives itself to an already massive vaetric well. Throughout the castle, illuminators, suntrackers, and other devices drew the power they needed directly from the walls and floor.

I grinned and nodded appreciatively. "It's marvelous. I can't imagine how long it took you to make that."

Ebnik chuckled and turned off the detector. "Almost six months, with a lot of research and many failed prototypes."

"That must have been frustrating."

"Actually, I had just retired from the Council, and it was the most fun I'd had in years."

The sounding staff was a fascinating device, but I wasn't sure what it had to do with my casting problem.

"Is this what you wanted to show me?"

"Not entirely. I have something else here as well."

Ebnik took the sounder back to the corner and returned with a different staff. This staff was about the same height as the sounder, but it was thicker. The top was carved into a concave hollow where I guessed a sphere would eventually go. It had two separate metal bands about two hand-widths apart. The bottom was capped with a metal spike, just like the sounder.

Ebnik handed the staff to me and said, "It's not done yet, as you can probably tell. I need to borrow Froth from you before I can finish it."

"Froth will go on top?"

"That's right. I'll make it so you can remove the orb whenever you want."

I held the staff at arms' length. "What does it do?"

"It's a combination of ideas. Most sorcerers who can cast always have an orb with them. The majority of us just carry one around in a pocket or coin purse to keep it hidden from mundane eyes. Others prefer something more decorative, so they mount the orb on a wand, staff, or neck pendant."

My face must have betrayed my dismay at the idea of putting Froth around my neck, as heavy as it was.

Ebnik chuckled and commented, "Most casting orbs are much smaller than Froth."

"Anyway, a sorcerer's staff typically has the orb mounted at the top, and it has a band that links the sorcerer's hand to the orb through a metal strip inside the staff."

I could see what Ebnik was talking about. Light glinted on a metal stub inside the bowl at the top of the staff. Presumably, that was where Froth would be mounted. One of the metal bands undoubtedly linked to that stub.

"Why does this staff have two bands?"

Ebnik smiled and wiggled his eyebrows. "That is where the combination of ideas comes in. My thinking was that you need a way to channel vaetra from an external source, right?" I nodded. "The sounding staff has a metal core just like a sorcerer's staff, but it connects to the metal spike at the bottom. When you dig the spike into a well, it can draw vaetra from the well. How it measures the available vaetra is a bit complicated, but what's important is that it can make that connection."

I thought I was beginning to see where he was going with this. If I could draw vaetra from a well through the staff, I'd be able to cast without being sucked into the Runedream.

I put my right hand on the lower band and my left on the upper band. The purpose of the design became instantly clear.

"I can draw vaetra through the lower band and cast with Froth through the upper band."

Ebnik clapped me on the back. "Precisely! The sounder is a single-purpose version of this design. The incantation built into it measures vaetra and illuminates the gems. You will provide the incantation for your staff. You can use it to cast whatever spell you want, and you never have to touch your internal well."

I grinned and held up the staff admiringly. "That's genius!" I handed the staff back to Ebnik and fished Froth out of my pocket. I wouldn't miss having the weight of the orb constantly pulling at that side of my clothing. I handed the orb to Ebnik.

"Froth's all yours. I can't wait to give the staff a try. You'd better watch out, or everyone's going to want you to make one for them."

Ebnik tilted his head as if to say maybe yes, maybe no.

"I'm probably not the first to think of this," he said. "The concept does have one serious limitation. You have to be standing right over a well. Most sorcerers just use their internal well, so the well tapping feature of this staff is unnecessary."

He was right, but the limitation was fine by me. It beat not being able to cast at all or having to suffer the embarrassment of borrowing vaetra from someone else. I just had to be strategic about where I positioned myself when I needed to cast a spell. That was probably easier said than done, but what other choice did I have?

"This is brilliant, Ebnik. Thank you. I don't know how I'll repay you for all the help you've been giving me."

Ebnik's face grew serious. "You can repay me by letting me help you learn everything we can about the Runedream. As much as I don't want the Council to interfere with your destiny, I do think you need to be careful. I know you are used to working independently, but you must learn to let your friends support you now."

I closed my eyes briefly and breathed a frustrated sigh. "There you go with that *destiny* stuff again. I'm not too worried. As far as anyone else knows, I'm just a broken sorcerer."

Ebnik held up a finger in warning. "As I said before, too many people know about the Runedream now for its importance to remain a secret."

He glanced at the two other men in the room, who appeared to be preoccupied with their own projects. He leaned toward me and spoke in a low voice.

"The Council won't be the only ones who are curious about what a runemaster might be able to do. And most of the interested parties won't even consider *your* best interests."

That disturbing thought stuck with me all the way back to my chamber. The more I thought about it, the more I started to believe Ebnik was right. I wondered how many of the runemasters who lived prior to the Wizard Wars had been serving their masters voluntarily.

CHAPTER 22

AUDIENCE WITH THE EMPEROR

Gregor watched his fellow councilor as the man's eyes roved the maps and tapestries around the emperor's conference room. Senior Councilor Boris Underwood had followed with wide-eyes and an open mouth practically since they'd entered the palace.

Back in the reception area, Councilor Underwood had quietly suffered the indignity of letting the guards pat him down. He had balked when the guard insisted he remove all jewelry, including a precious ring that was apparently a family heirloom. He finally complied with a glare at the unimpressed guard who waited patiently with his hand out.

After that, the councilor had stumbled along behind Gregor gawking at the palace architecture and the artwork that decorated it. He commented that the palace seemed more majestic when it wasn't filled with visitors, noise, and distractions, as it had been on his few previous visits.

Gregor had practically grown up at the palace, so he appreciated seeing it through the eyes of someone unaccustomed to it.

"Amazing," the councilor commented, still inspecting the contents of the room from his seat at the long conference table. "Each piece must be worth a fortune."

Gregor nodded. "I'm sure they are. As I understand it, some of the works are very old."

"Remarkable," the councilor mumbled.

"I'm glad you came with me, Councilor Underwood."

The change in subject distracted the councilor from his inspections. His eyes darted to Gregor. "I'm surprised to hear that. If you had wanted my company in the past, all you had to do was ask. Instead you kept these little visits of yours a secret. Forgive me if I doubt your sincerity."

Gregor nodded. He'd deserved that.

"The secrecy was a mistake. The emperor has almost always had a representative on the Archives Council. When the task fell to me, I was concerned about how it would be perceived by the other Council members, so I said nothing about my appointment. As time went on, revealing the truth became more difficult. I should have known that I'd have to tell you all eventually and that holding the information back would only make matters more awkward."

The councilor narrowed his eyes at Gregor. "Yes. You went from being an imperial ambassador to being an imperial spy."

Gregor looked down at his hands. "As I said, it was a mistake. I hope you'll see for yourself that I want what is best for both the Archives and the empire."

Councilor Underwood sat back in his chair and let out a deep breath. "That is my hope as well."

Gregor sat in silence while the councilor resumed his visual perusal of the wall hangings. After a few minutes, the back door to the room opened and a guard stepped inside. The burly man looked around the room and checked under the table. He motioned the two councilors to stand and checked them both a second time for weapons or implements of sorcery. Satisfied that the room was clear of danger, the guard motioned to a second guard at the doorway. The second guard came into the room as well, followed by two men and a tall woman.

The first man to enter after the second guard was ancient and bent. He cast a sour glance at the two sorcerers and curled his lip in undisguised disdain. Gregor knew the man well. He was Sorman Tanes, the emperor's seneschal, and a constant impediment during Gregor's visits to the palace.

The second man was the emperor himself. The worries of an empire rested on the man's shoulders, and today it showed. The emperor's rounded cheeks often dimpled merrily when he smiled, but at the moment his face was troubled. He clumped over to his seat while the guard held it back for him, and he dropped an armload of documents onto the table before settling in.

The last person was a tall woman with silver-streaked black hair. She wore a long, dark red robe trimmed with yellow along the hems. An eagle with its talons gripping a sphere was embroidered on the breast of her robe, indicating that she was an imperial sorceress. She glided over to the table and stood behind the seat that Gregor had previously occupied, to the left of the emperor.

Gregor eased further down the table away from the woman, knowing better than to contest her claim to the seat. Councilor Underwood shifted down a place as well so the seneschal could sit at the emperor's right. The guards remained standing along the wall behind the emperor's chair.

The emperor waved a hand, indicating that everyone around the table should sit down. With tension clipping his words, he got right to business.

"Councilor Rissik, Councilor Underwood, welcome to the palace. This is Seneschal Sorman Tanes, and this is Sorceress Dierdre Fleming. I understand that you have some important information to share?"

Gregor opened his mouth to respond, but Underwood spoke first. "Thank you, Your Majesty. We appreciate your taking the time to see us."

The emperor glanced at Gregor and then smiled at Councilor Underwood. "My pleasure, Councilor Underwood. I'm always interested in hearing whatever news Gregor brings me."

The emperor's hint was not lost on Underwood. The councilor bowed his head and glanced at Gregor with thinned lips. The seneschal snorted and shook his head, amused by the man's discomfort.

Gregor cleared his throat and spoke into the awkward silence. "I'm afraid I bring disturbing news, Your Majesty."

The emperor sighed. "I'm not surprised, old friend. I seem to be getting disturbing news from a lot of places right now."

The seneschal gave the emperor a warning glance and cleared his throat pointedly. Sorceress Fleming shifted uncomfortably in her chair as well.

The emperor rolled his eyes. "Relax, Sorman. The Archives network is second only to my own, so I'm not going to give away anything they wouldn't hear about eventually. Please go on, Gregor."

Gregor had practiced the way he would deliver the news, so there was no hesitation. "Yes, Your Majesty. We have evidence that Paeter Thoron is using sorcery to influence Governor Frederick Brachus of Sunset Province. We believe that he has used this influence to have his own son named Heir Designate."

The emperor stared at Gregor while he processed the information. He finally narrowed his eyes and said, "That's a serious charge. Using sorcery to manipulate the succession of a province is a direct violation of the Sorcery Accords and punishable by death. How were you able to acquire this *evidence?*"

Gregor could tell that the emperor believed him, but he needed to understand how the situation had come about. "We sent a team to Dusk and learned that the governor is wearing a mind control amulet. It is similar to the amulets that Sorcerer Thoron used to control the people of Buckwoods Village. Thoron himself was present and wearing the master amulet. We have no doubt that Thoron has the means to strongly influence the governor's decisions."

The emperor nodded and stroked his chin. "That explains Brachus's baffling decision to designate the child of a sworn enemy in place of his own son."

"That was our first clue, Your Majesty."

The emperor looked back and forth between the two Archives councilors, then settled a narrow stare at Gregor. "The last time you came to me bearing bad news, I warned you that there would be consequences if the Archives was unable to control Thoron and his accomplices."

Gregor looked down at his hands and thought about his response. But once again, Councilor Underwood spoke first. "We need more time, Your Majesty. We have been diligently investigating Sorcerer Thoron, and we've learned that the true mastermind behind the portal key theft and the activity in Dusk is Headmaster Dumont Fortenz of Thunderhead College. In fact, the headmaster's agents captured the Sword Sorceress, and she was injured during our rescue attempt. We are responding to the threat as quickly as we can with the resources we have."

Gregor closed his eyes and tilted his head back to the ceiling, letting out a quiet sigh. Underwood's panicked blather was exactly what Gregor was hoping to avoid.

The seneschal shook his head and mumbled, "Incompetents."

The emperor glared at the seneschal and then at Underwood. "What you're telling me is that you are out-matched. You have failed in your charter to defend the Accords and rogue sorcerers have taken over part of my empire." He slammed his hand on the table, making everyone in the room jump. "That is unacceptable!"

Underwood was initially shocked by the emperor's reaction. When he realized what he had done, he seemed to shrink into himself and he shot an apologetic glance at Gregor.

Gregor tried to control the damage. "Your Majesty, we just learned of the situation in Dusk, and that's the first evidence we've had that Thoron is breaking the Accords. We believe that the headmaster is helping Thoron, but we have no proof of that yet. This plan to return control of Sunset Province to the Thoron family has evidently been a long time in the making. As Councilor Underwood said, we need some time to respond."

The emperor held up his hand to interrupt. "Just tell me what the Archives is doing about all of this."

"We have started a training program that will expand our Guardian Corps ranks, and we have increased the proportion of sorcerers. We are also training a new Sword Sorcerer while Sword Sorceress Delano heals."

The emperor interrupted again. "Meanwhile, this so-called *Lightning Corps* from Thunderhead College spreads throughout my empire like a disease, carrying sorcery into the populace in the name of *integration*."

"That's why we are expanding the Guardian Corps, Your Majesty. The Lightning Corps hasn't done anything illegal yet, but we want to be ready should they step beyond the boundaries of the Accords."

The emperor shook his head. "You are too far behind. We have to put an end to this right now." He looked at the sorceress to his left. "Dierdre, I'm sending you with a detachment of guards to Dusk. The guards will arrest Paeter Thoron and you will remove the amulet from Governor Brachus."

Sorceress Fleming bowed her head. "As you wish, Your Majesty."

The emperor crossed his arms and considered Gregor. "I'm also going to send out an alert to every barracks in the empire. I want the Lightning Corps under constant surveillance, and I expect support from the Archives if I need it."

Gregor nodded. "You always have our support, Your Majesty."

Sorceress Fleming frowned and said, "Your Majesty, you have your own loyal sorcerers. Why not rely on us?"

The emperor smiled at the sorceress. "I do rely on you, Dierdre. You are family and you all belong here, protecting the palace. Besides, I have too few of you to make a difference. The Archives has sanctuaries filled with sorcerers across the empire."

The seneschal folded his arms and sneered at Gregor and Councilor Underwood. "Yes, but can you *trust* them."

The emperor fixed Gregor with a stare. Gregor knew that nothing he could say would make any difference. The emperor either trusted them or he didn't.

"Let's hope so," the emperor finally said.

Chapter 23

News from Cassandria

Talon came in low and fast in a maneuver designed to knock my staff upward and drive home a blow to my chest. After sparring with him for months, I could recognize most of his moves the moment he started them.

I angled the staff to deflect his attack to the side, but he altered his approach as he came forward to strike under my guard at my leg. I reacted without thinking and used the end of the staff to catch his sword and sweep it upward, adding a twist at the end. His sword clattered to the ground and he shook his hand where the tip of my staff had stung it.

"Nice move!" he said with a grin, leaning over to pick up his sword.

I stood back and rested the tip of the staff on the practice room floor.

"Thanks. I thought you had me there, but then that disarming move you taught me last week came from nowhere."

"That's good. That means you've internalized it. You seem to have a knack for the quarterstaff. I think you might be better with it than I am at this point."

I snickered. "Well, that's one thing, anyway. I guess you can't be the master at *every* weapon."

He laughed and shook his sword at me. "Hey, don't get too full of yourself. I'm not done with you yet."

I stretched the soreness out of my left arm. "No reason to worry there. Every session with you is a lesson in humility."

"And don't you forget it," he said with a wink.

Talon went to the weapons rack and hung up the practice sword. "Let's take this outside. I want to show you some vaulting tricks, but we need more room."

Before I could reply, the practice room door opened and a girl tentatively stepped into the room. She was dressed in a short, dark blue tunic trimmed with Council maroon. Her brimless cap did a poor job of containing a riot of brown curls. The tunic and cap identified her as a Council page.

Lissy followed the page into the room and met my eyes, dashing my brief hope that the message was for Talon.

"I'm looking for Jaylan Forester," the page said in the high, piping voice of a girl in her early teens.

"That's him over there," I said, pointing the staff at Talon.

The page faced Talon and reached up to push her cap more firmly onto her head before delivering her message. Lissy tapped on her shoulder right as she opened her mouth.

"Don't listen to him. He's just messing with you. That's Jaylan with the staff."

Blushing, the page gave Lissy a shy smile of thanks before sending a decidedly less friendly glare my way. The disarming grin and shallow bow I gave her in return did not appear to redeem me. She turned my way and spoke with a haughty tone that did a good job of expressing her displeasure.

"Jaylan Forester, the Council requires your presence. Please come with Sorceress Aragon and me immediately."

I sighed and tossed the staff to Talon, who caught it deftly. "Have fun," he quipped.

The page preceded us out of the room. As I came alongside Lissy, she punched me in the arm. "And try not to be a nuisance," she said in a loud whisper. The page looked over her shoulder at me and put her nose in the air to show her agreement.

I leaned forward as we walked and said, "Sorry," to the young lady's stiff back. She ignored me, but when I glanced at Lissy, her stern face had slipped and the corner of her mouth tilted in a smile that disappeared as soon as she saw I was looking at her.

Our young escort looked over her shoulder frequently to make sure we were still following. She led us to the antechamber outside Council Hall and stopped. "Wait here, please."

She looked tiny next to the huge double doors that opened into the hall, so I reached out to help her push the door open.

"I can do it," she said, shouldering my arm away. I raised my hands in apology and stood back while she leaned into the door and slowly shoved it open. As soon as the gap was wide enough, she slipped in and pushed the massive portal closed from the other side.

Lissy and I stood at the doors while the page announced our presence.

"Do you know what this is about?" I asked her.

She shook her head. "No idea, but Gregor was scheduled to visit the emperor this morning."

It was unusual for just Lissy and me to be called before the Council. I couldn't think of a scenario that ended well.

"Do you know if anyone else was summoned?"

"I didn't think to ask, and the page didn't say anything. She was quite a little chatterbox before *you* joined us. You really shouldn't have teased her like that."

"Sorry. She was just so serious. I was busy thinking about how little I wanted to have another visit with the Council, and I didn't realize she'd be embarrassed by my little joke."

Lissy giggled. "She is awfully cute in that little page outfit." Her face went stern again. "But she takes her job very seriously and you should respect that."

I held up my hand and swore, "I promise I'll never tease a page again."

We both broke into laughter just as the Council Hall door began to open. The page slipped out and looked at us both with suspicion. We kept our faces as straight as possible, but it was all I could do not to smile when she adjusted her cap again.

"The Council will see you now," she said in a clipped voice.

I pushed the door opening a bit wider so Lissy could walk in without having to squeeze through, and then I closed the door behind us. Our steps echoed in the large chamber as we approached the Council. All five Council members sat at the Council seat, which consisted of a long wooden table on a raised platform.

The psychology behind the arrangement wasn't lost on me. In fact, the sense of standing for judgment was one of the main reasons I hated coming here. It didn't help that, for most of my visits, I *had* been standing for judgment.

"Thank you both for joining us so quickly," Senior Councilor Underwood said in greeting.

"Your page was very efficient, Councilor," I responded with a droll tone. Lissy subtly elbowed me in the side. *Oh, right. Don't be a nuisance.*

Councilor Underwood ignored my response. He turned to Senior Councilor Gregor Rissik and said, "Would you mind filling in our guests on why we asked them here?"

"Certainly," Gregor responded. His gaze turned to us and he gave us a short nod of acknowledgment. He leaned forward and folded his hands on the table. "We recently received a disturbing report from the emperor. As you know, Councilor Underwood and I told the emperor about what you found in Dusk. He has dispatched a squad to arrest Paeter Thoron and remove the amulet from Governor Brachus."

Gregor had informed Lissy and me of the emperor's decision after he and Councilor Underwood returned from their visit to Cassandria two weeks ago. Upon learning that the emperor had decided to handle the situation without the Archives, I was both disappointed and relieved. I was disappointed because I wanted to be part of the team that took down Paeter Thoron, and I was relieved because Thoron had the annoying habit of coming out ahead in every one of our confrontations. From Gregor's tone, things hadn't gone so well for the emperor's team either.

"When the emperor's team arrived in Dusk, Governor Brachus had passed away and Paeter Thoron had left the city."

Lissy stepped forward and asked, "Passed away or was murdered?"

Councilor Velna Asher had been silent this whole time, but she spoke up at the accusation. "There's no evidence of murder. In fact, they didn't find an amulet either, so there's no evidence at all."

It sounded like Councilor Asher was questioning my claim that the governor had been wearing an amulet. I clenched my jaw, but Gregor went on before I could say anything, which was probably just as well.

"Imperial Sorceress Fleming led the team, and she was immediately suspicious as well. However, her team interrogated everyone at the governor's residence and came to the conclusion that he died unexpectedly from heart failure. I doubt we'll ever know what really happened."

Lissy instantly understood the current state of affairs. "With the governor dead, his appointment of Astin Thoron as heir designate can't be rescinded. Has Malcolm Brachus contested the appointment?"

Gregor shook his head. "Not yet. The young man is confused and understandably distraught."

I remembered from our brief meeting with him in Dusk that Malcolm Brachus had been concerned for his father's well being, but he didn't have much interest in becoming governor. He might actually be content to let the Thoron family resume control of the province.

"Is there anything we can do?" I asked.

Gregor shrugged and sat back in his chair. "The appointment followed proper legal forms, and unlike his father, Astin Thoron is qualified because he's not a sorcerer. As I understand it, Astin is not particularly enthusiastic about the turn of events either, but his mother is helping him cope."

So, Thoron wins again.

This was all very interesting, but it didn't explain why the Council had bothered to summon us. Lissy was apparently thinking the same thing.

"There's more, isn't there?" she said with trepidation in her voice.

Gregor smiled at her. "Indeed. We also learned that the Imperial Assembly has four new emissaries."

Lissy blinked a couple of times before saying, "Four? At the same time?"

I gathered from her reaction that the turnover was unusual. The Imperial Assembly consisted of five emissaries plus the emperor. The emperor represented Imperial Province and the other five members were appointed by the governors of their respective provinces. However, I wasn't familiar with how long emissaries typically served or the circumstances under which they might be replaced.

Gregor continued to explain. "The four new emissaries were all appointed in the past few weeks by the governors of Grassgate, Mineral, Bountiful, and of course, Sunset provinces. All four of them have shown remarkable enthusiasm for Integrationist policies. The emperor has had to step in personally several times to block odd appropriations and legislation. So far, the emissary from Lakewoods Province has supported him, but that could change."

Lissy's face went white and she looked at the floor. "He got to them all."

After her words sunk in, my heart started to pound. Paeter Thoron, or more likely, Headmaster Dumont Fortenz, was trying to gain control over *all* of the governors, not just Brachus.

Gregor confirmed her conclusion with a nod. "It looks that way. All except Governor Marrin Trask of Lakeshore Province. Meanwhile, the sanctuary in Northshore reports that the town is crawling with Lightning Corps." He looked at me. "They've also spotted your old friends Lohan and Peltor."

I closed my eyes and clenched my jaw. It was only a matter of time until Lohan would find a way to get to Trask. Then the five province emissaries would collectively be able to override the emperor's four votes. Headmaster Fortenz would control the empire.

I opened my eyes and looked at Councilor Asher and her compatriot, Councilor Shepherd. Shepherd was sitting back with his arms folded. I couldn't tell if he was gazing down at something on the table or if he was actually trying to catch a nap. Asher fidgeted in her seat, frowning and playing with an earring. Considering how often they had defended the headmaster's actions, I was surprised they didn't have smug expressions on their faces. Perhaps they realized he had finally gone too far.

Lissy slowly moved back until she was standing beside me and slightly behind. Her eyes were wide and her breath was shallow. Granted, the news was bad, but this was not the confident woman I was used to seeing.

I shook my head and spoke into the silence of the room. "We need to do something. We can't let them get to Trask or it's all over."

Gregor chuckled. "I'm glad you feel that way Candidate Forester."

His choice of title was deliberate. He was addressing me as a candidate for Sword Sorcerer.

"The emperor is mobilizing forces around the empire, with Archives assistance. He has tasked us to deal with Northshore, where his influence is weakest. The Council is sending a team to warn and to protect Governor Trask. You will lead the team and Sorceress Aragon will provide support."

Lissy looked at Gregor with pleading eyes. "Shouldn't we send a sorceress with more experience?"

Gregor sighed and then answered her. "I tried to suggest that, but you are the best choice. Marlene Delano is the only other experienced sorceress here who isn't too old or too young, and we need her to train the new guardians."

Councilor Asher raised an eyebrow at Lissy. "I'm surprised you're being so skittish. You and Sorcerer Forester worked so well together in Dusk."

Councilor Asher was being sarcastic, but I really did think Lissy and I had worked well together. Lissy had practically begged Councilor Rissik to let her go with me to Dusk, so this change of heart was puzzling.

Lissy frowned. "If only Sulana were here instead of at the refuge." As soon as the word left her mouth, she looked at me in shock and then embarrassment. In her distress, she had given away that Sulana was *not* getting help from an imperial physician in Cassandria as we had told everyone, but was with the druids instead.

Gregor was quick to step in before any of the other councilors could ask about Lissy's remark.

"It doesn't matter where the Sword Sorceress is just now. She will return when she can, and we can't wait for her. We need to act immediately."

Councilor Maris Torlon had also been silent throughout the meeting, but at this point she balled up her fists and said, "This is insanity."

Councilor Underwood rolled his eyes and waved a hand dismissively in her direction. When he did nothing more to stop her, she looked directly at me and went on.

"This mission is dangerous, Jaylan. You should not even be a part of it, much less leading it. It's foolhardy to put the only runemaster we've seen in three centuries at risk."

Gregor had explained the Runedream and what it meant to the Council during a routine report on my training progress. According to Lissy, he tried to play it down, but as Ebnik predicted, the Council had practically wanted to leash me to the castle. The night after our first discussion on the subject, I came close to sneaking away and hiding at the druid refuge with Sulana.

In the end, we compromised. I would be allowed to continue training to be a Sword Sorcerer and go on missions as long as I dedicated at least ten hours a week working with Ebnik and Maris (as I had begun to think of her) to learn and record as much as we could about the Runedream.

Maris was shy around me for some reason, but her quick intelligence and sense of humor made the research more interesting and fun than I expected. Being stuck with a Council observer wasn't so bad after all.

Unfortunately, the more we learned about the Runedream, the more protective Maris became. She seemed overly preoccupied with my status as a runemaster and urged me to dedicate more time to it. She thought I should give up the idea of becoming a Sword Sorcerer.

So, in spite of the fact that we were becoming friends, Councilor Maris Torlon didn't necessarily support my goals.

I considered defending my right to lead the team, but circumstances told me that wasn't necessary. The Council had already made their decision. I chose to say nothing.

However, Councilor Asher did have something to add. "For once, I have to side with Councilor Torlon, although not because I think we need to protect our precious runemaster. The quickest way to resolve this situation is to find Headmaster Fortenz and talk him out of his present course of action. I can't believe he is willing to start a war over integration. If we pick a fight with Thunderhead College in Northshore, *we'll* be starting the war."

Councilor Shepherd raised himself from his lethargy and thumped his fist on the table in time with his words. "We've … already … been … over … this." He gave Asher an exasperated look. "I agree with you, but the two Senior Councilors have made up their mind. We lose. Again."

Councilor Underwood looked back and forth, glaring at the junior councilors at both ends of the table. "Councilor Shepherd is correct. The decision has been made. Let's please maintain some decorum." He then turned to Lissy and me. "Please assemble your team and prepare to leave as soon as possible. We'll arrange for you to use the journey room so you can enter Northshore through the sanctuary. You are both dismissed."

Lissy and I left the Council chamber, and the page escorted us to the stairwell. We continued down the stairs on our own, and when we reached ground level, I asked Lissy to stop.

"What was that about? I thought you wanted to go on missions," I said.

Her eyes darted back and forth before settling on mine. "I thought so too. Until I went on one. Oh, Jaylan, I was so scared. It was fun until the soldiers tried to arrest us. I've never had to fight for real before."

"But you did just fine. It gets easier, you know."

She closed her eyes for a moment, and then opened them again. "I don't want it to get easier. I don't want to hurt anyone, and I don't want anyone to hurt me."

I'd seen this before. When I was with the Imperial Guard, young recruits would sometimes have a crisis of conscience after their first experience with lethal combat. The realities of mortality, whether your own or someone else's, can be a slap in the face.

I tilted my head at the stairwell. "You see those stairs behind us?" She nodded. "Either one of us could have just tripped and fallen, landing right here with a broken neck. Life is uncertain."

Lissy folded her arms and glared. "I understand that. But that doesn't mean we should go around putting ourselves in harm's way."

I nodded and smiled. "No one wants to put themselves in harm's way. But sometimes that's the only way to stand up for what's right and protect what's important."

Lissy frowned and looked down at the floor. "I just wish we had a better way to resolve our differences."

I sighed and shook my head. "Me too. I've spent most of my life trying to keep the peace without much success. It all seems so futile sometimes, but I can't give up. I won't stand by and let Paeter Thoron or Dumont Fortenz take away the things I've come to cherish. That means Sulana, and you," I opened my arms to encompass the Archives, "And even this crazy dungeon."

Lissy stepped into my open arms and hugged me, burying her face in my shoulder. I put my arms around her and squeezed back. Before the moment became awkward, she stepped back and wiped the moisture from under her eyes. "Thanks, Jaylan. I'll try not to let you down."

I waited until her eyes met mine before I responded. "Don't worry about that. The best way for us to return safely is to be prepared and focused. Let's go find Barek and Talon and let them know what's going on."

Chapter 24
Rollek's Amplifier

Dumont watched Paeter pace back and forth with a mixture of amusement and annoyance.

"Paeter, sit down. You are only working yourself up with all this pacing."

Paeter stopped and shook his head. "This is not working out like we planned."

"Oh, I don't know. Your *plan* was to put a Thoron back into the governor's office at Dusk, and you've done that."

Paeter's tone turned droll. "Yes, but I did not intend to become a fugitive in the process."

Dumont shrugged. "That was always a risk. I'm sure my sins against the Sorcery Accords will catch up with me eventually as well."

Paeter finally sat down, glaring at Dumont. "Then what is the point of all this? I face execution now, and so will you."

"The point, my dear Paeter, is to change the rules."

"Change the rules? How can we possibly do that? The Archives is already on to us and the emperor has gotten directly involved."

Dumont sat back in his chair and smiled. It did not escape his attention that Paeter had forgotten to respectfully pepper his speech with the honorific "Master." It was time to remind him of who was the master here and why.

"Laws are made by the victors, Paeter. In order to change the rules, we have to first be victorious. Your goal was to put young Astin in power, and I helped you make that happen. That was the end of your plans, but only the beginning of mine. Just who did you think the extra amulets were for?"

"The amulets were the price for your help. What you chose to do with them was your business."

Dumont shook his head and gave Paeter a disappointed look. "You can't truly be that naive. Your amulets have locked our fates together. We both win, or we both die."

Paeter went pale. "What have you done with the other amulets?"

Dumont nodded encouragingly. This was the kind of question Paeter should have asked long ago. "While you were so busy trying to recover control over Sunset Province, I moved toward a bigger prize."

"Bigger? As in Grassgate Province? The emperor placed a ruling proscription against your family. He would never allow you to take control."

"I'm sure you're right. But I wasn't talking about a bigger province. I'm talking about control over the empire."

Paeter laughed nervously. "Pardon my saying so, Master, but you're delusional. The emperor has thousands of troops around the empire and the backing of the Archives. We have, what, a few dozen sorcerers and soldiers?"

Dumont tolerated the insult because the word "Master" had crept back into Paeter's speech. The man was starting to realize just how much he had underestimated his master's ambition.

"Hundred, Paeter. We have several hundred now. Peltor and Lohan have been surprisingly efficient at churning out new Lightning Corps troops. We have loyal Integrationist agents in nearly every sanctuary, and we have a spy in the Archives Council. As for the Imperial Guard, they follow the orders of the provincial governors. The emperor's influence doesn't extend far beyond Imperial Province, the one province he truly controls."

Paeter's face was blank and uncomprehending. He was obviously shocked by the scope of Dumont's campaign. "Where did they all come from?"

"They come from the disaffected and the bitter. The Integrationist dream is irresistible to sorcerers who are sick of being treated with prejudice and disdain. Most will only admit to wanting equality, but the truth is that many of them want revenge. We can hardly keep up with the number of volunteers who have flocked to our banner."

"And the amulets?"

"It was your plan for Brachus that gave me the idea. If we could control one governor, why not all? I had expected it to take years for us to make any progress with our agenda, but you handed me the perfect shortcut."

Paeter blinked several times before sputtering, "But that's impossible! We'd never get close enough to the governors. The Archives and the emperor already know what I did in Dusk. They'll expect us to try the same thing elsewhere."

"Will they? You didn't. Besides, it's already done. Trask in Northshore is the only governor left, and Lohan is taking care of that as we speak."

Dumont almost felt sorry for Paeter. The man was having a hard time keeping up. He watched and waited while Paeter digested everything he had just learned. Sweat beaded on his brow and his breathing got shallow. He looked into Dumont's eyes with a haunted expression.

"We're dead men," he said, just above a whisper. "You're meddling with the imperial government. The emperor will have us burned at the stake."

The word "we" told Dumont that Paeter had finally accepted his culpability in recent events. The man was nearly ready to receive his next task.

"The emperor will have to catch us first, and prove what we've done. Through the governors, I control the Imperial Guard. I also control the appointments to the Imperial Assembly, which means I control the empire."

Paeter sat back in his chair, looking emotionally exhausted by the revelations. "What will you do with such power, Master?"

Dumont allowed a smug smile. "I'll fulfill my promise to our followers. Integration will be much easier with the passage of a few new imperial proclamations. I'll also solve our little problem of being wanted criminals."

"You'll give us clemency?"

"No. Think, Paeter. What would make integration possible and exonerate us at the same time?"

Paeter shrugged and shook his head, too tired to even make a guess, but then he sat up. "You mean to abolish the Accords!"

"Exactly. Three hundred years has been penance enough. It's time we took back the rights we deserve."

Paeter's brows drew together and his frown deepened. "But what about the mundane? We may be ready for integration, but the obstacle has always been convincing the mundane to accept our presence and our contributions."

"Convincing the mundane will take time, but I have an idea for making that process go quickly. And that's where you come in."

Dumont opened a desk drawer and took out an old book, which he gingerly placed on his desk. He turned the book toward Paeter and opened it to a page marked by a narrow strip of cloth.

Paeter's eyes absorbed the faded drawing on a page that was brown with age. He reached toward the book but held his hand back, reluctant to touch the ancient tome.

"What is this?" he asked.

"Those are the final ramblings of a nearly insane wizard. Possibly the greatest wizard our world has ever seen."

Paeter glanced up at Dumont briefly before continuing his study. "Rollek?"

"Yes. Just before his defeat ended the Wizard Wars, he designed the most powerful implement ever created. You are looking at the plans for a device he dubbed Rollek's Amplifier."

Paeter carefully paged backward and forward from the bookmark. "It seems to be incomplete. I don't see any runes, so there's no way to tell what spell it was meant to cast. The handwritten notes are nearly illegible."

"Look closer at the diagram I marked. If the device had runes, where would you expect to find them?"

Paeter concentrated on the diagram. As an accomplished smith, the device would be irresistible to him. After a moment, he pointed to a spot on the page. "The runes would be incorporated here. But there's a gap in the design."

"What else can you tell me about this device?"

Paeter cast him a sidelong glance. "If you know what it is, why don't you just tell me?"

"Because you are a better smith than I will ever be. I want your professional assessment without the influence of my assumptions."

Paeter searched Dumont's eyes. Satisfied with what he saw, he returned to the book.

Paeter mumbled as he reviewed the diagram. "This device was designed to be stationary. It draws vaetra from a well and focuses through an orb. With the right spell, it could operate continuously as long as the well had enough vaetra."

Paeter glanced up at Dumont, who nodded in encouragement. "What do you suppose goes in that gap you mentioned?"

Paeter flipped the page forward to a second diagram. "This appears to be an inset for that part of the device." His eyebrows went up and he glanced at Dumont again. "I think the device is some kind of framework. This slot is for a removable core. You could create multiple spell cores for it and swap them out, depending upon which one you wanted to use."

Dumont got into the same desk drawer he had opened earlier and took out a cloth-wrapped package. He gently laid the item on his desk and pulled away the wrapping. "Something like this, perhaps?"

Sitting on the cloth was a partially crushed glass rod, with the ends capped in metal. A thick metal bar ran through the glass. It was bent at an angle where the glass had been crushed, but it still held the rod together and connected the caps. Runes glinted along the surface of the bar.

Paeter reached for the rod, but arrested his motion. "May I?"

Dumont waved toward the item. "By all means."

The rod would have been about eight inches long when whole and it was about two inches in diameter. Paeter inspected the runes along the metal tab and smiled to himself.

"Ingenious."

Paeter looked down at the inset diagram again and then back at the rod. He gave Dumont a puzzled expression.

"This part seems rather large. I assume these diagrams aren't to scale, or this device would have to be ..."

"Huge," Dumont supplied.

Paeter gingerly set the glass rod back down on the cloth. "Are you telling me that this thing actually existed?"

"Indeed it did. It still does."

Paeter shook his head in confusion. "But it isn't practical. If it is as large as these diagrams indicate, it would be nearly impossible to move. You'd need ten sorcerers to power it, or you'd have to place it directly on top of an enormous basin."

"You are correct on all counts," Dumont confirmed.

"Then where is it?"

Dumont sat back and folded his hands across his midsection. "Before I answer that, let me ask you something. How much do you know about the retirement activities of Wizard Ebnik Vlastorus?"

Paeter frowned at the mention of Ebnik's name. "I have no idea what that old man has been doing with his retirement. Why would I care?"

Dumont ignored the petulant question and continued. "Vlastorus has been recreating a series of old charts that were lost during the Wizard Wars. The charts show the location of major vaetra basins and vaens throughout the empire."

"You think the device is at one of those basins? Did Vlastorus find it?"

"Yes, with a little help from Gregor Rissik and Emperor Tanes. The device sits on the largest basin in the empire, known from ancient times as the Confluence. Both are inside the Imperial Palace."

"*Inside* the palace?"

"I'm surprised you don't remember any of this, Paeter. When Ebnik and Rissik returned to the Archives with this document and the broken core about three years ago, it briefly caused quite a stir."

"Three years ago, I was researching the spells for the amulets. I lost interest in what was going on at the Archives long before that."

"It pays to monitor your opponents closely, Paeter. It's a lesson the Archives is learning the hard way right now."

Paeter squared his shoulders. "We all have our strengths, Master. Intrigue is not one of mine."

Dumont tilted his head in acquiescence. "You're right, of course. I apologize if my remark seemed critical."

Before Paeter could respond, Dumont waved away the digression and returned to the subject at hand. "In any case, the amplifier is stashed away in the palace basement." He chuckled and shook his head in disbelief. "This amazing device has spent the past three hundred years hidden in the fresh air shaft for the palace kitchen ovens."

Dumont watched as Paeter took in this additional bit of information. He scanned the diagram once more and then lifted his head to meet Dumont's eyes.

"Why are you telling me all this? Are you planning to steal the amplifier?" He picked up the core and turned it over in his hands. "If you are thinking of duplicating the device, I have to warn you that it would take a long time and might be beyond my skills."

"No, I think the device should remain exactly where it is. The Confluence gives it nearly unlimited power that would be impossible to duplicate elsewhere. From what I understand, the amplifier needs some repairs, but what it needs most is a new core."

Dumont leaned forward in his chair and pointed at the core that was still in Paeter's hand. "That, my friend, will be your task."

Paeter turned his head to the side and considered the broken core.

"I think I can do as you ask, Master, but how will we get access to the amplifier once we have a new core? And what do you want the new core to do?"

"Leave the access problem to me. As for the new core, I'm sure you'll find the spell work to be rather familiar."

Dumont took out a sheet of parchment and pushed the ink pot toward Paeter. "Pull your chair closer and take some notes. I'll tell you exactly what I've got in mind for Rollek's Amplifier."

CHAPTER 25

UNWELCOME VISITORS

Defender Marshal Nigel Shields sat at his desk in his office. He frowned over the latest reports from around the empire, growing more disturbed with every page he read.

His concerns about Dumont Fortenz were proving to be almost prescient. The headmaster's small army of Lightning Corps soldiers was spreading throughout the empire. The claims that these "representatives" were bringing magical assistance to the masses and sharing the hope of sorcerer integration didn't fool the marshal.

Reports of isolated mundane resistance indicated that not all of "the masses" were fooled either. None of the confrontations had become violent, but it was only a matter of time.

Nigel wondered if there might be a way to encourage and unify this resistance without exposing druid involvement. He was confident that his rangers could hold their own in a conventional fight, but taking on sorcerers was another story. As for fighting sorcery with blessings, the priests were mostly useless. They weren't trained for combat, and for the most part, they weren't temperamentally suited for it.

This wasn't a druid fight anyway. It was the Archives' problem to solve, and yet their own Sword Sorceress was languishing at this very refuge.

Was helping Sorceress Delano a mistake? He had visited her a few times over the past several weeks, and she seemed to be making good progress. But she admitted that her sorcery skills were still unreliable. She wouldn't stand a chance in a duel of sorcery.

He had reconsidered his decision several times. But every time he prayed for guidance, the spirits showed him the same image: Sulana in the robe of a druid priestess. The spirits clearly felt that she was somehow important to the druid cause. So far, he had let the spirits guide him, as he had sworn to do. But time was running out. Somebody had to stop Thunderhead College.

Hopefully, the Archives had the same intelligence he had and were preparing to do something about it. But if that were true, he wasn't seeing much evidence of it yet.

His ruminations were interrupted when the door flew open, scattering a few pages of his reports before he could clamp them to the table with his hand. He scowled at the lieutenant who stood breathlessly at the door, staring at the mess he'd just created.

"Sorry, Marshal. We've got armed riders heading this way. It's a fairly small group, but several more are waiting at the entrance to the refuge. They came in too fast for us to intercept."

Nigel stood and grabbed his sword belt. "Who are they, Lieutenant?"

"They look like Thunderhead College troops, sir. They're all wearing black."

Nigel slipped on his dark green leather armor, swiftly buckling the straps along the side. "Gather as many rangers and monks as you can and meet me outside the front gate. I don't want them to enter the preserve."

"Should I sound the alarm and alert the high priestess, sir?"

"Not yet. This should be a short conversation. Just follow my orders."

"Aye, sir." The lieutenant saluted Nigel and ran out of the room.

Nigel followed at a more dignified pace, but his stride was as long and fast as he could make it. As he exited the ranger headquarters building, he noticed a cluster of chattering monks coming out of the dining hall.

He whistled toward them to get their attention without breaking stride. "Arm yourselves and attend the gate," he shouted, pointing toward the open palisade gateway. "Now!"

The monks looked confused at first, but when they saw that it was the Defender Marshal who had called to them and that he was girded for trouble, they scrambled to obey his orders.

The Lieutenant was already across the courtyard sending every ranger or monk he could find toward the gate as well.

A young monk ran toward Nigel holding the reins of a horse. The animal's nostrils flared in alarm and it threw its head up and down, snorting. The monk handed the reins to Nigel.

"The lieutenant said you'd want to be mounted, sir."

"Thank you, Brother. The lieutenant was correct."

Nigel deftly leaped into the saddle and guided the horse through the palisade gate. Three other rangers were also mounted and already in position, facing the road beyond. They saluted him and he returned the gesture.

As several more monks and rangers filtered through the gateway and took up positions along the road, a group of riders rounded a corner in the distance. When they got closer, Nigel counted six men, all dressed in black with dark blue trim at the sleeve and collar. He didn't have to see the encircled lightning bolt symbol on the chest of their clothing to know he was looking at members of the Thunderhead College Lightning Corps.

He scanned the sleeves of their group and spotted two riders who deserved special attention. His reports indicated that Lightning Corps sorcerers distinguished themselves from their mundane brethren with a single silver stripe around the end of their long, loose sleeves.

Once again, he had sorcerers on the refuge.

The approaching riders came to a halt before they entered the funnel of druids alongside the road. One of their number, an unsavory looking character with a hooked nose, came forward slowly and stopped a little less than half-way between his party and the waiting rangers.

Nigel took the hint and urged his horse to move. He came to a stop about ten feet away from the stranger.

"I'm Defender Marshal Shields. Please state your business."

The man narrowed his dark eyes at Nigel. "I'm Captain Peltor Mullan. This is not a very friendly welcome, Marshal."

"I'm sure you are aware that we do not allow sorcerers on the refuge. I ask again, what is your business here?"

The man looked over his shoulder at his companions and grinned. "Ah, yes, sorcerers. An untrustworthy bunch, aren't they? In fact, I have information that one may be hiding out on your refuge right now. I may be able to help you solve that problem."

Nigel tried to keep his features impassive as the other man was watching his reaction closely. He shook his head slowly. "Your information is incorrect. As I said, sorcerers are not allowed on the refuge. I'm afraid you've wasted a trip."

Captain Mullan stared into Nigel's eyes for a long moment before replying, "Possibly, Marshal." Mullan looked around at the assembled druids, and then he turned his gaze back to Nigel.

"I guess we'll be on our way then. Good day."

Nigel didn't bother replying as Captain Mullan reined his horse around and rejoined his group. At the captain's command, the riders headed back toward the refuge entrance.

Nigel turned and spoke to the ranger who had warned him of the interlopers earlier. "Lieutenant, take every ranger here and follow them out. Make sure they all leave the refuge. If they stray, don't engage them unless they attack you, but keep them in sight."

"Yes, Marshal." The lieutenant waved the other rangers to follow him and started down the road.

Nigel waved one of the monks over. "Inform Her Grace of what happened here and tell her I believe we haven't seen the last of these men. I want the monks to escort two priests into the forest as quickly as possible. Have them set up barriers or entanglements at the major trail intersections and redirect all traffic back toward the main road." The monk nodded. "Tell her I'm going ahead to clear our people off the trails."

The monk's brow furrowed in concern. "Would you like some of us to accompany you, sir?"

Nigel reined his horse around to shorten the discussion. "That won't be necessary, Brother. The priests need your escort more than I do. I'm sure I'll find one of our patrols somewhere along the way." Nigel kicked his horse into a run without waiting for a response from the monk.

If he did run into one of his patrols, he'd send them to help deal with Captain Mullan. The last thing he needed was witnesses for the task he had to perform.

CHAPTER 26

HUNTED

The buckets were heavy, but Sulana welcomed their weight. The fact that she could carry both of them full of water without sloshing proved that her grip was as good as ever. Her shoulders strained under the load, but when she had arrived here, she wouldn't have been able to carry the buckets ten feet, much less all the way from the stream to the cottage.

The stream had become her haven. After her miraculous healing, she had spent time every evening sitting near the pool, absorbing the sounds of the forest. The trickle of the stream, the hoot of an owl, and the rustling of a squirrel searching through fallen leaves helped clear her mind and fill her with peace.

She also explored her new casting abilities every evening. The druids would probably call the pool her altar. Sulana wasn't sure if she found that idea amusing or disturbing. No matter how one labeled it, she could not deny that the spirits were responsible for her gift.

After some practice, she could create light bubbles at will. She had learned to control their size and duration by adjusting how much vaetra she fed to the spirits that assisted her. Using a cupped hand full of water as a focus, she could make a light bubble that would float nearby and shine brightly for several minutes.

Sulana had been careful not to flaunt her abilities in front of Karla, although the healer's curiosity had eventually gotten the better of her. Karla went with her to the pool one time to observe, and had been scandalized by what she saw.

"Sulana, you can't order the spirits around. You should be praying to them, asking them for their blessing."

That was the last time Karla visited the pool while Sulana was there.

After Karla's proclamation, Sulana had tried different ways of asking the spirits for help, but it didn't seem to make any difference. Prayer or command, the spirits understood what she wanted and helped her manifest it.

Light bubbles were not all Sulana practiced. She also tried weaving plants together to see if she could duplicate what she had seen at the boundary fence. Against Daven's strong objections, they had risked discovery and traveled to the boundary so she could try to get a sense of how it might have been created.

The result of her experimentation was positioned at the edge of the forest next to the pool. In a moment of inspiration, she had woven a nearby willow into a sturdy bench of swirling branches. It had taken her a couple of hours and all of her power to get right. Her hands had been frozen stiff from cupping the cold stream water by the time it was done. But the delighted look on Karla's face when she saw Sulana's gift to her made the project worthwhile.

As Sulana approached the cottage with her load, the scent of Karla's wonderful flatbread made her smile and take deep breaths through her nose. It seemed lunch was nearly ready. Sulana pushed her way through the front door, which was slightly ajar.

"You should have let me get the water," Daven commented. He took the buckets from her and poured them into a stubby barrel with a spigot at the bottom.

"That's okay. It was good exercise," Sulana said, rotating her arms to stretch them.

"Just in time for food," Karla said, flipping the last piece of flatbread onto a serving board. She carried the bread and a plate of roasted vegetables to the rough wood table.

Sulana sat down across from Daven while Karla grabbed a bowl of grated cheese. They were just starting to eat when hoofbeats approached the cottage. Someone was coming, and that someone was in a hurry.

The drill for dealing with visitors was familiar by then, so no one said a word as Karla got up from the table and headed toward the door. Sulana stayed seated, but glanced at her sword leaning against the wall about three feet away. Daven got up and strung his bow.

Karla's voice carried clearly through the half-open door.

"Marshal Shields! This is a surprise. What can I do for you?"

The hoofbeats halted, leather creaked, and boots thumped to the ground. At the Marshal's name, Sulana jumped to her feet and grabbed her sword belt. Daven was already buckling on his.

"Where is the Sword Sorceress? Is she here at the cottage?"

"Sword Sorceress? What are you talking about? Wait … where are you going?"

The cottage door swung open and Marshal Nigel Shields filled the open doorway, his face even more grim than usual. It took a second for his eyes to adjust enough so he could see Sulana and Daven standing at the end of the table.

"Good. You're here," he said, although his voice sounded far from relieved.

"What's going on?" Sulana asked, hand on sword hilt.

"We have to get you off the refuge immediately. Thunderhead College knows you're here. They sent the Lightning Corps to find you."

"You let them onto the refuge?"

"Not exactly. They came in unannounced and we stopped them at the preserve gate. I told them they were misinformed and insisted that they leave, but their captain gave in too easily."

The marshal had advanced into the room while speaking and Karla had slipped in behind him. Her eyes were wide with alarm and her hands were gripped together tightly at her chest.

Karla looked at the marshal incredulously. "You knew the Sword Sorceress was here? You let her stay?"

The marshal held up a hand to forestall further questions. "I don't have time to explain." He turned his attention back to Sulana. "Take only what you absolutely need for travel. My men and the priests will try to stall them, but I don't know how much time that will buy us."

Sulana and Daven both darted around the cottage collecting their belongings and stuffing them into their saddle bags. It was time for Stardust to work off some of the fat she'd accumulated during the long lazy summer of Sulana's treatments.

Sulana noticed that Karla was also packing and stopped to stare at the healer. Daven glanced over and stopped as well.

"What are you doing," he asked her.

"I'm going with you."

He stepped over to her and put his hands on her shoulders. "You can't. It's too dangerous. And this is your home."

She wiggled out of his grip and continued to pack. "I don't care. There's no reason for me to stay. I'm a healer. I can do that anywhere."

Sulana realized that Karla had probably been thinking about this for a while. It made sense. As the time approached for Sulana to leave, Daven and Karla would have to work out what that meant for their relationship. Daven would have to stay on the refuge somehow, or Karla would have to leave with him.

Sulana went back to packing, watching the confrontation between the two young lovers out of the corner of her eye. The healer seemed resolute, and Sulana wasn't sure what Daven could say that would change her mind.

Daven reached out and cupped Karla's face in his palm so she would stop packing and look into his eyes. To Sulana's surprise, he just smiled at her, nodded once, and went back to packing his own things.

The marshal crossed his arms over his chest, a frown turning down his mouth. "You don't have a horse, do you Adept Scoles?"

Karla paused in her packing, but Daven answered for her. "She can ride with me. I assume we aren't going on the main road, and we won't make much speed on the goat trails that run through the refuge anyway."

The marshal considered Daven's answer and let out a deep breath. He waved a conciliatory hand. "We'll all switch off to keep from tiring one horse."

While the rest of them gathered their belongings, the marshal got a sack from Karla and started loading it with travel-friendly food items. In a short time, they were headed out the door.

Sulana and Daven saddled their horses while the marshal watered his horse and loaded Karla's belongings. Sulana was putting the final adjustments on her cinch when a pair of hoof beats approached the cottage. She and Daven mounted and walked their horses around to the front yard, ready for trouble.

The new arrivals turned out to be two rangers who had stopped near the marshal to talk.

"Marshal Shields." The man saluted his superior. "We heard you were headed this way to warn the residents and clear the trails, sir. What are your orders?"

The marshal climbed into his saddle and subtly positioned his horse between the two rangers and Sulana before answering.

"We have intruders from Thunderhead College reported at the main gate and others may have entered the trail system somewhere between there and the preserve. We have priests going out to block the trail intersections so we can herd the intruders back onto the road. Lieutenant, I want you and the corporal to go escort the priests and help them identify the best places to do their work. Don't engage the intruders unless you have to defend yourselves or the priests."

The ranger lieutenant saluted again and said, "Yes, sir." As his hand tightened on the reins of his horse to turn it around, he looked over at Sulana and seemed to notice her for the first time. He gaze wandered over her saddle bags and her weapons before settling on her face. His eyes grew wide and his mouth dropped open.

Before he could speak, Marshal Shields barked, "Now, Lieutenant! You're wasting time."

"But sir. I know this woman. She's the Sword Sorceress from the Archives." He looked at the marshal with a confused expression. "You were there when Her Grace told them to leave."

Of course. Sulana hadn't recognized him at first, but this ranger was the same lieutenant who had escorted her party to the preserve that first day. He had grown a short beard since that time, but he had the same piercing eyes.

"You have your orders, Lieutenant Tanous."

"But sir, we can't leave her on the refuge."

"Exactly, Lieutenant. That's why I'm escorting her off the refuge myself."

The lieutenant looked back and forth between Sulana and his superior. He seemed to know that something wasn't right, and he was starting to put a few things together. His eyes narrowed and he lowered his voice.

"Sir, if the Lightning Corps is here for the Sword Sorceress, you might need our help to get her out of here safely."

The marshal stared at the lieutenant intently for a moment. He glanced over his shoulder at Sulana. The ranger already knew she was here. Sulana wondered if sending him away without an explanation was really the best course of action. Apparently, the marshal came to the same conclusion.

"You're probably right, Lieutenant. You know the back trails even better than I do, so you can take point. The corporal can take rear guard."

Lieutenant Tanous and the corporal both saluted the marshal and said, "Yes, sir," at the same time.

The small party moved out with Sulana riding behind Daven and Karla. Karla stared over her shoulder at the little cottage she had called home for the past few years. When they entered the forest trail, she laid her cheek against Daven's back and hugged him tightly. He reached down and patted her knee.

Sulana glanced back at the cottage too, just before it disappeared from view. The cottage had been her home during what might turn out to be the most significant discovery of her life. It was time to learn what that would mean for the future.

The trail that lay ahead represented so many things. She was relieved to finally be going home, and her heart ached to be with Jaylan. She was also terrified of being captured again by Thunderhead College. Most of all, she was excited to see what she could do with her new casting abilities.

If the rangers could escort her to Northshore, she and Daven should be relatively safe at the sanctuary. She looked forward to being back among fellow sorcerers and getting the latest news. Her last message from Jaylan had been a couple of weeks ago, and a lot could happen in that time.

In the meantime, they had to evade the Lightning Corps.

Chapter 27

Mission to Northshore

I thanked the spirits for the cool weather we were having. It made us less conspicuous in our long, hooded cloaks.

Barek led the way through the streets of Northshore. The other pedestrians automatically cleared his path long before he reached them. Lissy followed me, and behind her came one of our more experienced guardian recruits, a man hand-picked by Talon.

Sorcerer Hanlon Catcher hailed from Grassgate Province. He had experience with both sword and spell, so I was happy to accept Talon's recommendation that he join our team.

My casting staff thumped on the boardwalk every other step. I had removed Froth from the top, but worried that it still attracted too much attention.

We reached an intersection a couple of blocks away from the governor's residence when Barek came to a sudden stop.

"What's wrong?" I asked.

"Something is missing," Barek answered, scanning the streets slowly.

The town was quiet and calm. Residents and visitors went about their business as usual. Northshore looked just like I remembered from when I lived here what seemed like a lifetime ago. But that wasn't what we were expecting to see.

The last we had heard, Northshore was "crawling" with Lightning Corps. I hadn't seen a single black uniform since we'd arrived.

The old couple who maintained the sanctuary here didn't say anything about a reduction in force, but they had been keeping out of sight lately. Their son, who kept a closer eye on things, was on a message run to Riverview and wasn't expected back until later that afternoon.

So where were Lohan and Peltor?

"What should we do?" Lissy asked.

I shrugged. "We keep going. We still need to warn the governor."

Lissy grabbed my arm. "What if we're too late?"

That was a possibility. But it didn't explain why none of Peltor's men were around. The amulet was only useful if someone was there to guide the victim. My guess was Lohan. They wouldn't leave such an important target unprotected.

I turned to Lissy. Her hand trembled as she let go of my arm. I used my most reassuring voice to calm her. "We should be glad we don't have to dodge the Lightning Corps, but we do need to remain alert. Something has changed here. Until we figure out what that is, we have no choice but to continue."

She swallowed hard and nodded. Then she straightened her back and slipped a hand into a fold of her cloak where I knew her casting orb was hidden.

I smiled and tilted my head toward her hand. "Good plan."

We followed Barek to the governor's residence where we were stopped at the front gate by two guards.

"State your business," one of the guards asked in a bored voice.

I stepped forward and lowered my hood. "We are messengers from the Archives. We have come to speak with the governor."

The guard grew alert and looked closely at me.

"I don't think the governor is seeing anyone today, but I'll pass along your request."

The guard waved his companion toward the residence, which loomed against the back wall of the wide courtyard. The second guard jogged off, his mail and weapons jingling.

While we waited, I observed the people moving both inside and outside the residence walls. Every black outfit drew my eye until I could ascertain that it wasn't trimmed in blue.

Barek was just as vigilant. When our eyes met once, he shook his head slowly and frowned. His tense posture told me that he was just as spooked as I was about the lack of Thunderhead College presence. Was our information faulty? Or were we deliberately misled? If so, to what end?

The second guard returned and said we had been cleared to proceed. He escorted us to the big double doors of the residence before heading back toward the gate.

A third guard waved us into the reception area. Lissy started an incantation before we started inside.

As we approached him, the guard said, "Before ya can go in, I need to check ya for weapons. What's that yer sayin' miss?"

I heard Lissy's manifestation begin before the man finished speaking.

Lissy just stared into his eyes and said, "You don't need to check us for weapons. We're harmless. The governor wants to see us as quickly as possible."

The guard twisted his head to the side and looked us all over. "Ah, ya look pretty harmless. Let's go see the governor before he yells at me for keepin' ya."

I raised an eyebrow at Lissy and she winked at me. Paeter Thoron wasn't the only sorcerer who knew spells that could influence the mind.

The guard opened the inner door to the residence and swaggered down the hall beyond. He looked over his shoulder frequently to make sure we were keeping up.

At the end of the hall, we came to a heavy wooden door that sported a large disk carved with the governor's seal. The last time I had walked past the glaring eyes of the Trask family heron, I had been stripped of my Captain's rank and expelled from the Imperial Guard. I took a deep breath and closed my eyes to suppress the unwelcome memory.

The guard opened the door and announced us before stepping back to let us pass. As the door thudded closed behind us, Lissy dropped her enchantment. The guard's thinking would remain befuddled for a few moments longer, and he'd have some trouble recollecting what had just happened. We just had to hope he wouldn't be willing to interrupt our audience with the governor for an explanation.

I turned to face the man I'd hoped I would never see again in my life: Governor Marrin Trask. The middle-aged governor was rising from his seat at the far end of a long table. Two guards stood at the near end, between us and the governor.

One of the guards I knew from my time here. In fact, I had hired him. He looked at me curiously, my attire making it difficult for him to place me.

A huge fireplace dominated the left side of the room. In winter, long logs would crackle and pop in the gaping firebox, keeping the room comfortably warm. This early in fall, the fireplace sat dark and empty.

I stepped to the front of our group and bowed to the governor. "Greetings, Your Honor. I hope things are well with you."

The governor narrowed his eyes. "Well, well. If it isn't former Captain Forester. Or should I say *Sorcerer* Forester now. What brings you off the mountain and back to your old home town?"

I opened my mouth to answer and then closed it. I cocked my head to listen. Lissy was right. We were too late. The manifestation noise from her spell had masked another that was already in the room. And it was coming from Governor Trask.

Lohan had already gotten to him.

I decided to play it out. If necessary, we could probably overcome the guards and deactivate the amulet, although there was a decent chance we'd still end up incarcerated. But there was also a possibility that the amulet didn't have a strong grip on the governor yet. I might still be able to get through to him, since Lohan wasn't around. Where *was* Lohan?

"I came to warn you, Your Honor."

"Indeed? That sounds distinctly like a threat."

"Not at all, Your Honor. We believe you are the target of a conspiracy to take control of Lakewoods Province. Rogue sorcerers from Thunderhead College are using sorcery to influence the province governors."

"I see. That's a very serious charge. Do you have proof?"

"I believe the proof is hanging around your neck, Your Honor."

The governor looked down and pulled out the amulet I knew would be there. "You mean this old thing? I've had it for years and just took a fancy to wearing it again."

His eyes met mine and he sneered, daring me to argue with him. I could see the discussion was hopeless, so I readied myself for action even as I continued to banter.

"I know that isn't true, Your Honor. I can tell your amulet is enchanted and that it is operating even now."

The two guards sensed that a confrontation was brewing and drew their swords. However, the talk of an enchanted amulet seemed to confuse them, and they stole glances back at the governor with concern in their eyes.

The governor looked down at the amulet with doubt for just a moment before gripping it protectively in his fist.

At that moment, two dark shapes emerged from the far side of the fireplace. Lohan and a second Lightning Corps sorcerer had been hiding back there the whole time.

Lohan stood next to the governor and said, "I think we've heard enough, Jaylan. Your mission to assassinate the governor has failed."

"Assassinate?" I said. "Don't be ridiculous."

"Do you deny that you just used sorcery on the front door guard? Do you deny that you have entered the governor's chambers fully armed?"

The governor didn't bother waiting for my answer. "Seize them!" he barked.

The two guards hesitated a moment before moving forward. We used that moment to our advantage.

I activated the shield bracer I wore on my left arm and stepped in front of Lissy, who fell back to begin an incantation. Barek moved up next to me, drawing his broadsword in one smooth motion. Next to the door, Hanlon's sword also hissed free.

Lohan drew a wand and pointed it at Barek. The sorcerer next to him held forth an orb and began an incantation.

The guard who knew me approached with a strained look on his face. "Sorry, Captain. I never thought you'd do something like this."

I swatted aside his first strike with my staff.

"Don't believe them. I told the truth. That amulet is controlling the governor."

I saw doubt in the guard's eyes, but he had his orders. He needed to subdue me, and they could sort out the truth later.

I had different plans.

A manifestation hum arose from Lohan's wand, and the sound stretched toward Barek. The Winterman was exchanging blows with the second guard and seemed oblivious to the danger. Before the spell reached him, it faded to nothing. Lohan looked down at the wand in confusion while I thanked the spirits for defective implements.

While we battled, the governor leaped to the corner of the room and pulled on a rope that was hidden behind a curtain. A faint alarm bell tolled somewhere outside the room. We needed to get out of here before more guards arrived.

The guard who fought me was trying not to kill me, which gave me an advantage. The flat of his sword clapped me once on the forearm, nearly making me lose my grip on my staff. He had me on the defense until the numbness from the blow passed.

Our faces came close as I blocked another blow aimed at my head. "Tell Captain Pollard what I said." With that, I shoved the guard back off-balance and timed a strike to his head. The staff connected solidly, and his eyes rolled back in his head as he collapsed to the floor.

Hopefully, the guard would remember my request and give Pollard my side of what happened here today. Captain Pollard had once been my friend, and I hoped his respect for me transcended my becoming a sorcerer.

When Barek's opponent glanced over at his fallen comrade, Barek took advantage of the opening. He smashed his sword hilt into the man's face, and the guard fell back to the floor in a spray of blood. He groaned and rolled back and forth holding his hands to his face. His nose would probably never be quite the same.

Lohan had put away his wand and drawn a dagger. I thought it might be another implement, but he didn't point it and activate it. He simply threw it at me.

Fortunately, Lissy had put up a shield and the dagger ricocheted back toward the table, where it stuck into the back of a chair.

Hanlon had partially opened the door to the chamber and was peering out. "The door guard is coming back and I hear a lot of shouting. We need to go."

I nodded and waved him and Lissy out.

Lohan's companion started another incantation. In all the excitement, I wasn't sure what had happened to his previous spell. Lohan was reaching into his jacket for another hidden surprise. Barek took the expedient approach of stepping forward, grabbing a chair, and throwing it at the two sorcerers.

They easily dodged the chair, but it interrupted the incantation and gave us the opportunity to sprint out of the room.

The hall branched in two directions. To the right, we'd go deeper into the building. That was the direction the shouting was coming from. Going straight would take us back out the way we came. Hanlon and Lissy were already running that direction.

The door guard blocked our exit. He shouted, "Filthy sorcerers!" before charging Hanlon. Hanlon was knocked back by the ferocity of the man's attack, but he managed to hold his own against the larger foe. Barek slipped past Lissy and growled with frustration when the narrow hallway kept him from moving up to help Hanlon.

The shouts from within the building got louder. They were behind us this time, so Barek came back to stand with me.

"Trapped like rats," he said between gritted teeth.

Lissy started an incantation to help Hanlon, who was defending himself well enough but didn't seem able to turn the fight in his favor.

Two guards came around the corner behind us just as the door to the governor's office opened. Lohan and the Lightning Corps sorcerer peered into the hallway before stepping out behind the guards.

Neither opposing sorcerer had started a spell yet, so I took a calculated risk.

The governor wasn't the only one wearing a pendant. I slipped mine out from behind my shirt. Dropping my channel to the shield bracer, I powered the pendant instead. Barek saw what I was doing and stepped forward to protect me from the oncoming guards.

When Councilor Rissik had handed me the pendant before we left on our journey, Lissy had exclaimed, "Oh, how cute!" The pendant was a small, round amber globe with a laughing face etched into it. I had my doubts about how "cute" was going to help us until Councilor Rissik explained its function.

By prearranged signal, I yelled, "Eyes," just before I held up the smiling globe as high as the chain on my neck would allow and activated it.

Even though I had turned my head from the pendant and closed my eyes as tight as I could, the flash was stunning.

I hoped the rest of my team had heeded my warning and protected themselves.

When I looked around, our enemies were all rubbing at their faces and swearing. All except the guard who had been fighting Hanlon. That guard stood with his eyes wide and his mouth gaping open. Lissy must have completed her spell and immobilized the man before I triggered the flash.

Hanlon clutched his arm with a grimace of pain, blood welling between his fingers. Lissy had acted just in time.

Taking advantage of the confusion, we ran out of the governor's residence into the bailey.

I was relieved to find that the alarm bell had apparently rung inside the residence only, as no one was running in our direction to intercept us. That changed as soon as our group burst from the residence entryway and charged the open gate.

We got about half way to the gateway before the guards reacted. One guard shouted for help and ran to intercept us while the second started pushing on the heavy gate. If he got it closed before we reached it, we were done.

At the same time, two black-clad Lightning Corps agents came out of the jail house and turned to see what the shouting was about. The one with a sorcerer's silver stripe on his sleeve aimed his fist toward us while the other man drew a sword and ran to intercept.

Barek was in the lead, and I trusted him to take care of the advancing gate guard. Hanlon was injured, so that left me to take on the Lightning Corps swordsman.

A crash and a grunt told me that Barek had engaged his foe. I stepped away from Lissy and Hanlon with my staff ready as the swordsman reached us. The first quick parries told me this opponent was going to be a challenge.

Lissy started another incantation at the same time the black-robed sorcerer activated his ring. A narrow wave of force lifted a swirl of dust from the ground as it flew forward. The spell narrowly missed hitting me and the man I was fighting, but it caught Hanlon and Lissy solidly. I glanced over my shoulder to see that they were coughing and groaning after being blown off their feet.

My opponent growled at me and came in with a furious series of blows. But his confidence was his undoing. He came in low with one of his strikes and I used the same move that had disarmed Talon a couple of days earlier. My staff cracked loudly against the back of his head as he dove to retrieve his fallen sword, and he crashed face-first to the ground.

I checked on Barek to see that he had made short work of the first guard. He was already at the gate fighting the second. The gate was still partially ajar, thank goodness. That left me with the remaining sorcerer—the one who was holding a casting orb and starting an incantation. I activated my shield bracer again.

Movement at the front door of the governor's residence caught my eye as the two guards from the hallway, along with Lohan and his sorcerer, came stumbling out of the building. They were feeling their way and blinking repeatedly. I wasn't sure how long the effects of the flash would last, and I wanted to be long gone before I could learn the answer.

My shield bracer only protected me. If I was going to help Lissy and Hanlon, I needed to put my sorcerer's staff to work doing something other than bludgeoning people.

I shifted my position to put myself between the sorcerer and Lissy. At the same time, I took out Froth and plugged the mount Ebnik had added to it into the matching slot at the end of my staff.

I jammed the pointed metal cap at the end of the staff into the ground, but I couldn't sense any available vaetra in that spot. I needed to find some exposed rock or flowing water if I was going to use the staff. The only rock I could see was next to the flag pole at the front gate.

It was too far away. I might have to try casting through the staff using my internal well and risk triggering the Runedream. I moved my hand to the upper band that connected directly to Froth and prepared to create a wide shield between me and the sorcerer.

The high-pitched whine of an incoming manifestation told me I was too late. All I could do was defend with my shield bracer and hope for the best.

A powerful bolt of lightning arced straight at me. It met my shield and then cut right through it. In that instant, I realized that Thunderhead College had augmented the normal lightning spell. The strike that Headmaster Fortenz had used to take down Sulana was probably the prototype. Normal shields weren't effective against it.

I figured that thought would be my last, but the massive jolt I expected never came. Instead, my arm vibrated as the strike ground out through the lower segment of my staff with a loud crack and sizzle. I was a little dazed and partially deafened, but still standing.

I turned around to check on Lissy. She had gathered herself enough to sit up and start another incantation. Her face was a mask of anger as she spit out the chant and aimed her orb at the sorcerer. I stepped further to the side.

"I think I see them," Lohan said from the entrance to the governor's residence. The flash was apparently wearing off.

Barek was just stepping back from the horizontal form of the gate guard. He cast a grim look around the courtyard. He'd managed to keep the guard from closing the gate, but the rest of us were too far away. We needed a distraction. A big one.

I ran for the flag pole, hoping Lissy could keep the enemy sorcerer off balance for just a bit longer. Barek picked up a bow that leaned against the courtyard wall and pulled an arrow from the quiver that was next to it.

Lissy's spell launched at the Lightning Corps sorcerer. At first, I thought he'd had time to put up a shield to deflect it. He braced himself and then looked down, surprised that nothing had happened. His slow-forming grin turned to alarm as his clothes began to smolder. Small flames appeared at the ends of his sleeves and the bottom of his robe, and he batted at them franticly.

Lissy collapsed back to the ground, but her attack had given me an idea. I jumped onto a short, wide boulder near the flag pole and jammed the end of my staff into the rock. I prayed that the lightning hadn't damaged it somehow and felt for vaetra. Luck was with me. The stone was the top end of a massive rock formation that was part of a respectable basin. I had vaetra to spare.

For what I had in mind, that was a good thing. I began an incantation that I rarely used, hoping I'd get it right.

Manifesting fire was extremely expensive in terms of how much vaetra it consumed. Shaped fire, like what I was going to try, was even worse. Lissy had probably nearly drained herself just getting the sorcerer's clothes to burn.

While I chanted, the enemy sorcerer screamed and rolled on the ground to put out the flames. Barek had drawn his bow, and the moment the sorcerer stood up again, he released an arrow. The arrow came in a little low and took the sorcerer in the gut. The man doubled over and curled up on the ground.

Lohan heard me chanting and pointed in my direction. He pulled out his wand while the sorcerer next to him started an incantation. It was going to be close.

Barek nocked another arrow when the two guards near Lohan started moving my direction, following my voice. One of them diverted his course toward Lissy and Hanlon when he got close enough to spot them. That guard got an arrow in his shoulder, and he dropped his sword in agony.

Even though I was quickly running out of time, I chanted my incantation slowly to make sure I got it right. I'd only have one shot at this. Froth began a low, throbbing hum just as I finished the incantation. I channeled a month's worth of my own vaetra out of the basin, through the staff and myself, and into Froth. I cringed back from the ball of fire that formed a few feet away from me. When I launched the ball toward the governor's residence, the reaction force threw me back off the boulder and knocked the wind out of me. I narrowly missed slamming into the flag pole.

A huge boom was quickly followed by a rain of debris. I covered my head to protect it from the splinters of smoldering wood that fell around me. When I got up to peek over the boulder, my heart nearly stopped at what I saw.

The entrance to the governor's residence was blown apart and charred. Loose boards swung and smoked in the residual heat. A couple of small fires were growing inside the entrance, raising cries of alarm from those who came to investigate.

Lohan was lying on the ground, unmoving. His sorcerer companion was nowhere to be seen. Three more guards appeared from around the jail house, but they were focused on the fire and didn't seem to realize our part in it.

Seeing the guards go for buckets and water, Barek threw down the bow and ran to help Lissy and Hanlon. I did the same.

As I came around the boulder, I saw what had happened to the second guard that Lohan had sent for me. The poor man had the misfortune of being between me and the residence.

The fire ball must have passed right above him. His hair was mostly burned off and his face was badly blistered, as were the arms and hands he must have instinctively raised in a futile attempt to protect himself. He was still breathing, but he would be badly scarred for life if he survived. I wished there was something I could do for him. I didn't have anything against the guardsmen, who were only following orders. They didn't know the governor was under an enchantment.

"Jaylan, hurry," Barek called.

Barek picked up Lissy, who had fallen unconscious, and draped her unceremoniously over his shoulder. I could just imagine her reaction if she woke up in that position. Hanlon was looking a little dazed, but he was sitting up. He grinned at me as I helped him to his feet.

"Nice distraction," he said.

I looked over my shoulder at the destruction as we followed Barek to the gate. "I might have overdone it a bit."

He laughed and gave me a slap on the back. "Maybe. But it was sure fun to watch."

Barek went through the gate and we were just a step behind when a dull thud made Hanlon gasp. He turned to me with pain in his eyes and stared down at the tip of the crossbow bolt that stood out of his chest, dark and wet with his own blood.

I looked back and saw Lohan sitting up with a guard standing nearby. The guard was readying his crossbow for another shot.

Hanlon sank to his knees and pushed at me. "Go!" he insisted hoarsely, the word flecking blood onto his lower lip.

I couldn't carry him and his wound was beyond healing. Staying would only get me killed or captured. But I couldn't stand the idea of leaving him behind. Hanlon lost consciousness and started folding to the ground. I reached for him, but Barek grabbed my arm and pulled me through the gateway to the outside. He shook me when I continued to stare back through the opening at Hanlon.

"You cannot help him. Run."

The guilt of leaving Hanlon alone to die among enemies tore at me, but Barek was right. Hanlon would not want the rest of us to share his fate. We ran.

Along the way, we passed a guardsman who was jogging toward the governor's compound. He slowed and gave us a suspicious stare.

I waved toward Lissy's limp form without slowing down. "She was injured. We're getting help."

The guard reluctantly continued toward the shouts of the guardsmen fighting the fire.

We hastily answered the questions of the folks who operated the sanctuary as we ran downstairs to its journey room. We wouldn't be safe until we were back at the Archives.

When the effects from the translocation sphere faded and I beheld the interior of the Archives journey room, I finally allowed myself a sigh of relief.

Lissy moaned and Barek hastily sat her on the floor with her back against the wall. Her head lolled a couple of times before her eyes opened. We propped her up until she was able to remain upright on her own.

"How do you feel?" I asked.

She pressed her hands to her head. "Like I've been severely beaten." She looked up at us with a tentative smile. Then she looked past us and the smile faded. "Where's Hanlon?"

Barek answered, in his characteristic blunt style. "He died."

She blinked at him in shock. "When?"

"Just as we were about to leave through the gate," I answered. "He was hit by a crossbow quarrel."

"There was no hope?"

Barek and I both shook our heads.

She looked down at her hands. "He was the first of us to die for the Archives."

I stood and held out my hand to help her get to her feet.

"He was a good man. But he wasn't the first to die, and I don't think he'll be the last. With Northshore under the headmaster's control, I'm sure things are going to get a lot worse before they get better."

CHAPTER 28

EVASION

Sulana slowed Stardust to a stop behind Nigel's horse. The ranger who led their group had put up a hand for quiet. Voices carried from somewhere ahead, although the terrain made it difficult to determine distance or direction. The Lightning Corps was ahead of them in the forest.

Marshal Shields moved forward to confer with Lieutenant Tanous. Sulana crowded up as far as she could to listen in.

"They are ahead of us, Marshal. We can't take this trail all the way out to the road."

"I didn't think we would, Lieutenant. We need to take one of the border trails. Preferably one that will take us a couple of miles away from the refuge entrance."

The lieutenant frowned in thought for a moment. "I know of one, sir, but it's not much more than a game trail. It will be slow going, and our passage will be obvious."

"Let me worry about that. The main thing is to avoid contact. There are too many of them, and if they figure out where we are, they'll be relentless."

"Aye, Marshal. If I remember right, the trail I'm thinking of branches off just ahead."

Sulana broke into the conversation. "But won't we be heading *toward* them?"

The lieutenant looked annoyed at the interruption, but the marshal turned in his seat and responded casually. "It can't be helped. The voices we hear are still a ways off. Sounds can be deceiving in these woods."

Sulana nodded. "I'll take your word for it. Sorry for interrupting."

The marshal shrugged. "I understand your concern. But we do want to keep our chatter to a minimum from here on."

Sulana nodded, and when they started moving again, she fell back to pass the warning along to Daven and Karla. The ranger who was at the end of the party didn't seem to need the warning; he hadn't said a thing since they'd left Karla's cottage.

True to his word, the lieutenant found the border trail within another quarter mile. Unfortunately, the voices were getting closer as well.

When the lieutenant turned his horse onto the border trail, Sulana thought he had used some kind of druid spell. His horse simply vanished into the foliage. Then the marshal turned as well and she was able to make out the trail head more clearly. She had ridden on their current path a few times during her time on the refuge, and she'd never noticed this intersection.

As Sulana rode through the shrubs that obscured the trail, she pulled her legs in tight to avoid the branches that brushed against her and Stardust. No wonder she'd never seen this path. She could barely make it out while riding it.

After a short distance, the path opened up at the edge of a small meadow near the base of a rocky slope. The lieutenant and marshal stopped again and conferred briefly, but Sulana couldn't make out what they were saying.

The marshal waved everyone to move closer. When he spoke his voice was barely loud enough for them to hear.

"Everyone wait here. Our horses will have left a clear path, so I'm going back to hide our trail." The marshal dismounted and looped a waterskin over his shoulder.

Sensing that the marshal was up to something interesting, Sulana whispered, "I'd like to go with you," as he went by her.

He shook his head. "You can't help with this."

"Take her," Karla said, surprising both Sulana and the marshal.

He gave Karla an incredulous look. "You know I can't do that."

Karla stared intently at the marshal. "I know what you are saying, but you should take her."

Sulana expected the marshal to simply refuse and walk on, but he returned Karla's stare for a minute, and then he tilted his head in a motion for Sulana to follow.

Sulana scrambled from her horse and handed the reins to Daven. With excitement tingling in her chest, she followed the marshal's retreating back.

When they were about half-way back to the turnoff, the marshal stopped abruptly and turned to Sulana, who had caught up to him.

"Why did Karla think you should go with me?" he asked.

"I don't know. I was as surprised as you were."

"She knows that we don't allow sorcerers to observe druid rituals."

"Is that what you're about to do? A ritual?"

He stared at her with narrowed eyes for a moment before answering. He pointed to the symbol on his green jacket. "The star says I'm a ranger. The circle around it means I can also offer blessings like a priest."

"I didn't know you could be both."

"There's a lot you don't know about us. One of my duties is to keep it that way. I still haven't heard a good reason for you to go with me, so I'd like you to return to the others." He turned and started walking away.

Sulana thought through what she had just learned. It sounded like the marshal was going to cast a spell, or offer a blessing, or whatever the druids called it. Karla knew Sulana could cast in the druid way, but the marshal did not. The last time they had spoken, her channel had still been blocked. She decided to reveal part of her secret to him.

"I can help," she said to his retreating back.

He turned back around and took a few long strides to stand directly in front of her, uncomfortably close.

"I thought you were no longer able to use sorcery."

"The spirits healed me."

He stepped back and shook his head. "The spirits? That's unlikely. Even if it were true, using sorcery on the refuge would be sacrilege."

Sulana was tempted to just tell him she had learned to cast in the druid way, but she was pretty sure he wouldn't believe her, and if he did, she wasn't sure he would react favorably. If she could just *show* him, he might be more accepting.

For reasons he had never confided, he had helped her remain hidden on the refuge. He was probably the only druid who *might* be willing to teach her something about her new abilities. She couldn't let this opportunity go by without at least trying to see if he would help her.

"I don't know why you've been willing to help me, Marshal, but I'm asking you to go a step further and trust me now. Let the spirits guide you."

The marshal's brows drew together as he considered her words. Then with a shake of his head and a snort, he turned and walked away again.

Sulana's heart sank, and she was about to turn around and go back to the others as he requested when the marshal came to an abrupt stop a few feet away and put his hand to his head.

He strode back to her again and grabbed her arm, pulling her along with him toward the trail intersection. Sulana felt a tingle of hope and hurried to keep up. He released her arm and put his finger to his lips. The voices were getting nearer.

When the marshal and Sulana got within about twenty feet of the intersection, he stopped and kneeled. Sulana emulated him and watched closely.

The marshal opened his water skin and leaned it upright against his leg. He then detached something from the front of his armor. Sulana had thought it was a protective ornament, but it was actually a shallow metal bowl about the size of the marshal's hand. A glimmer of understanding began to form.

The marshal hesitated and looked at Sulana with a pained expression. His reluctance to continue was plain. Sulana returned his look, but she said nothing and didn't move a muscle, afraid to do anything that might make him change his mind.

With a sigh, he squirted water into the bowl.

Holding the bowl in both hands, the marshal closed his eyes and began to pray.

"Spirits of tree and meadow, spirits of stone and water, I humbly ask you for your guidance and your help. Intruders are on the refuge. Enemies are at our gate. Help me hide my companions from their sight. Help us leave this place in peace."

The hairs on Sulana's neck tingled as she listened to his prayer. She watched the pathway ahead for evidence of the blessing the marshal was about to invoke. The spirits were here; she could feel it.

The marshal opened his eyes and peered down the trail. Nothing happened. He repeated his prayer, more earnestly this time. Still nothing.

The marshal narrowed his eyes at Sulana and whispered. "I knew I should have left you behind. The spirits won't manifest for me."

The voices they heard earlier had fallen silent for quite some time. Sulana and the marshal shared a look of alarm when they began anew from fairly close by. If the searchers reached the intersection right then, they'd easily spot Sulana and the marshal.

Sulana held her hand out in silence. The marshal didn't understand what she meant at first. He looked down at the bowl in his hand and then handed it to her reluctantly.

Sulana opened a channel to the water bowl, and as quietly as she could, whispered her own prayer to the spirits. "Spirits, please heed my call. Our enemies approach and we need your help. Help me mend the forest where we have passed."

Sulana shivered as a couple of spirits responded to the vaetra she offered through her channel. She stared down the trail willing broken branches to heal, swept-aside leaves to right themselves, and the lowest branches of the trailside trees to droop into the open air space. She envisioned thicker foliage at the turnoff.

The spirits did everything she asked of them. While she watched, the path mended itself and became even more impassable than it had been before. Sulana grinned in elation and glanced over into the shocked face of the marshal. When she handed the bowl back to him, he was so disturbed that he nearly dropped it.

The marshal dumped the water from the bowl and signaled Sulana to stay low and retreat quietly with him. The voices were close enough for them to make out individual words.

"I swear this cursed forest is working against us."

"You're just mad because you've led us in circles twice now."

"Hey, you want to take lead? We'll see how much better you can do."

"You're doing fine. Just keep it down. Hey, what's that?"

"What?"

"I thought I saw movement over there."

"Probably just another squirrel. We haven't seen any other trails for a while now."

"Stop anyway. Let's take a look."

Sulana froze and looked over her shoulder in the direction of the voices. She saw just hints of movement in the distance. She reached to draw her blade, but the marshal put his hand on hers.

He poured some more water into the metal bowl and closed his eyes. His prayer was an inaudible whisper this time, but he had much better success. From about thirty yards away, a deer startled and crashed through the forest. At first, it ran toward the intruders, but it veered off when it saw them and disappeared into the trees.

"That was a big squirrel."

"Very funny. Keep moving. We've wasted enough time."

The marshal waited until the voices began to fade before continuing. He glanced over his shoulder at Sulana several times as they made their way back to the others. His expression was inscrutable.

Sulana was elated by her contribution to their escape. But had she just won or lost the marshal's support?

CHAPTER 29
EMISSARY ESCORT

"I'm sorry sir, but we can't let you into the assembly chamber without an appointment."

Dumont gave the palace door guard a disapproving frown. "Don't you think that's up to the emissary, officer?"

Before the guard could answer, the man standing next to Dumont interrupted the exchange. "It is my understanding that an emissary may invite a personal guest to assembly meetings. Is that not correct?" He pointed to the letter of appointment in the guard's hand as a reminder that it officially made him an emissary of the Imperial Assembly.

Dumont smiled. Jonah Lingen was following the script they had worked out on their way down to Cassandria. As well he might. He owed his new position in the assembly to Dumont's influence with Governor Trask. It was a position Jonah could never have hoped to achieve without Dumont's help.

The guard looked down at the letter of appointment and shrugged. "Yes, Emissary." He handed the letter back to Jonah. "I'll have one of my men escort you."

"Thank you," Jonah said shortly, as if he had expected no other answer.

The guard handed the letter of appointment to a second guard and ordered him to escort the emissary and his guest to the Imperial Assembly Chamber.

Dumont and Jonah followed the guard as he clinked and jingled his way through the palace and up a wide set of stairs to the second floor.

The guard stopped outside a large wooden door that was closed. "The assembly is currently in session. Please wait here and I'll announce you."

Jonah snatched the letter of appointment from the guard's hand and said, "That won't be necessary." Before the startled guard could react, Jonah opened the door and walked through.

The guard frowned and his face grew red, but it was too late for him to stop the new emissary. Dumont shrugged one shoulder and gave him a sympathetic look before following the emissary into the room.

A shrill voice called out, "What is the meaning of this intrusion? Who are you? Guard!"

The guard scurried into the room and bowed toward the thin old man who had stood to confront the newcomers.

"I'm sorry, Seneschal, but they didn't wait for me to announce them."

The seneschal narrowed his eyes. "Well? Out with it."

While the guard paused to gather himself, Jonah stepped forward and handed the letter of appointment to the twitchy old man.

"I'm Jonah Lingen, here to replace Zethar Trask as the emissary from Lakeshore Province."

A deep voice roared, "Lingen? That's impossible. My cousin would rather burn his own eyes out with a hot poker than appoint a Lingen. This man is a fraud." The man behind the voice was as tall and burly as Jonah was small and thin. He got up from his seat and came around the table to glare down at the smaller man. Dumont guessed that this was Zethar Trask. He had the same sturdy build as his cousin the governor and a similar lack of subtlety.

The seneschal looked over the document intently. With a frustrated shake of his head, he said, "It looks genuine to me."

Former Emissary Trask thrust his hand out toward the seneschal, demanding to see the letter for himself. The seneschal handed it to him, and the big man quickly scanned the letter.

"This is a forgery. It has to be." He threw the parchment back toward the seneschal, who deftly snapped it out of the air. "Save that as evidence for his trial."

"Let me see it, Sorman," demanded a quiet voice from the head of the table.

The seneschal handed the paper to a richly dressed man whose face showed lines of worry and whose eyes showed dark circles from sleepless nights. Two burly guards stood at rest behind him, one on either side of his chair.

"Of course, Your Majesty," the seneschal said with a bow.

The emperor reviewed the document, taking extra time scrutinizing the governor's seal at the bottom. He looked around the large oval table at the other emissaries, none of whom met his eyes. Dumont watched carefully as he passed the letter to the first emissary on his left. The emperor's mouth twisted into a smirk as each emissary passed it to the next with barely a glance. It was clear that the other emissaries had expected this eventuality.

"It seems we have yet another new addition to our august presence," he said with a wry tone as the letter made its way back to the seneschal.

"No!" shouted Trask. His face went crimson and he clenched his fists at his side as he leaned forward and put his face mere inches from Jonah's. "This little weasel is not replacing me."

"You will watch your tone when addressing the Emperor," hissed the seneschal. Although Trask could probably snap him like a twig, the big man quailed at the older man's glowering stare.

"I'm sorry, Your Majesty. But there must be some mistake."

The emperor took a deep breath and released it as a heavy sigh. "We'll look into it, Zethar, but for now, everything seems in order."

The seneschal waved toward the guard.

"Please escort Mr. Trask out of the palace."

The guard came forward and took Trask's elbow in hand, but the former emissary pulled his arm free and strode from the room without looking back. The guard closed the door on his way out, casting a disturbed and bewildered look toward the seneschal.

Uncomfortable silence reigned in the room for a moment after the door closed. The emperor extended a hand toward the recently emptied seat at the assembly table.

"Please sit down, Emissary Lingen, and kindly introduce your companion."

Jonah squared his shoulders and swept around the table to the proffered chair. Once he was seated, he tilted his head toward Dumont. "Thank you, Your Majesty. May I introduce Dumont Fortenz, Headmaster of Thunderhead College."

The emperor sat up as if stung. The seneschal immediately dipped into a defensive crouch and stepped between Dumont and the emperor. Dumont could not help himself from chuckling at the sight of the feisty old skeleton trying to protect his liege.

Dumont spread his arms in a gesture of peace and said, "No need for alarm, my good man. I am not armed and I have no wish to hurt anyone."

The seneschal growled back, "Forgive me if I don't take you at your word, sorcerer. Why *are* you here?"

The emperor interrupted. "You'll have to excuse Sorman. He has a pathological dislike for sorcery and those who practice it."

Dumont bowed toward the emperor. "I understand completely, Your Majesty. I hope to one day show your seneschal and others like him that sorcery can be beneficial to all, mundane and sorcerer alike."

The emperor huffed and rolled his eyes. "Don't count on it, Headmaster. Your colleagues have tried to win him over for years with no success."

Dumont twisted his head. "My colleagues, Your Majesty?"

"Ah. I suppose you don't think of the sorcerers at the Archives as colleagues."

It was Dumont's turn to snort. "Not exactly, Your Majesty. The Archives operates under a different ... agenda."

The emperor nodded. "Speaking of agendas, perhaps you could tell us what brings you before the assembly today."

Dumont bowed again. "I'd be happy to do so, Your Majesty. As you have no doubt heard, the Archives is having difficulties with their Sword Sorcerer program."

The emperor narrowed his eyes. "As I understand it, Headmaster, *you* are responsible for some of these difficulties."

"Yes, Your Majesty. I must admit that our disagreements have devolved into violence more than once, but the very fact that Thunderhead College has prevailed in most of these altercations shows you which of us is stronger and better able to serve the empire. I propose that Thunderhead College take over the duties of enforcing the Sorcery Accords."

The emperor's mouth dropped open briefly before he recovered himself. He smiled and shook his head. "I don't think so, Headmaster Fortenz. Isn't that rather like setting the wolves to watch the sheep?"

Emissary Lingen spoke up. "If by wolves you mean the Lightning Corps and by sheep you mean the mundane, Your Majesty, I must protest the unfair characterization. Integration is about sorcerers and mundane benefiting each other, not about sorcerers preying on the mundane."

The emperor waved a dismissive hand. "Spare me the politics, Emissary. I've heard it many times before, and I believe it less each time."

Dumont kept his face serious, but inside he was chuckling. The emperor was no fool, and Dumont liked him better for it.

"I'm sorry you feel that way, Your Majesty. I hope that in time, I can change your mind."

The emperor froze and stared intently at Dumont. For a moment, Dumont wondered if he had gone too far. The emperor knew about the mind control amulets. He had sent a team to arrest Paeter and free the Sunset Province governor from the influence of an amulet not long ago. Dumont had just used the words "change your mind" innocently, but the emperor might have suspected a double meaning.

Dumont kept his expression neutral and waited for the emperor to speak.

The emperor finally looked away and cast his gaze around the table. All of the emissaries were watching him, waiting for him to call for a vote.

The seneschal had returned to his seat. He leaned toward the emperor and said, "I'm no fan of the Archives, Your Majesty, but this proposal seems like a very bad idea."

In a tired voice, the emperor called out, "All in favor of transferring sorcerer custody of the accords from the Archives to Thunderhead College, please raise your hand."

All five emissaries raised their hands.

The emperor raised an eyebrow at the seneschal. His four votes meant nothing when the emissaries voted together. "It doesn't seem to matter what I think of the proposal."

Dumont grinned and then bowed toward the emperor and the emissaries. "Thank you, Your Majesty. Thank you, emissaries. I assure you that Thunderhead College will give the Accords the support they deserve."

Dumont had difficulty containing his glee as he left the palace. The four Lightning Corps agents who fell into step with him outside the palace gate had trouble matching his pace. One of them asked him if things had gone well.

"Yes, everything went exactly as planned. We should have the Archives off our back now. If they do interfere, *they* will be the outlaws." The irony made Dumont laugh so hard that passersby glanced his way with curiosity and concern.

CHAPTER 30

DETOUR

Sulana's respect for her ranger escorts grew during their cautious flight through the forest. Lieutenant Tanous took them around the Lightning Corps search parties and brought them back to the road several miles away from the refuge entrance. For the rest of the journey to Northshore, Sulana jumped at every sound and had a sore neck from checking their back trail. Thankfully, she hadn't seen another black uniform since the refuge.

Along the way, the marshal extracted her story about how she had healed her vaetra channel and experimented with blessings. At first, he had trouble believing her. Eventually he accepted that he had witnessed her offer a blessing firsthand. To the astonishment of his fellow rangers, he began to work with her and help her understand more about how blessings worked.

They moved as quickly as the horses could tolerate and covered a lot of ground. After one short and fitful night in a hidden camping spot off the road, the walls of Northshore finally came into view.

Sulana squinted into the distance. Was that smoke?

Nigel, as he'd asked her to call him, must have seen it as well. "It looks like there's a fire in Northshore." He kicked his horse into a gallop and the rest of the group did the same.

When they reached the eastern gate, a guard stepped into the center of the opening and held up his hands. The riders came to a stop, their horses huffing from the run.

The guard lowered his hands and stepped forward to speak with the marshal. "Good day, honorable ranger. Unless you have urgent business, we're asking everyone to stay out of the city until the fire is completely under control."

"Can you tell us what happened?" Nigel asked.

"Some sorcerer tried to assassinate the governor. We almost got him, but he used magic to escape and nearly blew up the residence." The man looked over his shoulder toward the governor's compound where white smoke still drifted into the sky. "It looks like they're getting it under control now. I should get the all clear soon, if you'd like to wait."

Nigel looked at Sulana. She wanted to ask more questions, but didn't think it would be a good idea to draw attention to herself until she knew more about what was going on.

Nigel seemed to understand her reservations and turned back to the guard. "That must have been quite a mess," he said conversationally. "Do you know anything about the assassin?"

The guard shrugged. "All I heard is that some former guard captain that the governor sacked a while back has turned sorcerer and came back for revenge."

Sulana's heart sank into her stomach. The guard was talking about Jaylan. What had he gotten himself into?

Nigel glanced at Sulana. "One man did all that? How did he get away?"

The guard shrugged again. "I wasn't there, but I heard he had other sorcerers with him and a warrior who may have been a Winterman. We took down one of the sorcerers, and another was injured badly enough that the assassins had to carry her off."

Sulana had to hold her breath and close her eyes to keep from pummeling the man with more questions. His information was obviously incomplete, and he wouldn't know what she was desperate to find out.

Who had been killed? Who had been injured?

The big man was undoubtedly Barek. The woman could be Lissy, but Councilor Rissik would never let her go on such a dangerous mission. And why had they come here in the first place? Surely not to assassinate the governor.

Someone at the sanctuary might know what was going on. If they could get into the city.

Meanwhile, Nigel tried to learn more. "What caused the fire?"

The guard scratched his head. "I know it sounds a little far-fetched, but what I heard is that the assassin threw a massive ball of fire at the residence. It blew away the whole front of the building."

"Is the governor okay?"

"Yeah, he's fine, but he's angry. The assassin escaped through the sanctuary, and the governor arrested everyone in the building. The black cloaks are guarding the place while our men fight the fire."

The black cloaks. That could only mean the Lightning Corps. Not only were they here, but they had the support of the governor, a man known for his intolerance of sorcery. An unsettling suspicion gnawed at the back of Sulana's mind.

Sulana decided it was time to leave. They needed to get out of here before someone recognized her. Also, it was only a matter of time before her pursuers realized she wasn't on the refuge and returned to Northshore. She couldn't let them find her here sitting at the gate.

She turned Stardust and said, "Our business here can wait. Let's continue on to Riverview." Without waiting for a response, she urged her horse into a trot. Daven and Karla followed her.

The guard looked over his shoulder again. "Really, I'm sure it will be just a few more minutes. There's hardly any smoke now."

Nigel followed Sulana's lead and waved toward the guard. "Thanks, anyway. We'd just be in the way until things settle down. If we leave now, we'll just have enough time to make the first road camp toward Riverview."

The guard was too surprised to say anything at first, but as they trotted away, he shouted, "Safe travels." Nigel waved back at him again.

Nigel and Lieutenant Tanous caught up to Sulana, who had slowed Stardust back down to a walk so Daven and Karla could keep up. The lieutenant continued past her and took up his position at the lead of the party. Nigel came alongside.

"What are you thinking?"

"Something is very wrong in Northshore."

"Uh, huh. Besides that. Do you know who might have attacked the governor?"

"I don't think it was supposed to be an attack. I think it might have been some kind of rescue."

"Rescue? How does blowing up the governor's residence constitute a rescue?"

"Something must have gone wrong. Jaylan would never have attacked the governor unless it was the only option."

Nigel was silent for a moment. When he spoke again, he kept his voice low. "What makes you think Jaylan Forester is responsible for this?"

"The guard said it was a former captain turned sorcerer. Jaylan is the only person I know who has ever fit *that* description."

Nigel went quiet again. Sulana suspected he was beginning to have doubts about his association with her.

"Is Jaylan really powerful enough to have cast the spell the guard described? Fire is a difficult element to control. Forgive me for saying that he didn't strike me as being quite that accomplished a sorcerer."

Sulana didn't know whether to laugh or cry in response to the marshal's remark. Her mind whirled with conflicting explanations for what might have happened at Northshore and what the implications would be. She put her hand to her forehead and took a deep breath to calm the panic that was building inside.

"Jaylan is full of surprises. His knowledge of sorcery is limited, but when he uses it, the results are often spectacular. And I don't mean that in a good way."

Nigel raised an eyebrow at her. "This is the man the Archives has chosen for Sword Sorcerer? And you for a mate?"

Sulana glanced at Nigel, wondering how much she could confide in him. And how much he already knew. He had made it possible for her to get the healing she needed and he had probably just saved her life by getting her off the refuge, but how far could she trust him when it came to matters of sorcery? His feelings on *that* subject were well understood.

There was one bit of information that might make him more positively disposed toward Jaylan.

"Jaylan thinks he may be getting help from the spirits."

The marshal started to smile and shake his head, but stopped and turned a sober look her way. "Are you talking about the first day you were on the refuge? When the spirits left you and entered Jaylan?"

"You saw that? You were spying on us?"

Nigel raised an eyebrow at her accusation. "I was debating throwing you off the refuge and making sure you left. Be glad I didn't."

"You're right. Sorry. What happened during my examination was unexpected, but that's not what I'm talking about. The messages Jaylan sent me over the past couple of months have been cryptic, so I'm not sure of the details. I get the impression that he thinks he has found a way to speak directly with the spirits. He mentioned one spirit, anyway."

Nigel's expression was doubtful. "What makes him think he is talking to spirits?"

Sulana rolled her eyes. "That's a funny question coming from a ranger priest. His note mentioned the name Tritia, which is why I figured he was talking about spirits."

After a minute or so of thoughtful silence, Nigel spoke again. "I normally wouldn't give such an idea a second thought." He gave Sulana a considering look. "But after the things I've seen over the past day or so, I'm more inclined to keep an open mind. It would be interesting to spend some time speaking with Sorcerer Forester one day."

Sulana smiled. "You can do that as soon as we reach the Archives." It would be interesting to see how Jaylan and Nigel got along.

Nigel shook his head. "I'm not going to the Archives. My men and I will escort you to Alpine Lakes Trail, and then you are on your own."

Sulana's smile faded. "I understand. I want you to know that I appreciate everything you've done for me. I don't know how I can ever repay you."

The marshal met her eyes and spoke seriously. "You can repay me by finding a way to put an end to Thunderhead College and its headmaster."

The coldness that crept into his voice when he spoke of Thunderhead College resonated with the anger and determination that had grown within her after nearly two days of being hunted by the Lightning Corps. She pressed her lips together and gave him a shallow nod.

"I'll do my best," she promised.

"May the spirits guide you," he rejoined.

They shared a knowing smile.

CHAPTER 31

GREATER SPIRITS

Normally, I would have been practicing potions with Lissy in the mid-afternoon, but she was still in the infirmary under observation. I stayed by her side after we got back until she chased me away, insisting that she was fine and the healers were being overly cautious. She was mostly just bruised from the spell that threw her to the ground during our confrontation at Northshore, and she was suffering a bout of dizziness from depleting herself so completely during the spell duel. I knew how that felt.

At loose ends, I went to the library and tackled our latest predicament. I was determined to find a way to fight the lightning spell that had so easily cut through my shield in Northshore. To do that, I had to better understand how both shield spells and lightning spells worked.

An hour or so later, I had three books open in front of me, and none of them were giving me any answers.

The door to the library opened and I looked up to see Ebnik and Councilor Maris Torlon enter. They came over to the table where I was seated and stood over me.

"Any luck?" Ebnik asked.

"Not so far. I thought a little research into shield theory would help, but so far, all I'm coming up with is more questions."

Ebnik gave me an understanding nod. "That's often how it goes at first. The gems of knowledge must be culled from the ore that obscures them."

I sighed and waved my hands at the reading material on the table. "So far, I have a lot of ore and no gems."

Maris bounced on her feet and said cheerfully, "We have an idea about that."

Considering who was standing in front of me and the familiar leather folder under Maris's arm, I had a fairly good notion of where she was headed. I'd been thinking about it myself. "You think the Runedream can help."

Maris's friendly smile faded from the lack of enthusiasm in my voice. "Sure. Don't you?" She took a chair and sat at the table opposite me. Ebnik did the same.

"I've considered it," I answered. "The trouble is that I need to be able to visualize the solution. I don't know what to visualize because I have no idea how they are penetrating our shields."

"How about Tritia?" Ebnik asked. "Can she help?"

"Maybe. But getting answers from her is like trying to catch flies with your bare hands. There's a lot of flailing around, and most of the time, you come up with nothing."

Maris let out a frustrated breath. "It's a shame she isn't more helpful."

I shrugged. "She seems to be more of a guide than a mentor. Once I know where I want to go, she can help me get there. In this situation, I have no idea where I'm going."

"Have you figured out *what* she is?" Ebnik asked.

"Whatever she is, she's related to the spirits. If she *is* a spirit, she's a powerful one. When I asked her about that, she said she was 'many spirits,' whatever that means."

"Is it possible that she's *the* Tritia?" Maris wondered aloud.

I shook my head. "Unlikely. She more or less said that she adopted a human form so we could communicate. I figure she chose a name that would make sense to me as well. I seriously doubt she's the same Tritia, Goddess of Water and Sprites, that the druids worship."

"Why not?" Maris insisted.

"Why would a spirit goddess help a sorcerer learn to cast spells?"

"Because you are the runemaster," Maris answered.

"Great. You make about as much sense as she does. Look, the druids claim that the spirits hate sorcery because we take without giving back. A spirit goddess would be more likely to smite me than support me."

Maris leaned forward and said in a lowered voice, "Maybe the druids are wrong."

"Maybe. But the spirits are the domain of the druids, so I'm inclined to trust their knowledge of the subject over our wild guesses."

Maris pouted, looking a little offended by my response. Her bubbly personality and easily offended sensibilities seemed at odds with her age, which I guessed at a little over thirty.

"Sorry, Maris. I didn't mean for that to come out so harshly. I promise I'll ask the next time I see her. Just don't expect me to come back with a straight answer."

Maris smiled and reached out to pat my arm. "That's okay, Jaylan. I know you are still trying to figure all this out. I'm just trying to help."

"I appreciate that."

I closed the books and stacked them into a pile. "You know, I'm not getting anywhere with this anyway, so maybe I *will* go see what Miss Enigmatic has to say." I got up and put the books back on the shelves where I'd found them.

"Do you want us to observe?" Ebnik asked.

"Absolutely." I still wasn't comfortable going into the Runedream without someone keeping an eye on me. Every time I stepped through the gateway, I recalled my first trip and the feeling of being trapped. I didn't know whether or not Ebnik would be able to do anything about it if that happened again, but his presence was reassuring nevertheless.

When I came out of the Runedream trance, Maris always asked innocent questions that turned out to be more insightful than I expected. She was good at helping me get a little extra out of each experience and suggesting things to try the next time.

The three of us went up to my chamber, chatting about what I'd learned during my research. I hoped Ebnik's lifetime of experience might help him see something I didn't, but all he was able to do was add a bit more "ore" to the pile that was already overloading my brain.

When we got to my chamber, I lay down and folded my hands across my chest. My chamber had two extra chairs that we had brought in specifically for sessions like this one. Maris and Ebnik each pulled a chair over to the bed. Maris put her folder down next to me and opened it, using the mattress as a desktop. The page was covered with her bold calligraphy.

"See you in a while," I said as I closed my eyes.

We never knew exactly how long the sessions would last. My sense of time inside the Runedream did not correspond to the passage of time in the conscious world.

Maris had helped me figure out that I didn't need Froth to invoke the Runedream. All I had to do was open a channel and *think* about casting a spell. The channel would automatically loop back through something within me that invoked the Runedream trance and brought the gray fog.

Without hesitation, I envisioned the gateway and opened it. I stepped into the dark tunnel and was immediately surrounded by about a dozen of the tiny lights that often followed Tritia around.

Their presence here without her was disappointing. I'd learned that Tritia didn't appear on every visit to the

Runedream. In fact, I'd only seen her one other time. When I asked her about it, "I am here when you need me," was the best she could do for an explanation. But the lights were always here, helping me see in the dark and offering incantations.

I tried to touch one of the lights with the end of my finger, but it wouldn't let me. It maintained a consistent distance, shifting its position as I moved around.

"Don't play with them," said a stern and unfamiliar voice from behind me.

I turned to discover that Tritia was here after all. And she had friends. Four other shapes stood with her, two on each side. They looked like Tritia did the first time I saw her: vaguely human-shaped clouds of light.

Tritia turned to the shape on her right. "Loralai, please have some respect for the runemaster. And everyone, please take your human forms."

All of the shapes shifted and twisted until they all looked more or less like human females. The one called Loralai had a long, green flowing gown and skin that looked like tree bark. Her hair was a cascade of willow leaves.

She looked down at herself. "Oh for goodness sake! Must our appearance be so ridiculous? I could curse the druids and their over-active imaginations."

The thin woman to Loralai's right smiled over her shoulder at a set of dragonfly wings and flitted them experimentally. "I think they're cute."

"You would," grumped the woman to Tritia's left. She was short and squat with hair that seemed to be modeled out of clay.

The last figure was the least attractive of all. Her human form seemed almost incomplete. Patches of skin were missing from her arms and face. Only half of her head was covered with hair; the other half was a mass of scab. She leveled a malevolent glare at me but said nothing.

Tritia turned back to me and smiled. "Runemaster, please meet my sisters." She pointed to the two women on her right. "This is Loralai and Arial." Arial fluttered her wings enough to rise a couple of feet and then smiled and bowed from the air. Loralai, gaping at her floating sister in disgust, buried her face in a hand and shook her head.

"On my left we have Umbria and Putra." Umbria folded her heavy arms over her considerable midsection and harrumphed. Putra just continued her unsettling glare.

Tritia had just named the four other greater spirits of druid lore. Either the spirits were playing an elaborate trick on me, or I was actually in the presence of the five druid goddesses.

Unsure of the protocol, I bowed deeply and said, "I'm honored by your presence."

Loralai sniffed. "You should be."

Tritia's shape had fully resolved as well. The first couple of times I had seen her, her lower half faded out before it reached the floor. She floated in position as always, but this time, the fins of a giant fish tail lifted into the air behind her.

"Get on with it," croaked the voice of Putra. It was a relief when she shifted the pressure of her gaze to Tritia.

Tritia rolled her eyes. "Very well." Her expression grew serious when she spoke to me.

"We bring grave tidings. The flow of life is in danger. Once again, someone threatens to awaken the parasite. That must not happen, or all of us will be destroyed."

Considering the source, I figured that the flow of life related to the vaenwork that Ebnik told me about. But the rest made no sense.

"What parasite?" I asked.

Loralai answered. "The parasite at the Great Basin, you fool. Your kind placed it there."

I searched my memory for even a hint of what she might be referring to, but came up empty.

"I'm sorry, but I don't know what you are talking about."

Loralai threw her hands in the air. "Gah! Stupid human. We are wasting our time here."

Tritia motioned with her hand for Loralai to settle down. Arial came to my defense.

"It was long before his time. The parasite has been asleep for centuries, and human memory is short."

Loralai shook her head. "Whatever. Get through to him if you can. I'm done."

Her attitude had been grating from the beginning, but I was getting tired of being blamed for not being able to decipher their cryptic method of communicating.

"Why did you come in the first place?" I mumbled half to myself.

Loralai narrowed her eyes at me. In a blink, she was inches away, her eyes burning into mine.

"I came because *you*," she paused to look me up and down with a sneer, "are our only hope." I took a step back, and she folded her arms. "Which means we are doomed."

With that, she was gone.

Umbria and Putra shared a glance and then disappeared as well, leaving just Tritia and Arial.

Arial gave me an apologetic shrug. "You must forgive them. They are frightened and unaccustomed to feeling that way."

"I wish I could help, but I don't know what to do."

Tritia swept her tail down once and coasted nearer.

"Loralai likes to have someone to blame. You are not our only hope. You are our only messenger."

"But I don't understand the message."

"You must find a way. Search the memories of your kind, living and dead. Rely on the talents of your friends, and let your mate be your guide."

"Sulana? What do you know about her? Should I go to her?"

"She comes to you," Tritia said.

I froze in panic. "She's on her way now?"

If Sulana was traveling from the refuge, she could not have seen my most recent message about what was going on in Northshore and elsewhere in the empire. Our past messages had taken about a week in transit because of the hand-off between the Archives network and the druid temple network. If she went to Northshore, she would be walking into a trap.

"I need to go."

Tritia nodded and smiled. "Good luck, Runemaster. We will be here if you need us."

That reminded me. I had come here to see what I could learn about our shield problem. However, having a goddess yell at me seemed like a good excuse for getting distracted.

The shield would have to wait. Sulana's safety was more important. I had to leave the Runedream and find her before the Lightning Corps did.

I bowed to the goddesses. "It was good to meet you Arial." She tipped her head toward me. To Tritia I said, "I'll try not to let you down."

She lifted a hand in farewell and both of them disappeared.

When I awoke back in my chamber. Ebnik was snoring softly in his chair, his head dipping toward his chest with each breath. Maris had folded herself at the waist and laid her head in her arms on the bed. How long had I been out?

I sat up, and the movement woke Maris. She rubbed at her eyes and yawned. "That took a while," she commented.

Her voice rousted Ebnik, who stirred with a final snort. He stood and stretched. "What did you learn?"

I raised an eyebrow. "Not what I expected. There's more to the Runedream than we thought. I learned that Sulana is on her way, and we're all supposed to stop some parasite from destroying the spirits."

Maris had her quill ready, but she stopped and stared at me in confusion.

Ebnik shook his head. "I think I'm still half asleep," he said. "Maybe you'd better start from the beginning."

I told them about meeting the five spirit goddesses and relayed as much of the conversation as I could remember.

"Spirits, Jaylan!" Maris exclaimed when I had finished.

"So it seems," I agreed with a smile.

She looked down at the papers on the bed and seemed to remember her part in these sessions. She found a new sheet of parchment and started writing furiously. "You are the messenger of the spirit goddesses? How extraordinary."

Ebnik folded his arms and gave me a self-satisfied smile. "Do you believe me now? Or are you still unwilling to admit that you have an important destiny?"

I got off the bed and waved a finger at Ebnik before stretching by back. "Don't start. Destiny is just a word they use to try giving purpose to a series of unusual events. Have you ever noticed that it is always applied in retrospective? If I fall down the stairs and die tomorrow, what does that say about my destiny?"

"It says you had a great destiny, but you were clumsy," Ebnik said with a grin.

"No, it says I'm just a man. Then as well as now. Unusual things have happened to me, but if not for a brief meeting with a thief on the run, I'd still be at the Snow Creek Inn mucking out stalls."

"But you aren't," Ebnik insisted, as if that proved his point.

"But I *could be*," I retorted. "You are basically saying that I *couldn't* be, and I don't buy it. I'm here right now because of a series of choices. Choices that *I* made."

Ebnik said, "You make choices because of who you are. You chose to help the young thief find his mentor because of who you are. You chose to learn about sorcery because of who you are. You chose to enter the Runedream because of who you are. All of this happened because you are the runemaster, messenger of the spirit goddesses."

Ebnik looked so earnest that I almost felt guilty for bursting into laughter at the end of his speech. Almost.

"You should hear yourself, Ebnik. You sound worse than a druid priest."

That comment brought both of them up short. Maris stopped writing and looked at me. Ebnik looked off into the distance and slowly rubbed his chin.

"The druids could be a problem," he finally said.

Maris nodded, catching on to his train of thought. She gave me a worried glance. "Maybe we should be careful who we tell about this session."

The druids worshiped the spirit goddesses and hated sorcerers. How would they feel about a sorcerer who claimed to speak for their gods? Ridicule would be the best I could hope for.

"You know, I'm not too excited about telling other sorcerers I talked with the spirit goddesses either."

All three of us went quiet as we thought through the ramifications of telling *anybody* else about the experience I just had.

Maris finally shook her head and pointed her quill at the notes she had been writing. In a scolding tone, she said, "This is too important to keep secret. We don't have that right. The whole reason I'm here is to witness and record. That was the deal with the Council."

Ebnik put a consoling hand on her shoulder. "Fine, continue to witness and record. Just skip over a few things when you report to the Council."

Maris looked at her notes and threw up her hands. "I'd have to skip this whole session," she complained.

"What session?" I asked pointedly.

She looked up at me and then to Ebnik, who nodded slowly.

Maris stared down at her notes with a doubtful frown. Then she gave a little shrug and said, "I suppose I could lose track of these notes for a while."

"Just until we know more," Ebnik encouraged. He looked at me and added, "If we can't figure out the puzzle for ourselves, we'll *have* to involve others."

I was just happy they were giving me a reprieve. I needed to find Sulana, and I didn't have time to get bogged down in theological arguments or more talk about the Great Destiny of the Runemaster.

"Agreed," I said. "Now, if you two don't mind, I need to see if Barek is up for another trip."

Maris got up and stood in front of me, worry lines wrinkling her brow. "Please be careful, Jaylan. I fear that something terrible is coming. We're going to need you more than ever."

"Don't worry. I'll be careful. You do realize that ambushing me hasn't been working out so well for the bad guys."

She clenched her hands together and sighed. "I suppose that's been true up to now. Let's just hope your luck holds out."

Chapter 32
Parting

Sulana and the others spent a tense and nearly sleepless night at a cold and dreary camp site well off the main road. In the morning, Lieutenant Tanous had once again taken the lead.

By then, the Lightning Corps had to know Sulana had left the refuge. If they had reached Northshore, talking to the gate guard might reveal that her group had ridden by and then left with haste.

Not knowing how far behind the enemy was made Sulana's skin crawl with the need to hurry. They pushed their horses as hard as they dared, but they couldn't overdo it because they still had a long uphill climb ahead.

Overnight, a misty rain had moved into the valley. No one carried a tent, so they had to make do by huddling under a few large cedars. The trees had protected them well, but as soon as they rode out into the cool, wet morning, moisture seeped into the shoulders and hood of Sulana's cloak.

A couple of hours later, they reached the Alpine Lakes Trailhead. The muddy trail went toward the base of the mountain and disappeared into trees that were wrapped in a thin fog.

"Well, Sword Sorceress Delano, this is where we part ways," declared the Defender Marshal.

His rangers moved their horses to stand next to his, flanking him on either side.

"Thank you, Marshal. For everything. If not for you, I'd either be dead or in chains probably wishing I were dead."

"We have a common enemy. I will try to convince the Hierarchy of that and do what I can to oppose Thunderhead College. I fear we both have a difficult time ahead of us."

That was an understatement. Sulana turned her head and looked toward the uninviting path that would take her up the mountain and return her to the relative safety of home. She shivered. The rain and fog would settle onto the trail and slicken the rocky sections. "We should get moving. I want to reach the Archives before nightfall, and it will probably be slow going."

The marshal nodded and raised a hand in farewell. "May the spirits guide you."

She returned the gesture and gave him the formal response he had taught her. "May their blessings sustain you."

The rangers left the trailhead clearing and turned north on Trench Highway toward Riverview. Nigel had told her he was planning to check in with the temple there, which had close ties to the mundane resistance that was growing in response to Lightning Corps activities.

Sulana urged Stardust toward the trail that would take her home. Stardust seemed eager to comply and Sulana had to hold her back for her own safety. Daven and Karla followed behind Sulana.

In spite of the fact that the sun had been up for a couple of hours, the dark clouds that sprayed a persistent drizzle draped the landscape with shades of gray. Banks of fog rolled downhill across the trail. The fog wasn't so thick that it forced the riders to stop, but it occasionally reduced their forward view to a few dozen paces.

Encountering a troll was unlikely this time of year because, in the summer, the trail crews would have encouraged any females in the area to move on during the trolls' search for new territory. But trolls weren't the only danger. Sulana made sure her sword was loose enough in the scabbard to draw quickly.

After about an hour of riding, the party reached a former avalanche path that had stripped the hillside of trees. It was one of the places where they had to proceed with caution, particularly with Daven and Karla riding double. The trail was mostly bare rock, and the weather could make it slippery.

As Stardust cleared the trees and clopped out into the open, a horse nickered from the trees across the clearing, followed by a muted curse.

Sulana reined in and stopped. She tried to see who might be approaching down the trail, but the fog obscured her view. All she saw were the tree trunks at the edge of the forest and dark shadow behind them.

She motioned low with her hand telling Daven to retreat. She pulled back on her reins and whispered, "Back up," to Stardust. The horse seemed to sense her tension and slowly stepped back into the protection of the trees.

Karla's eyes were wide and she was trembling, her arms wrapped tightly around Daven. His expression was one of desperation. There was no way he could fight with the frightened healer clinging to his back.

Sulana brought Stardust directly alongside Daven's horse. "Did you hear that?" she whispered.

Daven nodded. "Perfect place for an ambush," he whispered back.

It sure was. They would be out in the open while their opposition could shoot at them from the safety of the trees. However, it might just be an Archives crew clearing fall blowdown off the trail.

"Let's wait for a few minutes and see who it is," Sulana suggested. Daven nodded.

A couple of minutes went by and they heard nothing else. Sulana's sense of unease grew. "Get ready for trouble."

Daven turned in his saddle and met Karla's eyes. "We need to get down." She shook her head vigorously and gripped him more tightly.

Daven pulled at her fingers and forced her to release him. Holding her left wrist, he bumped her off the back of the horse with his right elbow, eliciting a squeak of protest, and he guided her gently to the ground. She pouted and rubbed her wrist while he climbed down to stand next to her.

"I'm going to get my bow. Then I want you to take the horse back toward the valley, and find a place to hide where you can still see the trail. Try to keep the horse calm so he doesn't make any noise. I'll come get you once we know it's safe. If you see anyone else go by, stay hidden."

Tears pooled in Karla's eyes. "I can't leave you here. What if you get hurt? I can't help you if I'm hiding. Besides, I'm not good with horses."

"You can help me after we get this sorted out. For now, I need to know that you're safe."

At first, Karla refused to get up into the saddle and Daven's pleas grew increasingly desperate.

Sulana decided to intervene. "We're running out of time, Karla. If you stay here, you'll get us all killed."

Her blunt comment seemed to get through to the healer. Karla reluctantly let Daven help her into the saddle. Daven retrieved his bow and quiver before grabbing the reins and pointing the horse back the way they came. He gave the horse's rear a gentle push and started it walking. Karla looked back over her shoulder at them with a bleak expression.

Sulana and Daven watched her go until she faded into the fog.

Daven strung his bow and nocked an arrow. "Any idea how many we're dealing with?"

She shook her head. "Let's see if a different angle gives us a better view. You go down the hill fifty paces or so and I'll go up. We'll meet back here and compare notes."

Daven nodded once and started picking his way through the trees, staying well back from the edge of the forest.

Sulana led Stardust back down the trail a short distance and found a spot where she could tether the horse. Then she followed Daven's example and threaded her way through the trees to a spot that overlooked the area where the trail crossed the avalanche path.

Across the gap, trees loomed behind a border of shrubs. Where the fog thinned, shadows would obscure anyone who might be waiting. The fog also dampened sound, so the forest seemed extra quiet. It was so quiet that Sulana couldn't tell if she was really hearing whispered voices across the way or if it was her mind playing tricks on her.

When two black-clad figures started picking their way across the gap much lower down on the hillside, she knew it wasn't her imagination. This was a Lightning Corps ambush, and the bastards were trying to flank them.

She needed to warn Daven, but she had no way to do so without giving away her own position.

She needn't have worried. Daven had seen them as well. One of the figures cried out in pain and fell over, rolling down the hill a few feet before coming to rest against a boulder. The second figure made a run for the forest edge as a retaliatory arrow sailed across the gap toward Daven. The incoming arrow must have distracted Daven because the second man made it across.

A moment later, a second arrow sailed across the gap, thrumming into the tree right next to her. She moved further back into the trees and activated her shield ring. It wasn't much protection against a sword in hand-to-hand combat, but it would certainly deflect arrows.

She reached for the lightning dagger she often carried, and cursed under her breath when she realized she hadn't put it on this morning. It was still in her saddle bag with Stardust.

Down the hillside, the clang of swords told her that Daven had engaged the enemy. The noise acted like some kind of signal for the others, as two more black-clad figures darted across the opening on the trail. Sulana headed back down through the trees to intercept them, wondering how many more waited on the other side.

The answer came in part when two more figures started across the gap from a position opposite hers. The first one had a bow ready. He fired as soon as he spotted her. She angled her shield ring toward him, and the arrow deflected harmlessly, clattering onto the rocks. The man threw his bow aside and drew his sword as he continued toward her.

Sulana stepped backward and was reaching for her own sword when her boot landed in a puddle of rainwater. Looking down, the bowl-like shape of the puddle caught her attention and gave her an idea.

Glancing toward the approaching swordsmen, she scanned the forest between her and them. She knew intuitively that she couldn't make the trees move fast enough to entangle the men. She also knew from her experience on the refuge that weaving the shrubs along the edge of the gap would take too long. She needed something … supple.

A sudden sense of urgency made her act without thinking. Sulana dropped to one knee and cupped her hands under the water. She asked the spirits for help and found her eyes drawn to a thin rope-like vine snaking up the trunk of a nearby pine. Honeysuckle. Perfect.

She concentrated on the honeysuckle stem as the attackers approached. With fluid grace, it unwound from the tree starting at the top and coiled near the base of the trunk.

The first swordsman came toward her in a crouch and grinned when he saw she was just kneeling there with her hands in the puddle.

"You picked a bad time for a drink, missy."

As he stepped next to the pine, the honeysuckle vine sprang across his chest and started winding around his torso. He shouted in alarm and raised his sword to chop at the vine. The end of the plant whirled around his arm and his sword fell to the ground.

The second man saw what was happening and ran around his partner straight toward Sulana. He obviously knew that the best way to fight against a spell was to take out the caster.

Sulana dropped the water and drew her sword, hoping her wet hand wouldn't affect her grip too badly.

Fortunately, the first man was still immobilized by the honeysuckle vine, which had gone dormant again. He twisted in the grip of the vine furiously, but was out of the fight for the moment.

The second man advanced with a determined but cautious look. He slashed at her as soon as he was within range. She easily deflected the strike and forced him back a step with two quick slashes of her own.

The caution in the man's eyes turned to respect. "It appears that the druids have healed you, Sword Sorceress. This fight will be more interesting than I expected."

"That's too bad," she rejoined. "*Interesting* probably won't work in your favor."

"We'll see."

He came at her with a series of attacks that demonstrated he was more experienced than the average swordsman. But the respect in his eyes became tinged with fear as the fight progressed. The little cuts she inflicted on him forced him to realize that he wasn't quite good *enough*.

From the trail below, a gurgling scream followed by the clang of steel told Sulana that Daven was still holding his own against the other two fighters who had crossed the gap.

She realized with a rush of guilt that she should be down there helping him. The man she fought was good, but she could have, and should have, ended the fight before then. This was no time to be testing her skills.

Her opponent's face had evolved into a mask of anger and desperation. He swiped at the sweat above his eyes and then lunged toward her when he saw the opening she deliberately gave him.

Sulana had activated her shield ring. She let the ring deflect his thrust while she raised her sword for a counter-strike. When his arm was fully extended, her blade took it off just above the elbow.

The swordsman collapsed to the ground writhing and screaming. He grabbed the stump of his arm in agony as his lifeblood streamed through his fingers. He fell back on his side and glared up at Sulana, who looked down at him with a mix of regret and pity.

The man's partner, who was slowly extricating himself from the vine, roared in anger and redoubled his efforts. He had managed to free his arm and was tearing at the remaining loops around his chest.

The dying man cursed her through gritted teeth, spittle spraying forth with every word. "The others will make you pay for this, sorceress."

"Maybe. But this was your doing. If you pick a fight, you'd better be prepared to lose."

The man screamed one more time before he lost consciousness and fell silent.

The swordsman who had been caught in the honeysuckle was nearly free when Sulana approached him. He went for his sword, but she stomped on the blade just as his fingers closed around the grip, knocking it from his grasp. As he straightened slowly to face her, she slammed the pommel of her sword into the base of his neck. He went limp, swaying in the inert vine that still encircled his waist.

Daven's duel on the trail continued, so she jogged down the hill to help him as fast as she could on the wet, slippery ground.

Near the bottom, she slid on a patch of wet leaves and sailed over the short berm that bordered the trail, her arms windmilling. She landed in a crouch just a few feet behind Daven, who had angled himself so he could see who was coming.

He blocked a slash from his opponent and said, "Thanks for joining me."

"Sorry. A couple more came across above."

The man fighting Daven glanced at Sulana and then did a double take. He parried Daven's next blow and then yelled over his shoulder.

"We found the Sword Sorceress! Get over here."

Daven growled and rained a series of angry blows on the man, who deflected the clumsy strikes easily.

"Talon would kick you in the butt if he saw you fighting like that," Sulana chided.

"Sorry. This guy is really getting on my nerves."

But all the hammering had taken its toll on the Lightning Corps man. When Daven's next strike came in, it wasn't clumsy at all. The end of Daven's blade slapped the other man's fingers, which reflexively opened. His blade clattered to the ground.

The man held his injured hand close to his chest in pain as he looked down at his sword. Then he turned and ran.

When the fleeing swordsman got about half way to the other side, two bowman appeared. They shot arrows at Sulana and Daven, just missing their cohort who yelled and crossed his arms over his face as the arrows streaked past him.

As soon as she saw the bowmen, Sulana ran forward and side-stepped in front of Daven with her fist held straight out. One of the arrows shattered when it hit her shield. The other arrow deflected straight down into the ground between Sulana's boots.

That was close. The shield was draining her vaetra and becoming less effective. *I can't keep this up forever.*

Sulana ran for the cover of the trees on the left and Daven went to the right, snatching up his bow and quiver as he passed.

Spirits! How many more of them are there?

From her position in the trees, Sulana saw at least four more soldiers on the other side, gathering to rush them. This time, she doubted she and Daven would prevail. She glanced across at Daven, who lowered his head and shook it when he saw what was coming. She was running out of tricks, and he was exhausted.

She readied herself for the inevitable attack when one of the black-clad bowmen stiffened and fell backward to the ground. The men standing next to him looked down in confusion before a shout from behind drew them all back into the shadows.

CHAPTER 33

REUNION

Barek had a second man down before the enemy realized they were being attacked from behind.

Meanwhile, my second arrow took the second bowman in the arm. I shrugged as I set the bow aside and drew my sword. *Close enough. That's why we leave the bow work to Daven.*

I brought my sword up just in time to parry an overhead blow from an enraged Lightning Corps swordsman. The man was poorly trained and managed two more frantic swings before I cut under his guard and left him moaning on the ground.

The last Lightning Corps man had the telltale silver stripe around his overcoat sleeves. His outstretched hand held an orb, and it was directed at Barek. He was chanting an incantation. I started running toward him.

Barek stepped over the body of the man he had just defeated and walked purposefully toward the enemy sorcerer. He was intercepted about half-way by the bowman I'd failed to drop. With an arrow still half-way through his arm, the man was panting and sweating from the pain, but he had managed to draw his sword and close with Barek.

Having to deal with the bowman slowed Barek and gave the sorcerer the time he needed to finish his spell. I was still several yards away when lightning flashed from his orb and cracked the air toward my friend.

I figured Barek was about to become fried Winterman, but miraculously, the lightning missed him and struck a tree, which instantly split in two. The two halves creaked apart until the upper branches got hung up in the other trees nearby.

As soon as the lightning strike left his orb, the sorcerer muttered another incantation and turned toward me. He didn't seem to realize that his strike had missed.

I swung my sword in a lazy arc forward until the blade met the resistance of his shield. I slashed the shield a couple of times just to watch him flinch.

I smirked at him and struck the shield a few more times. Every strike drained his vaetra a little bit more. "You can't hold that shield up forever, and while you are holding it, you can't cast anything else. You might as well surrender now before you start to annoy me."

What I said was true, but as Barek was sneaking up quietly behind him, my banter was more about distraction than mockery. Shields were almost always directional, and as long as he had to shield himself from me, he couldn't turn it toward Barek.

When Barek was close, I looked over the sorcerer's shoulder and smiled. The sorcerer froze, probably thinking I was trying to trick him, but not completely sure. Barek slapped the flat of his blade against the side of the man's head. His eyes rolled up and he folded to the ground.

"He was already annoying me," Barek commented, poking at the sorcerer with his boot.

"One of these days, you're going to have to explain how these spells keep missing you."

Barek met my eyes over the body of the unconscious sorcerer, but didn't respond.

I looked around us at the bodies littering the ground, marveling at the advantage a rear attack with surprise can give you. It was a rather nice change of pace to be the ambusher rather than the ambushee. The two of us had taken out seven Lightning Corps agents without a scratch. On top of that, we finally had three prisoners who might be able to give us some badly needed information about troop numbers and placement.

But first, I had to find out if that idiot who ran back from the other side knew what he was talking about when he yelled that the Sword Sorceress was there.

Barek kept an eye on the sorcerer and the two other men who were still alive while I went to the edge of the clearing. Careful to stay back in the trees, I squinted through the mist, but faint silhouettes against a shadowy backdrop was all I could see.

"Jaylan?"

Sulana's voice carried to me from the other side.

"Jaylan!" she cried, and then she was running across the clearing toward me.

I started running too and met her part way. She practically leapt into my arms, wrapping her arms and her legs around me in a full-body embrace.

She sobbed her relief into my shoulder just once before turning her face to mine and kissing me hard. The misty rain rolled down our faces, mixing with our tears. We ignored everything but each other.

After the kiss ended, I stared into her eyes, drinking in the details that I'd missed so badly. "Well met, Sword Sorceress," I said with a happy smile.

Daven appeared at the edge of the forest and I set Sulana back down on her feet.

"I'm going to find Karla," he called. Sulana waved an acknowledgment.

"Karla's with you?"

"It's a long story. I have so much to tell you, but right now I need to get Stardust."

Daven and Karla rode up right after Sulana and I rejoined Barek. Barek had found enough straps and rope to tie up the prisoners. When Sulana told him about the swordsman caught in the honeysuckle, he left to retrieve that man as well, but came back empty handed.

We kept our eyes open for the missing man in case he tried to free his cohorts, but by the time we were ready to leave for the Archives, we concluded that he was long gone. On the way back, Sulana and I didn't speak much because we had to keep a close eye on the prisoners and we didn't want them to overhear us. Catching up could wait until we were safely home.

We made quite a scene when we arrived at the Archives with three prisoners and a long string of horses. Two guardians took the prisoners off our hands and the stable master was ecstatic when we told him the horses were prizes of war.

It was the first time I had ever returned to the castle in triumph, and it was a moment to savor. Even more important, Sulana seemed to be in good spirits and her account of the ambush made it clear her fighting skills were back to normal, thanks to Karla.

She left me with a mystery though. She was sketchy on details about what happened with the swordsman and the honeysuckle. When I asked her about it, she said she'd explain later in private.

CHAPTER 34

PARASITE

Senior Councilor Gregor Rissik considered the two people seated across the desk from him. Ebnik was fidgety and kept looking away, which was unusual for him. Junior Councilor Maris Torlon was staring at her notebook and frowning like she had just received bad news. Both were here for the weekly report on Jaylan's progress with the Runedream.

"What is going on with you two? Did something bad happen? The last I heard, Jaylan's sessions were going well."

Ebnik and Maris exchanged an unreadable glance.

"They have been going well, but there's been an unusual development," Maris hedged.

Gregor's eyebrows went up. "That sounds promising. What's the development?"

"The last time Jaylan entered the Runedream, Tritia was not the only spirit who came to meet him."

"So there *are* others. We expected that to be the case."

Maris fiddled with the edge of the notebook. "Yes. Well … four others, to be exact."

Gregor didn't see the significance. What did it matter whether Jaylan met with five or fifty spirits within the Runedream? Shrugging, Gregor said, "Fine. So we have five entities now. Were they as helpful as the first one?"

Ebnik narrowed his eyes at Gregor and grew still. "I know you think all of this Runedream stuff may be the product of Jaylan's imagination, but I've sat in on the sessions. I've tested him myself. We've known each other a long time, Gregor. If you can't trust Jaylan, try to trust me."

Gregor raised a hand in apology. "Of course, Ebnik. If you say the Runedream is real, I'm willing to stipulate it's as good an explanation as any for what's going on. As for whether or not spirits inhabit this hidden realm, we can leave the theology to the druids and focus on the practical aspects of what Jaylan reports."

Maris shook her head slowly. "That may not be possible in the long run."

Gregor frowned at Maris. All this secrecy was becoming tedious. He snapped, "Out with it, Councilor. Why are you both being so mysterious?"

Maris took a deep breath and then spoke in a rush. "The spirits gathered as a group to give Jaylan a warning. The names they gave him were Loralai, Arial, Umbria, and Putra."

The four other greater spirits of druid legend. So the name of the first entity, Tritia, had not been just a coincidence.

The idea of *the* five spirit goddesses speaking to Jaylan through visions was so ludicrous that Gregor nearly burst out laughing. Respect for his friends was the only thing that held back his mirth. He masked his involuntary chuckle as a cough and then cleared his throat.

Ebnik caught the underlying reaction and sat back in his chair with his arms folded and a disappointed frown on his face.

Maris glanced at Ebnik and then back to Gregor. She slumped in her chair and sighed. "You still don't believe us."

"Oh, no. I believe Jaylan reported accurately to you. I also believe Jaylan is suffering from some kind of psychosis and that he is mixing legend with reality."

He leaned forward, putting his arms on his desk. "If you are asking me to believe that Jaylan is talking to *the* spirit goddesses, I'll need more than the word of an overwrought young man."

Ebnik nodded. "Fair enough. All talk of spirits and goddesses aside, we need your help."

Hoping to mollify his friend, Gregor spread his hands and said, "Certainly. What can I do?"

"Two things, really. First, your reaction was a good example of what might happen if word gets out about Jaylan's latest visit to the Runedream. Others will treat him as either a prophet or a pariah. We'd like to keep the goddess vision secret for now."

Gregor nodded his acceptance. "No problem. I'll be happy to let *you* try to explain it, when the time comes."

"The second thing relates to the warning Maris mentioned. It's a bit of a puzzle, and you are the only other person we can talk to about it right now."

Gregor braced himself. No doubt this puzzle would be more vague spirit drivel. But he'd try to give it a fair listen for Ebnik's sake.

Ebnik cleared his throat and continued. "The *entities*, as you call them, told Jaylan that their existence was threatened by something they called *the parasite*. They said that our kind placed the parasite on *the Great Basin* long ago, and that someone is going to reawaken it. Jaylan has to stop that from happening. Do any of those terms mean anything to you."

At first, the warning sounded exactly like the kind of nonsense Gregor expected. He made a show of giving it some thought. To his surprise, something about the warning caught his attention and he let himself fully explore the words.

The hair on the back of his neck stood up when he realized that it wasn't the individual terms that had caught his attention; it was the relationship between them. His eyes widened and he straightened in his chair.

Ebnik sat forward, looking intently into Gregor's eyes. "What is it? Does the message mean something to you?"

Coming from Ebnik, the question was a little annoying.

"Of course it does. It should mean something to you as well. Think, old man. Forget about spirits and goddesses. Forget about the words themselves and think about what they mean."

Ebnik sat still in thought for a moment, but when he didn't respond fast enough, Gregor continued.

"A long time ago, something was placed on the largest basin we know about. Something that is capable of draining a tremendous amount of vaetra. Almost like some kind of vaetric parasite."

Ebnik's face cleared. "You're talking about Rollek's Amplifier."

"Yes."

"But the amplifier is at the palace, and it's not in working condition. Besides, no one knows about it."

"Jaylan obviously knows about it."

Maris interrupted with a defensive tone. "Jaylan didn't know what the words meant. He was just as frustrated by the message as we were."

Gregor considered Maris's reaction. It wasn't the first time she had come to Jaylan's defense. He wondered if she was objective enough to continue sitting in on Jaylan's sessions. He shoved the concern aside. As long as she continued to report accurately, her feelings for the man didn't really matter.

Ebnik had been pondering in silence for a moment. When he spoke, it was in a musing tone. "Our investigation at the palace was about three years ago now. When we came back, we gave the Council a full report and sent a summary briefing to the sanctuaries. As I recall, it didn't stir up much interest at the time. It even slipped *my* mind, and I was the one who found the thing."

Gregor shrugged. "The amplifier was an academic curiosity. It wasn't functional, and the emperor gave us just that one opportunity to study it."

Maris said, "If we take the warning at face value, *someone* must have been interested. Someone who plans to use it."

Ebnik got out of his chair and started pacing. "I don't like where this is going. The device could only be operated by a sorcerer. You'd need a talented smith to repair it and you'd have to create a new spell core for it." He glanced over at Gregor with a raised eyebrow. "As I recall, the core we found was broken?"

Gregor nodded. "That's right. We analyzed it enough to learn that it was the original shield core that Rollek used to protect his keep. But I don't think it was salvageable."

"Where is the core now?" Ebnik asked.

"In the armory along with the Rollek's original notes."

Ebnik stopped pacing and frowned. "I think we should take a closer look at this. Would you be willing to find your notes from our trip and retrieve the amplifier artifacts from the armory?" Gregor gave him a nod. "I'll go get my notes and meet you in the library."

Ebnik held out a hand to help Maris up from her chair, and the two of them left Gregor's office.

Gregor went to a wall cabinet and rummaged for the information Ebnik had requested. When he found the right book of notes, he stopped and thought about the conversation they'd just had.

How had Jaylan known about the amplifier? Was it really possible that he was some kind of prophet? He hoped not, for Jaylan's sake. No one deserved that label and the trouble that came with it.

Still musing over what might really be happening in Jaylan's troubled mind and how much credence he should give this "warning" of the spirits, Gregor left his office and went down four levels to the armory. He checked in with the guard and opened the sealed armory door.

Rollek's Amplifier had been a remarkable discovery, and Gregor looked forward to inspecting the ancient items once again.

He knew roughly where he had placed the artifacts. Moving down one of the narrow aisles between the tall shelf units, his eyes scanned the shelves. Most of the armory's objects were stored in small wooden chests or had been tucked under a square of black cloth. As an artifact historian, he had studied many of the articles in this room.

Gregor stopped and kneeled when he reached the shelf he was searching for. Like nearly everything else in this room, the black cloth that protected the items was coated with a thin layer of dust. He carefully pulled out the bottom edges of the cloth and drew the corners together to trap the dust in the folds.

What was revealed when he lifted the cloth was not what he expected. A short section of a branch and a square block of bark sat in place of Rollek's notebook and the amplifier core.

It seemed that someone had secretly taken an interest in the amplifier after all.

Chapter 35

SPIRIT SORCERY

Sulana and I watched the swallows dip and soar over Castle Tarn as the sun went behind the peaks across from us. It would still be another hour or so before full dark. We stood at the water's edge, each with one arm hugging the other close for warmth. For the moment, we were above the clouds and rain that had settled into the valley.

I kissed the top of her head and said, "It's so nice to have you back. I'm glad to see you happy and relaxed again."

"I've never been so happy to *be* home."

The past couple of days had been filled with Archives business and friends welcoming Sulana back to the castle. The only chance we'd had to be alone before this was during dinner the previous evening. We'd both looked at each other over the table and said, "I need to talk to you about something," at the same time. After laughing over the coincidence, we agreed that the dining hall was not the place to share our secrets.

"So, do you want to go first, or do you want me to?" I asked.

"You go first. I'm really curious about your big secret."

So I filled her in on everything that had happened with the Runedream while we were apart. She knew some of it from our messages, but since we finally had privacy, I was able to give her the full story. She listened attentively and asked several questions along the way.

When I got to the most recent session, I hesitated. What would she think about me talking to spirit goddesses? I plunged ahead and gave her all the details, including

Councilor Rissik's interpretation of the warning and the latest news about the missing amplifier artifacts.

When I finished, she stood next to me looking at the lake in the fading light with a puzzled expression. I'm not sure what kind of reaction I expected. Maybe that she would tease me or be alarmed, but not this.

"Well, what do you think?"

"The spirits want us to work together," she mused, her eyes still roaming over the lake.

"What do you mean?"

She looked up at me and seemed to reach some conclusion. "I should probably just show you." She stepped down to the water's edge and kneeled. I followed and stood just behind her to see what she was up to.

She cupped her hands around some lake water and stood up. The water in her hands reflected dusk's dark purple sky.

At first I thought she was chanting an incantation, but the sounds weren't runespeech. She was asking the spirits to give her light. It sounded almost like a prayer.

Had Sulana spent too much time with the druids? I'd be disappointed if she had started worshiping the spirits while we were apart. We'd been over the subject of spirituality versus religion and agreed that worship was unnecessary.

To my amazement, a tiny sphere of light lifted from the surface of the water and grew to a bubble the size of her head. It floated above us for a moment and then winked out of existence when she tossed the water back into the lake.

She wiped her hands on her jacket and mumbled something about needing to get herself "one of those bowls."

I took a step forward and hugged her close. "Holy spirits, Sulana. You can *cast!*"

When she didn't respond, I held her back from me by her shoulders. "Aren't you happy?"

She shrugged under my hands. "Of course I'm happy. But it isn't exactly casting."

"What was it then? It sure looked like casting."

She looked through me with a considering expression and pursed lips. "I'm beginning to see why the druids try to distance themselves from sorcery."

She wasn't making any sense to me, but I was so excited about her new casting ability, or whatever it was, that I didn't care.

"Did Karla heal something that was preventing you from casting?"

"Karla didn't do it. The spirits did."

And then she went into detail about what happened to her on the refuge. She told me about how the spirits helped her fix her resistance and how they had helped her cast light the first time.

"And it's called *offering a blessing*, not *casting a spell*," she corrected.

She *was* starting to sound like a druid. "What's the difference?"

"No incantation. I can't offer blessings without the help of the spirits. They've been remarkably cooperative so far, but Defender Marshal Shields warned me that they won't just do whatever you ask. That's why the druids are so dedicated to the spirits: they can't work vaetra without them."

A shocking realization hit me. "You could have been a priestess. In fact, you still could."

Sulana stood next to me and put her arm around me again. "I considered that idea, but Nigel assured me that I would know if that were the path I was supposed to travel. He's convinced that it isn't."

"Nigel?"

"Sorry, Marshal Shields. We got to be on a first name basis when he helped me escape from the refuge and taught me about the nature of this new gift."

"Should I be worried?"

She pinched me. "Don't be silly. He's definitely not my type."

"Too old?"

"No, too druid."

"Ah." Her assurance made me feel better on multiple levels. The spirits needed our help, but they didn't need us to worship them. I could go along with that.

"I wish they would just come out with it and tell us what they want," I said.

"I think they have. The Defender Marshal of the Northern Region helped a sorceress hide on his refuge and then helped her learn how to offer blessings. Do you have any idea how remarkable that is? He said the spirits guided him to help us—*both* of us—fight against Thunderhead College."

"That is surprising," I agreed. "The Council should be thrilled to have druid support, although I'm not entirely sure they will be."

"But they don't have druid support. *You and I* have the support of a single druid Marshal. The druid Hierarchy is just as entrenched in their thinking as the Council is in theirs. The Hierarchy still sees sorcery as blasphemy and the Council still sees the priesthood as a bunch of charlatans."

"So it's all up to us?"

"I think it might be. We have help, but it's all rather low profile."

"What sense does that make? If the spirits want to fight Thunderhead College, why don't they mobilize the druids and gather the mundane resistance to help us?"

"Think about what that would mean. A war. A bloody, violent war. And *all* sorcerers would be the enemy."

She was right. We couldn't let it come to that.

I shook my head. "We can't do this alone, Sulana."

She gave me a squeeze. "We aren't alone. Dumont Fortenz may have the advantage now, but he has been making enemies along the way. We can get help from the marshal, the mundane resistance, and probably the Wintermen."

"It sounds like you've made some plans."

"Nothing specific yet, and we must be careful who we confide in. We still haven't identified Dumont's spy on the Council."

"My money's on Asher."

"Mine too, although no one has been able to prove anything."

"It's only a matter of time," I said. "She'll slip up eventually."

"In the meantime, let's keep what I just showed you to ourselves. It's enough for the Council to know that I'm back to my former self."

I chuckled. "You don't want to be known as the Priestess of the Archives?"

She answered me with a poke in the ribs.

Full darkness had fallen, and the waxing half moon rode high in the sky. Fortunately, it gave us enough light to follow the path back to the castle.

I took her arm in mine and couldn't resist teasing her. "Your light bubbles are pretty, but not very sorcerer-like. If we used one of those to get back to the castle, people would talk."

She squeezed my arm. "Yes, they would. We'll just have to walk in the moonlight."

I stopped and waited until she looked up at me, then I bent down and kissed her. "That sounds nice."

She put her head on my chest and hugged me. "So it is."

CHAPTER 36
AUTHORITY REVOKED

It was the first time the Council had called a full convocation of sorcerers since I had lived at the Archives. According to Sulana, the last one had been more than a year ago for her confirmation ceremony.

Some speculated that it was my turn to be confirmed, but Sulana assured me that confirmation wasn't something the Council would spring on me; they would have notified me first and instructed me on the proper protocol.

When information is lacking, people fill in the gap with stories. Rather than wait patiently to find out the truth, they prefer to argue about fictional possibilities.

Thus, Council Hall was abuzz with whispered speculation when Sulana and I took our seats at one of the many wooden benches that filled the hall. Heads turned our way, and we returned the nods of those who chose to acknowledge us.

The Council Seat was empty, but we were several minutes early. Ebnik entered the hall and we shifted over to give him room at the end of our bench.

I leaned past Sulana and asked Ebnik, "Have you heard anything about this?"

"No. The Council has been in session since yesterday afternoon when the imperial messenger arrived. The only breaks they've had were for meals and to relieve themselves. They've spoken to no one, as far as I know."

According to the large suntracker at the back of the room, it was exactly midday when the Council Chamber opened and all five councilors stepped up to their seats. Guards pushed the heavy main doors closed and the room began to quiet.

The faces of the councilors revealed nothing encouraging. They all had the rumpled and glassy-eyed look of exhaustion, and none of them looked out into the crowd.

When they were all seated, Senior Councilor Underwood slammed a wooden gavel three times and shouted for silence. Most conversation ceased immediately, and the few who dared to continue whispering went quiet when the councilor's glare fell upon them.

Underwood announced, "Yesterday, the Council received a message from Emperor Tanes. He regrets to inform us that our imperial charter for enforcing the Sorcery Accords has been revoked."

The audience burst into exclamations of disbelief. Councilor Underwood gave everyone a moment to process his announcement and then banged the gavel again. When the room quieted, he went on. "Effective immediately, enforcement *and interpretation* of the Accords will be the responsibility of Thunderhead College."

Shouts of, "Impossible!" and, "Outrageous!" filled the room. I looked around and noticed that even the sorcerers who professed Integrationist ideals looked shocked and uncertain.

Sulana's alarmed eyes met mine, but we didn't bother trying to speak above the din. We both went back to surveying the reactions around us.

Once again, the senior councilor waited until the shouts had died down on their own before he called for order. He had to know how hard it would be for his people to process this news. His grim face hinted that there was more to come.

"We also have reports that at least three sanctuaries are now under Thunderhead College control. The sorcerers who objected were arrested and are being offered in trade for the Lightning Corps bandits who attacked our Sword Sorceress."

Bandits. That's an interesting choice of words.

The councilor paused and cleared his throat. He looked up from his notes and out over the crowd for the first time. His eyes held sympathy and disappointment.

"What does this mean for us?" shouted a man from behind me.

The room went utterly silent, waiting for the answer to that question. The Council must have spent those hours in chamber deciding *something*. Most of the money that flowed into the Archives came from the sanctuary network, and the network was the Archives' communication link to the rest of the empire. Without the network, the Archives was isolated. Adrift. The journey room would become useless.

The councilors' faces revealed little of what they had decided. Maris closed her eyes, and a tear rolled down each cheek. Councilor Rissik's expression was stony and resolute. Councilor Underwood looked like he was about to give a stern lecture. Maybe he was. Asher was agitated and seemed almost frightened. Since things had turned in the favor of Thunderhead College, she probably wished she was no longer in the lair of her enemies. Councilor Shepherd was as unreadable as ever, mostly staring at his hands and occasionally glancing up in response to a comment from the audience.

After several seconds of silence that seemed to stretch for hours, Councilor Underwood spoke again.

"It is the conclusion of the Council that the revocation of our charter was made against the emperor's wishes. We believe that Headmaster Dumont Fortenz has found a way to influence the governors in every province. Most likely, he is using the same mind control amulets that Sorcerer Thoron used in Sunset Province."

Gasps of shock erupted in the audience along with several exclamations of indignation and more than a few comments disparaging the character of Headmaster Fortenz.

"We therefore reject the imperial proclamation and charge Headmaster Fortenz and his followers with using sorcery to take control of the Imperial Assembly in direct violation of the Accords."

Every sorcerer in the hall seemed to speak at once. Sulana looked at me and blinked a few times. I could barely hear her over the din. "The Council just declared war on the empire as well as Thunderhead College."

I nodded my understanding. It was nice to have the full support of the Council, but they had just positioned us all as outlaws.

Councilor Underwood's gavel slammed for order again and the crowd slowly quieted.

"We understand that our decision may lead to violent confrontations with the Lightning Corps, and potentially, imperial troops. Anyone who disagrees with us is welcome to leave the castle. If you do choose to leave, we recommend that you do so with haste, before word of our announcements here today gets out."

A small knot of the most vocal Integrationist sorcerers took the councilor's advice and rose to leave the hall. Their exit was tracked by several angry looks and a few comments along the lines of "traitors" and "good riddance." Councilor Asher watched their departure with dismay. Some of them were her closest friends.

After the guards closed the hall doors behind the departing sorcerers, Councilor Underwood continued.

"As we speak, Archives Guardians are securing and fortifying the castle. We recommend that everyone who remains at the Archives join the ongoing training sessions. Anyone who is knowledgeable in combat with arms or sorcery is encouraged to offer your assistance. We need all the expertise we can get."

The councilor paused to catch his breath. "We ask that everyone seriously consider the implications of what these announcements mean for our future. The Council welcomes your suggestions on ways to stop Thunderhead College and avoid what may become a war of sorcery, but we ask that you make an appointment through Weaponsmaster Destry. We will have more announcements soon, but that's all for now. Thank you."

The Council rose from their seats and returned to their private chamber. Several members of the audience stood and shouted questions at them, but to no avail. A glance around the room revealed a wide array of emotions, from anger, to fear, to dismay. Conversations started up around the hall and no one made an immediate move to leave.

Ebnik stood and looked down at us. "We need to talk," he said. "But not here."

Sulana and I both nodded and got up to follow him through the hall doors, which had been opened. Talon was standing at the exit and stepped into our path as we approached.

"Don't go too far. The Council wants to speak with you after they retire to get a few hours of rest. Be back here at sundown."

Sulana acknowledged his message with a nod and said, "It looks like we have our work cut out for us."

Talon didn't get a chance to say anything more because several people came up just then and started pummeling him with questions. We escaped the room while Talon fended off the desperate sorcerers whose lives had just been upended.

The three of us trudged silently to the Council guest chamber where Ebnik was staying. It was located on the Council level where we would not be disturbed.

I was closing the door behind us when long, hurried strides warned me of someone's approach. When I opened the door, Barek stood outside.

"May I join you?" he asked.

"Come in, Barek," Ebnik called out with a tired voice.

I closed the door behind the Winterman and sat next to Sulana on a plush couch. Set aside for visiting dignitaries, Ebnik's room was nicely appointed. Barek remained standing.

Sulana eyed Barek with a frown. "Do you know anything more about what's happening out there?"

Barek shook his head. "I do not. I may be able to find out numbers and positions of the Lightning Corps from my people, but no one warned me that this was coming."

"Numbers and positions would be helpful," I commented. "We can start with that."

"I'll see what I can do. It may take time."

Ebnik narrowed his eyes at the big man. "What's bothering you, Barek?"

Barek closed his eyes and took a deep breath before answering. "The empire's treaty with my people is clear on the subject of the Accords. The emperor must uphold the Accords, and we must help him do so. My people will not be fooled by this proclamation. The emperor is losing control of the empire to a sorcerer. That will not be tolerated."

Sulana nodded. "That's *good*. We can use their help to set things right."

Barek looked into Sulana's eyes and gave her a subtle shake of his head. "It's not good … for anyone who is a sorcerer."

"They know we've been fighting the headmaster for months now," Sulana protested.

Barek shrugged. "You are a faction competing with the headmaster. Sorcerers must not be allowed to rule, including sorcerers from the Archives."

"But we have no interest in ruling the empire. We are trying to return things to the way they were."

"I understand that, but my people may not. I must go to them and try to explain. I came here to tell you I am leaving for a while."

The rest of us sat quietly for a moment, looking at Barek. He watched each of us in turn, waiting for a reaction.

It occurred to me that the Winterman attitude toward sorcerers would be mirrored among the mundane and the druids. All sorcerers would be seen as a threat. After all, we had historical precedent. Even though sympathetic sorcerers had helped end the Wizard Wars, the mundane had never trusted them, which was why the Accords were created in the first place.

"Do you think they'll listen?" I asked. "Or will we have to fight Wintermen in addition to everyone else?"

"I will make them listen," Barek stated with determination. "But I cannot make them agree."

Ebnik nodded and sighed. "Do what you can, Barek. We appreciate your help, however it turns out."

Sulana folded her arms and crossed her legs, kicking her foot back and forth in agitation. "I won't have to face you on the battlefield, will I?"

Barek straightened to his full height and his face became a mask of indignation. "Never. I swore to protect you and the Archives. That is what I do now."

Sulana's foot stopped and her face softened. "I'm sorry, Barek. Please forgive me."

"There is nothing to forgive."

She nodded once in gratitude and smiled at him. "In case there's any doubt, you may feel free to fight sorcerers from Thunderhead College."

"Count on it," he answered with a grim smile.

I wanted to put reality on hold for a minute so I could catch up. Things were changing too fast, and Barek leaving made everything else we faced seem even more overwhelming.

I sighed and looked at Sulana. "Talon's busy here with overseeing the training program and castle security, so the team is down to just us and Daven."

Sulana shook her head and gave me a sad smile. "Nope. I just talked with Daven a little while ago. Karla wants to leave. She's uncomfortable here and wants to set up shop in Riverview. Daven is going with her. He seems to think he can do something to help organize the mundane resistance down there."

"You know, I'll bet he can. But that leaves us pretty short-handed."

"We'll see. Tonight's meeting with the Council should be interesting."

Barek left right after that, instructing us to pass along the news of his departure to Councilor Rissik in private. Rissik could decide how much to share with the rest of the Council. I wondered, and not for the first time, just how many secrets the Senior Councilor was privy to.

Ebnik, Sulana, and I spent the afternoon assembling all of the intelligence we had on Thunderhead College, comparing it to the resources we had available to us. Our situation didn't look promising.

CHAPTER 37

ALIBI

Deep in thought, Senior Councilor Gregor Rissik turned down the hall that would take him to his chamber. Another sanctuary had been lost, but the Archives still controlled nearly half of them. So far, the headmaster had not taken steps to officially appropriate them through imperial mandate. In some ways, it was worse knowing that he already had enough support for so many sanctuaries to be subverted from within.

A wet cough and a whimper drew Gregor's attention from his ruminations. *Is someone hurt?*

He stepped back from his office door and held perfectly still. Another whimper. It came from the partially open Council Library door at the end of the hall.

Gregor strode quickly to the library door and pushed it open all the way. It was a woman. She was lying on her side in a fetal position. Her blood pooled in the arc made by her twitching body.

Gregor ran to her and knelt at her side. It was Maris Torlon. Her breathing was ragged and shallow.

"Maris! What happened? Who did this to you?"

She opened her eyes, but had trouble focusing on him through the pain. "Shepherd. Headmaster's spy. Heard voices." It was all she was able to get out before her body clenched in a coughing spasm followed by another whimper of pain and a trickle of blood from her lips.

Gregor glanced around, looking for Councilor Shepherd, but they were alone. This had just happened. Had Maris stumbled upon Shepherd exchanging information with someone else?

Gregor started to rise. "I'll get help. Hold on, Maris."

She grabbed his arm, but her hand fell nervelessly to the floor as her strength failed her. "Wait," she breathed in a whisper. "He has a device."

"What device, Maris?"

But Maris was unable to answer as she clenched in pain and a fresh gush of blood pulsed from her body. Then, in a brief moment of lucidity, Maris looked up into his eyes. She took a deep breath, and with her last exhale, she croaked, "Talks to the headmaster."

Maris's eyes closed and she went limp. Gregor checked for a pulse at her neck, but she was gone.

He couldn't help Maris, but he might be able to catch Shepherd. He rose from her side and left the library, moving as quietly as possible and alert to every sound.

At least she had confirmed that the headmaster had a spy among them. Someone who was able to communicate with him directly from the Archives. That explained a lot. Outgoing messages had been screened for months with no sign of treachery. Yet still, the headmaster seemed to be prepared for every move they made.

Gregor passed his own room and listened at the door. Perhaps Shepherd lay in wait for him as well. But he heard nothing and moved on.

Recognizing the potential danger he was putting himself into, Gregor activated a shield amulet he wore under his shirt. He had taken to wearing it at all times since the fateful convocation of sorcerers. He reached into a pocket and fingered his casting orb as he progressed slowly down the hall.

At Councilor Velna Asher's door, he stopped again. Muffled voices leaked through. He moved his head closer to the threshold to see if he could make them out.

Asher's voice became clear first. "Why do you need me to lie for you? What have you done?"

Her Integrationist compatriot, Councilor Rikard Shepherd, replied in an urgent voice. "If someone asks, just say we were here talking."

"Okay, but you have to tell me what's going on. I need to know why I'm lying on your behalf," Asher insisted.

Silence.

Rikard continued. "I just found Maris Torlon in the library. She was dead. But if anyone knows I was there, they'll blame me. You know the rest of them are just looking for an excuse to kick us off the Council. Or worse."

"Maris? Who would hurt Maris? Are you sure she's dead? Maybe we should get help."

Rikard's voice took on a desperate edge. "Stop. You aren't listening. If we do anything, we'll get the blame."

"But we did nothing wrong."

Gregor had heard enough. Shepherd was trying to establish an alibi with Asher. Interestingly, she did not seem to know anything about Shepherd's spying activities. He rapped on the door a couple of times and eased it open without waiting for a response.

Velna stood with her hands tightly gripping her folded arms. Her face was white with agitation. "What are you doing here? No one gave you permission to enter."

Rikard had turned toward the door, and his suspicious eyes searched Gregor's face. Velna may not have noticed, but the dark spatter on the front of Rikard's robe drew Gregor's attention.

Rikard looked down at his own robe and his eyes narrowed. As he looked up again, he aimed a fist at Gregor, shouting a trigger word for the ring he wore on that hand.

The shield amulet drew from Gregor's strength when it absorbed Rikard's spell, but he had plenty to spare. Gregor tightened his grip on his orb. He would be vulnerable when he released the shield so he could cast, but the spell he had in mind was a quick one.

Rikard wasn't finished. He slipped a wand from a hidden sleeve pocket and pointed it at Gregor. "Your shield won't save you from *this*," he said with a sneer of contempt.

The contempt turned to shock when a heavy vase shattered on the back of his head. He toppled to the floor, his wand dropping from his hand. The wand flipped and bounced on its tip twice before coming to rest at Gregor's feet.

Councilor Asher held up the neck of the vase. She inspected the jagged edge where the vase body used to be. She threw the piece to the floor where it broke and added to the mess.

"I always hated that vase," she said, slapping the dust off her hands.

Gregor leaned down and picked up the wand, keeping his eye on Rikard and Velna. If his shield would have been useless against the wand, the device must have been enchanted with the shield-penetrating lightning that Jaylan had reported. Only Thunderhead College sorcerers had access to that spell.

Velna kicked at Rikard's unconscious form. "I don't think he's dead. You should probably get someone over here to take him into custody." She looked up at Gregor. "Did he really kill Maris?"

Gregor nodded. "I'm afraid so. He left her alive, but she didn't stay that way long."

"So he *was* lying to me."

"Yes. He's been lying to all of us for quite some time."

Velna had never been Gregor's friend. She opposed him on almost every point. But he had never faulted her intelligence. Her shrewd mind immediately made the necessary connections.

With wonder in her voice, she said, "Rikard was the headmaster's spy. Maris caught him at it somehow."

"That's what it looks like," Gregor affirmed. "If you don't mind getting a guardian, I'll keep an eye on Rikard."

Velna frowned at the unconscious sorcerer for a moment and then moved toward the door, skirting the vase shards.

As she came alongside him, Gregor spoke again. "And Velna, get help, but don't go too far."

She glared at him. "After I helped you, you still think I had something to do with this?"

"No, I believe you, and I'll testify on your behalf. But there *will* be an investigation, and Rikard may try to make things easier on himself by looking for ways to spread the guilt."

She glanced back at the prone form, working the muscles in her jaw. "I understand. And to think he was the only friend I had left." With that, she shivered, wrapped her arms around her torso, and left the room.

Gregor moved forward to stand over Rikard's body. Just to be sure, he cast a spell that immobilized the younger sorcerer before leaning down to search the man's clothing.

He felt the shape and weight of the object before he was able to find the hidden pocket that contained it. When he drew the item forth, he held a vaetric implement unlike any he'd ever seen. He had little doubt that this was the device Rikard used to speak with the headmaster. He transferred the device to his own pocket for later inspection.

Folding back a loose flap of cloak, Gregor exposed Rikard's sheathed dagger. He didn't need to draw it to see the thin red line of glistening blood where the blade met the handle. Maris's murderer had wiped the blade, probably on his victim's clothing, but he had been in too much of a hurry to do a thorough job.

Hurried footsteps approached. Gregor flipped the cloak back over the dagger and stood aside as two guardians entered. After he gave them a quick summary of what happened, they tied Rikard's hands behind his back and searched him, finding the incriminating dagger. Gregor released the spell that immobilized the still-unconscious man as the guardians raised him from the floor. They carried him out of the room by his arms, toe-tips dragging behind.

Finally able to return to his own chamber, Gregor started back down the hall.

Councilor Asher stood at the library door, looking in. Gregor softly walked over and stood next to her. They watched as a healer shook his head over Maris. The healer instructed the guardians to roll her onto a litter that had been placed alongside her body.

A sparkle at the edge of his vision caught his attention. Tears were rolling down Asher's cheeks. His face must have revealed his surprise when he turned to verify what he was seeing.

Asher frowned at him with a hurt expression. "Maris and I weren't friends and we fought a lot, but we worked together for a long time. She didn't deserve to die."

If it had been anyone else standing next to him, Gregor would have given her a hug or patted her arm. But their history was too contentious for a single shared tragedy to repair.

Instead, he simply turned to leave. As he walked away, he said in a sad voice, "No. She did not."

CHAPTER 38

INVITATION

Sulana and I enjoyed a sweeping view of Castle Tarn and the peaks that partially enclosed it. She shivered in my arms from the steady, cold breeze that whirled around the deck at the top of the castle tower. A few stubborn yellow leaves held on to silvery aspen branches, and the larch needles were beginning to turn orange. Birds, fewer in number every day, plucked at the last half-frozen huckleberries. A light, early snowfall dusted the ground and gathered in thin drifts around the tree trunks.

Sulana shivered again and pressed her back into my chest, snuggling for more warmth.

"You shouldn't dismiss the invitation out of hand, you know. It's quite an honor," she said.

"I gave it plenty of thought. But accepting the Council's offer to join them as a Junior Councilor is a short path to the asylum. I'm sure they only suggested it because they want 'the runemaster' to stay away from trouble."

"Do you think Lissy will accept?"

"Probably. I think she's had enough of field work, and Councilor Rissik has been pressuring her relentlessly. She's a good fit for the job."

"I think so too."

We were both silent for a moment. I suspected Sulana was thinking about the circumstances that led to my invitation, just as I was. Maris Torlon's death and Rikard Shepherd's treachery had been a blow to the morale of everyone who remained at the Archives. The headmaster's corruption had reached right into our haven and destroyed one of our most gentle spirits.

Confirming my suspicion, Sulana said, "I miss Councilor Torlon. She was always so quiet, but she stuck to her convictions."

I gave her a consoling squeeze. "I'll miss her too. I got to know her pretty well during our Runedream sessions. After you got past the initial shyness, she was funny and sweet. I counted her as one of my friends."

"I won't miss Shepherd, though. And I almost wish Asher had been implicated."

"Yeah, I guess we were wrong about Asher. I always figured Shepherd followed her lead, but he was apparently just using her as a distraction while he worked his own agenda."

"Speaking of agendas, we'd better get back down to Council Chamber. They are expecting your answer today."

She was right. Even huddled together, we were both starting to shiver, and my hands were becoming stiff and icy from the wind. I took one last look at the trees and the lake. The high clouds that obscured the sun muted all color with a gray tinge. Soon, multiple feet of snow would exaggerate the contrast and complete the landscape's transition to black and white.

We separated and hurried inside. The tower stairwell gave us some protection from the bite of the wind, but the constant draft that flowed down the stairs encouraged us to hurry toward the Archives proper. We shook off the remaining chill when we closed the door on the drafty tower and proceeded down a relatively warm hallway.

"When winter arrives, we'll be practically trapped here," I commented. "The journey room won't be worth much if we keep losing sanctuaries."

Sulana took my hand. "The only good thing to come from Councilor Torlon's death is that everyone wants to take action now, whether we are ready or not. The change in attitude may be partly a desire for revenge, but I'll take it."

"Councilor Rissik is certainly wasting no time. He scheduled a Runedream session with me today to see if we can learn anything about Shepherd's implements. Lissy is taking over Maris's duties as scribe."

Sulana pulled back on my hand and slowed us both to a stop. Her eyes met mine and her voice was serious. "Are you sure you don't want to accept that Council position and stay here where you can use the Runedream safely? You said yourself that you think you may be able to find a way to stop the headmaster."

I started shaking my head before she finished. "No way. The spirits have convinced me that both of us need to work together to defeat Thunderhead College."

Sulana let go of my hand and hugged me. "I'm glad to hear you say that, even if it may not always be practical."

"We'll make it work. Never mind the spirits—*I* can't stand the idea of us being separated again. The time you were with the druids was awful. Now that I have you back, I don't want to let you go again."

The truth of my words surprised even me. The idea of letting Sulana disappear on missions she might never return from was unbearable. The only time I was happy was when I was with her. My mind leaped to the next logical conclusion and I spoke without really thinking.

"We should get married."

"Okay," she said with a smile.

The implications of what we'd just said finally caught up with me. "Wait. What did we just decide?"

She raised an eyebrow. "We're engaged. But I want a ring."

I stared into her smiling blue eyes, a tingle of excitement coursing through me. I had just proposed. And she accepted. I grinned back at her.

"Sure, no problem."

CHAPTER 39

LIGHTNING WAND

We moved the Runedream session to Ebnik's quarters. So many people were attending that it would have been standing room only in my chamber. It was strange to be lying on the bed with everyone else sitting around as if this were some kind of social event. I felt like an observer at my own wake.

Sulana and Ebnik sat on a couch across the room from me. This was my first Runedream session since Sulana had returned, and she was curious about it. I assured her it was a boring process for everyone else, mostly sitting around waiting for me to wake up again, but she insisted that she wanted to be there.

Lissy sat in a chair next to the bed with Maris's notes. She skimmed through the notes of previous sessions and stopped when she got near the end of the leather folder.

"What's this about goddesses?" she asked.

I had forgotten that she was the only person in the room who didn't know the full truth about my last session.

Gregor stood next to Lissy and waved her on. "I'll tell you about that later. We need to get on with this."

Lissy narrowed her eyes at him and then shrugged. Finding a clean sheet of parchment, she started a new session diary using Maris's past work as a guide.

Gregor handed me the wand he had taken from Rikard Shepherd. To my untrained eye, it looked brand new or very well cared for.

He said, "I tested the wand and verified that it emits the Lightning Corps shield-breaking lightning. Shepherd claims that the headmaster himself invented the spell. We could take the wand apart and analyze the runes he used, but that kind of reverse-engineering would take a while and destroy the implement in the process. I'm hoping you can use the Runedream to figure out how it works so we can devise a way to defeat it."

I could see the doubt in his eyes. He didn't have much hope this would work, and I had no assurances to give him to the contrary.

"I've never tried to take anything into the Runedream with me. Most of what's there seems to manifest from my own experience and imagination. The wand may not be any more familiar to me in there than it is right here."

Gregor nodded and sighed. "I understand. Just do what you can."

I clutched the wand tightly and rested my fist on my chest. I opened a channel and started the incantation cycle that would bring on the Runedream. The creak of Gregor settling into a chair accompanied the soporific effect of the Runedream fog as my consciousness faded.

I opened the Runedream gateway and went into the tunnel beyond. As usual, the dancing lights flocked to me as soon as I stepped through. Was each light an individual spirit? Or were they something else? They never spoke coherently, but they seemed to understand me.

Remembering why I was there, I held up my hand and found that I still gripped the wand. I inspected it and was relieved that it appeared to be the same one Gregor gave me.

"I see you brought a toy," came a teasing voice from behind me.

I turned around to discover Arial floating and dipping in time to the slow movement of her huge dragonfly wings. She smiled at me and then her eyes dropped to the wand.

I bowed to her and said, "Greetings, Arial. I'm surprised to see you. I expected to find Tritia."

"The answers you seek relate to my domain, so Tritia asked for my help."

"Thank you."

"Thank her."

Of the spirits I met the last time I was here (I still wasn't comfortable thinking of them as goddesses), Arial seemed the most friendly. Nonetheless, I got the distinct impression she'd rather be somewhere else.

"You already know why I'm here?"

She shrugged a delicate shoulder. "More or less."

I held up the wand. "I need to know how this works."

"No, you don't."

Her response confused me. "I thought you were here to help. If I don't know how it works, I won't know how to defeat it."

"Ah, that's a different problem."

"What is?"

Her lips twisted into a chastising frown. "Defeating it."

I hung my head and sighed. *What is it about spirits? Can't any of them speak plainly?*

I tried a new approach. "What do you suggest?"

"Use your experience," she answered, as if that explained everything.

I looked at the wand. "But I've never cast this spell. We've been over that. I don't know how it works."

She let out a breath of exasperation. "What is it you wish to do?"

"Ultimately? Figure out a way to improve our shields so this spell can't cut through them."

She raised her arms and let them fall. "Finally, we are getting somewhere."

Arial was proving to be as annoying as Tritia. With Tritia, most of what she said only made sense in retrospect. Maybe the same was true with Arial. I thought back over our conversation. She seemed to be saying that I didn't need to know how the spell worked to defeat it. I needed to use my own experience.

I didn't have experience casting the spell, but I did have experience defending against it. I knew firsthand how poorly a normal shield resisted its effects. But how would *failing* to shield myself be helpful? Maybe I could try shielding myself in the Runedream and get a better feel for how the spell got through. That sounded like an unpleasant experience. I shrugged. *If that's what it takes …*

I took a step forward and held the wand out to Arial. "I think I understand. Here, you fire the spell at me and I'll shield against it."

Arial fluttered back, maintaining her distance. Her expression became decidedly cross. "No, you *don't* understand. Perhaps Loralai was right about you. I don't know how Tritia puts up with this."

"Why don't you just tell me what you want me to do?"

"I already did. Use your experience."

"Every time I've shielded myself against this spell, it has cut right through. I don't know how that experience could be helpful."

"Your memory is faulty. It's a wonder you can learn anything."

What was I forgetting? I had been attacked twice with the spell: once by the headmaster and once by the sorcerer at Northshore. The first time, Sulana had nearly been killed. The second time, I got lucky because the lightning hit my staff instead of me, and the staff directed it into the ground.

Wait a minute.

A shield deflected and fractured a normal lightning bolt. That form of protection failed against this new spell. But what if the shield acted more like my staff and *grounded out* the lightning instead?

Arial was watching me think through the problem. She flitted closer when she saw my eyes light up with the grounding idea.

"What are you thinking?" she asked.

"I'm thinking I need to figure out a way to ground our shields."

She squealed with glee and clapped her hands together. "Oh, this is so much more fun when you aren't an idiot."

I rolled my eyes. "Gee, thanks. Why didn't you just make that suggestion in the first place?"

She shrugged as if the idea had never occurred to her. "I'm a guide, not an instructor. Your answers must come from within."

Once I knew what I needed to do, I got to work on the problem. With the help of Arial's tiny spirit lights, I created a shield and kept altering it until I had it anchored into the ground.

Arial reviewed my work and declared that something was missing. She asked for the wand and discharged a low-powered bolt at my shield to demonstrate. The bolt went through and zapped me hard enough to knock me on my butt. Arial doubled over with laughter.

Point taken.

The shield was grounded, but the lightning still went through. What was the difference between my staff and the shield? My staff had a metal core. It was conductive. Could I make the shield conductive?

By the time I finished tweaking the shield to my satisfaction, I was exhausted.

Arial didn't look much better. She no longer floated and her wings drooped listlessly on her back. Her body was becoming transparent. She fired the wand one more time, and both of us sighed in relief as the lightning spread across the shield and flowed into the ground.

She held the wand out to me. "Nice job, Runemaster. Tritia will be proud."

On a whim, I reached out and took her slim hand in mine. I opened a channel to her and gave her most of the vaetra I had left. It wasn't much, but it was everything I could spare.

Her appearance solidified again, and she gave me a shy smile. "That was unnecessary, but thank you nonetheless."

"It was the least I could do."

She gave me an appraising look. "Perhaps Tritia was right. You aren't so bad, for a sorcerer."

"I'll take that as high praise."

She flitted her wings and floated backward. "You should probably get going. Your strength is waning."

The gateway pulled at me, reinforcing her suggestion. Visiting the Runedream was a drain on my internal well, and the drain was much worse when I "made things happen." This session was probably the most demanding I'd ever attempted.

"Thank you for your help, Arial. I hope we meet again."

"Perhaps we shall," she said with a shallow bow. She winked at me and then disappeared.

I woke up to disorienting smells and voices in low conversation before I remembered that I was in Ebnik's chamber.

I was so tired that I kept my eyes closed and just listened for a minute. Sulana was in the middle of saying something.

"To be honest, the people in this room are the only ones I trust with this information. For now, I'd like to keep it a secret."

Gregor said, "I'm not sure anyone else would believe us if we told them. I don't think *I* would have believed it if you hadn't demonstrated."

Ah, Sulana had shared the secret of her new casting abilities. I would loved to have seen the reactions to *that* demonstration.

"I'm happy for you Lana," Lissy said. "But isn't it kind of scary? No one has ever heard of anything like this happening before. What do you think it means?"

I opened my eyes and sat up. Before anyone else could answer, I said, "It means the spirits need our help."

Lissy sat forward with eager eyes. "Did you speak with the goddesses again?" While I was out, someone had apparently told her about my previous trip into the Runedream.

"Just Arial this time. She helped me with the shield problem."

Ebnik stood and brought a plate of food over to me. "That was your longest absence. We had dinner brought in and we were starting to worry."

The food was cold, but it looked wonderful. My stomach growled loudly in anticipation as I took the plate from him. Ebnik raised an eyebrow and I said, "That means, 'Thanks,' in starving stomach language."

Ebnik chuckled and patted me on the shoulder. "I suspected as much," he said as he returned to his seat.

Sulana came over and sat next to me on the bed. She started eating the cucumber slices off my plate, knowing they would upset my stomach.

"How did it go?" she asked between bites. "Were you able to figure it out?"

"I think so. We won't know for sure until we try it for real. I got it to work in the Runedream, but it was complicated. I need Lissy to record the incantation before I forget it."

Everyone listened in while I chanted pieces of the incantation for Lissy and explained how the new shield worked.

When I was done, Gregor shook his head, his expression one of amazement.

"If that works, I'll take back every doubt I've had about the Runedream. It would have taken weeks of research to assemble that spell. Maybe months. I'm not even sure it could be done. I know the Sorcerer's Encyclopedia as well as anyone, and I don't think it has all of those incantation elements."

Ebnik got a thoughtful look and tapped his chin. "The origin of sorcery," he mused.

Gregor turned his head toward the old wizard. "What was that?"

"Oh, it's just something that came up during our initial research into the Runedream. One of our sources claimed the Runedream was 'the origin of sorcery.'"

His comment made everyone in the room go silent with thoughtful stares.

My ruminations were interrupted by a huge yawn. It was still fairly early in the evening, but my eyelids were getting heavy from the draining expedition into the Runedream and the meal that had followed.

Gregor took my yawn as his cue to leave. He stood and addressed me. "I'd like to have you get started on the new spell first thing tomorrow morning. I have other things to attend to, but I'm sure Lissy and Ebnik can give you all the help you need."

Sulana raised a hand, "If I might make a suggestion, you should get my mother's help as well. She would love to be involved in the creation of a new spell."

Gregor nodded. "Good idea. No one is better than Marlene at incantations. Sulana, I need you to participate in our strategy sessions. We need to stop the headmaster before he becomes entrenched in the capital."

Sulana nodded. "I just hope we aren't already too late."

CHAPTER 40
SURRENDER

Lohan strutted into Council Hall with a smug expression. The guardians who escorted him kept a wary eye on his every movement. His step faltered when he saw Sulana sitting with the Council and me standing next to the Council Chamber door, but he recovered smoothly with a gloating smile.

The lead guardian came to a halt about twenty feet away from the Council Seat and bowed.

"Esteemed Council, may I present Adviser Lohan Fletcher of Northshore."

About an hour ago, I had been with the Council discussing the current status of the new lightning shield spell. Refining the incantation took longer than we had hoped, but it was ready at last. We no longer needed the wand for testing, so we could safely take it apart and see how it worked. We would have a tremendous advantage against the Lightning Corps if we could shield against their lightning and then hurl their own spell back at them.

Our meeting had been interrupted by a guardian who informed us that an imperial delegation waited at the gate. It seemed they had a proclamation to deliver. The "delegation" turned out to be Lohan, Peltor, and two dozen or so Lightning Corps troops.

The Council allowed Lohan to enter the castle while his retinue waited outside, and then they made him wait while we finished our discussion. The Council moved into the Council Hall to receive him. I stood to the side of the Council seat as an observer.

To the guardian's annoyance, Lohan stepped around him and flourished a parchment, which he began to unroll. He did not bow.

"Yes, greetings, *esteemed* Council. I carry a proclamation from the Imperial Assembly demanding that you surrender the Archives castle to Lightning Corps control immediately. You have one full day," he glanced up at the suntracker, "from this moment, to collect your personal effects and vacate the premises. All Archives property, including everything in the armory and classrooms, must remain in the castle."

Lohan looked up from his parchment to find a collection of unreceptive faces. He narrowed his eyes and waved the proclamation at them, as if they needed a reminder of the document's significance.

Senior Councilor Underwood gave Lohan his best scowl, the one that nearly drew his eyebrows together into a single bushy line. He motioned his hand in a circle, indicating that he wanted to see the parchment. Lohan started to move forward, but the lead guardian snatched the parchment with his right hand while his left pressed against Lohan's chest to keep him in place. The guardian delivered the parchment to Underwood's outstretched hand.

The councilor's eyes scanned down the parchment slowly. When he reached the bottom, he passed it to Councilor Rissik and then folded his hands.

"That document is invalid," he declared. "It does not include the Emperor's seal."

Lohan's neck grew red and he drew himself up. "That proclamation was sealed by the majority vote of the Imperial Assembly. The Emperor's vote was not necessary."

Underwood leaned forward. "Don't try to play games with *me*. A decision of this nature requires a Quorum of Nine. The Emperor's four votes must be counted, even if all five province emissaries vote against him. Without the Emperor's seal, this *proclamation* is worthless."

To underscore his fellow councilor's point, Rissik wadded the parchment into a ball and tossed it to the floor where it rolled to a stop at Lohan's feet.

Lohan stared down at the crumpled parchment, his breath came in huffs and his pulse was visible on his neck. He looked up sharply at Councilor Rissik.

"It doesn't matter what you think. Integration is coming and you can't stop it."

Councilor Rissik responded to Lohan's outburst. "We wouldn't dream of stopping it, if the mundane supported the idea *of their own free will.* However, that hardly seems the case with your group of bandits assaulting the province governors and forcing Thunderhead College *advisers* on the citizenry."

Lohan frowned. "All of that is temporary. The mundane would never have given us the opportunity to prove how integration would benefit them. Once they see the value of integration, they won't *want* to go back to the way things were."

Sulana snorted. She was temporarily serving on the Council in place of Maris Torlon, a rarely exercised duty of the Sword Sorceress. "That's not what we hear. How do you explain the mundane resistance?"

"The mundane resistance is a tiny, vocal minority. Their paranoid ravings don't worry us. There will always people who resist progress."

Lissy laughed. "Where do you get this stuff? Do you memorize all of this ridiculous propaganda from some kind of Integrationist Manifesto?"

Lohan clamped his jaw closed and glared at Lissy. She had officially replaced Rikard Shepherd as a Junior Councilor and was thriving in her new role.

"I don't expect you to understand," Lohan responded bitterly. "In time, the headmaster's vision will correct the imbalance that has kept our society from moving forward."

Velna Asher had been quietly observing Lohan throughout the conversation. After his last remark, she glanced at Sulana with a look that said, "Is this what I sounded like?" Taking a deep breath, she leaned forward and addressed Lohan.

"I think we understand the headmaster's *vision*. You've been duped if you think his agenda has anything to do with Integration. He is using Integration as a rallying point to gather the gullible. The only *progress* Dumont Fortenz cares about is his own."

Lohan's eyes showed his surprise at hearing such a statement from Asher's mouth. He sighed and his shoulders fell.

"I'm wasting my time here. Enjoy your tiny bubble of isolation while you can. In time, the Archives will fall just as your sanctuaries have fallen."

"You'd better hope you're right," Councilor Rissik said with a steely tone. "Your master has gone too far. If he fails, it means the gallows for him and everyone who used sorcery against the mundane. We'll see how well you rationalize your actions from the end of a short rope."

Lohan face distorted in rage and his fists clenched at his sides. "Don't threaten *me*, old man. By the time this is through, I will be the one gloating over *your* body twisting in the wind."

Councilor Underwood shook his head in disgust. "Get him out of here," he ordered.

The lead guardian was happy to comply. He grabbed Lohan's arm and escorted him from the room. Lohan tried to tear his arm away, but the guardian's grip was too strong.

A second guardian took his other arm and the two of them practically carried the struggling sorcerer out of Council Hall.

"That was unpleasant," mumbled Councilor Asher after the door closed behind Lohan's undignified exit.

I walked around to the front of the Council seat and picked up the crumpled proclamation. I couldn't decide if I wanted to set it on fire or hang it on the wall as a reminder of how far things had gone.

Councilor Rissik sat back and stared down at the proclamation in my hand. "Lohan was right about one thing. Time is against us. If we don't stop the headmaster soon, we won't be able to stop him at all."

"It's time we put Thunderhead College on the defensive for a change," Sulana said.

"And how do you intend to do that?" Councilor Asher snapped.

Sulana returned the councilor's stare and answered in an even tone, "By attacking the origin of all our troubles."

"You mean Thunderhead College itself? You're insane!"

"Actually, now would be an excellent time. The headmaster has moved his headquarters to the Cassandria sanctuary. Lohan is *adviser* to Governor Trask in Northshore. Peltor also seems to spend most of his time in Northshore, although he moves around a lot. Paeter Thoron is the only unknown at this point. He may be at the college or he may be in Cassandria. Wherever he is, he's staying out of sight."

Asher was unconvinced. "The place is still crawling with Lightning Corps."

"Yes, but their recruitment is finally slowing, and they are spreading everyone they have across the empire. All that remains are a couple dozen trainees and a skeleton staff."

"How do we know this?" asked Councilor Underwood.

"I received a message from Riverview just before the meeting that Lohan interrupted. Former agent Daven Prost is leading the Riverview resistance now. They have been spying on the college and he shared what they've observed."

Councilor Underwood's bushy eyebrows rose in surprise. "I thought the resistance was disorganized and that Peltor had them completely out-manned."

"That was true several weeks ago, but once Daven pulled them together, they shaped up quickly. Daven also found out how Peltor was able to anticipate their every move; Minister Bogard was under control of an amulet. When Peltor came through Riverview, the minister reported what he knew about the resistance."

That explained a lot. Elerus Bogard had been strangely tolerant of the Thunderhead College operations in his area, given that he had such a bad history with the headmaster. Riverview was supposed to be a "sorcerer free zone" by his own decree, yet the Lightning Corps was frequently seen in and around the township.

But getting one of Thoron's amulets off a wearer against his will was no simple matter, as I knew from my own experience.

"Daven was able to deactivate the amulet?" I asked.

Sulana smiled and looked down at the table. "Not exactly. He convinced the lieutenant in charge of the guard garrison to hold on to the minister while he removed it."

I drew in a sharp breath. "That was risky. We've never tried to remove an active amulet. He's lucky it didn't transfer its influence to him."

Sulana tilted her head, acknowledging my point. "Knowing Daven, he would have worn leather gloves, just in case. As you can imagine, the minister was livid once he was freed, and he pledged to support the resistance in any way he could."

Councilor Rissik stroked his chin thoughtfully. "So, what you're saying is that the resistance can help us with a campaign against the college."

Sulana tilted her hand back and forth in a "maybe" gesture. "I don't think they'll participate, but if Peltor is in the area, they'll find a way to distract him for us."

Councilor Asher was still frowning. "This is starting to sound feasible, but how will we keep control of the college? We can't afford to maintain a defensive force both here and there."

Sulana gave Asher a bland look. "I don't plan to *take possession* of the college. I intend to burn it to the ground." She smiled and threw an impish grin my way. "With a little help from my friends."

Lissy looked back and forth between Sulana and me, like she was considering something. Her lips thinned as she seemed to reach a decision.

"Before we start planning any campaigns, I think we need to get something out of the way. Something the Council has been putting off for too long."

Lissy had everyone's attention.

"I think Jaylan has adequately demonstrated that he is a competent sorcerer and swordsman. There is no reason to put off his confirmation as Sword Sorcerer. I propose that we confirm him now and hold the official ceremony within the next few days."

The room was silent as all eyes turned to me.

Councilor Underwood shrugged and raised his hand. "All in favor of Councilor Aragon's proposal?"

Sulana raised her hand. "Aye," she voted with a smile. Councilor Rissik and Lissy held up their hands at the same time, leaving just Asher, who stared at me intently.

Asher's vote was unnecessary at this point, but she raised her hand anyway and said, "Aye."

Everyone looked at her in surprise.

"Don't look at me like that," she complained. "I had good reason to doubt his suitability in the past, but I'm not too proud to admit he exceeded my expectations."

And with that ringing endorsement, I finally earned the title of Sword Sorcerer.

CHAPTER 41

STRIKE FORCE

Crouching at the forest's edge, I peered around a thick tree trunk and gazed upon the training facility of my enemies.

"They *have* made improvements since the last time we were here," I commented.

Daven's message had warned us of the new construction. A wooden palisade had been erected on top of the rock wall and three guard towers had been added: two on either side of the gate and one at the back of the compound.

Sulana was kneeling just below me, sharing the protection of the same tree. "No slipping over the wall this time," she said.

"That's okay. I'm pretty sure they know we're here."

A soft thump was followed by a crossbow quarrel falling to the ground at the base of the next tree over. They definitely knew we were here.

"Sorry I gave away our advantage of surprise," I said.

As we had moved through the forest to our current position, I was so busy looking for traps at ground level that I had failed to notice the alarm ward hidden in a tree at shoulder height. Sulana saw it and grabbed my arm to warn me, but she was too late to stop me from triggering the ward.

The experience taught me something though. I was relying too much on my ability to hear manifestations to warn me of vaetric traps. The alarm ward gave off a high pitch that blended in perfectly with the cacophony of morning birdsong. If we had approached at night, I might have heard it, but during the day, the natural sounds of the forest were perfect camouflage.

Sulana shrugged. "It doesn't matter. This wasn't going to be a sneak attack anyway."

Our plan had been to approach the gates and demand to speak to the person in charge. We would tell them they had thirty minutes to gather their belongings and leave the college on foot. All implements of sorcery had to be left behind.

They would never comply, of course. We came expecting a fight and we were prepared for one. Besides Talon, Sulana, and me, our strike force had eight Archives Guardians and eight sorcerers of varying skill. If our intelligence regarding their manpower was correct, our group was more than powerful enough to defeat them. Particularly if we didn't care too much about the condition of the place at the end of the fight.

Sulana and I backed away from our vantage point and rejoined Talon, who had stayed back with the others. I got back on Patches and patted his neck.

Sulana mounted Stardust and spoke to Talon. "It looks like things are just like Daven reported. The place has been fortified, but not heavily. And they know we're here."

Talon nodded. "Do you think they'll come out after us?" he asked hopefully.

I answered him. "No. The gate is closed tight and the guards seem content with showing their disdain by firing their crossbows from the guard towers."

Sulana gathered her reins. "Well, we'd better get on with this. No point giving them more time to ready their defenses."

Our group rode out of the forest with Sulana and me in the lead. We both enabled our shields as Thunderhead College came into view.

The college guards fired a few more quarrels at our group as soon as we came into range, but our shields easily deflected them. They finally decided to stop wasting ammunition and let us approach.

A man appeared in the guard tower on the left. The towers were so small that the crossbowman who was already there had to step back so the second man could address us. "What do you want?" he demanded.

"We want you to surrender this facility," Sulana shouted back.

"On whose authority?"

"By the authority granted to the Archives by the emperor. The leadership of Thunderhead College will be tried for treason and for violating the Sorcery Accords."

The man in the guard tower laughed. "You don't have that authority. It was transferred to us. Leave now or you'll be the ones arrested."

To back up his threat, the man drew an orb from his pocket and began an incantation.

We had practiced for this moment, so several things happened at once. Sulana moved Stardust as close as she could to Patches and we both deactivated our normal shields. I activated a second shield bracer on my other arm. We'd only had time to make one implement that could generate the new lightning shield, and I was wearing it. Most of the other sorcerers on our team could cast the spell using an orb, and behind me their chanting told me that was exactly what they were doing.

As anticipated, lightning arced from the guard tower straight at Sulana. When it hit my shield, it sparked and spread to the edges of the shield where it followed two paths into the ground.

Patches didn't like the pyrotechnics and started to back away from the shield. One of the down sides of the new shield was that it wasn't mobile, so I had to drop it before Patches' movement pulled me out of the saddle. The buzz of Sulana's normal shield came just in time to deflect another quarrel from the guard in the right tower.

Our own people hadn't been standing still. We had four archers of our own and they opened fire on the towers. The enemy guards had to duck to avoid getting hit. The sorcerer who had cast the lightning wasn't quite quick enough and yelled in agony as an arrow pierced his shoulder.

One of our sorcerers fired a low-powered lightning bolt at the wooden gate, but as we anticipated, the gate was shielded. Unfortunately, we hadn't yet reverse-engineered the shield-breaking spell for our own use, so we'd have to find the gate shield and disable it.

Sulana and I moved on to phase two of our attack plan and left Talon in command. Along the wall on the far side of the gate was a small pond surrounded by bare cottonwood and birch trees. We positioned the horses behind the relative safety of the tree trunks on the far side of the pond and dismounted. I slipped my staff from a special leather sheath I'd made for carrying it on horseback.

As we hoped, the tower guards focused on the main body of our group and ignored us. Sulana knelt next to the pond and cupped her hands under the water. I stood next to her, ready to use either of my shields in case anyone decided to send trouble our way. Sulana asked the spirits for help while I watched the wall.

It turned out that the towers weren't the only improvement to Thunderhead College's walls. They had apparently installed wall walks on both sides of the gates as well. Several heads peeked briefly above the wall to assess the position of our forces. A few moments later, the defenders stood and hurled both physical and vaetric missiles toward us.

I held my breath, but everyone survived the first round behind hastily raised shields. Our archers returned fire and took down another of the defenders who had stayed above the wall too long.

A deep hum from the pond told me that the spirits were answering Sulana. Her job was to breach the gate or the wall somehow, so I wasn't sure exactly what was about to happen.

I wasn't the only one who noticed that something was happening at the pond. One of the enemy sorcerers raised his head long enough to look our way and glare. The next time he rose above the wall, he did so several feet further along, anticipating the arrow that whizzed through the space he had occupied a moment before. I grinned at the marksmanship and tactics our guardians were demonstrating even if that particular shot had missed.

It was time to employ some tactics of my own. When the sorcerer popped up again, I needed to be ready to defend both Sulana and myself. Casting a spell meant he would be exposed above the wall too long, so I guessed he would use an implement. Even though it seemed that all Lightning Corps trainees were taught the shield breaker spell, implements were time consuming and costly to create. I gambled that the implement he used would throw something else at us.

It mattered because the new grounded shield worked great against all forms of lightning and physical missiles, but not as well as a standard shield against most other spells. I had to choose one or the other, so I moved as close to Sulana as I could and gambled on activating my standard shield bracer.

The enemy sorcerer pointed his fist in our direction and spoke a trigger word. His ring emitted a whirling vortex of force that spread as it came toward us, whipping through tree branches and sucking some of the weakest stems into the wind stream.

I increased the flow of vaetra to my shield to strengthen it and braced myself as loose branches slammed into the shield like a barrage of arrows and spun off in every direction. But even the strengthened shield wasn't enough to absorb all of the force from the vortex. I staggered back several steps as some of it bled through my shield.

Sulana glanced up at me, but didn't interrupt her spell or blessing or whatever she called it. I picked a small branch out of my hair and gave her a grim nod to let her know I was okay.

The enemy sorcerer popped up again to see how well his spell had worked, but forgot to change position. He fell silently from the wall walk with his hands covering his face and the fletching of an arrow protruding between his fingers.

Sulana continued to work while I watched for evidence of what she was doing. When the wall next to the gate started to crumble, it took me a moment to understand why. The ground along the base of the wall was getting wet. The stone wall sagged into the softened soil and the old mortar couldn't hold the stones.

The right gate tower lurched sideways, leaning toward the disintegrating wall section it had been built against. The wooden ramparts built on top of the wall groaned and twisted. Panicked shouts came from inside the wall as the gate tower creaked and shifted again.

Sulana's part was almost done, so I searched the edge of the pond for a good location to launch our next attack.

The pond had been an important component of our strategy. Sulana used its water as a giant focus device for her blessing. I was going to use the granite basin that formed it as a source of vaetra.

The supports for the leaning guard tower cracked loudly and the tower crashed to the ground, pulling half of the gate down with it. The wall under the tower sloughed into a low pile of rubble. Through the gap, I could clearly see the college manor.

Sulana stood up and wiped her hands on a sash she had taken to wearing specifically for that purpose. I admired her practicality, although I hadn't been able to resist teasing her about her wearing a dish towel for a belt.

"Are you ready?" she asked.

"Yep." I pointed toward a smooth rock face that angled into the pond. "Right over there should do nicely."

Sulana took over shielding duties while I moved to the rock and drove the tip of my staff down into the surface. I closed my eyes and placed my hands on the metal bands. Opening a channel to the pond's basin, I tried to get a sense for how much vaetra was available. My senses were nowhere near as sensitive or accurate as Ebnik's sounding staff, but I could tell the difference between *none*, *some*, and *a lot*. *None* would be bad. In a basin of this size, even *some* would be plenty.

We were in luck. I had power to spare. Certainly enough for what I had in mind.

I took one last look at the battle scene before beginning my incantation. The enemy was gathering at the sides of the wall gap to defend it. They peeked out in confusion, not understanding why our forces hadn't moved in yet. One of them pointed at me and made a rude gesture in my direction.

"Go ahead. I've got this." Sulana said.

This spell was for her. When I told her about our escape from Northshore, she was disappointed that she "didn't get to see the fireball." It wasn't a spell one threw about casually, so she asked if I'd be willing to demonstrate it again today.

She asked for the favor as if we were going to see a fireworks display. "Anything for my betrothed," I promised. She bestowed a sweet kiss upon me as a reward.

I drew a deep breath and began my incantation. That was the signal for our archers and sorcerers to lay down covering fire. The figures at the wall gap leaped back in alarm as a small storm of arrows sailed through the opening or shattered on the stones. A lightning bolt sizzled through as well, throwing down one defender who didn't back away fast enough.

Hearing my incantation, a defender did try to reach me with an arrow, but Sulana easily deflected it with her shield ring.

I raised my voice for the last syllables of the incantation, and Sulana took the hint to step well aside.

From my previous experience in Northshore, I had a better feel for how much vaetra I should use to generate the fireball. I also knew to be careful about how fast I pushed it toward the target.

I drew nearly twice as much vaetra from the pond basin than I had in Northshore, creating a massive ball of fire about three feet in diameter. Unfortunately, the spell manifested the flaming ball at the same distance every time, which quite frankly, wasn't far enough. The hairs of my eyebrows curled and singed, forcing me to lean back from the monstrosity I'd created.

I launched it toward the college, pushing just hard enough to get it moving at walking speed. Even so, the reaction force made me stumble back several paces. Sulana ran over and steadied me, absently patting at my smoking sleeve while she watched the fireball float toward our enemies.

At first, I don't think they believed what they were seeing. The fireball covered half the distance between us and the wall before they reacted. An arrow disappeared into it, consumed instantly by the heat. When it passed through the gate opening every bit of wood near it exploded into flaming splinters. It barely grazed the rock wall, cracking stones into shards. The shrapnel of its passing pelted the defenders, forcing them to back away with exclamations of shock and pain.

One brave sorcerer stood between the fireball and the manor. He held up his casting orb and chanted, probably trying to use a shield to stop or deflect the approaching ball of flame.

Bad idea. Once launched, a fireball flies forward until one of two things happen: either it goes far enough to lose all of its energy and dissipate, or it encounters an obstacle and explodes. This sorcerer was turning himself into an obstacle.

The explosion was deafening. Sulana and I cringed away from the flying debris, covering our heads with our arms. When the shock wave reached us, it pushed both of us back a step and took our breath away.

I think half the manor collapsed just from the blast, but fire quickly began to consume the rest. The defenders who were still conscious crawled through the gateway with groans and bleeding ears to escape the intense heat inside the courtyard. Most of the wooden rampart had collapsed outward and even the original stone wall was cracked and leaning in places. The second guard tower had collapsed into a shattered pile of lumber outside the wall.

I looked over at our group to make sure they were all right. Most were rising from a defensive crouch and staring at the destruction with gaping mouths. Talon shook his head and whistled then gave me a thumbs-up.

Sulana looked up at me with wide eyes. "Wow. You sure know how to show a girl a good time."

I squeezed her close and stared at the destruction I'd wrought. As much trouble as Thunderhead College had given us, I didn't feel good about killing people. Even knowing they would have killed *me* without a second thought. I wished there were another way.

Sulana must have read the regret on my face. She glared at the burning manor and said, "Just think about me being chained in that dungeon for days. Think about me lying dead on the ground about a half mile from here. It's us or them, and they picked the fight."

Pounding hooves from behind the wall drew everyone's attention. A horse and rider turned sharply through the destroyed gateway and bolted across the strip of land between the wall and the pond. The horse stumbled when it hit the section Sulana had softened, but it got its feet back under it and thundered off into the trees. The escape happened so fast that no one had a chance to react.

Two of our guardians started to go after the man, but Talon held them back. The ground was marshy in that area, and you'd have to know where you were going to navigate it safely. Instead, he ordered everyone to secure the college and watch out for defenders lying in wait.

It took a while to clean up the mess I created. A burial detail took care of the dead, none of which were ours, thankfully. Our group suffered a few wounds from the initial missile exchange, but none were mortal. The college healer had survived our attack, and we allowed him to tend to the wounded Lightning Corps personnel.

The college had expanded the stable, which was in danger of fire spreading to it from the main building. We guided the frightened horses to the edge of the pond outside the wall.

We were deciding what to do with the seven college survivors when several horses charged down the road toward us from the direction of Riverview. Everyone ran back to the relative safety of the walls, our backs warm from the blaze still consuming the manor. Talon quickly arranged a defensive line along the rubble of the wall and at the sides of the gate opening.

When the riders came into view, they brought their horses to a sliding stop and stared in awe at the broken wall and the flames of the manor, which licked up into a roiling column of black smoke.

"Sulana!" called the man on the lead mount. It was Daven. He walked his horse forward.

Talon gave the signal for everyone to stand down and we went out to meet the riders.

Sulana and I jogged up to Daven. He leaned on his forearm while his horse huffed from the hard run. "Nice bonfire. We could see the smoke for miles."

Sulana smiled and then raised an eyebrow. "You're a little late to the party. We weren't sure if you would meet us here, so we went ahead without you."

"Sorry about that. We were delayed. Our old friend Peltor showed up in Riverview. I had to sneak out without him seeing me, and a few of the guards who were going to come with me had to stay behind to protect the Minister and avoid suspicion."

Peltor was that close? He would undoubtedly see the smoke eventually, just as Daven had. He would know something was very wrong at the college.

"How many people were in his party?" I asked.

"About fifteen. Two were not in uniform, so I think they were students being brought here for training."

A loud crash made me cringe reflexively as the last standing wall of the manor collapsed in a shower of sparks. "They may want to reconsider that plan."

Daven sent a concerned look over his shoulder. "They might not be far behind us. The minister was going to pretend that he is still wearing an amulet, but he may not fool Peltor. Also, by now someone in Riverview will have spotted the smoke."

"A Lightning Corps man escaped not long before you arrived. Did you see him?" I asked.

"No. We'd have stopped him. That clinches it. Peltor is going to know exactly what happened here."

We took Daven's warning to heart and prepared for Peltor's arrival. As the fire died down, we moved the college horses around to the back of the complex. They were still outside the walls, but hidden from anyone approaching on the road. We brought everyone else inside what was left of the courtyard, avoiding the section where smoke still swirled before it was carried away by the light breeze.

We waited for over an hour, but Peltor never showed up. Instead, a rider from Riverview arrived and told us that Peltor had turned back toward Northshore. Apparently, he didn't think a facility that had been burned to the ground was worth the fight. After another hour, we left the surviving Lightning Corps captives with Daven's group and started back for the Archives.

I looked around our group as we headed back up the trail. Even the injured among us seemed to be in good spirits. The truth was that our successful attack would only temporarily slow down the headmaster's training program. The change in our morale was the real benefit from taking down Thunderhead College. Our guardians' faces reflected pride and determination, where yesterday there had been worry and uncertainty.

I hoped that their improved attitudes would sustain them. The battle may have been won, but the war had only begun.

CHAPTER 42

HEADMASTER'S IRE

The Lightning Corps sorcerer who stood before Headmaster Fortenz struggled to catch his breath. He bowed awkwardly and gulped audibly when his eyes met Dumont's.

"Well, out with it," Dumont said.

"Yes, Headmaster." The man took a deep breath to collect himself. "We just received word from Northshore. Archives forces attacked Thunderhead College two days ago." The man gulped again, reluctant to continue. "The corps fought valiantly, but the college was destroyed. One of the survivors escaped and warned Captain Mullan." The man set a message tube on the table next to Dumont. "This is the captain's full report."

Dumont dismissed the man with a curt wave of his hand. "You may go." The sorcerer bowed deeply and fled the room.

Dumont ripped the seal off the message tube and extracted the parchment inside. Unrolling it, he squinted to read Peltor's crude penmanship. The message didn't say much more than the guard had already told him, except it added that Peltor believed that the minister was no longer under their control.

Finishing the message, Dumont glanced at a double-sphered instrument sitting on the desk across the room. Why hadn't Councilor Shepherd warned him of this attack? The device had been silent for over a week, and with this news, he was starting to believe that it would remain so indefinitely.

He tossed the parchment onto the table and closed his eyes to calm himself. Losing the college was not really a problem. What was more disturbing was that the Archives was finally going on the offensive. He no longer had a way to anticipate their actions.

Overall, things were going well, but several unexpected obstacles made the timing of his master plan more critical and delicate than ever. He controlled the Imperial Assembly. His emissaries could overrule the emperor on any issue. But the emperor had found a clever way to prevent Dumont from influencing much more than trade and law enforcement matters.

For the assembly to change imperial law, they needed a Quorum of Nine. The emperor had to be present for the vote, even if the emissaries voted against him. By refusing to set foot in Assembly Hall, the emperor had effectively kept all Quorum of Nine decisions off the table.

At the same time, Dumont's emissaries were starting to show an unpleasant tendency toward independent thinking. Their power, the power *he* had given them, was starting to go to their heads. He might have to remind them that he could still take away the power they so relished.

Dumont stood and began to pace the room. These were minor details. The fact was that he was too close to his goal for the Archives or the emperor to stop him. He may not yet be in the palace, but he was in Cassandria.

He had taken control of the Cassandria sanctuary with little effort and no bloodshed. When the Lightning Corps arrived at the gate, his supporters within the sanctuary had already secured the building. The few sorcerers who resisted his occupation, including the former housemaster, had been thrown out into the street where they received little sympathy from the mundane populace.

There was one simple solution to all of the problems that currently plagued him: Rollek's Amplifier. With the amplifier and the new spell core Paeter was working on, he could influence every mind in Cassandria. He could abolish the Accords and establish a new empire where sorcerers received the respect they deserved. Integration would come, whether the mundane wanted it or not.

But time to consummate the plan was running out. The mundane resistance was gathering support and the Archives would eventually find a way to free the governors from their amulets. The Imperial Guard was fragmenting as the resistance seeped into their ranks. He needed to take firm control before conditions turned fully against him.

With decisive steps, Dumont grabbed his traveling robe off its wall hook and opened the door of his office. "Masterson," he shouted. A young man at the reception desk in the sanctuary foyer jumped to his feet. "Have horses readied for my traveling party. We leave immediately."

"Yes, Housemaster," affirmed the secretary. He ran toward a back room where the lieutenant in charge of Dumont's personal guard would be.

The secretary's habitual use of the term "housemaster" reminded Dumont that Tolby Masterson was one of the sorcerers who had chosen to stay at the sanctuary and serve Thunderhead College. The young man followed orders and seemed capable enough, but he was jumpy and wary, which made his decision to remain suspicious.

Dumont made a mental note to have one of his most loyal followers keep a close eye on the secretary.

He fingered the portal key, which was hidden in a wand pocket in the sleeve of his traveling robe. No more delays. It was time to bring in reinforcements and knock down the remaining obstacles.

CHAPTER 43

GRAND ENTRANCE

Dumont walked through the main palace doors accompanied by six heavily armed Lightning Corps sorcerers. The two entryway guards stepped forward with expressions of suspicion and alarm. To their credit, both men stood their ground, and the senior guard demanded to know Dumont's business.

"I'm here to visit the emperor," Dumont replied in an even voice.

"Have you made an appointment with the seneschal?"

The lie came easily. "Yes I have."

The guard narrowed his eyes at Dumont and backed away toward the door to the Great Hall. "Allow me to announce you, Headmaster Fortenz."

"That won't be necessary," Dumont replied.

All six Lightning Corps soldiers went into motion. Two of them immobilized the guards with spells. The senior guard froze in place while other slid to the floor unconscious.

The commotion attracted the attention of the four guards manning the main gate. Two of them drew their swords and ran toward the palace, but they were both knocked to the ground and rendered unconscious by spells from two Lightning Corps sorcerers. Before the two remaining gate guards could react, they were overwhelmed by a dozen more black-cloaked swordsmen and sorcerers who stormed through the gateway.

Dumont opened the door to the main hall and let his soldiers surround him as he strode down the carpeted walk that stretched toward the emperor's throne. The six guards who stood duty against the walls of the hall ran forward to challenge him, lowering their halberds menacingly. Sorman, the old seneschal, looked up from his work with a frown. When he saw the multitude of black cloaks, he threw down his quill and scurried toward the back of the room.

The lead Lightning Corps sorcerers took down three of the guards with their first round of spells. The other three guards yelled and charged.

A blinding flash and crackling boom left a residual odor of ozone in the room as a bolt of lightning slammed into two of the emperor's soldiers, throwing both the floor. They slid backward a foot or two from the force of the blast, smoke curling from their clothing.

The remaining guard managed to reach the front line and skewered a sorcerer who failed to complete his incantation. Two of Dumont's swordsmen flanked the guard and took him down in a spray of blood.

One of Dumont's men kneeled at the side of the fallen sorcerer. He looked up and shook his head.

"Leave him," Dumont ordered. "We follow the seneschal. He will lead us to the emperor. Everyone stay together. It's all or nothing now, so don't hesitate to eliminate resistance using whatever means necessary."

Dumont pointed toward the back of the hall where the old seneschal had disappeared. He smiled with anticipation as his men formed up around him again. When the group moved forward, their boots synchronized in a determined march that echoed throughout the hall.

CHAPTER 44

ESCAPE PORTAL

Senior Councilor Gregor Rissik waited patiently for Emperor Tanes to respond. Assimilating bad news took time. It took even longer when the news was a mixture of good and bad.

The emperor finally spoke. "I should never have allowed you and Vlastorus to inspect the device. I wish we had left it hidden."

Gregor had warned the emperor of his suspicions that the headmaster's ultimate goal was to gain control of Rollek's Amplifier. "I understand, Your Majesty. But there was no way we could have anticipated our current circumstances."

"So you don't think destroying the Thunderhead College headquarters will slow them down?"

Gregor shook his head. "It was more a symbolic victory, Your Majesty. They already have alternate training facilities in Sunset and Grassgate provinces."

"I'm guessing your visit today was for more than just to give me this status report. You have an urgency about you."

"You are perceptive, Your Majesty. Fortenz may have already received the same news I delivered to you. I'm sure he knows that his supporters are spread too thin across the empire to maintain control everywhere. The resistance is gaining strength and even the druids speak out against him. Imperial guardsmen are becoming suspicious of their orders. He must do something soon or be exposed for the criminal he is and face the rope."

"That will be a happy day," said the emperor.

"I quite agree, Your Majesty. However, that day has not come. Fortenz has entrenched himself here in the capital, and may even try to take the palace by force."

"He wouldn't dare such treason! The Tanes have ruled the empire for generations."

"He dares plenty, Your Majesty. The chaos he has created is the perfect environment to do something bold and unexpected. I recommend that you increase palace security as soon as possible." Gregor cast a glance at Imperial Sorceress Dierdre Fleming. "I also recommend that you bolster your defenses against attack by sorcery."

Sorceress Fleming nodded her head in agreement.

The emperor let out a heavy sigh. "I suppose you're right, although I'm not sure where I'll find the guards. We've been at peace for too long. Most of the guards are on the borders watching for *external* dangers. I can't believe Fortenz has become such a threat in such a short period of time."

"His advantage has been planning and speed, Your Majesty. But it is also his weakness. His plan only continues to work if we stay on the defensive, responding slowly and predictably. Our attack on Thunderhead College shows we aren't playing along any more. We hope that changing the rules will force him to make a mistake."

A muffled yell came from the main hall through the nearly soundproof door of the emperor's conference room. When the door latch clicked, the captain of the emperor's personal guard drew his sword and stepped from behind the emperor's chair. The second guard followed his lead.

The door flew open and Seneschal Sorman Tanes practically fell into the room. He stumbled around the door and pushed it shut, sliding home additional security bolts.

The old man was puffing air like a bellows and shaking like he had just stepped out of a freezing bath. He pushed aside the blades of the startled guards and placed his hands on the table near the emperor, trying to catch his breath. The emperor sat back with a frown.

"What is going on out there Sorman?" the emperor demanded.

"Majesty … sorcerers … dozens attacking the guards," wheezed the seneschal.

One of the guards reached for a security bolt.

"Stop!" yelled Gregor. "It's too late for that. We must get the emperor to safety."

The guard looked at the emperor for confirmation. The emperor put up a hand, indicating the guard should wait. "We might be able to put an end to this right now," he said to Gregor.

Gregor leaned forward. "Your Majesty, if Fortenz is here with dozens of fully armed Lightning Corps swordsmen and sorcerers, we can't stop him."

"I will not be routed from my own palace," the emperor said with a growl.

A deep boom shook the room, causing tapestries to shiver on the walls and dust to sift out of the seams in the ceiling.

In a breach of protocol, Gregor got up from his seat before the emperor. "Your Majesty, we must leave now. That door will not hold them for long."

The emperor opened his mouth to object again, but the old seneschal had caught his breath enough to put his hand on the emperor's arm. "Please, Meritus. He's right. Listen to him."

The emperor got up slowly, uncertain of his decision. "You think Fortenz would actually try to assassinate me?"

Gregor motioned everyone toward a second door that opened into the emperor's private access hallway. "I don't know, Your Majesty. We can ask that question at his trial."

Emperor Tanes tilted his mouth in a wry smile. "If he takes the palace, you may be the one put on trial."

Ushering everyone through the door, Gregor's face grew grim. "Taking the palace is one thing, Your Majesty. Keeping it is quite another. We escape now so we might fight another day on our own terms."

Two more guards waited on the other side of the door with anxious expressions. In terse commands, the guard captain took the lead and got everyone moving away from the conference room. No one had to tell him where they were going.

The captain led them to a stairwell that went down into the palace basement. They marched through a couple of turns in the basement hallway and stopped when they reached two more guards standing on either side of a tunnel entrance. The captain ordered the additional guards to fall in, so the party had three guards in front and three in back. After everyone had moved forward into the tunnel, the last guard closed a massive door made of thick wooden beams and slammed home a series of six metal bolts, three on each side of the opening.

A second boom rattled the door bolts as the guard rejoined the group, inciting them all to stride swiftly down the tunnel toward the other end.

Gregor had heard of this tunnel, but he had never used it before. It supposedly connected the palace to the Tanes family manor.

The palace had been designed more for conducting imperial business than for the comfort of its residents. The sleeping quarters were mostly given over to the guards and serving staff. The emperor had an opulent office with a comfortable bed, but most of the Tanes family lived at their ancestral home in the Nobility Quarter of Cassandria.

At the far end of the tunnel, another pair of guards peered into the passage with their swords drawn, having heard our hurried approach. Once again, the guard captain added them to our protection detail.

The captain turned to the emperor.

"Your Majesty, the manor is not fortified to withstand attack. We are vulnerable here."

Gregor spoke up. "Your Majesty, if I may, I suggest you come with me to the Archives. The castle is designed to resist both conventional and vaetric attacks. We can protect you there."

"How will we get there?" asked the emperor.

Gregor glanced at the captain. "We can go back the way I came. There's a portal about a mile outside the city walls."

The guard captain shook his head. "It's too risky, Your Majesty. We'd have to sneak through the city and hope we didn't encounter any Lightning Corps patrols that may be looking for you."

"Your Majesty, we believe Sorcerer Fortenz's goal was to take the palace, not to assassinate you," Gregor objected.

The guard captain rounded on Gregor. "I'm not willing to take that chance with His Majesty's life. This position is weak, but it is better than running in the open. We must set up our defense here as best we can."

Gregor bowed to Emperor Tanes. "The decision is yours, Majesty."

"Wait," interrupted Sorceress Fleming. "There is another way. Another portal. Here, at the manor."

The seneschal was scandalized. "What? A secret portal here at the manor? Why was I not informed? A portal is a serious security risk to the royal family. It should have been destroyed."

Sorceress Fleming ignored the old man and spoke to the emperor. "The portal is no risk, Your Majesty. It is blocked, so it can't be opened from within the keep. It has been that way for over a hundred years."

"If it is blocked, how will we get through?"

"We tear down the obstruction, Your Majesty."

The guard captain was just as stunned to hear the news of a secret portal as the seneschal had been. He was unable to muster any arguments against the new plan.

The emperor stood silent for a moment. He finally shook his head.

"If we run, we leave the empire in the hands of this usurper. My strength is *here*. I can't fight him from the Archives." The guard captain agreed with a nod.

Gregor sighed. "Your Majesty, the Imperial Guard is brave and capable, but you will need sorcery to defeat the Lightning Corps. Even though Fortenz played this move well, his hold on the empire is tenuous. Let the Archives," he glanced at Sorceress Fleming, "and your own sorcerers, help you take back your empire. If the guard fights back without us, the losses could be horrific."

The emperor was silent again, and his frown deepened. When he finally looked up at his guard captain, his eyes held a determined glint.

"Gather the empress and the children. Assign two men to help Dierdre clear the portal. We leave for the Archives immediately."

Twenty minutes later, two guards had cleared decorative blocks out of the center of a large garden arch. The arch itself was not the simple decoration it appeared to be. It framed a portal, which Gregor opened with his key.

One of the guard lieutenants begged to remain behind so he could inform and organize the remaining loyal guards in the city. The captain made the man promise that he would help maintain order, but not directly oppose Sorcerer Fortenz until support arrived from the Archives. From the look in the man's eye when he agreed, Gregor knew he would find ways to *indirectly* oppose Fortenz' rule.

A dozen members of the royal family, frightened by the turn of events, stepped tentatively through the portal, gawking at the interior of the ancient and unfamiliar tower. Gregor and the Emperor entered just before the last two guards who were accompanying them.

"Well, Your Majesty, it seems that our fates are intertwined."

The emperor put his hand on Gregor's back as they stepped through the portal together. "I'm beginning to think they always have been, my old friend."

Chapter 45
War Council

The air in the Council Chamber was warm and stale. I had a strong desire to escape the tight quarters, but Sulana's hand in mine anchored me to my chair along the wall.

All of the seats at the Council's round conference table were occupied, including the "guest seat" where Emperor Tanes was sitting. In the center of the table was a long tube of rolled leather and a small wooden box. It almost looked like everyone had sat down to play a board game of some sort.

The emperor! I couldn't believe I was in the same room with him. Two guards stood at ease behind the richly dressed monarch, their eyes flicking to every movement within the chamber. No one else in the room was supposed to be armed, but after the attack on the palace, the guards were taking no chances.

The emperor cleared his throat and everyone gave him their attention. "I would like to thank the Council for its assistance and hospitality. I shall try to minimize the inconveniences my entourage will undoubtedly impose upon the Archives."

Senior Councilor Underwood sat stiffly in his chair and wore a serious expression. The slight tremor in his hands and his voice gave away his nervousness. "You and your family are welcome here, Your Majesty."

"Thank you, Councilor Underwood. I also appreciate your invitation to sit in on Council sessions during these difficult times. I assure you that I have no interest in Archives affairs except as they relate to regaining control of the empire. My staff and I are available to you as resources, and you may feel free to exclude us from discussions that do not concern the empire."

I suppressed a snort. That was the emperor's way of asking the Council not to waste his time with trivial details.

Underwood's wry smile told me he caught the same subtext. "I understand, Your Majesty. Perhaps I should start by introducing our councilors."

The senior councilor introduced the emperor to the Council members sitting at the table, including their newest member, Marlene Delano, Sulana's mother.

Professor Delano had accepted the appointment as Junior Councilor only after assurances that her students would be well taken care of. Fortunately, several experienced sorcerers had taken refuge at the Archives after Thunderhead College appropriated their sanctuaries. Two of the new arrivals had been assisting with Marlene's sorcery class and Lissy's potions class, and they were willing to take over.

During the introductions, the emperor shared a private smile with Lissy that made me wonder if they knew each other. Lissy was from a prominent family in Cassandria, so it wouldn't be a surprise if they had met previously.

Underwood went on to introduce the rest of us sitting around the edge of the room, which included Barek, Talon, Sulana, and me. We each stood and bowed when our turn came to acknowledge the emperor. During the introductions, the emperor's gaze lingered on Sulana. A quick glance was the only indication he gave of noticing my introduction.

"So, this is the famous Sword Sorceress I've heard so much about. It is a pleasure to finally meet you, Sorceress Delano."

Sulana tilted her head in a shallow bow. "Thank you, Your Majesty. The pleasure is mine."

The emperor's intent gray eyes shifted to me. "And you, Sorcerer Forester. Congratulations on your confirmation. For the first time in many generations, we have two Sword Sorcerers. That's good. It looks like we're going to need them."

Several polite chuckles came from his audience.

I nodded and said, "I'm afraid you're right, Your Majesty."

"Never be afraid to agree with your emperor, Sorcerer Forester," he advised in a mock-serious tone.

My face heated as nearly everyone chuckled in appreciation of his joke.

Barek, sitting across the room from me, frowned and shifted in his seat. His movement caught the emperor's eye.

"Yes, I know, Barek. We should get on with this. Why don't we start with you? I understand you have good news."

Barek stood, and in so doing, made the room feel even smaller. "Thank you, Your Majesty. My people have agreed to help the Archives fight the usurper. Our treaty with your empire demands it. The Accords demand it."

It was a subtle thing, but Barek's voice had a disturbed edge to it. I doubted that anyone who didn't know him well would notice it. But the emperor caught on immediately.

"What is it Barek? You sound as if there was some question that they would help."

"There was … debate, Your Majesty. The tribal elders were not eager to fight alongside the sorcerers of the Archives."

The emperor nodded knowingly. "Let the magicians take care of themselves. Or something like that."

"Yes, Your Majesty. But the headmaster's attack on the palace ended the debate. We cannot allow a sorcerer to control the empire."

"I agree wholeheartedly, no offense intended to present company," the emperor said, glancing around a room filled with sorcerers.

Underwood smiled. "None taken, Your Majesty. The Accords exist for a reason, and the Archives has defended them since they were established."

The emperor gave Underwood a stern look. "Indeed. We'll discuss the effectiveness of that defense at another time. In the meantime, I would like to know how things are progressing with the mundane resistance and the druids."

All of the councilors turned to look at Sulana. She stood and faced the emperor. "If I may, Your Majesty." She waited for his nod before continuing. "The druids refuse any direct involvement, but their priests speak out against integration. They encourage the mundane resistance, which has done more to swell the ranks of the resistance fighters than anything else. My contact within the resistance tells me that their primary strategy at the moment is interference rather than direct confrontation. If the frustration of the Lightning Corps is any indication, they're doing a good job."

"Thank you, Sorceress Delano." He motioned for her to sit. "Now, would the Council please tell me how the Imperial Guard and I can help the Archives remove Thunderhead College and its headmaster from my empire?"

Councilor Rissik sat forward. "The main thing we need from you, Your Majesty, is the support of the Imperial Guard that remains loyal. Our best bet at this point is to use the headmaster's own tactics against him. We strike hard and fast, everywhere at once. It divides our forces, but his are spread thin as well. A concentrated, province-by-province approach gives him too much time to prepare a defense. Also, as our forces moved forward, he'd be able to use the Portal Keep to slip behind us."

The emperor considered Rissik's suggestion and looked over his shoulder at his guard captain. The soldier frowned, not looking pleased with the approach, but shrugged to indicate he'd be willing to consider it.

The emperor waved toward the captain. "Please include Captain Lutwin in your military strategy discussions. He will represent the empire and coordinate the Imperial Guard's participation in the campaign."

Gregor nodded to the emperor and the captain. "Of course, Your Majesty."

The emperor looked around the table. "If that is all, I need to see to a nearly hysterical empress who is dealing with several petulant children. The Archives has done an admirable job of accommodating us, but some members of the royal family have become too accustomed to the luxuries of Cassandria."

Councilor Underwood checked around the table, but none of the other councilors had anything to add. "I believe that is all, Your Majesty."

The emperor stood and waved the rest of us down when we started to rise as well. "No need to get up. Please carry on. Captain Lutwin will return shortly."

Everyone was silent until the emperor left the room with his escort. When the door shut behind him, the tension in the room dropped a few notches, and we released a collectively held breath in one big sigh.

Councilor Rissik stood and leaned over the table to unroll the leather tube, which as I suspected, turned out to be a map. The map depicted the empire and its six provinces. He flipped open the lid of the wooden box to reveal three compartments with colored markers in each. Referring to a sheet of notes he had in front of him, he began to place green markers around the map.

"These are the last known locations of Lightning Corps units," he said.

He went on to place red markers to represent concentrations of loyal guardsmen and resistance groups. Last, he placed the blue markers where sorcerers loyal to the Archives were holed up.

By the time Captain Lutwin returned, Rissik had the map well populated with markers. The captain sat in the guest chair and listened while the councilor explained the arrangement.

Once the captain had been briefed, the Council got down to the business of planning our campaign to recover the empire. Barek fielded questions about the Wintermen, and Talon shared the status of the Archives Guardian Corps.

Sulana and I would coordinate the five-prong strike into the Lakewoods, Sunset, Grassgate, Mineral, and Bountiful provinces. Our mission was to free the governors from Sorcerer Thoron's amulets and cut the headmaster's support out from under him.

We'd be able to give the Lightning Corps a nasty surprise at the same time. Losing so many sanctuaries to the enemy had resulted in a concentration of refugee sorcery talent at the Archives. The shield-breaking spell from Rikard Shepherd's wand had been reverse-engineered faster than any of us had hoped. We could hurl the headmaster's own spell right back at his Lightning Corps—and they didn't have the benefit of our improved shields.

The Portal Keep and journey room were critical to our plans. When the time came, we had to move faster than the Lightning Corps could react. We couldn't afford the time or the manpower it would take to fight against a prepared defense for an extended period. We needed to take action with minimal casualties—on both sides.

The Lightning Corps had at least a half-dozen soldiers at every strategic portal. That was enough firepower to make real trouble for anyone trying to exit the keep. However, that same force could easily be overwhelmed from *outside* the keep. That's where our contacts among the resistance and Wintermen would come in.

As for the journey room, it's use was limited. All of the sanctuaries in the province capitals had been taken over by the Lightning Corps. We controlled only one sanctuary that would get us reasonably close to one of our targets. But one was better than nothing.

Going back into the palace through the portal in the royal family garden was not an option. Upon investigation, we learned that the headmaster's men had found the portal and sealed it up again. The only way we were getting in was through the front door.

By the time Sulana and I left the room, we were exhausted but satisfied with the progress that had been made. The Council and Captain Lutwin were optimistic in spite of the challenges we faced, and that attitude probably did more for our chances than anything.

CHAPTER 46

GOVERNOR THORON

Sulana and I hunkered down at the forest edge. Only a few tenacious yellow leaves clung to the silvery branches of the aspen and birch. The rest had become a colorful carpet on the forest floor. For a couple more weeks, the rusty-gold needles of the larch would continue to contrast against the evergreens. I thanked the spirits we didn't have rain in addition to the cool temperatures, although a light fog from last night's deluge condensed on the pine needles and dripped occasionally onto our wary group.

Our trek across the Merciless River Valley had been swift but cautious. For stealth and logistical reasons, we'd chosen not to bring horses. We stayed as low as we could and moved forward in short bursts of small units. The fog helped us cross the Merciless River bridge unobserved, or so we hoped.

We waited in the shadow of the mountain about a quarter mile from the Dusk main gateway. The Wintermen in our group had scouted ahead.

"Please, let the gate be open," Sulana mumbled.

I squeezed her shoulder in agreement just as a low whistle alerted us to the return of the Wintermen.

I signaled our lookouts to stand down as Barek and one other Winterman loped toward us.

"The gate is ours," Barek declared the moment he reached us.

"Already?" I asked.

"We were fast. They weren't. Only two Lightning Corps men. Once we took them down, the gate guards helped us tie them up."

Sulana and I shared a grin. "Sounds like the Lightning Corps hasn't been making many friends," she observed.

"It's a good sign," I agreed. "Let's see what happens when we reach the city."

Getting intelligence about the situation in Dusk had been difficult. Its sanctuary had been one of the first we lost. We knew the resistance had representation in the city, but the rebels were understandably coy about revealing anything to the few contacts we'd managed to sneak past the Lightning Corps. Of all the provinces, Sunset was the only one that had a governor who was *voluntarily* supporting the headmaster.

The fact that the gate guards were less than sympathetic to the Lightning Corps was noteworthy. The attitude of the guards often reflected the attitude of their leadership. We came prepared to fight the combined forces of the Imperial Guard and the Lightning Corps if we had to, but I'd be happy to let the guard stand aside.

"Move out," Sulana ordered with a forward wave of her hand, and everyone started trooping toward the gate. We had decided that she would lead this mission and I would be second in command, even though we were both Sword Sorcerers. The chain of command would be clear and I would be free to offer advice to her.

When we passed through the gate, the guards from Dusk were tied up next to the unconscious Lightning Corps men. One of the men nodded soberly in our direction as we passed. Their bindings confused me as I thought Barek had said the guards were helpful.

Turel, First Sword of the Winterman squad trotted past, so I tilted my head toward the guards and asked him, "Why'd you tie them up?"

He answered without slowing. "They insisted. If we fail, the black cloaks won't know they helped us."

Ah, Good thinking.

We scuttled to the first switchback road that would take us up the mountain to Dusk. I scanned the mountainside above us, checking for anyone who might be taking an interest in what was happening below. From what I could see, there weren't many good observation points. A plateau halfway up the mountain was probably the bench at the top of the second switchback, and in the distance, the back sides of a couple large homes on the city level loomed over the valley.

We traversed the first incline with no problems other than the occasional mud puddle from the prior night's rain. We also encountered no traffic, which wasn't a surprise as harvest season was long past and the weather was hardly inspiring.

Slowing down for the second incline, we came upon the first houses. Smoke puffed listlessly from the chimneys, and nearly everyone was inside. A couple of men were outside splitting wood together. The splashing water of the roadside creek masked the sound of our approach.

The two men were so absorbed in their work that they didn't look up until we came alongside their homes. Both men moved their axes into a defensive position and shifted backward when they saw the Wintermen.

"No need for alarm," Sulana called to them. "We aren't here to harm you."

Neither man looked convinced, and I couldn't really blame them. To these men, our group of heavily armed swordsmen looked like a raiding party. Which we were, except our raid wasn't aimed at the city. We moved on.

When we reached the next switchback, I looked back to see that the two men were following our group at a distance, axes at the ready.

My heart sank with the thought that we might have to fight our way through the townspeople to reach the sanctuary.

Barek led the way up the third incline. About half way, he slowed to a stop. He made several rapid hand signals indicating trouble ahead and telling us to take cover.

I ran toward the cover of a shop to our left with Sulana following closely. I activated my standard shield bracer as I moved. Unfortunately, not all of us could shield ourselves.

The buzz of arrows was followed by a cry of pain. One of our number had been hit.

After we ducked into the alley along the side of the shop, my shield bumped into the wall and Sulana, so I dropped it. I peered around the corner of the building and searched the street for the person who had been hit, but the victim must have made it to cover. Instead, Barek and Turel caught my eye as they sneaked forward. A Lightning Corps sorcerer stepped out in front of them with an orb in his hand and the final words of an incantation on his lips.

I shouted a useless warning. From where I crouched, I was helpless to do anything for the two Wintermen. Sulana pulled me back from the corner as an arrow splintered the wood where my face had been. I lost my balance and sprawled to the ground, taking her with me. Before she pulled me away, I had spotted where the bowman was hiding. He had ducked behind some crates across the street after loosing his shot.

A crack of thunder was followed by groaning wood and a splintering crash. I crawled back to the corner of the building, keeping my head low. The front overhang of the building had collapsed on top of the spot where Barek and Turel had been standing. The two Wintermen and the sorcerer who had attacked them were gone.

My breath caught as I realized that Barek was probably buried under the debris. I bolted from my hiding place and ran forward, just as the enemy bowman rose from behind the crates for another shot.

My unexpected movement spoiled his aim. The arrow twanged into the wall just behind me. Before the man could duck back down, one of our guardians fired an arrow that struck the man low in the throat.

A second bowman stepped out from behind the next building. I slid to a stop and activated my shield bracer. He narrowed his eyes at my half-raised arm, seeming to recognize that I was shielded. He tossed his bow aside, drew his sword, and advanced on me with a grin.

I dropped the shield and reached under my long coat to draw my own blade. *You want to fight with swords? No problem.* His grin faded and he slowed his approach. Apparently, he did not expect me to be both sorcerer and swordsman.

The clash of arms told me that I wasn't the only one engaging in hand-to-hand combat. As my blade came up to deflect his initial strike, members of our team surged forward from their hiding places to find and engage the remaining ambushers.

The bowman who faced me should have spent more time practicing his swordplay. I let him take the offensive, but he scored no hits on me while I managed to draw blood with every counter strike. The desperation in his attacks increased along with his fear until he got so sloppy that I simply disarmed him and punched him in the face hard enough to knock him out.

I looked around for more opponents, but saw none. The sounds of battle were subsiding and the other members of my team were gathering back at the street. I sheathed my sword and started throwing aside chunks of wood, searching desperately for a sign of the buried Wintermen. I was joined by several guardians who ran over to help.

I gripped the end of a heavy beam, took two deep breaths, and nodded to the burly swordsman at the other end. With a strained grunt, we shifted the beam off the pile. As soon as we threw it aside, the boards underneath tilted and rose. Barek and Turel stood up, shaking their heads and shoving away the broken boards that had held them down.

"Thanks," Barek said. "It was getting hard to breathe."

"What happened?" The last I'd seen, they were about to get blasted by a lightning bolt. I'd missed how they ended up under a collapsed overhang.

"He missed."

"How? You were, what, ten feet away from him?"

Barek shrugged. "Maybe he was aiming for the support posts."

Yeah, maybe. "If you have a way to deflect lightning, I sure wish you'd let me in on it."

Barek just stared back at me. His trademark impassive expression told me we'd had this discussion before and I wasn't going to get any further this time. Turel gave Barek a considering look followed by a slow nod of comprehension.

"Magebane," he said.

Barek turned to him and silenced him from saying more with a stern glance.

As much as I wanted to ask Turel for an explanation, I kept my mouth shut. At least I had a term to research. I might be able to figure out more on my own. For the moment, I would respect Barek's desire for secrecy.

Sulana walked up, sheathing her sword, just as a guardian called out, "Found him."

The guardian pushed aside the last few boards and raised the body of the sorcerer by the armpits. He leaned the corpse against the front wall of the building. The guardian pulled on the hilt of a long dagger that stuck out of the man's chest. Wiping the blade off on the sorcerer's black robe, he stepped over to Barek and held it out hilt-first. "I believe this is yours?"

Barek took the dagger with a nod and returned it to his belt. Bending down, he picked up something from the debris and tossed it to me.

It was the sorcerer's casting orb; a prize of war. I tucked it away, deciding that it might come in handy. I'd left Froth attached to my staff back at the Archives, thinking that both would just be in the way for this mission.

Once the action had subsided, residents started opening doors and peering out at us. The shopkeeper who ran the business that had lost its overhang came out and glared at the dead sorcerer with his hands on his hips.

We all turned our heads in response to a shout from further up the street. Two black-clad men on horseback raced out of a stable several doors up and kicked their mounts into a full gallop toward the city. Our two bowmen scrambled to get a shot at the retreating figures, but the horses rounded the next turn and disappeared before either could get off a shot.

My eyes searched the hillside above us for a way to reach the next level and cut them off, but the incline was too steep and covered with shrubs and trees. I tracked their progress helplessly as they charged up the next switchback leaving exclamations and curses in their wake.

"So much for sneaking up on the sanctuary," Sulana commented.

We hadn't really expected to get all the way to the sanctuary without alerting the Lightning Corps, but it would have been nice. The weather was keeping most people indoors, so before the ambush, I had been daring to hope.

Sulana raised her voice so everyone could hear her. "Form up, everyone. We may have lost the element of surprise, but that doesn't mean we should give them any more time than necessary to prepare for our arrival."

Sulana's sweeping glance lingered on the two men who had been hurt during the encounter. One had taken an arrow through the shoulder and the other had suffered a leg wound. Neither were in any condition to double-time it up the next incline and into the city.

"We have Lissy's healing potions," I reminded her.

"Yes, let's give one to each of them, but I don't want to wait." We looked around for a place the men might be left behind safely, and we were startled to see that the two axe-wielding residents from earlier had come up behind us.

I reflexively reached for my sword, but stopped with my hand on the hilt when I saw that both men had lowered their axes to a less threatening position. One of the men took a step forward.

"You're here to fight the black cloaks?"

"Yes," Sulana answered.

"We can tend to your men for you."

I believed them. Apparently, so did Sulana. She immediately ordered potions for the two injured men. The axemen set their weapons aside and helped the two guardians inside the home of a stout woman who stood at the door and waved them in.

The rest of our group formed up quickly and continued up the road to Dusk at a jog. The few residents who were on the street either stopped to stare curiously or ran inside. We had just reached the top level where a low rock wall framed the entryway to the city. A group of armed men filled the gap and more men stood behind the wall, crossbows and bows aimed our way.

I sighed with defeat. We'd never get to the sanctuary if we had to fight through that crowd. Besides, Sulana hadn't lied before. We weren't here to fight the residents, just the Lightning Corps. It was starting to look like our mission had failed.

One of the men stepped forward several paces. His gaze was directed at me. "Jaylan Forester?"

A flicker of hope for our mission returned. It was Malcolm Brachus, the former governor's son. I pushed past Barek to stand at the front of our group. Sulana followed and stood next to me.

"Hello, Malcolm. Yes, it's me."

The young man started walking toward us and a few of his men muttered in protest. He raised his open hand behind him to quiet them. Sulana and I met him about half way, and I introduced her.

"Why are you here?" he asked.

"The emperor sent us to purge the Lightning Corps from the city and return control of the province to its rightful heir."

Malcolm lowered his voice. "And you think I'm the rightful heir?"

"Aren't you?"

"It doesn't matter. What matters is what's best for our people."

I blinked a couple of times in confusion. If not for the headmaster's meddling, Malcolm would have become governor upon his father's death, not Astin Thoron. It sounded like he was willing to let things continue as they were.

Sulana narrowed her eyes at him and spoke sharply. "You believe the Lightning Corps represents what's best for your people?"

Malcolm laughed. "Not in the least. But I want you to consider separating the issue of governorship from the goal of defeating the Lightning Corps. We'll help you get the black sorcerers out of the city, but we won't let you arrest Governor Thoron."

His offer to help sent a tingle down my spine. He had about twenty people in his group. Only a few had the look of professional soldiers, but they would do. I had no qualms about accepting his terms.

"We have no intention of arresting Astin Thoron," I said, "Although we do have a proclamation from Emperor Tanes that gives you the authority to replace him as governor."

Malcolm grew still and narrowed his eyes at us. "May I decline that offer?"

His response surprised me. After years of enmity between their parents, Malcolm was willing to let Astin remain governor?

Sulana answered for us. "I don't see why not."

"Good. Then it's a deal." He held out his hand to each of us, and we shook on the agreement.

"Malcolm! Black cloaks coming!" a man back at the entryway shouted. He pointed toward the town square.

The area between our position and the buildings around the square was mostly filled with flower beds, which offered little cover. Five Lightning Corps soldiers and six men in Imperial Guard uniform marched around the corner of a building and came our way. The group was led by a robed sorcerer who carried a wand in his right hand. The leader's step faltered when he spotted the stand-off between Malcolm's group and mine, but then he squared his shoulders and lengthened his stride.

The sight of the overconfident sorcerer made me flush with anger. Malcolm shook his head in dismay and started back toward his group. Sulana and I followed him. She signaled our team to move forward, and Barek was at our side within a few more steps.

Malcolm's men grew agitated as we approached, looking back and forth between the Archives troops and the oncoming Lightning Corps sorcerer. Malcolm gave them a calming gesture as he walked past the wall toward the sorcerer.

Sulana and I stopped just before reaching the wall. She turned to Barek.

"Get everyone ready for trouble. Jaylan and I will go see what he has to say."

The Winterman nodded and immediately started positioning our people behind the wall with hand signals. Malcolm's soldiers watched nervously from their side of the wall, but they seemed more concerned about the presence of the Lightning Corps.

Sulana and I hurried to catch up with Malcolm. We had just done so when he and the enemy sorcerer came to a stop a few paces apart. The sorcerer kept his wand pointed at the ground, but his knuckles were white around the thin strip of wood.

The sorcerer addressed Malcolm first. "I'm surprised to see you here, Brachus. I wouldn't have expected your help in detaining these ... invaders."

Malcolm bowed gracefully to the man and introduced him. "This is Sorcerer Drake, Dean of the local Thunderhead College campus."

Sulana and I did not bow. Drake and his crew had appropriated the local sanctuary and turned it into the *campus* Malcolm was talking about.

"And this must be Sword Sorceress Delano," the so-called dean continued with a sneer in his voice. "I suggest you take your band of ruffians back the way you came. You are not welcome in Sunset Province."

"I get the impression that it's *you* who has worn out his welcome," I retorted.

Sorcerer Drake's calm and superior expression didn't waver. He glanced at Malcolm. "We've had our differences, but the people of Dusk are learning how sorcery can ease their burdens."

Several grumbles including phrases like, "at what cost?" and "for those who can afford it," came from Malcolm's men.

Drake's demeanor changed to one of wariness and he shifted his stance, turning slightly so he presented his right side toward us. I could see his wand more clearly, and the newness of it convinced me that I should activate my lightning shield bracer if he attacked.

Sulana took the verbal offensive. "Your time here is over, Drake. The emperor has charged us with removing Thunderhead College influence over the government of this province."

The smile that spread across Drake's face was unpleasant to witness. "Forgive me for doubting you, but that seems unlikely," he said.

Sulana whipped out a small message tube and impatience crept into her voice. "I have the orders from Emperor Tanes right here, if you care to see them."

"Ah. I see the misunderstanding," Drake replied. "I'm not surprised you haven't heard the news. I myself just learned this morning. Meritus Tanes is no longer emperor.

Since Tanes abandoned his people, the Assembly crowned Dumont Fortenz in his place."

Gasps and mumbled comments erupted all around. Even the imperial guards in Drake's party looked at each other with uncertainty. Sulana and I exchanged a worried glance, but it was Malcolm who spoke up.

"They can't crown a sorcerer as emperor. The Accords forbid it."

I wouldn't have thought it possible, but Drake's grin grew wider. "The Sorcery Accords have been abolished. It is the dawn of a new age where sorcerers will regain the respect that was stripped away by the Accords. You should rejoice with us," he added, addressing Sulana and me.

I didn't like Drake's implied association. We might both be sorcerers, but I saw nothing but disaster down the road Fortenz was taking. Drake seemed oblivious to the reaction of the mundane who stood around us, while I was never more aware of the fact that they saw me as a sorcerer first and a fellow citizen of the empire second.

Malcolm's stance was rigid and he looked me in the eye. When he spoke, his question was a challenge. "What say you?"

I returned his stare and spoke carefully. "Dumont Fortenz is a criminal and a traitor. We support the rightful emperor, Meritus Tanes, and we will give our lives to restore him to his throne."

Malcolm relaxed and nodded once.

Drake sneered and said, "So be it."

As soon as Drake started to raise his wand, I activated my shield bracer. Sulana stepped behind me as the shield came up, just as we'd practiced. A spark at the end of Drake's wand turned into a flash of lightning that arced toward Sulana and me. It struck my shield, flared, and drained into the ground.

Drake narrowed his eyes at my bracer. He muttered, "So it's true." I saw his mouth form the words more than I heard them since my ears were still recovering from the noisy attack.

He stowed the wand and raised his fist to activate one of his rings. That was when Malcolm crashed into him, bearing him to the ground.

The Lightning Corps swordsmen drew their blades and advanced on Malcolm, but Malcolm's men charged forward and slammed into them, weapons flailing. Drake's sorcerers stepped to the side to get a clear shot at us, but to everyone's surprise, the guardsmen from their own group stepped up behind them and knocked them to the ground. The guards stood over the sorcerers, sword points at their throats.

It was all over in a few seconds. Malcolm lifted Drake to his feet and two of his men searched the sorcerer for weapons and vaetric implements. They found and took his dagger, his wand, and his casting orb.

Drake's face was twisted into a snarl of hatred. "You'll pay for this. When the emperor hears what you've done, he'll have you flogged and hanged." He turned and looked at the guards who had arrived with him and then changed sides. "You'll all pay."

Given the circumstances, his threats didn't concern me. The guards didn't look impressed either. I shook my head, unable to accept his use of the term "emperor" when referring to Dumont Fortenz.

Sulana was apparently thinking along the same lines. "Controlling the palace does not make Fortenz an emperor. It makes him a usurper and traitor. His residency at the palace is temporary."

Drake laughed. "Taking control of this backwater is one thing. Taking back the other provinces and Cassandria is another matter."

I ached to tell him that the other provinces were being taken care of at that very minute, assuming things were going as planned. But that information needed to remain secret until all of our teams had completed their missions.

Sulana glanced at me, probably struggling with the same desire to rub our plans in Drake's face, but she restrained herself as well. "We'll see about that, Drake. In the meantime, let's find out if your people at our sanctuary will come out peacefully or if we'll have to take it by force."

Marching through Dusk to the sanctuary, our combined forces filled the streets from side to side. When we arrived at the sanctuary, we surrounded the building and stood at the entrance with Drake in hand.

Fortunately, Drake saw the futility of resistance, so he encouraged his few remaining people to evacuate the poorly fortified structure. Within five minutes of our arrival, we had regained control of the sanctuary.

In the meantime, more city guardsmen had arrived to investigate the disturbance. They were happy to take all of the Lightning Corps personnel into custody, ignoring Drake's repeated threats of retribution.

That left us with one more stop.

~

Governor Astin Thoron stood at the entrance to his residence with a ring of guards and his mother, Uriel, at his arm. He put on a brave face, but the tremor in his voice as he demanded our business gave away his unease. His mother glared at us in barely controlled fury.

In our march through the city from the sanctuary to the governor's residence, we collected more people who were drawn to Malcolm's group and more guards who joined their fellows. Governor Thoron faced Archives sorcerers, a handful of Wintermen, and a large crowd of his own citizens.

Sulana stepped forward.

"Greetings Governor Thoron. I am Sulana Delano, Sword Sorceress of the Archives. We are here because Emperor Tanes has ordered us to restore Sunset Province to its rightful heir."

Astin sighed and lowered his head in an attitude of defeat. His young face showed relief more than disappointment.

Seeing her son's reaction, Uriel Thoron drew herself up and shouted in indignation. "My son *is* the rightful heir. Governor Brachus legally appointed Astin as the heir designate before his death."

Sulana responded, keeping her voice even. "Governor Brachus was a victim of sorcery. You and your husband will be tried for your roles in his manipulation."

Uriel gripped Astin's arm, anger and fear warring for dominance over her expression.

Malcolm started to speak but Sulana raised her hand to stop him and interrupted. "It has come to our attention that Malcolm Brachus supports your claim to the governorship, as do the majority of Dusk's citizens." Voices from the crowd behind us chimed in with exclamations and comments supporting Sulana's statement.

"We will confirm their wishes with the emperor, but we see no reason to remove you from office for now."

Uriel's face broke into a happy smile and she leaned her head on Astin's shoulder briefly in affection.

But Sulana wasn't done. She pointed at Uriel and continued. "However, we must insist on the arrest of Uriel

Thoron until she stands trial for violating the Sorcery Accords."

Astin pulled his arm out of his mother's grip and signaled his guards to take her in hand. His mother looked up into his face incredulously. "You would arrest your own mother?" she asked.

The young governor looked down into her eyes and spoke with sadness in his voice. "I never wanted this, Mother. Our family was doing perfectly well, but you and Father couldn't be satisfied." Astin glanced at Malcolm's sympathetic face. "I'll accept this responsibility because it seems I must, but I'm not doing it for you and I'm not doing it for Father. I'll be governor for the people of Sunset Province, and I'll do it my own way."

Astin turned toward Sulana. "My mother will remain under house arrest until an imperial judge arrives, if that is acceptable to you, Sorceress Delano."

Sulana gave the young governor a shallow bow and said, "Thank you, Governor Thoron. I see your people's faith in you is well-placed."

The governor shrugged and looked once again at Malcolm. "Are you sure about this? We know the truth now." He waved an arm toward the doorway of the residence. "All of this should be yours."

Malcolm smiled as he replied. "I'm sorry to disappoint you, Governor, but you are the better man for the job. Your judgments have been fair and you put the interests of our people ahead of your own. You just proved that to all of us."

Astin stared at Malcolm for a moment before responding. "Fine. As long as you agree to take me hunting with you once in a while."

Laughter broke the tension around the residence courtyard as Malcolm strode forward to shake Astin's hand. The guards escorted a subdued Uriel inside the building.

Sulana spoke over the buzz of conversation that was starting to gain volume. "One more thing, if you please, Governor." Astin and Malcolm both turned their attention to her. "We have a few *guests* who need secure lodging. Do you think you can accommodate them?"

Governor Thoron's mouth twisted up on one side in a sardonic smile. "I'm sure something can be arranged. Leave them with my guard. I'll make sure they are taken care of."

"Thank you, Governor."

"I assure you, Sorceress Delano, it will be my pleasure."

~

Our team helped the city guard take all of the Lightning Corps men into custody. Back at the sanctuary, the sorcerers we'd brought from the Archives gleefully set about reclaiming the home that the Lightning Corps had forced them to abandon. Most of our team would stay in Dusk until Emperor Tanes was back on his throne.

Barek, Sulana, and I planned to use the journey room to return to the Archives. At secret, pre-scheduled time windows, the translocation orb for Dusk would be placed on a pedestal at the Archives, allowing us to employ its twin at the Dusk sanctuary.

When the next scheduled time arrived, Barek, Sulana, and I said our goodbyes and went downstairs to the small journey room in the basement. The three of us stood on the circular grate of the translocation sphere and set the Archives translocation orb onto the pedestal.

Sulana did the honors and activated the orb. Moments later, we were back at the Archives, hurrying through the halls to find out how the other teams had fared.

CHAPTER 47

THE PROMISING PATH

Dumont ran his hand down the silvery surface of the long metal rod that extended up from the floor and disappeared into the ceiling. The workmen had done a fine job of restoring the link between the amplifier on the floor below him and the giant focus sphere located several levels above on the roof of the palace.

Smiling with satisfaction, Dumont descended the stairway that curved along the outside wall of the ancient wizard tower to the bottom level where Paeter was working. He ran his hand along the stone wall, marveling at how well the tower had withstood the ages.

Who would have guessed that Wizard Rollek's old tower was hidden all this time *inside* the palace? That old fool Vlastorus must have nearly soiled himself when he rediscovered it and the treasure it held. All these years, such incredible power lay wasting away in the palace basement.

Rollek's Amplifier had been silently waiting. Waiting for a sorcerer powerful enough and clever enough to give it purpose once again.

And here I am.

The body of the amplifier lurked at the lowest level of Rollek's tower. The restored metal rod descended from the ceiling and disappeared into the top of the wide, blocky stone base. The base was about the size of a large oven with a cavity in the top where they would insert the finished spell core. A heavy blade switch that would complete the connection between the core and the focus link was mounted next to the cavity.

All that remained to restore the amplifier to its full potential was the spell core.

Paeter Thoron labored feverishly at a work bench they had moved into the tower for his research. With access to the Confluence, Paeter had more vaetra than he could possibly need for his smithing. He was concentrating so hard on his task that he hadn't noticed Dumont's presence in the tower yet.

Looking over the shoulder of the hardworking sorcerer, Dumont asked, "How goes the battle, Paeter?"

Paeter jumped and nearly knocked over a crucible that was poised over an oil burner. Dumont took a step back when Paeter glared over his shoulder.

"Please don't do that, Master … I mean Your Majesty. This is delicate work and easily spoiled."

"I was hoping for a progress report. Our opponents have finally made their move. It's only a matter of time before they are roaring at our gates."

Paeter put down his tools and wiped his hands on the heavy smock he wore over his regular clothing. He turned to Dumont with a pensive look.

"What of Dusk? Did they arrest Astin?"

"Curiously, no. It seems they were content to recapture their sanctuary and purge the city of the Lightning Corps, but your son remains governor."

"What of Uriel?"

"That I don't know. She hasn't made contact with any of our agents, but I think we'd have heard about it if she'd been arrested."

Paeter nodded absently, frowning and staring off into the distance. His eyes refocused on Dumont's face.

"Where do we stand now?" he asked.

"I'll admit the Archives surprised me. I expected them to gather the Wintermen and the mundane resistance into an army that would sweep through the provinces. We would have had plenty of time to complete the spell core and whittle down their forces at the same time."

"So what happened?"

"They took a risk. They sent small teams into every province and attacked in concert. It was an impressive demonstration of planning and logistics, but it wasn't entirely successful. They failed to take Grassgate Province, so I still control the Assembly."

Although Paeter seldom kept abreast of current events, his sharp mind quickly understood the implications when presented with the facts. "Nothing stops them from marching on Cassandria now."

Dumont nodded. "You must accelerate your efforts. I don't know how much time we have, but you must complete the spell core before they arrive."

Paeter shook his head, doubt creeping into his voice. "I have to get this exactly right, and I can't work any faster."

Dumont frowned and spoke sharply. "Surely the Confluence gives you all the power you need."

Paeter's voice took on a pleading tone. "Yes, certainly, but it's not a matter of power. Power doesn't help me craft the right spells for the core or the master amulets. Power doesn't help me design a core that can stand up to the flow of vaetra that will pour through the amplifier. What I need is time, Your Majesty."

Dumont let out a harsh breath in exasperation. "Your perfectionist ways will be the end of us, Paeter. You've had plenty of time. I know how you work. You investigate every possible path before choosing one. You must learn to work more intuitively."

"You mean, *guess?*"

If he weren't so annoyed, Dumont might have laughed at Paeter's horrified expression. "No, I mean take a calculated risk. You are probably the most talented smith of your generation. Use your experience to skip the paths that are likely to lead to a dead end. Go back to them later if you must, but follow the most promising course first."

Paeter stared at Dumont, considering his master's words. After a moment of silence, he blinked rapidly a few times and bowed. "I'll do my best, Your Majesty."

Dumont put a hand on the other man's shoulder. "Just do it quickly, Paeter. I want that spell core in place when the Archives and Meritus Tanes arrive on our doorstep."

"You think the emperor … former emperor will be with them?"

Dumont gave Paeter a conspiratorial smile. "I certainly hope so. Just imagine how much easier it will be to solidify my control over the empire with Tanes himself helping me do it."

CHAPTER 48

PORTAL TO NORTHSHORE

I waited with Sulana at the rocky overlook near the Archives portal. We had a lovely, snow-encrusted view of the narrow valley sweeping down and away from us. The rock under our feet was sheathed in ice, so we stayed well back from the edge and safely in the zone that had been sanded this morning.

After exchanging a few cursory greetings with the poor shivering archers, swordsmen, and sorcerers assigned to guard the portal, we'd settled into enjoying the beauty while we waited for Ebnik. I had my arm wrapped around Sulana's shoulders, and she huddled close with her arms folded up next to my chest.

"Jaylan. Sulana. Are you ready to go?" said the familiar and unexpected voice of Councilor Velna Asher. We turned to find her all bundled up and carrying a pack over her shoulder.

"We're waiting for Ebnik," I said. "He's going to use his portal key to take us through to Northshore."

Asher looked over her shoulder at the trail that led back to the Archives. "He isn't coming after all." She took off a glove and showed us that she was wearing Ebnik's portal key ring on her thumb. "I told him that I decided to join the march on Cassandria. He seemed relieved that he didn't have to come out into the cold."

Sulana narrowed her eyes at the councilor. "How will we get Ebnik's ring back to him if you come with us? His ring needs to stay here at the Archives. It's one of the few we have left."

Asher glanced back at the trail again. She then looked around at the guards, who didn't seem to have any interest in our discussion. "People are still going back and forth all the time. He said to just give it to the next person coming this way. In fact, there's probably someone waiting at the other side right now."

I understood Sulana's frown. It was unlike Ebnik to part with his portal key. He had rarely taken it off since the last one was stolen out of the Archives armory. But his intolerance for cold was one of the things that made him retire to the milder climate of Plains End, so his reluctance to venture out into the icy weather was not a surprise.

Asher stamped her feet and blew on her hands. "Can we go now? I'm freezing."

Sulana and I exchanged a glance and shrugged. We picked up our belongings while Asher pointed the ring at a well-trampled area near one of the ravine's rock walls and triggered the portal key. I slid one pack strap over my shoulder and leaned on my sorcerer's staff. Sulana shouldered her pack as well and cradled her favorite crossbow under one arm.

Asher opened the portal door and motioned us inside while she held it open. Sulana and I stepped in cautiously, looking all around and up at the higher levels. It was rare to encounter anyone else traveling through the keep, but Sorcerer Fortenz (I refused to call him Emperor) still had a key, so we could never be sure.

No one could stay in the tower for long and remain conscious, and the only sorcery that seemed to function were the illuminators that lit the interior and the portal controls. Still, one could rotate conventional ambush teams into the tower if you had enough men and were willing to dedicate a portal key to the task.

"It looks clear," I said, giving Asher the cue to come in and close the door.

The door closed off the silvery light from outside, leaving only the dim light from the keep's illuminators. My eyes were still adjusting, but I knew where the door to Northshore was located, so I took a step toward it.

A swish of cloth and searing pain at the base of my neck sent me crashing to the floor. The last thought to spark through my awareness as I collapsed was that we'd been fools to trust Velna Asher.

CHAPTER 49
INFIRMARY

Gregor burst into the infirmary and rushed over to Ebnik's bedside. The old man's head was wrapped in a bandage and his face was deathly pale. His eyes were closed, and if it weren't for the steady rise and fall of the wizard's chest, Gregor might have thought he'd arrived too late. An abrasion on Ebnik's cheek glistened from some kind of healing cream, and his stockinged feet hung out over the end of the bed that was far too short for him.

"How is he?" Gregor asked the nurse.

The nurse looked down fondly at Ebnik, who opened his eyes and winked at her. "Oh, he'll survive. The old bird has a tough noggin."

"What happened?"

"The guards found him in the hall with a nasty whack on the back of his head. He scuffed his face when he fell. Anything more, you'll have to get from him." The nurse gave Gregor a stern look and shook her finger. "But don't be long about it. He needs rest."

Gregor nodded his understanding and slid the visitor chair as close to the side of the bed as possible so they could converse quietly.

"Do you know who did this?" Gregor asked the old wizard.

Ebnik nodded and then grimaced in pain. "Yes," he said with a hiss. "It was Asher. My portal key is gone, and I think she took it. The guardians are looking for her."

Gregor closed his eyes briefly and sighed. "They won't find her. The portal guardians say she left for Northshore with Jaylan and Sulana."

Ebnik's eyes came alert at the news. "They never arrived?"

"Correct." Gregor put his head in his hands. "I should have had someone watching her. Asher has been jittery and agitated ever since Fortenz took the palace and we informed the Council that he may be restoring Rollek's Amplifier."

Ebnik raised a hand and patted Gregor's arm. "We've *all* been jittery and agitated." Then his expression became serious. "We need to find them, Gregor. They are our link to the spirits, and the spirits are deeply involved in this somehow."

A flash of annoyance made Gregor frown. "If Jaylan has some kind of destiny, why would you worry? Maybe this is part of it."

Ebnik sighed. "I'm worried because *everyone* has a destiny, and fate decides which destiny prevails."

Gregor let out an impatient harrumph. "That sounds positively chaotic. And no different from having no destiny at all."

Ebnik put up a hand in surrender. "Fine, Gregor. I agree that either way, it's out of our hands. But I can't help wondering about the timing. Why would Asher wait until now? Do you suppose she was a spy all along?"

Gregor shook his head. "I don't know. Perhaps. Or maybe she just started thinking that she might be on the losing side."

Both men retreated into their own thoughts for a moment. Gregor reflected on what a disaster this abduction was turning into. Should he have foreseen it?

Ebnik broke into his reverie, "I can't imagine Jaylan and Sulana would have gone with her willingly. They knew Talon was expecting them in Northshore to help lead the Archives

Guardian Corps. *I'm* just a silly old fool, but for Asher to surprise those two would have been a challenge."

"I agree. If she really has chosen to betray us, her most likely destination would be Cassandria. Jaylan and Sulana would have instantly known something was wrong."

Ebnik reached up and touched the bandage on his head. "Assuming they were conscious."

Gregor stood and pushed the visitor chair back toward the foot of the bed. "We'll keep looking for a while, but the march on Cassandria can't wait. If they *have* been captured, the sooner we get to them the better. Using the keep is going to become more dangerous as well. If Fortenz has a second portal key, he can afford to dedicate one to rotating troops into the tower and making our lives miserable."

Ebnik raised an eyebrow. "Maybe we should beat him to it."

"How? My key is the only one we have now that yours is gone."

Ebnik gave Gregor a knowing half smile. "Talk to Sorceress Fleming. I know the royal family had one, and I seriously doubt she would have left it behind."

Gregor agreed with Ebnik's assessment of Dierdre Fleming. If anyone knew where the royal family's portal key was, it would be her. Whether she would part with it was another story.

"I'll see what I can do." Gregor reached down and squeezed Ebnik's arm. "Take care, old man. We may have to pull you out of retirement yet."

Ebnik rolled his eyes. "Ha. Some retirement. I saw less action *before* I retired."

Gregor chuckled and waved goodbye as he walked toward the door.

His face grew somber as soon as he left the infirmary. With purposeful strides, he headed toward Sorceress Fleming's quarters. The emperor and his guards would be the last to go through the keep to Northshore. Once Fleming knew of the increased security risk, she should be willing to loan her key to keep the tower free of assassins.

In the meantime, Gregor hoped Jaylan and Sulana were alive and well. The thought brought on an unexpected surge of emotion that made his breath catch in his throat. Lissy would be devastated when she heard the news of their disappearance. Through their friendship with her, the young couple had become more dear to him than he'd realized.

He wasn't a religious man, and he still had his doubts about Jaylan's stories of the Runedream, but he uttered a silent prayer to the spirit goddesses anyway.

Jaylan and Sulana have followed your guidance as best they can. Please keep them safe.

CHAPTER 50

BETRAYAL

Pain. Everywhere.

My senses swam in a sea of confusing input. I was sweating, but a chill shivered through me. The scene that was revealed when I opened my eyes was dim and unfocused. A horrible stench worked its way through my blocked sinuses. Although I was lying on my back, I seemed to float in a fog of dizziness.

I coughed and then groaned in agony as a sharp pain shot across my chest. At least one rib was probably cracked. My tongue probed a puffy split on my bottom lip and gave me an answer for the metallic taste in my mouth. Someone had worked me over good.

"Jaylan! Thank the spirits you're still alive. Are you okay? Say something!"

It was Sulana's voice. She seemed to be in much better shape than I was.

A second voice said, "Yes, thank the spirits. His snoring was driving me insane."

The other voice triggered a dim memory of walking into the Portal Keep with Councilor Asher. I could blame her for at least one of my throbbing aches.

Sulana shouted, her voice tight with suppressed fury. "Shut up, Asher! He was nearly killed, thanks to your stupidity." Her voice softened. "Jaylan, answer me. Please."

I cleared my throat of bloody phlegm and croaked, "I'm alive." When the pain subsided from forcing out those first words, I softly added, "But I've felt better."

Sulana blew out a breath of relief. "I'm not surprised. Those cowards took the loss of Thunderhead College out on you, but didn't have the guts to do it while you were conscious."

Worry twisted my stomach, which was already a bit queasy. Sulana had attacked the college with me. "How about you?"

"I'm fine. They slapped me around, but Sorcerer Fortenz didn't let them go too far. You were Mister Fireball, after all."

My relief eased the tension in my stomach, but the abuse I'd taken caught up with me. My stomach lurched, so I hastily twisted onto my side. Big mistake. Pain cramped every muscle in my body, curling me into a fetal position. I vomited onto the straw flooring of the cell. I tried to scoot back from the noxious mess, but that only brought more pain. I froze in position until the heaves subsided and my muscles unknotted.

Asher grumbled, "Great. As if this place didn't smell bad enough already."

Being on my side was even more painful than lying on my back, so once I had recovered enough to move again, I slowly unfolded and flattened myself out with a sigh of relief. I was sure it was going to be days before the bruises and stiffness would begin to fade. My movement had also alerted me to the fact that my right leg was manacled to a chain.

Feeling slightly better, I turned my head to the side. Dim torchlight flickered through the grate of the cell door opposite me. I craned my neck up to look toward the wall to the right of the door and found Sulana staring anxiously at me. She was as close as she could get, her leg extended behind her, stretching the chain that restrained her to its fullest extent.

She had a red mark on her left cheek that would turn into an ugly bruise, and a nasty split on her forehead that left a dried streak of blood all the way down the right side of her face.

When her eyes met mine, she swiped at her tears and cleared away some of the blood stain. A tentative smile appeared on her face and I smiled back.

She sniffed and self-consciously wiped at her nose. "Sorry if I look scary. I'm fine, other than a nasty headache from this." She reached up and gently touched the cut on her forehead and glared across the room. "Thanks to Miss Traitor over there."

Turning my head to follow the direction of Sulana's glare, I focused on the wall opposite hers. There sat Velna Asher, looking much less arrogant than usual, with straw sticking out of her hair and a heavy manacle on her leg. She had her back pressed up against the wall and her arms curled around her knees, which were folded against her chest. Her dirty face was streaked from recent tears.

When my eyes met hers, she looked away and pressed her forehead onto her knees.

I wanted to shout at her, but I couldn't muster the strength for it. All I could manage was to ask the one question that was foremost in my mind.

"Why?"

She looked over at me again with a bored expression. *There* was the arrogance I was used to. Then she actually shrugged. The adrenaline that surged through me from my anger did nothing but send my heart pounding and elevate the pain. If I'd been capable and unrestrained, I would have crawled over to her and slapped her hard.

She finally chose to answer my question. "We were doomed anyway. Fortenz is the greatest sorcerer of our age. With the amplifier in his hands, we never stood a chance."

"So you figured you could buy your way back into his good graces by delivering us to him," Sulana growled.

Asher returned Sulana's glare with that same infuriating bland expression. "There was no *back*. I was never his spy. I tried to be a good little sorceress and work within the system at the Archives. I want integration, but I never trusted Fortenz or his college of malcontents."

Sulana clenched her fists and her voice rose nearly to a scream. "So you changed sides just because you thought we were going to lose? Have you no integrity whatsoever?"

Asher's eyes flashed and she shouted back. "I panicked! I thought Emperor Fortenz would have mercy on me if I gave him a way to end the conflict peacefully."

"So you gambled with our lives."

"And my own. With the amplifier in his control and you two as hostages, I figured the Archives would have to surrender."

"I think you overestimated our value," I mumbled.

She glanced at me with a wry twist to her mouth. "Apparently. Fortenz wasn't interested in seeking surrender. He said something about using you as bait instead. He knows the Archives forces are on the way here, and he's not worried."

The constant pain was exhausting, and I was having trouble keeping up with the conversation. I started to drift off, but Asher's next comment reawakened me.

"For what it's worth, I'm sorry. I'm sorry I panicked and I'm sorry I involved you."

The bitterness and sincerity in her voice convinced me that Asher truly regretted her actions.

"You're only saying that because it didn't work," Sulana shot back.

Before anyone could say more, I interrupted with a whispered, "Apology accepted."

"You can't be serious!" Sulana exclaimed. "Her cowardice and poor judgment nearly got us all killed, and it may come to that still. How can you forgive her?"

I cleared my throat and met Sulana's angry eyes with mine. "Who said anything about forgiving her? I'll testify at her trial and support whatever sentence the Council deems appropriate. But I believe she's sorry, and that's … something."

My words trailed off as weariness overtook me. Sulana's tight and angry face softened into an expression of tender concern. "Get some rest. I promise I won't go anywhere."

My mouth curved into a smile and I nodded just enough for her to see the motion. "We aren't dead yet," I whispered before sleep pulled me away from her.

Chapter 51
South Pass

Gregor rode near the front of the main body of the army alongside Talon and Captain Lutwin. After two frantic days of preparation, they had finally left Northshore that morning. Gregor's sense of relief as they started their journey had given way to anxiety when he realized how slowly they were moving. If Fortenz got Rollek's Amplifier working before they could stop him, there was no telling what they might face when they arrived at Cassandria.

The first day of the march had delivered both blessings and curses. The bright sun warmed his robe, and the storm that had passed through two days before saved him from choking on road dust. But his ears ached from the deep chill left behind by the clearing clouds. The half-frozen mud bogs his horse easily stepped around presented a challenge for the supply wagons and the emperor's carriage. What would normally be an easy two day's ride was undoubtedly going to turn into three. And that assumed they didn't encounter opposition along the way.

Gregor looked over his shoulder and was amused by the odd assortment of soldiers they had collected at Northshore. Imperial guardsmen in maroon livery walked alongside mundane resistance fighters dressed in homespun earth tones. The dark blue robes of Archives sorcerers were littered in small clumps throughout the ribbon of marchers that stretched behind him. A few mercenaries from the Raven Company had joined their ranks as well, although they had left their black tabards behind to avoid being confused with the enemy.

All told, the army numbered about six hundred fighters and sorcerers. A few additional volunteers from the resistance were still joining them as they progressed through the countryside. A larger army would be better, of course, but Talon was confident that they had enough soldiers to defeat the Lightning Corps forces at Cassandria. The real trick would be taking the palace without destroying it.

A commotion drew his attention back toward the front of the host. One of the scouts was returning at a full gallop.

Gregor's heart started to beat faster. The hurried scout's news was unlikely to be good. As the scout approached and turned his lathered mount to ride alongside Captain Lutwin, Gregor eased his horse closer to them so he could hear.

The scout reported. "Captain, rangers approached us. They say South Pass is blocked by forces from Grassgate. They want to speak to you."

"Rangers? Where are they?"

"Over the next rise, sir. Just before the road starts down into the pass."

Captain Lutwin checked the sun's position in the sky. It was no more than an hour above the horizon. "We'd best stop here." He gave the command to halt. The order was repeated like an echo toward the front and rear of the column. Two of his lieutenants turned in their saddles, awaiting his next orders. The captain pointed toward the apex of the rise in the road ahead. "I want a defense perimeter along the rise and into the forest on either side. Set up camp about a half mile back. There's a good chance the enemy already knows we're here, so stay alert." The lieutenants acknowledged his orders and rode off to comply.

Gregor appreciated the captain's leadership and experience. When they met in Northshore, he and Talon agreed that the Imperial Guard should manage their forces with the captain in charge. The Archives Guardian Corps would provide support under Talon's command, and Gregor would advise the captain on how to deploy their sorcerers.

Although they were allies intent upon the same mission, the guard and the mundane were uneasy about having sorcerers in their midst. A few unpleasant exchanges had been cut short by the lieutenants, but a lifetime of suspicion and distrust was not easily put aside. The captain had wisely recommended keeping the sorcerers in groups of two or more to reduce the likelihood of "accidents."

Captain Lutwin turned to Gregor. "Do you want to attend this meeting? You know how druids feel about sorcerers."

Gregor shrugged. "I'm sure the rangers know sorcerers are present. I won't be a surprise to them. I'm curious to find out what they want. The druids have avoided getting involved in the conflict up to now. This warning is out of character."

"I agree. Well, let's see what they have to say."

Captain Lutwin led the way to the shoulder of the rise. At the forest edge, several resistance men used their axes for the original purpose of cutting and trimming small trees. Guardsmen dragged the trees to the rise and set up barricades. It would take hours to block the entire rise, so they settled for several short barriers that would protect them from enemy archers. At the top of the rise, they could see far down the road into the canyon until it curved to the right and out of sight. The captain nodded his approval. If the enemy tried to storm up that hill, his men would have the advantage of high ground and plenty of warning.

The company of rangers had moved to the near side of the rise by the time the captain stopped his horse in front of the lead man. The leader's intense grey eyes took in the telltale robe of Archives blue and his gaze locked with Gregor's. With a surge of uneasiness, Gregor wondered if coming along had been a mistake. But then he noticed the Marshal's star on the man's leather breastplate and the circle around it that denoted a ranger priest.

Taking a calculated risk, he said, "Defender Marshal Shields, I presume?"

The marshal's eyes narrowed. "You have me at a disadvantage, sir."

"I'm Councilor Gregor Rissik of the Archives. This is Captain Lutwin and Weaponsmaster Destry. Sword Sorceress Delano speaks highly of you, Marshal. I would like to personally thank you for your part in restoring her health and helping her get back to us."

Marshal Shield's face tightened and his eyes darted to the side. Two of his men looked down and fidgeted in their saddles, while the others turned curious gazes upon him. He frowned at Gregor and asked, "Speaking of Sorceress Delano, where is she? I expected to find your Sword Sorceress and Sword Sorcerer at the head of the army."

Captain Lutwin shot a warning glance at him, but Gregor had the feeling that the truth would serve them best in this situation. "Sorceress Delano and Sorcerer Forester have been missing for three days. We have reason to believe they may be prisoners of the Lightning Corps."

The marshal jerked back in his saddle as if struck, and his face paled. His horse shifted under him in response to his agitation. "That cannot be. The spirits would not allow it."

"The spirits work in mysterious ways," Gregor said, regretting the words as soon as he spoke them. The marshal's eyes widened in outrage. It was clear he did not appreciate a sorcerer quoting a common druid saying back at him. The man would undoubtedly see it as a mockery of his faith.

"I apologize, Marshal. I meant no disrespect. What I should have said is that we don't know exactly where Sulana and Jaylan are. They may yet serve the purpose of the spirits."

The marshal took a deep breath to calm himself and nodded once at Gregor, accepting the apology.

Captain Lutwin wisely chose that moment to take control of the conversation. "My scout tells me you warned him of an ambush in the pass. We appreciate that, Marshal Shields."

The marshal gave him a wry smile. "Yet you can't help but wonder why." The captain tipped his head to the side in concession.

The marshal explained. "I've been instructed to help Emperor Tanes regain his throne as quickly as possible using whatever means I deem necessary, short of committing druid resources to direct combat."

The captain rolled his eyes. "You won't help us fight."

"That's correct. But I think we've just demonstrated that we can provide valuable intelligence. We can assist in other *passive* ways as well."

Gregor immediately saw the value of having the druids on their side. "Thank you, Marshal. Your assistance is sincerely appreciated."

The captain seemed to come around to Gregor's line of thought. "Yes, thank you, Marshal. Can you tell us how many soldiers are in the pass?"

The marshal reported that he and his men had counted approximately two hundred soldiers. The troops appeared to have come from Grassgate Province.

The road through South Pass split into two forks. The west fork went high along the side of the canyon and was the preferred route during the summer and fall. The rest of the year, the east fork, which was longer and ran through the bottom of the canyon, was safer and easier to keep open.

The bulk of the Grassgate forces was positioned on the east fork of the road, although they could move to the west fork readily enough. They had chosen their position well. From the higher road, they could cover both routes through the pass.

The captain thought for a moment about the information Marshal Shields had supplied. "So, we have no choice but to fight them head-on."

Gregor's chest tightened with anxiety. A battle for the pass could take days. They didn't have days. The enemy had to know they would lose eventually, which meant the purpose of this ambush was to slow down the emperor's army.

"We don't have time to fight them for the pass. We must get to Cassandria without delay. Every hour counts."

The captain's eyebrows rose in surprise. "What do you suggest? Does sorcery give us a solution?"

Gregor shook his head impatiently. "No. They have sorcerers as well, no doubt." He glanced at Marshal Shields and received a nod of confirmation.

Talon moved his horse forward so he was alongside Gregor. He had stayed back and observed up to then. "Perhaps Marshal Shields has a suggestion."

Marshal Shields smiled at Talon. Apparently, he did indeed have an idea.

Gregor had tremendous respect for Talon, but the weaponsmaster was so quiet most of the time that he still tended to underestimate the man. Talon was used to enhancing conventional tactics with sorcery. If anyone could foresee a way to use unanticipated resources to create an unorthodox solution, it would be him.

"If you don't want to fight them, go around them," the marshal said.

The captain waved a hand in frustration. "How? Taking an alternate road to Cassandria would delay us a week or more."

"The east fork is only covered by a few sentries and runners. Under cover of night, you could take out the sentries and slip past."

The captain shook his head incredulously. "Our torches would light the entire canyon like a bonfire! And we'd give the enemy perfect targets for their arrows."

Marshal Shields shrugged. "So don't use torches."

The beginnings of a smile tugging at the corners of the marshal's mouth told Gregor that he was baiting the captain. He seemed to enjoy the captain's frustration as he revealed his plan in bits and pieces.

Gregor decided to have mercy on the poor confused captain.

"Marshal, would you kindly just let us in on the full plan here?"

The marshal pursed his lips and then nodded. "Of course. Here it is. With some help from the spirits and a little sorcery, we walk past the enemy tonight without torches."

Excitement coursed through Gregor as he caught on to what the marshal was suggesting. "You're talking about using night vision."

"Exactly."

Gregor's excitement quickly faded to disappointment. What the marshal suggested was just as impossible as sneaking past with torches. "We don't have anywhere near enough night vision potions to distribute to the entire army. We've barely enough for the sorcerers."

"That's where the spirits come in."

Marshal Shield's filled them in on his plan as the sun eased below the horizon. They would get started as soon as it was full dark, and they'd have to be on the move as quickly as possible. They had to get well beyond the enemy and set up camp before the night vision wore off.

The horizon turned golden and then faded until the first stars glimmered against a dark purple backdrop. During that time, Marshal Shields requisitioned a twenty-gallon cask of water and collected the two other ranger-priests on his team. The trio took the cask into the forest for a private blessing of the spirits.

While the rangers worked, the captain conferred with his lieutenants, and Talon passed along the plan to Daven and Barek. They gathered everyone, except the lookouts along the rise, into a sinuous line that wove down and across the valley.

When they were told what was coming, some of the soldiers refused to participate. A few changed their minds when they learned that they would have to stay behind and join the volunteers who would tend the fires to make it look like the army was still camped behind the rise.

Gregor rounded up all of the sorcerers and made sure everyone had the ability to invoke night vision. Since they were sorcerers, the marshal would not allow them to participate in the ceremony. Gregor was relieved to learn that a few of them knew the incantation or had implements they could use. If not for that, he would have run short on potions.

The rangers returned from the forest carrying the casket of blessed water and set it on a table near the front of the line. One by one, every soldier went by the table and drank a small cup of water, carefully measured out with a ladle.

After receiving their water, the soldiers formed a new line that circled back on itself. Men and women soldiers stared across the fires at one another, their faces revealing their attitudes about the druid ceremony they were about to endure. Some were amused, and some concerned. The more pious among them were excited about participating in a genuine miracle.

The three ranger priests removed their shoes and splashed into a long but shallow pool of water that the storm had left behind alongside the road. Their position had been strategically reserved at the head of the loop. The marshal gave the signal for everyone to join hands. Groans and protests from the soldiers were shushed by their lieutenants. Gaps closed quickly where soldiers lost their nerve and stepped out of the loop. At last, everyone in the loop formed a continuous human chain.

The three rangers began to pray. Most of the soldiers looked down at the ground and closed their eyes in respect. Many joined in the prayer, asking the spirits to support their cause. After about a minute, Marshal Shields looked up in consternation and Gregor knew something was wrong.

Gregor had his doubts about the plan, but he'd kept them to himself. What the marshal intended was so different from what could be done with sorcery that he didn't understand how it would work. And Marshal Shields was not very forthcoming with explanations.

Calling for everyone to stay where they were, the Marshal left his position and walked over to where Gregor waited to the side with the other sorcerers.

The marshal pulled Gregor away and kept his voice low, but he spoke rapidly. "I need a favor."

"Name it. Is the ceremony not working?"

"I miscalculated. The spirits have blessed me with night vision on many occasions, but I'm having difficulty getting across what I want them to do."

"How can I help?"

"Do you have any extra night vision potions?"

"I think I can spare one. Fortunately, some of us have other means." Gregor put his hand into his pocket to retrieve the potion.

"Stop," commanded the marshal. Gregor's froze, his hand still in his pocket. "If you don't mind, I'd rather no one else know about this. Could you pass the potion to me as we shake hands?"

"What are you going to do?"

The marshal stared into Gregor's eyes. Gregor guessed he was considering how much he was willing to share. "I'm going to pretend that I forgot to drink some of the blessed water myself. But instead of the water, I'm going to drink your potion."

Gregor was shocked. A druid accepting a product of sorcery? He'd never heard of such a thing.

The marshal smiled at Gregor's blank expression. "Yes, I know. But I need a way to show the spirits what I need."

Gregor suddenly understood what the marshal had in mind. "You're going to turn the blessed water they just drank into a night vision potion."

The marshal nodded slowly. "In essence, yes." He held out his hand as if to shake Gregor's. "Please. I must act quickly. Thank you for your help."

Gregor removed his hand from his pocket and passed the potion to the marshal while pretending to shake the man's hand. The marshal turned and walked swiftly to the table where the cask of water still sat. He took a ladleful of water from the cask and poured it onto the table next to the cup. Gregor was the only person close enough to observe the deception. The marshal poured the potion into the cup as he reached to pick it up. Downing the contents of the cup in two swift gulps, he went back to the circle and joined his fellows, who looked at him with curious expressions.

After ensuring that all hands were still joined, the rangers began their prayer again. This time, Gregor saw the violet glow of vaetric manifestation build in the water around their ankles. The breeze increased and plucked at his clothes as the prayer grew in intensity. Within moments, the breeze had grown to a forceful wind that whipped around the line of soldiers and stoked the camp fires into tall, sparking infernos.

Many of the soldiers glanced around, eyes wide with alarm. But no one dared release the hand of his neighbor. Soldiers were starting to lean back from the growing flames when the violet glow flowed up around the bodies of the rangers and flared down each side of the loop from one hand to the next. For a second, the fires went out completely as the druid blessing completed the loop at the far end of the line.

In the next blink, the glow had disappeared, the breeze was a mere breath on Gregor's cheek, and the fires once again flickered normally. The shift from tempest to calm was so sudden that he shook his head, his mind rejecting what he'd just witnessed.

A moment later, the valley filled with gasps, exclamations, and the excited chatter of soldiers who realized that they could see in the dark. Most took several steps back from the fires and shielded their eyes.

To Gregor's sorcerer vision, the soldiers' eyes glowed the same eerie violet that had flowed from the rangers. He turned and signaled the Archives sorcerers to activate their own night vision. The clock was ticking.

As previously planned, everyone who was going through the pass gathered into three columns. A forward unit left immediately, armed with crossbows and daggers to silence the sentries who had been posted to watch the west fork. It was possible that some of the sentries had night vision as well, so the scouts would have to approach the pass cautiously.

Within ten minutes, the army began marching over the rise and down into South Pass.

The new moon was only two days past, so that night the moon was a thin crescent sitting just above the Western horizon. What little illumination it granted their enemies would be gone shortly.

Gregor was amused to note that most of the soldiers seemed pleased by the blessing the rangers had called for them. The few who were frightened by the experience were cajoled into acceptance by their more enthusiastic fellows. There was brief talk of attacking the enemy while they were settling down for the evening, but the lieutenants warned them to be careful what they wished for. The night vision would only last so long. Engaging in melee along a cliff on a moonless night would be deadly for both sides.

When they reached the point where the road split, they saw the first evidence of their advance party at work. The bodies of several sentries were prone by the side of the road. Four horses had been left tied at the center of the fork.

Everyone of rank was mounted, but most of the soldiers were not. The horses went to four lieutenants who were instructed to assign the animal to the subordinate who could make best use of it.

A tall ridge separated the east and west roads for the first part of the journey, so it went without incident. They startled several deer, but otherwise the canyon was quiet and dark.

About half an hour later, the ridge melted into the east wall of the canyon, and the first torches of their enemies flickered along the edge of the other road high above. To Gregor's relief, the river flowing at the bottom of the canyon was loud enough to help mask the sound of six hundred boots attempting to march quietly.

Fifteen minutes later, the army had reached the place where the roads joined back into one. The advance team waited for them there, having dispatched another group of sentries. The rangers, who had left the staging area even before the advance team, met up with them as well and reported that the rest of the pass was clear ahead.

Gregor peered over his shoulder, smiling at the distant camp fires of his unsuspecting foes. His smile faded when a shadow broke free of the shrubs along the road and started running toward the encampment yelling at the top of his voice. The advance team had apparently missed a sentry.

He reached for his lightning wand, but realized it would give them away. Before he could alert anyone else to the danger, Daven kicked his horse into motion after the escaping sentry. The horse's hoof beats were like thunder after all their stealth, making Gregor wince in trepidation.

But Daven didn't plan to try catching up to the man. After he covered about fifty yards, he pulled his horse crosswise to the road and nocked an arrow. His shot was one smooth pull with only a brief pause to aim. Even with night vision, Gregor could not track the arrow's flight, but the sentry tensed in mid stride and hit the ground face first. He didn't move again.

Everyone held still and went completely silent. Had the enemy heard the sentry's warning? After about a half minute with no reaction, Daven turned his horse and headed back. In spite of the need for silence, a few whispered cheers greeted Daven when he trotted into the main group. Soldiers patted his legs and whispered their congratulations on his excellent shot as he rode past.

The army continued through the pass, leaving their own sentries behind to watch for enemy movement. By the time they neared the far side of the pass where it opened out onto a forested plain, the night vision was wearing off. They didn't get as far as they'd hoped, but their position was defensible so they stopped for a rest.

Gregor wrapped himself in a blanket and leaned against a tree, settling in for a nap. He smiled to himself when he thought about how far they'd managed to go on the first day, thanks to the rangers. Marshal Shields was an intriguing man. He hoped they would meet again some day.

The army ate a cold breakfast and started out the next morning as soon as it was light enough to make out the road.

Only two more days to Cassandria, Gregor thought as he mounted his horse.

CHAPTER 52
THE TEST

The Great Hall buzzed with tension, and Dumont reveled in it. About fifteen feet away, four leaders of the most powerful families in Cassandria stood in a tight cluster whispering to each other. They would never have behaved so rudely to Emperor Tanes, but these families were the ones who were most critical of Dumont's ascension. Anias Rissik and Melody Aragon stood stiffly at the forefront while the other two patriarchs cowered behind them.

Dumont lounged in the comfortable chair that served as the emperor's throne behind a long, elevated desk. Some day soon, he would have to replace the arrangement with something more impressive. For the moment, he had more important matters at hand.

Paeter sat next to him, fiddling idly with his new amplifier core. He had temporarily affixed a casting orb to one end to serve as the focus for today's exercise. Dumont stroked the chain of the master amulet he wore to protect his mind from the effects of the core. A similar amulet glinted at Paeter's neck.

Dumont decided that his guests had stewed long enough. "Thank you all for coming today," he greeted them.

He wasn't surprised that Melody Aragon, known in social circles as "Aragon the arrogant," was first to speak. She huffed at his greeting and said, "You say that as if we had a choice. Your guards practically dragged us here. What do you want, *Emperor* Fortenz?"

Dumont ignored her rude mockery of his title. She would bow in time. His guards weren't as forgiving and stepped forward to chastise the woman. She looked down her nose and dared them to touch her. Dumont held up his hand to forestall his men.

Dumont steepled his fingers and tapped them together a couple of times. "I wish to negotiate an agreement with you."

Aragon squinted at him and crossed her thin arms under her breasts.

"What did you have in mind, Your Majesty?"

Lady Aragon had been one of the great beauties of her time, and her well-maintained figure still enthralled men twenty years her junior. Her charms did not sway Dumont in the least. Poison came in the prettiest of bottles.

"In exchange for your support, I will grant each of your businesses a reprieve from the new taxes that are scheduled to begin next month."

The tax increase was minimal, but for these families, even a small increase would add up to a substantial sum. Dumont regretted losing the income, but he was willing to pay well for any consideration from this group.

Aragon pursed her lips in thought. The other three representatives leaned toward her and offered their opinions in low whispers. She shook her head and took a step away from them, effectively quieting them.

"What kind of support are you asking for, Your Majesty?"

"You would all swear fealty to me and cease this endless rhetoric criticizing my rule."

Aragon gave him a slow insolent smile. "Debate is good for the government, Your Majesty. It keeps our leaders on their toes. Accepting a bribe to ignore our concerns would be a disservice to the people of Cassandria."

Dumont had no expectation that these aristocrats would accept his offer. If he had, he would have made his initial offer even less palatable. He had an experiment to conduct after all.

Having established the baseline attitude of his subjects, Dumont turned to Paeter and nodded subtly. Paeter had been watching for the signal. After a brief hesitation, he spoke the trigger word for the core and activated it.

Aragon gave Paeter an uneasy glance and slipped back into place next to Anias. Her fear seemed to make her angry. Dumont guessed that being fearful was an unusual experience for her.

"What is that?" she snapped. "Some kind of weapon? We must lie for you *or else?*"

Dumont waved a hand in dismissal. "Not at all, Lady Aragon. This is a device of peace. We all want the same thing: peace and prosperity for Cassandria. Your families have served Cassandria well for generations."

Paeter had warned Dumont that he would need to help the spell along. Dumont had to associate himself with something the targets cared about and praise them for their loyalty to it. Once the association was in place, the spell would reinforce it and make them susceptible to any suggestions he might make.

Dumont glanced at Paeter. The sorcerer's eyes had glazed over a bit as he fought the effects of the spell. One of the limitations of their test was that Paeter couldn't operate his master amulet and the spell core at the same time. Being the inventor of the spell, Paeter was able to resist its effects better than most people, but ultimately it would slip through the cracks of his will and he would be as suggestible as the rest.

The faces of his guests had the same disoriented look people got when they stepped out of a bright sunny day into a dark pub. Dumont waited for them to relax and return their attention to him before he spoke again.

"Now that you've had a few minutes to think about it, I'm sure you can see that taking an oath of loyalty to me is the best way to protect Cassandria."

Her voice had lost some of its venom, but Aragon still shook her head in refusal. "I will never swear loyalty to a sorcerer."

A mild jolt of panic shot through Dumont. They didn't have time to craft a new core. Their enemies would be at the gates of the city within a few days. He turned to Paeter with a furrowed brow. Whispering behind his hand, he said, "The spell does not appear to be working."

Paeter smiled. "Oh, it's working, Your Majesty. It just hasn't had enough time to overcome their resistance to your rule. For now, try something more in line with their own desires."

Dumont straightened his shoulders and cleared his throat. He adopted his most severe expression and looked down into Aragon's eyes.

"Surely you do not want our beautiful city torn apart by war, Lady Aragon."

The woman's eyes widened in shock at the suggestion. "Certainly not, Your Majesty."

"Then perhaps you would be willing to help me unify the people of Cassandria against anyone who threatens us."

Lady Aragon pursed her lips and looked down while she deliberated. Dumont wanted to prompt her for an answer, but held his tongue. He wasn't asking for her loyalty, but he *was* asking for an alliance, something she had already proved she would not agree to even when bribed.

Dumont kept his face straight, but he wanted to smile triumphantly when the three others with Lady Aragon started nodding their heads. He was not surprised to learn that her mind was the strongest at resisting Paeter's spell.

Finally, she looked at him with hooded eyes, not quite trusting her own words. "Cassandria must be protected, Your Majesty. Of course we will do what we can to keep it safe."

She was not agreeing to the kind of alliance Dumont had in mind. He needed a stronger commitment from her. "Can we agree to suspend our differences and work together for the good of the city during this time of crisis?"

Lady Aragon bowed slightly and said, "I'm sure we can come to an agreement, Your Majesty."

Dumont could not have stopped the grin that came to his face if he'd tried. *This* was the kind of respect he deserved. Once the core was installed in the amplifier and activated, the entire city would bow to him.

An area spell like the one the core radiated affected everyone, mundane and sorcerer alike. Only he and Paeter possessed the master amulets that shielded their minds and made their suggestions irresistible to anyone within range of the spell.

When Emperor Tanes and the Archives showed up outside the gate with their little army, they would fall under the influence of the spell and bow to him as well. In fact, he could hardly wait for them to arrive.

CHAPTER 53

THE GATES OF CASSANDRIA

Gregor caught up to Captain Lutwin and reined his horse in alongside of Lutwin's. The captain was staring into the distance at the high walls of Cassandria. Gregor could see that the north gate was closed, as they had expected it would be. More than one black-clad lookout had ridden off in haste upon seeing their advancing force.

Daven joined them and inclined his head toward Cassandria. "Do we surround the city?"

The captain shook his head. "We don't have enough soldiers to cover all four gates and break through their defenses at the same time. We'll concentrate our attack on the north gate."

Daven furrowed his brow. "Aren't you worried the headmaster and his henchmen will escape through one of the other gates?"

Captain Lutwin snorted in disgust. "Let them escape. We can always hunt the traitors down later. All that matters now is regaining the palace."

Gregor interrupted. "Sorcerer Fortenz will not leave the palace. His strength lies with the amplifier. In fact, if he's managed to get it working, we could have a nasty surprise waiting for us."

Captain Lutwin glanced at Gregor, his confident demeanor slipping. "Do you have any idea what we might be facing?"

Gregor shrugged apologetically. "There's no way to know. Wizard Rollek shielded his fortress with it, but the original spell core was destroyed. Fortenz would have had to create a new core, and only the spirits know what kind of spell he might have put into it. If Thoron is with him, it could even be some variation of the amulet spell. I suggest you keep the emperor well back from the city for now."

The captain looked over his shoulder at the emperor's coach. Emperor Tanes peered out of the coach window, casting a questioning look at his military commander.

"I agree, but I doubt he'll go along with that idea. He intends to enter the palace in triumph and spit in Fortenz's face, assuming the usurper survives our attack."

Gregor raised an eyebrow. "The emperor's optimism is commendable. I believe we'll have to get into the city first."

The captain nodded and urged his horse forward. "Let's take care of that right now."

The army moved forward through the empty fields north of Cassandria. It was slow going over soft, muddy ground that had been roughly tilled under for winter. Captain Lutwin set up his command post well back from the walls, out of bow and spell range.

There was no question of parlay or discussion. The enemy lined the high walls, ready with arrow, quarrel, and spell. They had seen the army coming and had no intention of giving up peacefully.

Most of the Lightning Corps troops who had escaped the raids in the other provinces had fallen back to Cassandria. Although the forces loyal to Emperor Tanes outnumbered them by a wide margin, the Lightning Corps had the advantage of a strong defensive position. Time was also on their side.

After spending a few moments assessing the gate and its defenders, Captain Lutwin turned to Gregor. "Do you have a way to breach the gate with sorcery? Or should we ready a battering ram?"

Gregor considered the gate for a moment. It was probably fifteen feet high at the apex of the stone archway and at least as wide. "If we can get close enough, sorcery can help weaken the gate, but a battering ram will deliver the most force in a concentrated area. I think the best use of sorcery will be to protect the ramming crew."

The captain nodded and gave orders to two of his lieutenants. One would harvest a suitable tree from the forest beyond the fields while the other put together a team.

While they worked, the enemy was not idle. Soldiers along the wall sluiced water down the surface of the gate to protect it from fire. Arrows occasionally arced uselessly back and forth between the opposing forces, testing their range. The air was charged with anticipation for the battle to come.

A small group of overeager resistance fighters moved closer to the walls for a better shot and were punished with a bolt of lightning from a sorcerer on the walls. The strike was at maximum range, so all it did was burn one bowman's arm, but the point was made and the rest of the group hastily scrambled backward.

Before long, a group of ten men returned from the forest with a thick tree trunk. The soldiers carried the heavy log by branch stubs that jutted from both sides at uneven intervals. They set the log down near the captain with a thud.

Captain Lutwin praised the men for their handiwork and turned to Gregor with a grin. "I never thought I'd be excited about battering down the gates of my own city. Are your sorcerers ready to do some shielding?"

Gregor had collected a volunteer team of eight sorcerers who would shield the ramming crew. It was dangerous duty. Missiles and spells were likely to come in from many angles, and gaps in the shielding were inevitable. Of course, the rest of the army would be doing its best to distract the defenders and make them keep their heads down.

Soldiers and sorcerers gathered around the ram and the first group of attackers readied their bows. The men with long shields took the lead, followed closely by the bowmen and a few additional sorcerers who would fire spells at the defenders and help shield the men around them.

Captain Lutwin gave the command to attack and the first wave moved forward. As soon as they were within range, arrows arced out from the defenders along the city wall. The attackers returned fire, and from there it was a free-for-all.

Gregor held his breath as the men charged forward with the battering ram. One man went down before they had gone twenty steps and was immediately replaced by a nearby soldier. Once the sorcerers and shieldsmen figured out how to synchronize their forward movement with the men carrying the ram, arrows and lightning strikes deflected harmlessly from their protections.

Captain Lutwin signaled the line of archers and sorcerers to move forward and begin their attack. "Long live Emperor Tanes!" he shouted, and the army echoed his call with a roar.

The defenders along the wall targeted the oncoming battering crew but were forced behind the battlements by the arrows and spells that speared through the air around them. With a loud boom, the ram struck the north gate and the battle for Cassandria was on in earnest.

Captain Lutwin glanced at Gregor with his lips pressed into a grim frown. His haunted eyes betrayed his feelings about attacking his own people and the city that had been his home for most of his life.

"Fortenz will pay for this," he stated in a voice husky with anger.

Gregor nodded once and turned his attention to the walls. He scanned for familiar faces among the bobbing defenders. At this range, it was unlikely he'd be able to recognize anyone, but he had little doubt that a few members of his own family were among the defenders.

The ramming crew backed up for another run at the gate. As they started forward again, several cries went up from the defenders and the rain of arrows and spells from the walls ceased. The ram struck the gate unopposed and the crew backed up for another strike.

Captain Lutwin signaled the archers to hold their fire. The defenders had disappeared from the walls and sounds of battle came from within the city. The ramming crew hesitated.

Two heavy thumps came from behind the gate. A moment later, one of the wide doors opened part way. The ramming crew dropped the ram and drew their swords.

Gregor watched in disbelief as someone waved a white handkerchief through the door opening and called out to the soldiers. The door opened further and a woman on a brown appaloosa rode out to address the ramming crew. After a brief conversation, she galloped across the field toward Captain Lutwin.

Gregor recognized Lady Aragon as soon as she had emerged from the gate. He shook his head and smiled. It didn't surprise him that she would be at the head of a resistance movement within the city.

She slowed her horse and stopped within a dozen feet of Captain Lutwin. The captain called back the soldiers who stepped forward to block her approach.

Lady Aragon inclined her head toward the captain and smiled. "Good day, Captain Lutwin. If you wanted to enter the city, all you had to do was knock."

The captain leaned back in his saddle with a mock-innocent expression. "I thought we just did."

Lady Aragon glanced over her shoulder at the battering ram. "Yes, I suppose you did at that." Her face grew serious. "We need your help, Captain. We hold the north gate for the moment, but it won't last. The Lightning Corps still controls most of the city."

Captain Lutwin immediately gave orders for the army to enter the city and help Lady Aragon's men hold the north gate.

Gregor interrupted. "Excuse me, Lady Aragon. Have you heard anything about the headmaster's progress with something called Rollek's Amplifier? We believe it is the main reason he moved on the palace when he did."

Lady Aragon met Gregor's eyes. "Hello, Councilor Rissik. All I've heard are rumors, really. Craftsmen repaired part of it, but they were ushered in and out past a canvas wall that blocked their view of the lowest chamber."

Gregor's heart lurched when he heard that repairs to the amplifier's link had been completed. All that remained was the creation of a new spell core. "Have you heard anything else? Like what he might be planning to do with it?"

Lady Aragon shook her head, but then she got a thoughtful look with her eyes focused in the distance. "No, although a strange thing happened a couple of days ago. The usurper summoned me and three other business leaders to the Great Hall. He wanted us to swear fealty to him, but of course we refused. He then asked that we swear to help him protect the city. At the time, his second request seemed reasonable, but after we left, we realized he had tricked us into supporting him somehow. When your army showed up outside the gates, I knew it was time to show that fool just how I thought our city should be protected."

Alert for clues, Gregor latched onto her comment about being tricked. "You aren't, by any chance, wearing an amulet that he gave to you?"

Lady Aragon pulled a necklace free of her blouse. Hanging from the center was a fine rendition of a daffodil in gold, but it had no gems that Gregor could see. "I just have this, which has been in my family for years," she said.

Gregor let out a breath of relief. Fortenz could be a smooth talker at times. Perhaps that explained Lady Aragon's temporary confusion.

Lady Aragon's supporters opened the north gate fully so the loyalist army could start pouring into the city. A few moments later, the sounds of battle resumed as the troops encountered Lightning Corps reinforcements.

As Gregor rode toward the gate alongside Captain Lutwin and Lady Aragon, she turned and spoke privately to him. "I trust you are keeping my niece safe?"

He smiled. "Lissy is back at the Archives, as safe as she can be at the moment."

Lady Aragon nodded in acknowledgment, and then looked over her shoulder at the carriage slowly rolling forward a ways behind them. "I wish we could say the same for the emperor."

Gregor followed the direction of her glance. "Emperor Tanes wants to be here when we take back the city. Captain Lutwin and I aren't happy about it, but he is, after all, the emperor."

Lady Aragon threw her head back and let out a small laugh. "I'm quite familiar with the man's stubbornness. I just hope you can keep His Majesty out of trouble."

"So do I, my lady. So do I."

CHAPTER 54

RESURRECTION

It was impossible to tell the exact passage of time, but my best guess was that we'd been confined to the dank cell for three or four days. The only visitor we'd had was the Lightning Corps guard who delivered our food and squirted water into our mouths from a water skin. No matter what we demanded or how we pleaded, the man never said a word.

Our captors were taking no chances. Water wasn't the best focus for a spell, but a caster might be able to do something useful with even just a handful. Our guard ensured that we swallowed every mouthful.

I didn't need a focus to enter the Runedream, but my three brief visits had been a waste of time. None of the goddesses appeared, and I really couldn't blame them. What use did they have for a prisoner? I had failed them, just as Loralai predicted.

The worst of the pain from my injuries had faded, but I couldn't tell if it was because I was healing or if I was just getting used to it. Maybe it was a bit of both. I'd pulled up my shirt to inspect the side of my chest and Sulana gasped when I revealed a massive reddish-purple bruise. Whether the ribs were cracked or just bruised, I couldn't tell. All I knew was that every movement was painful and no position, sitting or lying down, improved matters.

To make matters worse, Sulana had come down with some kind of cold or flu. She returned my concerned looks with reassurances that she was okay, but her feverish eyes told a different story. None of us were sleeping well due to her uncontrollable coughing.

My silent pondering of our grim situation was interrupted by Asher's dispirited voice. "How long do you think he's going to keep us here?"

I knew the question was addressed to me. Sulana had stopped speaking to the former councilor long ago, and not just because her throat was sore. "I think that depends upon *why* he is keeping us here," I answered.

"What do you mean?" she asked warily.

"I mean, why are we still alive? He must want us around for some reason. Our army should reach the city any day now, but Emperor Tanes won't back down just because Fortenz holds a few Archives sorcerers hostage. We have no trading value, at least, not for anything important. Yet here we sit."

"Maybe he's just not a murderer," she said with disdain.

"In his mind, we're traitors. There's only one sentence for that crime. Execution, murder, call it what you want. It's all taking a life. Some labels for it are just more acceptable than others."

Sulana sighed and spoke in a hoarse voice. "Whatever he's going to do, I wish he'd do it. I'm getting sick of rotting in this cell." She doubled over in a coughing spasm with the last word.

I hated to hear the fatalism in her voice. "Don't give up yet. As long as we live, there's hope."

Sulana shrugged and cleared her throat noisily. "I'm not giving up. I'm just hoping for a chance to *do* something. So far, sitting in this cell hasn't given us many opportunities for action."

Her comment seemed prophetic when a key rattled in our cell door lock.

"Be careful what you wish for," I whispered with a raised eyebrow.

We had just been fed about an hour before, so this visit was unexpected. After being here for several days, we knew our jailers' routine.

The door opened and three guards moved into the room. Two of the guards drew their swords and stood at either side of the doorway. The third man carried three sets of manacles.

"Prisoner, get up and step forward," he said to me.

I levered myself off the floor, wincing at the familiar ache in my side. I stepped forward as far as my chain allowed.

The guard dropped all but one set of manacles behind him and took a step forward, placing his face within a foot of mine. "We are taking you for a short walk. If you try to escape, we have orders to strike you down."

The man kneeled and clamped the manacles on my ankles. He was vulnerable in that position. I longed to take advantage of it, but the second I glanced down at his exposed back, one of the swordsmen stepped forward, glaring at me and hefting his sword.

The four manacles were linked to a center chain in an "I" formation. After the guard stood back up and clamped the cold manacles onto my wrists, my reach was severely limited. I would have to crouch just to scratch my nose.

The guard went to Sulana next and repeated the process. All of the manacle sets were the same size, so being much smaller, she still had considerable freedom of movement. She coughed onto his chest just as he finished binding her wrists, making him step back quickly with an expression of disgust.

Asher was last. She insisted that manacles weren't necessary and that she wasn't an enemy of Emperor Fortenz, but the guard grabbed her by the neck and told her to shut up and stay quiet. Cowed by his manhandling, she nodded and obeyed.

The three of us were led, jangling and clanking, out of the cell and into the bright, torch-lit hallway beyond. It seemed bright to us anyway, after a few days of semi-darkness. The guard who had restrained us was in front and the two swordsmen walked behind. The pace was a little fast for those of us wearing leg restraints, but the swordsmen were quick to poke us in the back if we failed to keep up.

Fortunately, we didn't have far to go. The lead guard took us down the hall and through a warm, fragrant room containing a series of wood-burning stoves. The cooks working the stoves looked over at us curiously before wrinkling their noses and waving their hands at the odor we'd carried with us from our cell.

At the far side of the room along a curved, stone wall, two Lightning Corps soldiers guarded a stout wooden door with three ventilation grills. When the soldiers opened the door and stood aside to let us pass, I realized where we were going.

A small gasp escaped my lips and Sulana glanced over at me. "Rollek's tower," I whispered. Her eyes widened when she recognized Ebnik's description just as I had.

I got a particularly vicious jab in the back from the guard behind me. "No talking," he growled.

Anger made the muscles in my shoulders bunch and a trickle of blood rolled down my back under my shirt. I resisted the urge to round on the man, thinking I'd either get a chance to exact revenge on these people or I wouldn't. For the moment, all I could do was be patient and wait for an opportunity.

Besides, I wanted to see this legendary artifact that had everyone so agitated. Crafted by the last great sorcerer/king from the Wizard Wars, Rollek's Amplifier had power that surpassed any other implement in all of recorded history.

We stepped into the ancient tower. To our left, a stairway curved up along the wall to the level above. To our right was a workbench littered with the tools of a vaetric smith and a sturdy storage cabinet. Straight ahead sat the object in question. Rollek's Amplifier was an unimposing box made of stone blocks positioned at the center of the room. A shining metal rod extended from the top of the box up through the ceiling. According to Ebnik, that was the link to the focus sphere on the roof of the palace.

Dumont Fortenz stood to the left of the amplifier, resting his hand on it possessively. His smug expression turned to a sneer as we clinked into the room behind our escort.

My old nemesis Paeter Thoron stood to the right of the amplifier. His twitching eyes and fidgeting hands gave a much less confident impression than Dumont's arrogance. Paeter's nervousness both pleased and worried me.

Something momentous was afoot. With a sinking feeling, I began to suspect we were here to witness a demonstration.

The escort bowed to Dumont. "The prisoners, as ordered, Your Majesty." The man moved to the other side of Sulana from me.

Dumont patted the amplifier. "Doesn't look like much, does it? The most powerful vaetric implement ever created, and Rollek made it look like a brick oven. He apparently lacked the design talent of Sorcerer Thoron here."

Paeter gave his master a thin smile and inclined his head to acknowledge the compliment.

Dumont turned his attention back to his guests. "It's too bad former Emperor Tanes didn't bring the amplifier back into service for his own purposes. I probably wouldn't be standing here today if he'd had any foresight."

Sulana made tiny strangling noises trying to hold back her cough, but she finally couldn't restrain herself and burst into a coughing jag that left her red-faced and winded.

Dumont frowned at the interruption. "That was unpleasant." He pointed to a pewter goblet on Paeter's work bench. "Guard, give her some water. I don't want her coughing through the entire demonstration."

Paeter's eyes widened in alarm. "Is that wise, Your Majesty? She's a sorceress."

Dumont waved away the concern. "She doesn't cast." He watched the guard pour some water into the goblet and take it to Sulana, who accepted it gratefully and took a sip.

"As I was saying, you are all here to witness a historic demonstration. For the first time in three centuries you will see Rollek's Amplifier in action."

I glanced at Sulana. She had the cup to her lips with her eyes closed, as if she were savoring the cool water. But I could see the concentration in the set of her features. I turned my attention back to Dumont, keeping Sulana in my peripheral vision.

Paeter was watching Sulana suspiciously, so I spoke to deflect his attention. "The amplifier didn't do Rollek much good in the end."

A guard came up from behind and kidney punched me, driving me to my knees. "You will address the emperor as Your Majesty and speak only when spoken to," he growled into my ear. "Now get up."

Dumont waited until the guard had lifted me back to my feet. "You are correct, Sorcerer Forester. Like Tanes, Rollek also suffered from a lack of vision. His mistake was using the amplifier for defense. He hid behind a shield when he should have blasted every enemy who defied him."

A light buzzing sound, like that of a fly zooming by, came from Sulana's direction, and I caught a fluttering motion out of the corner of my eye. A quick glance revealed reddish dust falling to the floor. Light glinted through a hole in her manacles. Somehow, she had rusted the pin that kept them locked. Fortunately, corroded hinges kept the two halves of the shackles from swinging open and giving her away. She kept both hands around the cup with her wrists together just in case.

Shifting my eyes back to Dumont and Paeter, I hoped neither had noticed Sulana's surreptitious blessing. Paeter was looking back and forth between the two of us, seeming to sense that something was going on, but he said nothing to interrupt his master.

Asher leaned forward to look past me toward Sulana. Had she seen something? Her eyes narrowed in suspicion and then she looked at me. Our eyes locked and I knew she had figured out what Sulana was doing. I willed her to silence, but her desperation must have overcome whatever loyalty she might have once had for other members of the Archives.

A wicked smile twisted the corner of her mouth and she raised her head to address Dumont. As she opened her mouth to speak, I drove an elbow into her side, knocking the wind out of her. I rammed her as hard as I could into the wall, satisfied with the clunk when her head hit the stone. She collapsed to the floor unconscious.

A boot kick to my lower back drove me to the floor. The guard placed a boot between my shoulder blades and set the tip of his sword at the nape of my neck.

Dumont glared down at me. "If you keep interrupting, I may reconsider letting you watch my little demonstration. Believe me, you won't like the alternative."

It was hard to breathe against the pressure of the guard's foot, so my answer was strained and pitiful. "I apologize, Your Majesty, but she had that coming."

Dumont laughed. "I suppose she did. Traitors can be so irritating. Guards, take her back to the cell."

The head guard pointed to the man who was holding me down and the other guard behind Sulana, and he motioned them to take care of Asher. He remained at the foot of the stairs on Sulana's left.

I slowly got onto my knees and stumbled to my feet, my chest aching anew from the body slam to Asher and the subsequent kick from the guard.

Sulana watched me get up with an unreadable look on her face. A single tear rolled down one cheek, but her jaw was clenched and she gave me a nearly imperceptible nod. She coughed and took a quick sip of water to quell it. I hoped she still had plenty of that water left and could figure out some way to use it. We were rapidly running out of time and options.

Dumont returned to his speech. "As I said, Rollek lacked vision. The amplifier is a tool of nearly unlimited power and deserves to be used for something worthy. What could be more worthy than inspiring loyalty in my subjects? Rollek was defeated by treachery. You've both experienced firsthand how dangerous traitors can be. When I activate Rollek's Amplifier with Paeter's new spell core, there won't be a single traitor in all of Cassandria."

So that was it. Paeter had adapted the spell he used in his amulets to create the new spell core for the amplifier. I was still learning about the relationship between the different types of spells and the vaetra required to power them, but my mind went numb thinking about how much power it would take to blanket Cassandria with such a charm for an extended period of time. It didn't seem practical. Was the Confluence truly unlimited?

Thinking back on my conversations with the spirit goddesses, I knew the answer was "no." They said the amplifier was a parasite; one that threatened their existence. Vaetra was their "flow of life." If the amplifier consumed all of the vaetra from the Confluence, or the "Great Basin," as they termed it, they would be destroyed. The ramifications of that possibility were unfathomable.

Dumont grinned in a way that made me shudder at what he might say next. "It might interest you to know that your army has arrived. The latest report said they entered the city through the North gate. They should be approaching the palace about now, and best of all, the patriarch of the Tanes line came with them."

The army was here. Emperor Tanes was here. Just in time to become vassals of Emperor Fortenz. I went light-headed with panic, but what could I do? I ached to run forward, tear the core out of the amplifier, and destroy it somehow. But the guard would be on me in a second. Paeter, who was watching me closely in smug silence, looked prepared to strike me down as well.

I looked over at Sulana in despair. She held the water cup at her chest and glared at Dumont, her eyes twitching with hatred. Why wasn't she using her power to do something? What were the spirits waiting for?

Dumont seemed to notice my distress. "Don't worry, Forester," he said with an indulgent smile. "You'll soon feel much better about things. In fact, you have an important role to play in my demonstration. You will prove that the amplifier is working properly. I considered having you eliminate Ms. Asher for me, but she's not here now, and having you dispose of the Sword Sorceress would be a much better test anyway, don't you think?"

Sulana and I exchanged a fearful glance. Could the amplifier really be so powerful that it could force me to do something so abhorrent? Had my attack on Asher doomed Sulana in her place?

He reached over and gripped the handle of a lever on the top of the amplifier. "Paeter, it's time." He and Paeter touched the ornate amulets around their necks and activated them.

Dumont lowered the lever until it slid between the prongs of a connector embedded in the top of the amplifier. "Loyalty," he said with reverence, and activated the device.

Dumont, Paeter, and Sulana winced and averted their faces from the light produced by the amplifier, but for me the manifestation was much different. I bent over to slacken my chains and plugged my ears with my fingers, uselessly trying to block out the sound of a thousand horse-drawn carriages racing past.

Next came a familiar sensation that I had hoped to never experience again. The feel of Paeter's new "loyalty" spell was disturbingly similar to the "member" spell of his amulets. I became aware of the other people around me, near and far, and I was drawn to the magnificent leader before me. My concerns fell away and my sense of purpose was cast adrift. I longed for some kind of guidance.

Some deep down part of me screamed in frustration and anger, but my higher self suppressed those negative feelings with curious delight. Everything was going to be okay. We were all in this together.

Dumont raised his arms toward the ceiling, addressing the entire city through his master amulet. The power of his voice was mesmerizing, his love for us boundless. "Welcome, citizens. Today is the beginning of a great future for all of us. Together we will build a new empire. A better empire. An empire where the old prejudices are gone and the obstacles to progress are erased."

The manifestation noise faded somewhat as the spell took hold. I started to ease my hands away from my ears when a small cold hand grabbed my wrist and held it. I looked over at Sulana to see her staring at me in concentration. Like snow melting off a warm window, the loyalty spell slid away from my consciousness. I tried to pull my wrist away from her because I didn't want to lose the warm sense of belonging, but her grip was stubbornly firm.

Her relief was apparent when I was finally able to hold her eyes with clarity and awareness. Dumont continued his exhortation to the masses, fully involved in his own voice. However, Paeter watched us closely, his expression uncertain. I had only a few seconds before he would realize that neither of us were affected by his spell.

Hoping Sulana would understand and cooperate, I opened a channel through our physical connection. After a brief moment of resistance, she let me tap into her internal well. I linked to the goblet of water in her hand and started an incantation as quietly as I could while I stared into her eyes. I hoped Paeter would think I was talking to her and that Dumont's speech would continue to drown me out. With the last syllables of the incantation, I looked over at the amplifier and directed a weak lightning bolt at it. Water was not the best focus for sorcery, but it was all we had, and I pushed it to the limit. The remaining water in the cup evaporated in a puff of steam as the lightning manifested.

Paeter was ready for me. He brought up a shield just as the lightning fired across the chamber. But Paeter didn't anticipate that I would use Dumont's own shield-breaker lightning. It easily cut through the standard shield he raised and struck the core in a shower of sparks and a loud sizzle.

Dumont stopped in mid-sentence and leaped to the amplifier, checking it for damage. Paeter pulled a wand from his robe and kept an eye on us while he anxiously looked over the amplifier as well. The guard next to Sulana, his eyes dulled by the loyalty spell, stepped forward and slapped the empty goblet from Sulana's hand. It clattered to the floor, as useless at that point as my spell had been.

My lightning interrupted whatever Sulana was doing to protect us from the amplifier. As the loyalty spell started pushing its way back into my conscious, I met Sulana's disappointed eyes in defeat.

Dumont swung toward us, panting with anger. "You fool! You could have killed us all."

Paeter raised his wand and looked to Dumont for permission to strike. Dumont gathered himself and straightened his robes. He waved toward us in dismissal and said, "Go ahead, Paeter, this demonstration is over for them."

Before Paeter could open his mouth to trigger the wand, a loud pop and a spray of sparks erupted from the center of the core. Dumont and Paeter cringed and shielded their faces with their arms. The glass rod surrounding the core had cracked, and a visible arc of power jumped from one end to the other.

Dumont and Paeter lowered their arms and stared in horror as the arc grew and twisted toward them. Both tried to step away, but the arc leaped across the remaining gap and connected with the amulets they wore. They screamed in agony as power flickered and twitched over their bodies. The stones in both amulets shattered and the odor of burnt cloth and flesh filled the room. The screaming stopped abruptly and both men tipped stiffly away from the amplifier like felled trees. As they dropped, the arc snapped away from them and resumed jumping and sizzling across the damaged core. A tendril of smoke arose from the cloth near their amulets, which had melted to slag.

The moment the arc destroyed Dumont's amulet, a searing pain shot through my skull. I went to my knees, breaking contact with Sulana to clutch my head. She crashed down beside me, crying out in agony and curling into a ball. The guard was similarly incapacitated.

Staring at the two bodies on the other side of the room, I knew that Dumont was right. By damaging the amplifier, I had doomed us all.

I sensed that everyone in the city was experiencing the same agonizing end. A dreamlike sense of separation came over me and the walls seem to shimmer and disappear. One moment the wall would be solid, and the next I could see out into the city where people littered the streets in writhing distress. I wondered if this was what it was like to die. It was like I was shifting into and out of the Runedream.

In my delirium, Tritia appeared between me and the amplifier. She was so transparent that I could barely make her out. She seemed to be sharing our terrible doom and reached toward me with a shaking hand. Her mouth formed words, but I couldn't make them out. She cried with despair and reached both arms toward me, screaming a whisper that said, "Stop the parasite." And then she disappeared, leaving me staring at the twisting arc of power through the space where she had been.

Getting shakily to my feet in spite of the mind-searing pain, I realized that Sulana had dissolved the pins on my shackles too at some point. I opened the clamps and threw the chains aside as I stumbled toward the amplifier.

The glass rod of the core was blackened and cracked. There was no repairing it. The ends of the rod were fused with the connectors that cradled it. I tried to raise the lever that the headmaster had used to engage the device, but it too was fused in place.

I couldn't concentrate on a solution with the amplifier melting my brain. All I knew was that I had to stop it somehow. With a scream of frustration, I reached under the deadly arc and grabbed the core with both hands. It was still hot enough to sear my hands, and glass splinters grated into my skin as I yanked on it as hard as I could.

But it was no use. The core refused to budge. As I let go, the crackling arc dipped and connected with my hands.

Power. Raw vaetra like nothing I'd ever dreamed could be possible. It coursed through me like a river going over a waterfall. My heart beat so hard that I thought it would burst from my chest, but just as the pain faded from my head, my heart began to calm.

Everything became clear. I understood how the spell of the core had been corrupted by the damage my lightning caused. I suddenly had full control over my strange double vision and could shift my awareness to see across the entire city. Sulana cried my name, and I looked over to see her crawling toward me with tears streaming down her face. I could sense her spirit slipping away and death coming to take her from me. I alone was unaffected at the center of a raging storm of death.

All of the spirit goddesses appeared just behind Sulana. The tiny lights that always seemed to follow them around were dim and barely moving. The goddesses gazed upon me with expressions that varied from expectation to fear to loathing. The amplifier was draining the Confluence as well as every vaen and basin connected to it. To the spirits, that network was the flow of life, and when it was gone, they would be gone as well.

Arial's look of hopeful expectation inspired me, but what could I do? I had managed to make myself part of the flow, but how could I stop it?

If I couldn't plug the leak, perhaps I could put a bucket under it. How could I store the vaetra that was streaming out of the Confluence until I could figure out a way to stop the flow?

An image came to me then. An image of a fish. It was the spirit fish Sulana had shown me at Castle Tarn. I knew what I had to do and asked the spirits for help. Arial flew to my side and supplied the incantation, which I repeated aloud as she spoke it into my ear. Never before had I so effortlessly repeated the required vocalizations. I got it right on the first try.

The manifestation noise shifted to a higher pitch as the amplifier replaced the damaged spell with my incantation. Sulana slumped to the floor unconscious, and a glance across the city with my enhanced vision showed everyone else doing the same. They were hurt, but their minds were no longer under attack.

The goddesses immediately started to look more solid. My spell had redirected the flow of vaetra so it fed directly into them and every spirit in the area.

Taking full control of the amplifier was exhilarating. I could destroy my enemies with not much more than a thought. I could heal every wound or level every wall.

Loralai folded her arms and frowned at me. When she spoke, I could hear her clearly. "So what next, Runemaster? You had the courage to take the power, but do you have the humility to give it up?"

Arial, still floating at my side, gave me a look of warning and said, "You must stop the flow. The land still bleeds, and there's a limit to how much we can hold."

As if to underscore her point, one of the bright spirit lights floating next to her flashed and winked out of existence. Arial herself was not only looking solid, but she was becoming brighter as well.

I looked down at the amplifier for a solution. All of the parts were still fused together. I could blow the whole thing up, but I'd kill myself and probably Sulana in the process. I suspected that breaking any of the individual connections would just result in another arc.

The link rod that extended from the top of the amplifier into the ceiling caught my eye. Although it had been recently replaced, small spots of rust had already appeared along its length where the humidity of the underground room had condensed on the metal surface.

Arial followed my gaze and smiled at me, seeming to read my mind. She leaned forward and once again spoke an incantation into my ear. Repeating her words verbatim, I directed the spell Sulana had used on our manacles at the link rod.

The rust spots grew and joined until the entire rod was discolored. The rust ate deeper and bits of the rod began to flake off. Tiny arcs of power flickered along the length of the rod as if the amplifier were resisting my efforts.

As the link rod continued to disintegrate, the flow of power from the Confluence weakened encouragingly, and the arc of vaetra through my hands began to shrivel. Finally, a long, thin length of the remaining rod shattered and broke free, collapsing into a crusty pile across the top of the amplifier. It sprayed bits of rusted metal and forced me to avert my face and close my eyes. The arc died out, spitting one last, spiteful spark at my hand.

~

"Excellent work, Runemaster." Arial had gone back to float alongside her sisters. The goddesses were so bright by then that I had to squint when I looked at them.

Sulana groaned and rose to a kneeling position. Noticing the shackles dangling from her arms, she pried them off and let them clatter to the floor. I went to her and helped her remove the shackles from her ankles. When we stood together, she threw her arms around me and hugged me tightly.

We surveyed the destruction that surrounded us. The amplifier was a mess of fused and corroded parts. Dumont and Paeter lay dead where they had fallen. The smell of cooked meat turned my stomach.

When we turned toward the spirit goddesses, Sulana gasped.

I looked at her in shock. "You can see them?" I realized that the double-vision of the Runedream was gone, yet the goddesses were still visible.

The guard, who had collapsed at the base of the stairs, groaned and stirred. With a few quick strides I went over to him and had his sword in hand before he could fully regain consciousness. The man looked around in confusion, resting his gaze on me, the dead sorcerers, and Sulana. When his eyes found the goddesses, they grew round with fear and he scrambled from the room as quickly as he could manage.

Sulana was still gaping at the goddesses, apparently at a loss for words. I went back to her side and took her hand in mine.

"Sulana, I'd like you to meet Arial, Tritia, Loralai, Umbria, and Putra."

Sulana bowed deeply and spoke in a shaking voice. "I'm honored."

Loralai considered me with a less critical eye than usual. In a begrudging tone, she said, "You have surpassed my expectations, human. Perhaps you are worthy of the title Runemaster after all."

Before I could thank her, she turned to Tritia. "Are we done here?" Pointedly looking around the chamber with distaste, she added, "I've had enough of this place."

Tritia smiled at her. "Yes, the danger is past. Thank you for your assistance."

Without another word, Loralai simply disappeared.

Umbria stepped forward and looked directly into Sulana's eyes. In a deep, grating voice, she said, "You have done well, daughter. Be true to your heart, and your path will remain clear."

"Th-thank you," Sulana said, clearly uncertain of how else to respond.

Umbria then looked at me. "Protect and support her, Runemaster. You have won this day, but more days lie ahead."

I dipped my head in acknowledgment. "I gladly promise to do so."

Then Umbria disappeared and Putra vanished an instant later.

With just Arial and Tritia present, I felt more comfortable asking the question that was nagging me. "Why can Sulana see you? Have you brought her into the Runedream somehow?"

Tritia smiled and shook her head. "We are not in the Runedream. The power you bestowed allows us to manifest in your world, for a time at least. After we restore the flow of life to the Great Basin, we will return home."

I chuckled at the thought of one of the goddesses of legend walking into a temple full of spirit worshipers. "If you stuck around for a while, you could start quite a revival among the mundane."

Tritia shrugged. "We don't seek worship, but we are content to let the druids do as they must to protect the flow of life." She reached out to Arial and took her hand. "We should go now. The land still aches and we must use your gift to heal it."

I spoke quickly, before they could disappear. "Thanks for your help, Arial. I couldn't have done it without you."

Arial winked and said, "Until we meet again, Runemaster."

Arial and Tritia disappeared, leaving Sulana and me standing hand-in-hand in the chamber, alone except for the corpses of our enemies.

CHAPTER 55
BEGINNINGS

The Grand Hall of the palace was a sea of faces; some I knew and many I didn't. A band of troubadours played on the other side of the room and the din of conversation seemed to fill every corner. Sulana and I stood in front of a table heaped with gifts, sipping wine from two beautifully detailed silver goblets. Looking over my shoulder at the neatly arranged pile of brightly wrapped presents, I shook my head.

"While there are certain advantages to having the emperor host our reception, I'm not sure what we are going to do with all that … *stuff.*"

Sulana smiled up me. "We'll figure something out. There are worse problems to have."

I put my arm around her waist and gave her a squeeze. "Yes, and we've had them." She went up onto her tiptoes and gave me a quick peck on the lips.

"We can't leave you two alone for a minute." We turned our heads in response to the familiar voice.

Daven approached hand-in-hand with Karla. The healer looked radiant in a long green dress, and Daven cut a handsome figure in an embroidered jacket of a similar shade.

The two had married within a month of our victory at the palace and settled down in Riverview. After the members of the mundane resistance melted back into the empire and returned to their normal lives, Daven opened a craft shop and helped Karla start a small healing clinic. Minister Bogard was thrilled to have them join his community.

I shook hands with Daven and hugged Karla. "I hear a rumor that you're wasting no time starting a new generation of Prosts," I said while Sulana hugged them both.

Karla rubbed a hand across her abdomen and looked up at Daven with glittering eyes. "We'll see. It's still early days."

Daven tilted his head toward Sulana. "What about you? Now that you've bankrupted the empire with this little gathering, are you planning the pitter patter of tiny feet?"

Sulana and I glanced at each other. Daven was about the one hundredth person who had asked us about our plans for children. Sulana answered for both us. "I think we'll get a dog first and see how that goes."

Sulana wasn't joking, but Daven and Karla laughed as if she were. When they saw Talon and Barek waiting to speak to us, they waved goodbye and moved on.

"Nice ceremony," Talon said. "It pays to have friends in high places."

I chuckled at the understatement. "Yes, Her Majesty outdid herself."

When the emperor's wife found out that Sulana and I were engaged, she insisted on hosting our wedding and the reception at the palace to thank us for putting an end to the headmaster's brief reign. In the past three months since the destruction of the amplifier, we lived at the palace recovering from our ordeal and then helping to plan the wedding. Both of us looked forward to returning home to the Archives soon.

Barek angled his head toward the table of presents. "You'll have to hire a sleigh to get all that loot up to the Archives."

I rolled my eyes. "Yeah, we tried to say, 'no gifts,' but the empress wouldn't hear of it. She claimed that everyone needed a way to express their appreciation and that it would be cruel to deny them that opportunity."

Talon grinned. "She's one savvy negotiator."

"Yeah, I'm starting to understand what's behind that nervous look the emperor often gets when she's around."

"When do you return to the Archives?" Barek asked.

"Next week. It will probably take that long just to recover from all this excitement. Sorry we stuck you with all the cleanup duty."

Barek shrugged. "No problem. It was my kind of fun."

After the fall of their leadership, the Lightning Corps mostly dissolved. A few bands retreated to Grassgate Province where they still had supporters, but the emperor made it clear that anyone wearing a Lightning Corps uniform would be arrested as a traitor, as would anyone who aided them. The black cloaks disappeared quickly after that, and Integrationist rhetoric was at a low ebb for the time being.

Our personal enemies disappeared as well. Lohan and Peltor vanished from Northshore and were rumored to be hiding in Grassgate Province with the other Lightning Corps refugees. If the two of them were still together, they'd probably kill each other off eventually. Asher took her own life rather than face trial for her crimes. Although, if it hadn't been for her interference, the conflict with the headmaster might have turned out quite differently.

Talon and Barek led raids on the sanctuaries that had been taken by the enemy and eventually restored the Archives sanctuary network to normal. I was mostly healed toward the end of that effort and wanted to help, but Sulana told me there wasn't going to *be* a wedding if I abandoned her to deal with the empress by herself. When she flipped it around and suggested that she go and I stay, I quickly understood her position.

Sulana's mother walked up and hugged the both of us while congratulating us on our marriage. She stepped back to stand next to Talon, threading her arm into his. She had a glint in her eye that Sulana caught onto right away.

"What is it, Mother? You have your *I've got a secret* look."

"I was just speaking with Seneschal Tanes and heard the most interesting rumor. Apparently, the emperor has decided what he is going to do with the Thunderhead College facilities that the headmaster funded with imperial coin."

I'd assumed he would tear them down, but I guess it made better sense to re-purpose the structures. Sulana urged her mother to continue.

"He and Councilor Rissik have worked out a plan to turn the facilities over to the Archives. But they won't be turned into sanctuaries. They are to become emporiums that will fulfill their original intent of finding ways to use sorcery to assist the mundane."

When the headmaster built Thunderhead College campuses around the empire, they had mostly been a smoke screen for what were really Lightning Corps training camps. The declared purpose of integrating sorcery back into the lives of the mundane had never been attempted, much less realized.

Barek looked skeptical. "But will the mundane *want* that kind of help?"

Marlene shrugged. "Time will tell. Sorman seemed pretty negative about it himself, but the emperor insists on trying the experiment. I believe there's a bit of spite involved as well."

I chuckled. "It would be ironic for the Archives to implement an Integrationist vision."

Sulana had been thoughtful during her mother's revelations. She finally spoke in a musing tone. "Maybe it's time sorcerers stopped fighting each other. As long as the Accords are respected, we can offer our help and let the mundane decide how much sorcery they want in their lives. Maybe nothing will change, but maybe we can prevent something like this from happening again."

Barek harrumphed. "Maybe. My people will be watching this *experiment*."

Talon put a hand on Barek's shoulder. "We wouldn't have it any other way, old friend."

After exchanging a few more pleasant words, Talon, Marlene, and Barek wandered off to mingle with the rest of the crowd.

Within a few seconds of their departure, Defender Marshal Nigel Shields appeared before us with two of his rangers in tow. The two rangers nodded in our direction and congratulated us before stepping back and turning to face the room.

"They don't mean to be rude," the marshal apologized. "I asked them to give us some uninterrupted privacy. I have something to give you."

The marshal was carrying a wooden box under one arm, but the item he held out toward Sulana had come from a pocket.

Sulana set her goblet down and accepted the necklace from him and peered at the pendant that hung from the long chain. The chain and pendant were both made of silver. The pendant was a circle with a star in the center. The symbol was a match for the one the marshal and his rangers had on the breast of their jackets.

Sulana turned the pendant in her hand, admiring the way the light played across it. "It's beautiful, Nigel. Thank you."

The marshal glanced over his shoulder and lowered his voice. "It's more than a pretty bauble. With it, the Archdruid has authorized me to grant you a field commission as an Honorary Ranger Lieutenant."

Sulana shook her head in confusion and moved the hand with the necklace away from her. "Wait. What does that mean? I already have responsibilities at the Archives."

The marshal reached out and closed her hand over the necklace. "Your only responsibility to the Hierarchy is to use your abilities with discretion. I'm sure you understand what I mean."

Sulana nodded and slipped the necklace over her neck. She dropped the pendant into her cleavage where it disappeared behind the lace at the neck of her wedding dress.

I understood what he meant as well. Only a few people knew that Sulana could cast in the manner of druids. They wanted her to continue keeping that secret.

"Good. To make that responsibility easier, I have another gift for you."

The marshal handed the wooden box to Sulana. It was about six inches square with a hinged lid. A golden latch on the front kept the lid closed. I could tell by the way Sulana's hands dipped when he passed it to her that the box was heavy.

Sulana unlatched the box and tilted open the lid. I craned my neck to see into the box. It looked like a large crystal ball nestled in purple velvet.

"Please don't take it out right now," he cautioned. "I'd rather you inspected it in private."

"Thank you again. It's a lovely crystal ball," Sulana said as she tilted the top of the box toward the light.

"It's not crystal," Nigel corrected. "It is a reinforced glass ball filled with blessed water. It has a metal cap on the bottom that works like my spirit bowl. You can offer blessings with it, but to an observer, it appears to be a sorcerer's casting orb, albeit a large one."

Sulana grinned at Nigel and latched the lid closed. "That's brilliant! Thank you so much."

He gave her a slight bow. "My pleasure, Sword Sorceress Delano. If not for you and your new husband, we would all be at the mercy of that megalomaniac, Dumont Fortenz."

Sulana glanced at me. We'd had many conversations about what happened and she knew I didn't feel particularly heroic about my part in it.

She met Nigel's eyes and said, "It was a team effort, Marshal. We all had our parts to play."

Nigel nodded once. "So it was. Your humility becomes you."

The marshal congratulated us both and shook hands with me. When he offered his hand to Sulana, she leaned forward and gave him a brief hug instead. The marshal collected his men and slipped back into the crowd as suddenly as he'd appeared.

Daisy's bubbling laughter carried across the room, drawing my attention to where she stood with Ebnik and her brother. She waved her wine cup in an exaggerated flourish that slopped wine over the rim and onto the floor. Ebnik snatched it from her in mid-wave and set it down on a nearby table. With a stern look, he said something to Ben, who reluctantly set his cup down as well. Ben unsteadily guided his sister to a bench at one of the dining tables. I predicted that the twins would be indisposed for a good part of the next day.

Before anyone else could head our way, a gong sounded, echoing throughout the hall. The music stopped instantly and all conversation quickly hushed. Everyone turned toward the dais as the emperor stepped up onto the platform with his empress by his side.

The emperor's voice was not particularly strong, but it carried well nonetheless. "Thank you all for being here on this joyous occasion. I'm so glad we could show our appreciation to Sulana and Jaylan for helping us defeat a most powerful enemy. Please raise your cups and join me in a toast." The emperor raised his goblet toward Sulana and me. "To Sulana and Jaylan, heroes of the empire. May your future together be a happy and peaceful one."

The crowd broke out into various cheers of "huzzah!" and "Hear, hear!" before sipping their beverage of choice.

The emperor left the dais and the buzz of conversation resumed along with the music.

For a moment, Sulana and I were left alone in a semi-circle of peace cut out from the milling, noisy crowd.

I took her into my arms and looked down into her eyes.

"What next, my beautiful Sword Sorceress, Trollbane, and now Honorary Ranger Lieutenant."

She smiled up at me and winked. "We must bow to tradition, my handsome Sword Sorcerer and Runemaster. I believe we must observe a period of social abstinence called a *honeymoon*."

I nodded sagely and spoke in a mock serious tone. "Social abstinence sounds pretty good about now. But what is this honeymoon you speak of? Will it be strenuous?"

Duplicating my serious tone, she responded, "Only if we do it right."

I laughed and held her close while she giggled into my neck. I thanked the spirits for bringing us together. No matter what path our lives might take, the most important thing was to have Sulana, my love and my best friend, at my side.

Right then the musicians struck up a lively tune that had always been one of my favorites. Many of our guests were unable to resist the song's beat and part of the hall cleared for those who began dancing. I put my right hand on Sulana's hip and raised her right hand in my left. "Shall we?" I asked.

"Let's do," she agreed.

As we twirled in with the other dancers, I thought back on how far things had come in such a short time. In less than a year, I'd experienced a lifetime of adventure. I'd ridden out of Northshore a mundane innkeeper with an uncertain future on that cold spring morning so many months ago. Since then, I had become a Sword Sorcerer of the Archives, with a future I looked forward to exploring.

Best of all, I got the girl.

THANK YOU FOR READING

Thank you for dedicating some of your reading time to the Vaetra Chronicles. I hope you enjoyed the adventures of Jaylan and Sulana and the exciting conclusion of the trilogy.

If you would like to be notified by email when I release a new book, you can sign up for my New Releases email list at the series website, Vaetra.com. The signup form is right at the top of the home page.

I know that not everyone likes to write book reviews, but if you are willing to spare the time to write a sentence or two about what you thought of *Vaetra Unleashed*, I encourage you to post a review at your favorite book vendor site or share a message with your social networking friends.

If you would like to share your thoughts with me privately, you can reach me through the contact page on Vaetra.com. Those messages go straight to my inbox. I look forward to hearing from you.

Happy reading,
Daniel R. Marvello

ACKNOWLEDGEMENTS

No one has done more to encourage and support my dream of becoming a fiction writer than my wife. That goes double now that she shares the dream with me! I'm more thankful than I can ever express for her love and for the joy she brings to my life every day.

Special thanks to my alpha and beta readers, Susan Daffron, Cynthia Daffron, Nancy Brashear, Paul Sheriff, Becca Mills, "Aimless," Ken Rahmoeller, and Lynda Wilcox. Their excellent feedback helped me refine *Vaetra Unleashed* into a worthy end to the Vaetra Chronicles trilogy.

Although I've long dreamed of writing a fantasy trilogy, it would not have been as fun to create if no one read it. Thank you to all of my readers for making the Vaetra Chronicles a satisfying chapter in the story of my writing career.

I'm blessed to have family and friends who encourage me. Among those friends, I count my fellow writers at the Writer's Pub. Special thanks to Susanne O'Leary for founding the Pub and for populating it with such a great group of supportive authors.

About the Author

Daniel R. Marvello writes fantasy adventure stories from his log home on forty acres of forest and meadow in the North Idaho panhandle. The setting for his Vaetra Chronicles book series was inspired by the scenic beauty of his surroundings. Daniel shares his home with his loving wife of 20 years and several wonderful animals.

Visit the Vaetra Chronicles Web site at:

www.Vaetra.com

Visit Daniel's blog at:

www.DanielRMarvello.com